# THAT
# FATEFUL
# LIGHTNING

# THAT FATEFUL LIGHTNING

## A NOVEL OF ULYSSES S. GRANT

## RICHARD PARRY

BALLANTINE BOOKS ★ NEW YORK

A Ballantine Book
The Ballantine Publishing Group

Copyright © 2000 by Richard Parry

All rights reserved under International and Pan-American Copyright Conventions.
Published in the United States by The Ballantine Publishing Group,
a division of Random House, Inc., New York, and simultaneously in
Canada by Random House of Canada Limited, Toronto.

Ballantine and colophon are registered trademarks of Random House, Inc.

www.randomhouse.com/BB/

A copy of the Library of Congress Cataloging-in-Publication Data
is available upon request from the publisher.

ISBN 0-345-42728-9

Test design by Mary A. Wirth

Manufactured in the United States of America
First Edition: June 2000

10 9 8 7 6 5 4 3 2 1

To my wonderful friend and companion
of thirty-five years, my wife, Kathie.

*May your days be filled with the blooms of the roses you so dearly love.*
*Certainly, I've supplied you with enough of the thorns.*

## ACKNOWLEDGMENTS

All an author does is write the manuscript. In bringing it to life in terms of ink and paper, many hands guided the process. I wish to sincerely thank all those at Ballantine who worked to make *Fateful Lightning* a reality.

A special thanks to my editor, Gary Brozek, for his thoughtful suggestions which greatly improved the manuscript, and to my agent, David Hale Smith of DHS Literary, Inc., for his faith and support.

Two other people deserve special mention: Heather Kern for creating the cover design that captures so eloquently the sense of the book, and Alexandra Krijgsman, the managing editor, who guided the production process with a sure and steady hand.

# THAT
# FATEFUL
# LIGHTNING

# APPOMATTOX

GENERAL: The result of the last week must convince you of the hopelessness of further resistance on the part of the Army of Northern Virginia in this struggle. I feel that it is so, and regard it as my duty to shift from myself the responsibility of any further effusion of blood, by asking of you the surrender of that portion of the Confederate States army known as the Army of Northern Virginia.

U. S. Grant, Lieutenant-General

GENERAL R. E. LEE

APRIL 7, 1865

GENERAL: I have received your note of this date. Though not entertaining the opinion you express on the hopelessness of further resistance on the part of the Army of Northern Virginia, I reciprocate your desire to avoid useless effusion of blood, and therefore, before considering your proposition, ask the terms you will offer on condition of its surrender.

R. E. Lee, General

LIEUTENANT-GENERAL U. S. GRANT

APRIL 8, 1865

GENERAL: Your note of last evening, in reply to mine of same date, asking the condition on which I will accept the surrender of the Army of Northern Virginia, is just received. In reply, I would say, that *peace* being my great desire, there is but one condition I would insist upon—namely, that the men and officers surrendered shall be disqualified for taking up arms again against the Government of the United States until properly exchanged. I will meet you, or will designate officers to meet any officers you may name for the same purpose, at any point agreeable to you, for the purpose of arranging definitely the terms upon which the surrender of the Army of Northern Virginia will be received.

U. S. Grant, Lieutenant-General

GENERAL R. E. LEE

APRIL 8, 1865

GENERAL: I received, at a late hour, your note of to-day. In mine of yesterday I did not intend to propose the surrender of the Army of Northern Virginia, but to ask the terms of your proposition. To be frank, I do not think the emergency has arisen to call for the surrender of this army; but as the restoration of peace should be the sole object of all, I desire to know whether your proposals would lead to that end. I cannot, therefore, meet you with a view to surrender the Army of Northern Virginia; but as far as your proposal may affect the Confederate States forces under my command, and tend to the restoration of peace, I should be pleased to meet you at ten A.M. tomorrow on the old stage-road to Richmond, between the picket-lines of the two armies.

R. E. Lee, General

LIEUTENANT-GENERAL U. S. GRANT

APRIL 9, 1865

GENERAL: Your note of yesterday is received. I have no authority to treat on the subject of peace; the meeting proposed for ten A.M. to-day could lead to no good. I will state, however, general, that I am equally anxious for peace with yourself, and the whole North entertains the same feeling. The terms upon which peace can be had are well understood. By the South laying down their arms they will hasten that most desired event, save thousands of human lives, and hundreds of millions of property not yet destroyed. Seriously hoping that all our difficulties may be settled without the loss of another life, I subscribe myself, etc.

U. S. Grant, Lieutenant-General

GENERAL R. E. LEE

---

FARMVILLE, VIRGINIA, EIGHT MILES EAST OF
APPOMATTOX COURTHOUSE. APRIL 9, 1865

---

Ulysses S. Grant, General-in-Chief of the Federal forces, rode slumped forward in his saddle. Avoiding the worried glances of his staff, he struggled against the headache that threatened to split his skull. Normally, Grant rode as if he and his horse were one, but not today. His faithful mount, Cincinnati, recognized the uneven pressure of his rider's legs and tossed his head nervously. Grant noted thankfully that the animal was picking its way over the battle-torn road with infinite care and with an easy gait, something his other mount, the little pony Jeff Davis, would never have done.

Colonel Horace Porter, his trusted aide-de-camp, followed closely at his general's side, half expecting his leader to pitch from his saddle onto the muddy road. Porter gnawed his lower lip, and his fingers twisted his reins into endless knots while he watched Grant suffer.

Since noon yesterday the headache had plagued the general. Mustard plasters to his neck and wrists did nothing to ameliorate the attack, nor did soaking his feet most of the night in hot water laced with mustard. At four in the morning Porter found Grant sitting on the sofa in the abandoned hotel in Farmville, throbbing head in hands and bare feet shuffling his boots about the floor.

Porter had even suggested that his general ride in an ambulance this morning to avoid the sun as well as the jostling. But Grant refused.

Plodding along with his jaw clenched, Grant reviewed the events of the last day. Despite the flurry of notes, Lee's last letter clearly showed that the Confederate general still meant to fight. Grant ground his teeth, forcing the insistent smell of the mustard plasters from his mind.

Did the man not realize that his army was surrounded? Grant wondered. Lee was in a bottle with Sheridan's cavalry corking the opening. Good old Sheridan could be relied upon to hold the door shut even if Lee threw his whole army at him, and he, Grant, was rushing Ord's command and the Fifth Corps to reinforce Sheridan. When they got there, the cork would be driven firmly in place with Lee's army trapped inside. What was left of it could scarcely amount to more than twenty thousand men, thirty thousand at the most. And those men were presumed to be starving. Reports saying they were boiling the leather from their bullet pouches came with each new batch of rebels who surrendered. One captured wag related that he'd eaten his shoes months ago and his Sunday-go-to-meeting hat over a year before.

*Was I wrong to ask for their surrender? Was I premature or hasty? Not if it puts an end to this useless slaughter.*

Grant's mind wandered back to the gaunt and haggard man who had turned up at the headquarters in Farmville two days ago. Wearing the threadbare uniform of a Confederate colonel, the man claimed to be the owner of the hotel Grant's staff used. He was the sole remaining member of his regiment, which had been raised from Farmville and the surrounding area—the last of all those men. Obviously defeated, the man's only request was to look after his property. When Grant told him to stay there and no one would bother him, the man's eyes filled with tears and he could only nod his head in silent reply.

And there was Dr. Smith, the captured Virginia medical officer, who related to Grant what General Ewell told him after the Federal troops crossed the James. The South was licked after that and should surrender, Ewell had said, and every man killed in subsequent battle was little better than murdered. The responsibility for those murdered ought to weigh heavily on the consciences of their generals and those they reported to, Ewell stressed.

Now General Ewell himself was their prisoner, captured after the battle at Sayler's Creek along with eight other generals and five thousand men. The victory there drove another nail into the coffin of the Army of Northern Virginia, for it severed Longstreet's corps from the body of Lee's army.

Grant rode along with two crumpled letters in his pocket. One had been captured from Confederate Colonel William B. Taylor, who wrote with simple eloquence, *Dear Mama, our army is ruined, I fear.* The other scrap of paper was a telegram sent from President Lincoln urging them on. *Let the thing be pressed,* Lincoln implored.

Well, Grant thought, my conscience is clear. I've made the first move. *Then, why doesn't this headache let up?*

The general twisted his neck and shrugged his shoulders, attempting to ease the constant pain behind his eyes. But his movements only ratcheted the level of his discomfort another notch higher. Why is Lee stalling? he wondered. Clearly, his last two letters to me changed their tone. Playing with words. I asked him to surrender, and he requested my terms. I gave him fair ones. Then, suddenly, he slipped peace negotiations in when I was clearly only writing about surrender of his army. He knows I have no authority to deal with the Confederate government.

*Lee's counting on resupply!* He must have got word that supplies were on the way. That's what he's trying to do, lull me into inaction, hoping for one more day. Lee expects those supply trains from Lynchburg to arrive at Appomattox Station today. Seven in all, I think. Food, medicines, powder, and percussion caps, one last infusion of supplies to prop up his tottering force. Then he'll attempt a breakout and join with Joe Johnston's army.

Grant smiled grimly. Sheridan and Custer had dashed those hopes. They captured all of the precious railroad cars late last night. Sheridan reported that the rebels mounted a fierce counterattack to carry the train, but Custer burned what he couldn't send back through the Union lines.

Custer managed to find engineers to drive the captured trains from among his Third Division cavalrymen. Euphoric at being returned to their former occupation, the reconstituted train men raced their locomotives up and down the track, blowing their whistles most of the night. Not until Sheridan threatened to burn their engines did the engineers follow orders and withdraw to the safety of Union-held territory. No relief would reach the Army of Northern Virginia.

Lee will know that by now, Grant realized. All that's left to him is a breakout.

Salvos of gunfire erupted ahead and off to his right, causing the general to rein in Cincinnati and stand in his stirrups. The sound of the musket fire, like yards of some giant's cloth being ripped, rolled over the distant hill in staccato clusters.

That must be Lee's advance guard contacting Custer and Sheridan's cavalry, Grant thought. The crackling sputtered and died away into isolated batches of fire. In his mind's eye he could see the battle as clearly as if he were there: the dismounted Union cavalry, crouching amidst whatever cover the torn fields and scattered split rail fences could offer, crouching and firing, falling back under the weight of the advance force, falling back as the Confederates moved forward. Grant held his breath.

As if on signal, a hundred more bolts of cloth ripped apart just over the rise. Then, what Grant was waiting to hear: the dull thump of artillery added to the sounds of the rifles. He sighed in relief, and his tense shoulders drooped into their normal slumped position. That artillery belonged to Ord and the Fifth Corps. They had got there in time. Lee's advance guard could not have brought up their own artillery so quickly. Sheridan had engaged the enemy, fallen back, and drawn them into the waiting jaws of Ord's infantry and heavy guns. The cork was driven firmly into the mouth of the bottle.

As abruptly as it started, the gunfire ceased.

Porter edged his mount alongside Grant and pointed to a lone rider galloping toward them down the route they had just taken. The general nodded. He had seen the blue-coated rider an instant before his staff. Within minutes the rider drew abreast. Covered with a curious mixture of mud and dust, he saluted, a broad grin spreading across his face.

"Lieutenant Charles Pease on General Meade's staff, sir! With a dispatch, sir."

"Good morning, Lieutenant." Grant returned the salute. "Have you good news for me this morning?"

Pease's face beamed. "I do indeed, General." He pulled a letter from his gauntlet and presented it to Grant as if it were the keys to the kingdom. "From Lee himself! He has the white flag out, sir!"

A murmur swept through his officers. Grant took a deep breath and issued a silent prayer: God grant that this bloodshed will be over. With so slight a twitch of his cheek that his staff never noticed, he opened the dispatch with steady hands. His staff, lost in the moment, forgot their manners and crowded about him, jostling Cincinnati. The proud horse shook its mane in protest and stomped its hooves.

Grant looked around at the anxious faces surrounding him and read the dispatch out loud.

APRIL 9, 1865

GENERAL: I received your note of this morning on the picket-line whither I had come to meet you and ascertain definitely what terms were embraced in your proposal of yesterday with reference to the surrender of this army. I now request an interview in accordance with the offer contained in your letter of yesterday for that purpose.

R. E. Lee, General

LIEUTENANT-GENERAL U. S. GRANT

A wild cheer broke the silence, and hats filled the air. Grant blinked. His headache had vanished. He slid from his saddle, produced his message book and a worn pencil from his pocket. Quickly, he wrote:

APRIL 9, 1865

GENERAL R. E. LEE, COMMANDING C. S. ARMIES:

Your note of this date is but this moment (11:50 A.M.) received, in consequence of my having passed from the Richmond and Lynchburg road to the Farmville and Lynchburg road. I am at this writing about four miles west of Walker's Church and will push forward to the front for the purpose of meeting with you. Notice sent to me on this road where you wish the interview to take place will meet me.

U. S. Grant

LIEUTENANT-GENERAL

Colonel Babcock galloped directly toward the Confederate lines with the reply, waving a white flag high above his head. Grant walked back to his horse. He grasped the saddle horn and paused as he looked at the worn-out saddle. He'd had it continuously since the fall of Fort Donelson; the saddle showed heavy signs of hard use. The leather was worn paper thin and smooth in the center, and the pommel chafed clean of all stain until it gleamed like exposed bone. Worn down by this war just like me, Grant thought. And just like Lincoln.

At their last meeting at City Point, the President appeared years older, as though he'd aged decades in little more than weeks. While Grant directed the tightening noose around Richmond and Petersburg from his cabin at City Point, Lincoln anxiously awaited the inevitable end aboard the steamer *River Queen*, anchored in the harbor.

How the President could stand to live those last two weeks on the dank and rocking boat was a mystery to Grant. But he did, choosing to be close to the action, as he put it. While they met often, old Abe never interfered.

Grant ran his hand over the worn leather. Which one would give out first, Lincoln, the saddle, or me? he mused. His part was almost over. But Lincoln's task was only half done, and the President knew it. Clearly, Lincoln worried now about returning the South to the nation.

Grant mounted easily and spurred Cincinnati into a trot which the spirited animal, happy that his rider was back in fit form, took to with relish. Heading toward Appomattox Courthouse, the group shortly encountered Colonel Newhall, adjutant general of Sheridan's staff, with a duplicate message from Lee.

At one o'clock the party crossed a rise and entered the outskirts of Appomattox. Grant reined in his horse and rose in his stirrups to study what lay ahead. Situated on a rise, the town overlooked a broad valley. Grant's eyes followed the curve of the land. Past the town the land dropped gently away to expose the curve of the forest to his right and a wide-open plain of poorly tended fields and broken fences to his left. The arcing road from town divided the two just as surely as war now split their nation. Scattered peach and apple trees dotted the fields, covered with pink and white blossoms as if in celebration. Flitting among these blossoms, scarlet cardinals and blue jays darted into clumps of sweet gum, white oak, and ash, ignoring the armies drawn up below them.

The faintest scent of the apple blossoms reached Grant's nose, a delicate and wistful fragrance out of place amidst the heavy odor of sweating horses, soiled leather, and smoke-stained uniforms. He sniffed appreciatively, his nose seeking the flowers' perfume instead of the smells of war.

Grant blinked, drawn to the defiant gesture of the blossoms and the birds. As always, nature continued its supreme indifference to war. The days of greatest killing were always sunny.

But it *was* a gorgeous day, and this was the first time he had noticed. A ray of optimism flickered inside him. Spring was here, and already the earth was repairing the damage of winter and the war. With spring came renewed hope. How often had Lincoln stressed to him the necessity of letting the defeated South up easy? With Lincoln in charge, the nation would repair itself just as the land before him was doing.

Grant shook away his feelings when his eyes caught sight of the army in the valley. Lee's army. Too many years of fighting prompted the hairs to raise on Grant's neck and his senses to quicken as he appraised the columns of wagons and rows of infantry drawn up near the curve of the Appomattox River. Ragged and starving, but still drawn up in good order. Exhausted, yet still proud, just like their commanding general. And with plenty of sting left. Lee's army could—and would—fight if ordered. Thousands more would be killed or crippled for life. But the end would be unchanged; the Army of Northern Virginia would be destroyed.

Dr. Smith's words, relating what General Ewell had said, echoed in Grant's ears. Any men killed at this point would be nothing less than murder.

With grim satisfaction, Grant noted a far greater number of blue soldiers arrayed in battle order before him. Holding the high ground that rimmed the bowl containing the Army of Northern Virginia, he recognized the fluttering guidons of the Fifth Corps, General Ord's soldiers, and Sheridan's cavalry. Carpeting the south and west hills, the Union troops surrounded the Confederates. There was no way out for those weary men in the hollow. If they fought, they would be slaughtered.

While Cincinnati moved easily down the road, his rider studied the town ahead. The Lynchburg-Richmond stage road cut straight between a two-story, redbrick house with white railings rimming both the first and second floors and a white frame store. Straight as an arrow the road led to the octagonal patch of lawn with its white picket fence surrounding the brick courthouse of Appomattox. Orderly whitewashed fences lined the stage route. Beyond the imposing courthouse with its chimneys at all four corners, the road exited the town and curved down into the valley to where the rebel forces waited.

The war seems to have missed this town, Grant realized. How different from Richmond, with its blackened buildings and starkly poignant smokestacks standing alone against the spark-filled sky. As the houses burned to the ground there, they left their brick chimneys, pointing like accusing fingers at the sky, mute testament to the bitter fruits of war. Grant knew the inhabitants of the rebel capital blamed his men. What would they say if they knew the fire that burned Richmond started when the retreating Confederates burned their ammunition stores? They would not believe it.

Grant twisted his neck against the chafing of his soiled collar and tightened his hands on his reins. If Lee backs out now, he thought, this peaceful town will vanish. My artillery pieces will rut the road, the orderly fences will disappear—used for fortifications—and the handsome buildings will sag and crumble, pitted with round shot, or be burned to the ground.

Ahead he recognized General Ord. With him, he saw Phil Sheridan, wearing his flattened porkpie hat, surrounded by his staff and seated on his handsome black charger, Rienzi. Only Sheridan could wear his hat at such a jaunty angle and not lose it during a charge, Grant mused. Sheridan was the consummate warrior, always at the forefront of his troops, unafraid of death, and graced with that luck only an Irishman could claim. Grant nodded to Porter. "Sheridan," he said softly.

Porter's face gleamed as he saw the jaunty figure. "General Sheridan, the Murat of our cavalry. Why, at the Battle of Five Forks, I heard he raced ahead of his men, yelling: 'Go at them with a will, boys. Move on them with a clean jump, or you'll not catch one of them!' Then he jumped Rienzi over the rebel breastworks and landed smack in the middle of the startled defenders."

"And those men surrendered without a shot," Grant said, finishing the tale. He thought, Sheridan's lucky he didn't get his head blown off. Little good he'd be to me then, just when I needed him the most.

As they approached the jaunty general, Grant thought back to events of the evening of the fourth, just five days ago. While riding parallel to the South Side Railroad on the road linking Burkeville and Nottoway, a horseman in full Confederate dress had emerged from the trees to their right and calmly trotted directly toward General Grant and his staff. Startled officers had spurred their mounts to intercept this sudden threat.

But Grant had recognized the rider as Campbell, a spy attached to Sheridan. Campbell produced a ball of wax paper from within his mouth, which carried a tissue paper message from Sheridan. No doubt, if necessary Campbell would have swallowed the evidence, which would have gotten him shot on the spot. The message from Sheridan read: *I wish you were here yourself.*

Then Grant had done the unexpected—as one might expect. With Porter and only three other officers as guards, he'd ridden off with Campbell in search of Sheridan. Straight through rebel-held territory. Wending their way in the dark, they encountered fresh signs of Confederate cavalry moving nearby. As Campbell led them on his circuitous route, Colonel Porter constantly wiped his sweaty palms on his blouse and kept his pistol free of its holster, mindful that many spies were double agents, working for whichever side paid them last.

But Campbell had proved true, and soon they reached Sheridan's lines, where a startled picket blurted out: "Great Scott! The old chief's out here himself!" Grant only smiled when another added: "Uncle Sam's joined the cavalry sure enough. Boys, this means business."

That nighttime conference between Grant and his chief of cavalry led to this iron snare that now held the Army of Northern Virginia.

What a contrast the two men made that night: the fiery, bombastic Sheridan and the level, practical Grant.

"Lee is in a bad fix," Grant had said without a trace of emotion, stating a fact as he saw it, with no thought of embellishment. "It will be difficult for him to get away."

With that Sheridan jumped up, slammed his fist into the palm of his hand like a hammer and shouted. "Damn him! He can't get away! We'll have his whole army. We'll have every goddamned one of them!"

Calmly and quietly, the Commander-in-Chief shook his head, saying, "That's a little too much to expect. I think if I were Lee, I could escape with at least some of my men."

And Lee almost did slip out of their grasp, burning the elevated railroad trestle, and the wagon bridge over the swollen Appomattox River to block the Union troop's pursuit. Only the prompt arrival of their advance guard, using their hats and whatever else could carry water, saved the bridge. With the wooden spars still smoldering, Meade's foot cavalry stumbled after the retreating Army of Northern Virginia. Like hounds hot on the scent of a fox, the men smelled victory, and nothing these last days could hold them back. Marching twenty miles to fight a battle each day, they still clamored to press on.

Now here was Sheridan in position as promised, the cork in the bottle. Grant drew alongside his cavalry commander. He touched the brim of his floppy hat. "How are you, Sheridan?"

The little man rose in his stirrups, his eyes sparkling, and a broad grin spread almost from one ear to the other. "First rate, thank you! How are you?" Sheridan cried with full voice. His élan was not lost on his own staff, who patterned themselves after their jaunty commander. Brigadier General Custer grinned as well, still basking in the warm glow of his capture of the rebel supply trains, which had sealed the fate of their foe. The boy general doffed his wide-brimmed hat like a Royalist Cavalier, and a murmur of approval issued from the cavalrymen.

Sheridan had been chafing at the bit since early morning; when Lee's army stepped into the snare, his fighting instincts let loose. The white flag had gone up so promptly on the Confederate side, Sheridan admitted to a twinge of disappointment that no battle would be fought. But sitting astride Rienzi, he could not contain his pride. And the acute angle of his flattened hat readily manifested that feeling, as did the fresh polish of his knee-high boots and shoulder straps.

Moreover, as he looked from Custer, with his ridiculously wide hat, embroidered gauntlets, and flowing red scarf, to the slumped, mud-spattered man who was their commander-in-chief, Sheridan wished Grant would dress more like the victorious general he was and show more enthusiasm for his triumph. By God, Grant deserves that! he thought.

But Grant was all business, as usual. Without answering Sheridan's inquiry as to his well-being, he got straight to the point. "Is Lee over there?" he asked, gesturing with his head to the town ahead.

Sheridan twisted in his stirrups and pointed to a two-story building with a double-tiered white porch, the customary whitewashed fence, and a curious white gatehouse blocking the front path. "Yes. There is his army down in the valley, and he's in the brick house, waiting to surrender to you."

Grant nodded. His eyes caught sight of a magnificent gray horse nibbling contentedly on the grass by the fence. A dark mare grazed alongside, while a Confederate orderly watched them. Always a connoisseur of horses, Grant admired the lines of the animal. He next noticed the gold stars on the animal's saddle blanket. That must be Traveler, he thought. I'd know him anywhere from his descriptions. Almost as famous as his rider, I'd imagine.

Grant looked down at Cincinnati. Well, old boy, you don't have to take a backseat to any animal yourself, he thought fondly, and he patted the horse's strong neck. But maybe you warrant a fancier rider. Cincinnati swung its head and looked back as if to disagree.

A curious change came over Grant, though outwardly he gave no evidence of it. The jubilation that followed the surrender notice delivered by Lieutenant Pease had soured. Instead, he felt depressed at the sight of that notable animal and its empty saddle. A sadness settled on his shoulders, to replace the weight that had lifted with Lee's last note. Inside waited Robert E. Lee, the legendary leader of this rebel army, a man whose tactics had paralyzed and confounded so many of Grant's ill-fated predecessors.

For any one twist of fate, I might be in his shoes, waiting to surrender my command, Grant thought. Am I a better general, or am I just luckier? No, I do not believe in luck in war. War is progressive. Luck may affect a battle or even a movement, but not the outcome of a campaign. I beat Lee because my plan was better than his. Lee is a master of maneuver, exquisitely skilled in field movements, but not at attacking. But I always attack.

Grant shrugged his shoulders as if unconsciously adjusting the weight this new sadness carried. As he nudged Cincinnati forward, he looked at Sheridan impassively. "Well, then, we'll go over," he said matter-of-factly.

As their chief and his entourage rode by, passing through the battle lines, scores of soldiers rose from their positions. Some removed their caps, but most urged Grant not to go farther. "Don't go, General. It's a trick," one man shouted to a chorus of agreeing shouts. "Let us finish them off!" another added. One lone voice said, "I reckon they've learned their lesson, General. If they are of a mind to return to the fold, you've got my blessing to let them in." Grant nodded to that man as he rode toward the brick house.

Sheridan followed, holding his breath as they approached the Confederate lines. His dark eyes darted from tree to tree. All sorts of mischief and misunderstanding followed the flag of truce, and the cavalry officer feared some diehard still might open fire on Grant. As Sheridan had ridden toward the Confederate general Gordon earlier that day, he was amazed to see Gordon's flag bearer struggling with a tattered rebel soldier who rushed forth and tried to capture the banner. It took the word of Gordon himself to convince the soldier that he was the one who was surrendering, not the Union soldiers.

And there was the matter of General Geary's brigade of cavalry, who kept firing in spite of the cease-fire. When Sheridan, at Gordon's urging, sent his own staff officer, Lieutenant Vanderbilt Allen, under a white flag to declare the truce, Geary took Allen prisoner. "I do not care for white flags," Geary swore. "South Carolinians never surrender!" It took a concerted attack of overwhelming force to free Allen and discharge Geary of his foolish last-stand notions.

Fortunately, the Union generals now reached their destination unobstructed. Grant dismounted, tied his horse to the fence, and climbed the seven steps to the first landing with his entourage close behind. The long hallway was lined with doors on each side. Instantly, the first door on the left swung open, and Colonel Babcock ushered his commander inside the room.

Grant stepped inside and looked around. The white walls were decorated with paintings of hunting scenes, duck hunters, and stags, hung in heavy gilded frames. A thick Persian carpet, predominantly burgundy with a contrasting gray-green medallion pattern, covered the floor. A bookcase of dark oak hugged one corner, and a mantel of darker wood covered the fireplace, while a sofa, upholstered in red velvet similar to the rug, occupied the other wall. Two tables, each with a single chair, had been pulled hastily into the center of the room.

Grant realized that the tables were placed so they would not have to directly face or confront one another. Instead, one was located at right angles to the other. Grant approved. Someone with enough sensibility left after all this horror, whether Colonel Babcock of his army or Lee's aide, Colonel Charles Marshall, sought to ease some of the stress of this encounter.

All eyes turned to the man who rose on their arrival. Drawn stiffly erect to his full height of over six feet, General Robert E. Lee gazed down at Grant. His clear blue eyes studied every detail of the stoop-shouldered man standing before him without revealing the slightest hint of emotion. Neither trace of smile nor frown marred Lee's firmly pressed lips.

This is my just punishment, Lee thought, for as I have written my wife, I have been truly sinful. That this man, who has not the civility to wear a fresh uniform or clean boots, should vanquish my army can only be through the hand of Providence. It is God's will, he resolved, that the South should lose, that the South with all its patriotism and spirit should fall before the commercialism of the North.

As Lee stood before Grant, a passage his father, Light Horse Harry Lee, wrote ran through his head. At times of great distress, like this and after Longstreet's corps broke upon the rocks of the Federal fire at Gettysburg, he quoted those lines to himself to stiffen his resolve. " 'A man ought not to be only virtuous in reality, but he must also always appear so'; thus said the great Washington."

Grant extended his hand in a quick straightforward thrust so characteristic of the man himself, a move that broke Lee's moment of reflection. "I met you once before, General Lee," he said, "while we were serving in Mexico, when you came over from General Scott's headquarters to visit Garland's brigade, to which I then belonged." Grant smiled warmly. "I have always remembered your appearance, and I think I should have recognized you anywhere."

Lee took the hand—as a matter of courtesy more than anything else. He studied the face before him. A plain face, he thought, but one fixed with firm resolve that shows in the clarity of his eye and the grim set of his jaw. More like a farmer set upon saving his principal crop from the impending storm. A sudden chill of understanding ran through Lee as he sampled the firmness of Grant's grip. I am mistaken, he realized. Not like a simple farmer at all, more like a Cromwell! And I like Charles the First.

"Yes," Lee responded. "I know I met you on that occasion, and I have often thought of it." He paused hoping to see a glimmer of pride rise into Grant's face, willing his adversary to take the bait, so that he might have some small victory from all this. But Grant remained impassive, so Lee halfheartedly launched his petty barb. "And I tried to recollect how you looked, but I have never been able to recall a single feature."

An audible murmur rose from Grant's staff at this slight. But their general took no notice.

Suddenly ashamed of his shallow actions, Lee cut to the painful reason for their meeting. "I suppose, General Grant, that the object of our present meeting is fully understood. I asked to see you to ascertain upon what terms you would receive the surrender of my army."

"The terms I propose are those stated substantially in my letter of yesterday. That is, the officers and men surrendered to be paroled and disqualified from taking up arms again until properly exchanged, and all arms, ammunition, and supplies to be delivered up as captured property." Grant looked past Lee to Colonel Charles Marshall, Lee's secretary. Straight as his master but thin as a rail, Marshall's narrow face with its sparse goatee and pince-nez glasses gave the man the look of a misplaced French instructor rather than an officer in a rebel army. Dressed in a spotless uniform also, Marshall looked ready to cry.

Lee nodded slowly. "Those are about the conditions I expected would be proposed." His voice remained deep and flat and devoid of all emotion.

Grant continued evenly as if clarifying a point. "Yes. I think our correspondence indicated pretty clearly the action that would be taken at our meeting." I don't think I left any room for misunderstanding, he thought. These are generous and simple terms. "I hope it may lead to a general suspension of hostilities, and be the means of preventing any further loss of life." Again, the words of Dr. Smith echoed in his mind.

Lee bowed his head. Whether he meant it as a sign of agreement or not, the act struck Grant as similar to that of a man hearing his death sentence being pronounced. He sought to soften the effect, but Lee pressed on with the unpleasant task.

"I presume, General Grant, we have both carefully considered the proper steps to be taken, and I would suggest that you commit to writing the terms you have proposed, so that they may be formally acted upon."

Grant studied Lee's implacable face, entrenched behind its white beard and veiled eyes. Proper steps? What proper steps? he thought. You surrender to me, and that's the only step needed. That's what Pemberton and Buckner did.

Lee's actions were not in keeping with what Grant knew of his operations. Lee relied on general orders, verbal orders, affording his field commanders wide discretion in their implementation. His adversary rarely wrote an order himself, unlike Grant, who personally wrote most of his commands. Lee was not one to fret over crossing t's.

Suddenly, it became clear to Grant: There is more than this man's great personal dignity at stake here. There is the matter of propriety. Lee is presiding over the surrender of an army of which he has become the prevailing cause.

It was no secret that men of the Army of Northern Virginia fought for Lee as much as for anything else. Lee, with his almost mystical righteousness, personified the soul of his force. *He was their cause.* He had shared their meager rations, suffered with them, and held them together when no one else could. He had led them to victory, and now he would lead them to defeat. But *he* alone would do it, no one else. Subordinates would not handle this momentous undertaking.

Grant reached out his hand. "Very well. I will write them out. Colonel Parker, my order book." Grant moved to the small table behind him. Settling into a comfortable padded leather swivel chair, he looked over at the table behind which Lee now sat. That table was a massive pedestal affair of what appeared to be highly polished cherry. Gracefully carved filigrees decorated the edges and the base. Grant looked down at his cramped surface, then back to Lee's handsome table. Well, it matches his uniform, he thought. A plain table fits a plain uniform like mine.

Then he saw the chair Lee had. A straight-backed cane chair with thin arms, it looked like something pulled from the porch at the last moment. The Confederate general sat stiffly, as if the chair were too small to contain him. Lee's table is grander than mine, Grant mused, but my chair is more comfortable.

Suddenly, he realized he had not given any thought to wording the surrender terms other than what he had written to Lee in their dispatches. I suppose others would couch this in grandiose terms, but I won't, he vowed. Quickly, he wrote from his heart.

> APPOMATTOX COURTHOUSE, VA., APRIL 9, 1865.
>
> GENERAL R. E. LEE, COMMANDING C.S.A.
>
> GENERAL: In accordance with the substance of my letter to you of the 8th inst., I propose to receive the surrender of the Army of Northern Virginia on the following terms, to wit: Rolls of all the officers and men to be made in duplicate, one copy to be given to an officer to be designated by me, the other to be retained by such officer or officers as you may designate. The officers to give their individual paroles not to take up arms against the Government of the United States until properly, and each company or regimental commander to sign a like parole for the men of their commands. The arms, artillery, and public property to be parked and stacked and turned over to the officers appointed by me to receive them.

Grant paused and looked up. His eyes moved directly to the beautiful sword hanging from Lee's belt and stopped, captivated by the fine weapon. Light glinted off the decorated scabbard and the jeweled hilt. Obviously, this was a presentation sword of great value that Lee wore. Grant raised his eyebrows ever so slightly. No need to add insult by asking for that sword, he thought, that would be an unneeded humiliation. So, he continued:

> This will not embrace the side-arms of the officers, nor their private horses or baggage. This done, each officer and man will be allowed to return to his home, not to be disturbed by the United States authorities so long as they observe their paroles and the laws in force where they may reside.
>
> Very respectfully,
> U. S. GRANT,
> Lieutenant-General

Colonel Parker leaned over his general and pointed to where Grant had written one word twice. Grant grunted in embarrassment and ordered Parker to strike it out. He rose from his chair and extended his arm with the order book to Lee. But Lee remained frozen. Quickly, Colonel Porter took the papers and carried them to General Lee.

Where Grant's table was bare, a pair of brass candleholders and a book rested before Lee. Almost violently, Lee's arm cleared a space on his table, his action sweeping the candleholders and book brusquely aside while he slammed his hat and gauntlets onto the open space. As rapidly as his tiny burst of frustration flared, it just as quickly vanished. The silver-haired man once more resumed his imperturbable facade. His face remained placid, almost serene, while he slowly removed a pair of steel-rimmed glasses from his inside breast pocket, polished the lenses attentively, and placed the spectacles on his face.

With legs crossed, he read the terms as a heavy silence filled the room. Marshall hovered at his superior's side, his eyes blinking rapidly with emotion.

Lee readjusted his glasses, but not before giving his military secretary a mindful glance, as if to order him to regain his composure. That look did wonders, and Marshall straightened his back and squared his shoulders. Almost like a schoolteacher who had discovered a pupil's error, Lee looked up, tapped a place on the paper and said: "You seem to have omitted the word 'exchanged' after the words 'until properly.' I presume you omitted the word inadvertently."

Grant's frown deepened, making his left eye appear to drop even lower than his right one. "I thought I had put in the word 'exchanged,'" he said. Behind him, Colonel Parker grimaced at the omission he had also missed.

Lee recrossed his legs. "With your permission," he said slowly, "I will mark where it should be inserted." His soft Virginia accent grew more pronounced. He patted his uniform jacket as if looking for a pencil, only to accept one Colonel Porter offered him.

As Lee studiously read the rest of the draft, he tapped the pencil on the table from time to time and twirled it between his fingers. The twirling

stopped when he read the passage allowing him and his officers to keep
their side arms. His face softened and he nodded his head slightly. "This
will have a happy effect upon my army," he commented. "But there is one
thing I should like to mention. The cavalrymen and artillerists own their
own horses. In that respect the organization of our army differs from that of
the United States."

The men in blue standing silently behind General Grant shifted uneasily at this last comment. Sheridan's face darkened while General Ord
pulled at his golden mustache and shook his head.

Grant chewed thoughtfully on his lip and absentmindedly stroked his
beard as he considered Lee's prescient remark: *from that of the United States.*
Through all four bloody years they had looked upon their foe as rebellious,
contumacious, and contrary, yet still Americans. Lee's statement drove
home the realization that the South really considered itself a different
country. Lincoln was right to worry about mending this awful breach. His
work would be arduous. At that moment Grant understood the magnitude
of responsibility that aged his president more each day.

Lee pressed on with no evidence that he recognized the distress his
words had caused. He looked over the rim of his glasses directly at Grant.
"I should like to understand whether these men will be permitted to retain
their horses," he asked.

Grant hunched forward from his chair, bent in his characteristic
crouch with both arms resting on his table. "You will find that the terms as
written do not allow this," he said flatly. "Only the officers are permitted to
take their private property." From the corner of his eye he saw Sheridan
and General Custer nod vigorously in agreement. There was no question
his staff agreed with the terms. They were too generous for most of the
Union officers as it was. Except ... The words of Lincoln rang in his ears:
*Let 'em up easy.*

Lee's eyes dropped to the paper in his hand. "No, I see the terms do
not allow it. That is clear." A notable edge of tension filled his voice. His
men had suffered for so long and fought so valiantly for their cause, a cause
he still considered just. In serving their conscience, they had lost everything, their health, their wealth, and their honor. Now they were to lose

their animals, the only possessions most had of any value. How could he face them if he did not fight for the horses that might restore their ruined homelands?

Grant stroked his beard as he noticed the marked change in Lee's countenance. The face that moments before appeared almost haughty, now looked worn and tired. A vessel alongside Lee's right temple pulsed visibly, and plainly his eyes looked anxious. His lips moved slightly, and Grant feared the old man was steeling himself to plead for his broken soldiers.

Before Lee could speak, Grant said. "Well, this subject is quite new to me. Of course I did not know that any private soldiers owned their animals. But I think we have fought the last battle of the war—I sincerely hope so." He paused to look directly at Marshall and then at Lee. Without that gray-haired man seated across from him, the Confederacy and its remaining troops would sue for peace. "And that the surrender of this army will be followed soon by that of all the others." He paused again to let his words sink in—as much for his own men as for Lee.

His gaze drifted out the window at the front of the room to the flowering trees on the hillside. Spring, a time for rebuilding, a time for planting. "I take it that most of the men in the ranks are small farmers."

Lee nodded.

"And as the country has been so raided by the two armies, it is doubtful whether they will be able to put in a crop to carry themselves and their families through the next winter without the aid of the horses they are now riding."

Grant paused again, and his men thought he was considering the problem. But he was thinking of those hard times when he was pitied by all in St. Louis, forced to cut and haul firewood to keep his family from starving. He would not hinder a man feeding his family, he vowed. He had been there, and he knew how it felt.

"I will arrange it this way. I will not change the terms as now written. But I will instruct the officers I shall appoint to receive the paroles to let all the men who claim to own a horse or mule take the animals home with them to work their little farms."

Lee sighed. The corners of his mouth turned upward into the slightest smile, and his eyes filled with tears which he blinked hurriedly away. "This will have the best possible effect upon the men," he replied. "It will be very gratifying and will do much toward conciliating our people."

The tension within the room dissolved. A frantic search for ink delayed the needed copies until Colonel Marshall produced a boxwood inkstand from his pocket. Lee signed a letter of acceptance, then rose to his feet while Grant presented his staff. The old general bowed silently to each man introduced until he came to General Seth Williams. The balding Williams had been Lee's adjutant at West Point in better times. The two men shook hands sadly. Williams attempted a lighthearted banter about their days at West Point, but Lee's stern visage silenced him.

When General Grant presented his secretary, Colonel Ely Parker, a full-blooded Indian, Lee blinked in amazement at the dark-skinned officer. A reigning chief of the Six Nations and grand nephew of Red Jacket, Parker's Indian name was Donehogawa. With a degree in civil engineering, Parker was a complex and educated man, standing astride the two worlds of his heritage and the industrial world.

A surprised look crossed Lee's face as he mistook Parker for a Negro holding the rank of Colonel in the Union Army. Parker smiled obtusely. That mistake had been made before, but he had no wish to enlighten General Lee.

Now, General Grant became acutely aware of the disparity between his dress and the elegantly attired Lee. The Confederate's gray dress uniform was spotless, adorned with gleaming rows of buttons and a handsome sash. His hat matched his coat perfectly, as did his gauntlets. The presentation sword glittering at his side reminded Grant poignantly that he was not even wearing one.

Grant looked self-consciously at his mud-encrusted boots. The clumps of dirt covered the knee-length leather, spilling onto the trousers tucked into the tops of the boots. Even his coat was worn and shabby, a private's coat, without the double rows of brass buttons arranged in clusters of threes befitting a general officer. Only the soiled shoulder straps with their faded three stars identified this short, stoop-shouldered man as Ulysses S. Grant, Lieutenant-General and Commander-in-Chief of the United States Army.

For some reason, Grant felt compelled to explain his attire to Lee, something he rarely did. Even standing before Lincoln that day in Washington when the President promoted him to the rank of Lieutenant General, Grant wore his customary plain uniform. But it *was* clean, Grant reminded himself, and the President was just as simply dressed with his black frock coat. But the granite visage, the rigid bearing, and the immense personal dignity of his vanquished foe demanded an explanation. He wanted Lee to understand his attire was not a sign of disrespect but a matter of circumstance.

"I started out from my camp several days ago without my sword," he explained, "and I have not seen my headquarters baggage since." He looked down at his coat and patted his empty pockets. "I have been riding about without any side arms."

Lee listened attentively. What sort of a commanding officer rides out without his sword, he thought, whatever the circumstance? A sword is as essential to an officer as his trousers.

Grant cocked his head slightly, sensing the reproach. Tell the truth, he reminded himself. You hardly ever wear a sword. You hate them. After all, what use is one to a commanding general except to get tangled in his legs? I'd be a fool to lead a charge, wouldn't I? That's for men like Custer and Sheridan. Let them have their swords, I'll give the orders.

"I have generally worn a sword, however, as little as possible—only during the active operations of a campaign," he admitted.

Lee inclined his head while his hand rested on his weapon. "I am in the habit of wearing mine *most of the time*—when I am among my troops moving about through the army."

Grant nodded his head at this bit of instruction. Lee extended his hand to Grant, bowed to the others, donned his hat and gloves with studied care, and walked out of the room. Silently, the Union officers filed onto the porch.

Lee paused on the bottom step and turned his head toward the valley where his army waited. If things had been different, he thought. His right hand curled into a fist. Three times he struck the palm of his gloved left hand. *If only ... only ...*

Around him Union soldiers rose to their feet in silence, but he ignored them. Only the arrival of Traveler recalled him to the present. He mounted and turned his head toward General Grant, who descended from the porch to look up at him. Tension charged the air as the soldiers waited to take their cue from Grant. If he cheered, a thousand voices would join him. Muskets would fire and fill the air with smoke.

Instead, Grant simply raised his hat in a silent but elegant salute.

Lee returned the gesture with his own hat, and Grant's staff did the same. The thousands of surrounding soldiers fell silent as the defeated general rode in a slow trot toward his lines.

You are but an instrument of the hand of Providence, Lee reminded himself as he rode. This is God's will that the South and I have been brought so low. I must satisfy myself that I have done my duty as God has seen fit to allow me to do. I shall speak no more about this war, but shall endeavor to rebuild Virginia and myself. This conflict is ended for me.

But the dark looking glass of the future held more surprises for all that day. Abraham Lincoln, the one man who single-handedly held the Union together, would fall from an assassin's bullet. The youthful, long-haired General Custer standing on the porch would be massacred with all his men in a battle that would rock the nation. And even Lee and Grant would not go untouched.

On September 28, 1870, barely five years later, Robert E. Lee, returned home to share tea with his family. Stricken as he rose to give thanks for their meal, he found himself unable to speak. Calmly accepting the will of God, as he always did, Lee took to his bed. On October 12 he died.

Now, as Ulysses S. Grant stood watching Lee ride off, he also assumed his task in life was finished. Always practical, his thoughts turned to a white mule tied nearby that reminded him of a similar animal during the

Mexican War. Then he reminded himself to cancel supply orders to save his government money. He would like to see his family waiting in their log cottage back at City Point, he realized. Beyond that he had no plans.

Little could he imagine what fate had in mind for him. Rising even higher than at this moment, he would serve two disastrous terms as president of the country he and Lincoln saved. His fortune would be taken from him, leaving him more impoverished than when he eked out an existence selling firewood. To save his wife from crushing poverty, he would wage one last, desperate battle—the most important of his life.

# THE BIOPSY

Dr. George Shrady adjusted the wire-rimmed pince-nez glasses on the bridge of his aquiline nose and studied the glass slide in his hand. A minuscule lump of violet tissue rested on the center. Tentatively, his right hand dropped from his glasses to touch the lump. He gently pressed the specimen against the glass. Its firmness, resisting the pressure of his finger, told him more than he wanted to know. It was almost as if the biopsy wished to proclaim its virulence, its deadliness. He precisely applied the methylene blue stain and slipped the specimen underneath his microscope.

Closing his left eye, he squinted into the eyepiece while he fingered the heavy knob of the brass microscope, coaxing the field into focus. Begrudgingly, he admired the brightness of the scene from the new Zeiss microscope from Germany. The microscope was in keeping with this office—everything was first-rate. The wood floors sported a lustrous polish, the glass cabinet held gleaming, stainless instruments, and even the air carried the cleansing bite of carbolic acid, the latest antiseptic. Dr. Shrady studied the slide.

The dark stain of the closely clustered nuclei in the sample confirmed what his finger already knew. Scattered whorls of unruly cells streamed like raiding parties into the space of normal cells. Here and there the raiders broke through the walls of blood vessels that coursed throughout the specimen. As if determined to launch an amphibious assault, rafts of the darker cells flooded the twisting channels.

Cancer.

Shrady straightened from his task, sighed, and removed his glasses. He wiped the back of his hand across his mustache, turning it over in the process to stroke the narrow goatee that drooped from his chin. His colleagues chided him that his beard and mustache made him look like Napoleon III, but Shrady liked the effect. The linearity of his Vandyke served to accentuate his narrow, angular face and deep-set eyes, giving him the look of a Roman aesthete not to be expected in one of New York's most prominent surgeons.

The expectant stares prompted him to return to the matter at hand. "This specimen comes from the throat and base of the tongue and is affected with cancer," he said.

"You are sure?" asked Dr. George Elliot, who glanced knowingly at the two other men in the room.

"Perfectly sure. The patient has a lingual epithelioma cancer of the tongue."

"Do you think surgery might hold out a chance for cure?" asked one of the men, who bore a striking resemblance to the poet Henry Wadsworth Longfellow.

Shrady pursed his lips as he turned to face John Hancock Douglas. Taller and more imposing than Shrady, Douglas's shock of white hair and full, flowing beard covering his cravat made him resemble the dead abolitionist John Brown, except Douglas's eye bore none of the madness that once filled Brown's. Even though Shrady and Douglas had crossed academic swords on occasion, each man respected the other. Douglas was recognized as the foremost authority on throat ailments, while Shrady's fame as one of the leading proponents of the new science of plastic surgery grew with each passing day.

"Would you describe to me the findings of your examination again, Dr. Douglas?" Shrady asked.

"Dr. Barker?" Douglas deferred to the other man.

Standing slightly behind and to the left of Douglas, Fordyce Barker stepped closer. While dressed somberly, except for the heavy gold watch chain that crossed his waistcoat, one could have easily mistaken Barker for a poet laureate or a misplaced romantic rather than a physician. Enormous white muttonchop sideburns coursed down both cheeks like frosty waves raging against a stern coastline. With their milky exuberance, they brushed his stiff, starched collar and flanked both sides of his neck. Silver hair set in ringlets crowned his head, and, to complete the picture, a wavy forelock offset his melancholy eyes.

Dr. Fordyce Barker was one of the most progressive and modern physicians of his time. Each year, he made a pilgrimage to Europe in search of the latest medical advances, and he was the first physician in America to use the hypodermic needle and syringe.

As if lecturing his students, Barker grasped the lapels of his black broadcloth jacket and spoke. While he took pains to speak softly, his deep voice rolled forth, and his words filled the room. "The lesion occupies the base of the tongue on the right side. It appears to have grown rapidly from a pea-sized nodule, which was first discovered last June."

Fast, indeed, Shrady thought. But such growth was consistent with the virulent appearance of the tumor cells.

Barker paused and looked at his colleague. Douglas nodded in accord. "I confirmed Dr. Barker's examination using the new reflecting head mirrors." He pointed to a circular mirror with a central hole, which was fastened to a leather head strap that lay on the counter to his right. Beside it an alcohol lamp still flickered. "There is also congestion and inflammation of the soft palate, as well as ulceration of the right tonsillar fossa and the hard palate." Douglas paused to let his information sink in. "And three nodules invading the hard palate."

Shrady watched John Douglas's eyes cloud. Obviously, this patient was well known to Douglas—and a friend. "And he has a palpable lymph node in his neck?" Shrady guessed the obvious.

"The right neck ..." Douglas nodded sadly. "He is in much discomfort, finding it most painful to swallow. I cleansed the ulcerations and swabbed them with Lodoform, the newest derivative of chloroform, and that brought the patient some relief. Just now I administered hydrochlorate of cocaine for this biopsy. Please, Doctor, what is your prognosis?" Douglas tried to keep his voice steady, but his clenched fists spoke far more eloquently of his own distress.

Shrady winced at the outpouring of emotion. "Your patient is doomed, I'm afraid," he said flatly. He saw little sense in denying the obvious, as these men were trying so hard to do. After all, they had solicited his expert opinion.

"The patient is General Grant," Dr. Barker blurted out.

Shrady gasped. "Surely, that cannot be! Why, as I was arriving in my cab, I saw your patient disembark from the streetcar and climb the steps to your office. The former President of the United States taking the streetcar?"

"He rides the streetcar twice a day to my office for treatments," Barker went on. "He does so to save the cab fare. The general is in dire financial straits since the collapse of Grant and Ward. He—"

"There is no need to discuss the general's financial situation in this medical conference," Dr. Douglas said sharply. "Dr. Shrady, what you have learned here is of a highly private nature. Both the medical and the financial aspects," he interjected sternly, "and must be kept strictly confidential. I trust that is clearly understood. General Grant is entitled to whatever privacy can be provided him in this distressing period."

"I agree wholeheartedly," Shrady replied.

"Good." Douglas smiled within the confines of his luxurious beard, but only the slightest elevation of the ends of his mustache betrayed the fact that he had grinned. "Would you care to meet General Grant?"

"Indeed, I would be honored."

Without further discussion, Douglas grasped Shrady's arm and ushered the younger man through the door into his inner office, where a smallish man sat slumped in an overstuffed leather chair. A silk top hat obscured the upper half of the man's face, and when he looked up at the doctors, he bore no resemblance to any of the well-known pictures of the famous man that Shrady had ever seen. Were the man to pass within two feet of him, Shrady thought, he would not have recognized him as the hero of the Great War and former President.

Grant rose to meet them, removing his hat.

The transformation was nothing short of miraculous. Without that hat shading the face, the broad forehead, furrowed brow, and fixed look of grim determination came clearly into view. Now, Dr. Shrady saw the curious twist to the general's features that set his left eye lower than his right, and the wart resting on the right fold of his cheek, just like Abe Lincoln's. Equally plain was the perpetually furrowed brow that many said gave Grant the look of a man determined to drive his head through a brick wall.

Grant's clear blue eyes fixed them sharply. Unclouded as the purest river ice, those eyes studied the doctors in detail, as if analyzing the topography of a battle map, probing the strengths and weaknesses of an enemy's position. To Shrady's surprise, the color of Grant's eyes shifted from blue to gray, filling with warmth, as he spoke: "I see Dr. Douglas has called a staff meeting on my behalf." Grant chuckled. "My case must be a hard nut to crack."

Even the voice caught Shrady off guard. He did not know that Horace Porter, one of Grant's staff officers during the war, described Grant's voice as having "a singular power of penetration." But Grant's words, spoken softly and with some discomfort, resonated clearly throughout the room.

Because of his past experience with elected officials, Shrady was prepared to dislike Grant—a feeling, he reminded himself, that would never affect his medical opinion. But now he found himself warming to this little man.

"General," Dr. Douglas said, "may I present Dr. George Frederick Shrady, one of our foremost authorities in pathology and plastic surgery."

Grant shook Shrady's hand with a soft grip that again caught Shrady off guard. The general retained his grasp of Shrady's hand while he studied the physician. "Yes, Dr. Shrady? Were you not consulted during the assassination of President Garfield?"

"Why yes, General. Yes, I was," Shrady blurted. He had also consulted during the difficult illness of Frederick III of Germany. Both experiences formed the basis for Shrady's intense dislike of politicians and the intrigue that covered them like a poison mist, making proper medical care all but impossible. Only Dr. Douglas's pleading had persuaded him to see another "special" patient.

"Dr. Shrady has also founded the *Medical Record*, a journal debunking hoaxes and charlatans in the field of medicine," Dr. Douglas added.

Grant smiled, a wistful, corkscrewed grin that raised the drooping corner of the right side of his mouth and added to the asymmetry of his face. "Have you come, then, to guard my flanks against Dr. Douglas? I must warn you that Douglas and I go back a long ways. Back as far as his 'pickles and sauerkraut' days, and I trust him implicitly."

"Pickles and sauerkraut, sir?"

Douglas nodded excitedly at this warm compliment, his beard bouncing spiritedly. "Yes, Shrady, I served in the Sanitary Commission during the war. I am pleased to say that I ordered pickles and sauerkraut to prevent scurvy among the National troops. Highly effective it was, too. My medical brethren ridiculed my choice, but the troops embraced it wholeheartedly. Perhaps, because a great number of them were German, they took to the sauerkraut eagerly. Perhaps because it offered a welcome change from salted beef and moldy hardtack."

Grant stroked his beard, as he often did while deep in thought. "Almost two hundred thousand of them were German. That was due in great part to Carl Schurz, Lincoln's friend. Some of their regiments spoke no English at all. Dr. Douglas did as much to win the war as any general, myself included." Grant grasped Douglas's arm and shook it warmly. "Dr. Douglas worked tirelessly for the army. Without his help, the field hospitals would have lacked cots, bandages, medicines. His efforts saved many a wounded soldier on both sides."

Douglas grinned with obvious pleasure and embarrassment at this compliment. He hung his head and shuffled his feet on the rich Persian carpet that covered the floor of his office. He felt strangely like a schoolboy praised for doing his homework correctly yet worried that his peers might scoff at him.

Grant sensed this instantly. Evidently, direct praise was something that a physician like Douglas avoided when surrounded by his associates. Strange, Grant thought, I would have imagined they liked to be commended, just like my generals. Even if they didn't deserve it. There is nothing so fragile or demanding as a general officer's pride, he reminded himself. Except Sherman and McPherson. Those two were cut from a different bolt of cloth; he sighed—a bolt of scarce material, indeed. McPherson was dead, killed in the war by a sniper's bullet.

So many good men are gone, Grant thought as he ran his hand absentmindedly over his close-cropped beard. The gesture brought his fingers into contact with the throbbing lump on the right side of his neck. The mass responded by shooting an electric bolt of pain upward into his jaw. Grant winced. He was learning to live with the constant soreness of his throat and the incessant throbbing in his neck as he endured the neuralgia that plagued his every step. Swallowing solid foods was becoming more difficult.

He said, "Where was it we first met, Douglas? I believe while I was investing Fort Donelson, was it not?"

"It was, indeed, General. Fort Donelson."

"I was fortunate enough to have Douglas at Shiloh and during the Wilderness campaign. But Meade got him for Gettysburg."

Douglas flushed again at this offhanded praise, then shook it off, raising his chin toward Dr. Shrady. "General, would you be so kind as to allow Dr. Shrady to examine you?"

Grant loosened his tie and collar in response, and the younger surgeon stepped forward and felt the general's neck. His fingers ran across the skin and collided with the hard lump beneath the angle of Grant's jaw. The general's lip twitched. Several smaller, softer nodes on the left side raised Shrady's anxiety as well. With practiced patience, George Shrady removed his reflecting mirror from his coat pocket, settled it on his head, and inspected the back of Grant's throat. He moved a lighted alcohol lamp closer to provide the needed light.

*Both sides! Douglas was right. It had spread to both sides already!* Shrady ordered himself to give no outward sign of the gloom that welled up inside him as the beam of reflected light danced over the afflicted palate. But his findings were unmistakable: General Grant was incurable. A slow, painful, protracted death awaited this man.

Shrady removed his mirror just as Grant asked him directly. "Is it cancer?"

"Well, um ..." Shrady faltered.

Grant looked directly at Shrady, and his blue eyes turned dark. It was not a threatening look, but one of warning, telling the doctor that he would tolerate nothing less than the truth.

"Doctor," Grant related, "when I was a lad, I wished to purchase a pony from a man. I went to him and I said: 'My father says I am to offer you twenty dollars for this animal, and that if you won't accept that I am to offer twenty-two dollars. If that is unacceptable, then I am to say I will pay twenty-five dollars.' So, you see, I am a plainspoken man, used to dealing with the simple facts and the truth, whether or not I find them to my liking."

A startled look filled Shrady's face, and he looked from Douglas to Barker for help.

Grant moved to soften his blow. "The man was so taken back by my openness that he sold me the pony for the lower price. So being straightforward has its advantages. It served me well during the war. Nothing is so essential to a general's success as accepting the cold, hard facts. Only then can you formulate a working plan which has any chance of succeeding." Grant shifted his weight from his sore leg. "I don't do well with vague and indirect answers or the half-truths that politicians hold so dear." He paused to grin wryly. "My two terms as President have proven that. Truth and openness, I ask for nothing more and nothing less, Doctor. So, I'll ask again. Is it cancer?"

An embarrassed silence filled the room. Only the ticking of the

brass clock on the mantel provided any sound other than the breathing of
the men.

"Well?" Grant asked. "What is your answer?"

I know already, Grant told himself, from the cast on their faces. They
look like my field commanders did after General A. S. Johnston overran us
at Shiloh. Defeated.

Dr. Douglas fielded the question. As the older physician, he feared
the younger Shrady might blurt out something brash to this man whom
Douglas loved. "General, the disease is serious, epithelial in character." He
hoped substituting the word "epithelial" for "cancer" might soften the
blow. Somehow, he knew it was wasted effort. "Sometimes it is capable of
being cured—"

"But not in my case." Grant finished the sentence.

The three doctors shook their heads sadly.

"And how much time do you give me?"

"A year—at most."

Grant nodded slowly. He readjusted his tie and settled his hat back on
his head, straight and low over his eyes, in the no-nonsense way he always
wore it, far from the jaunty angle that Phil Sheridan used. Straightening his
broadcloth jacket, Grant touched his hat brim as he bowed slightly to the
three men. "Thank you for your time, gentlemen. I trust we will be seeing a
lot of each other in the future."

With that he turned and made his way out the front door. Standing outside the brownstone building, Grant paused to study the bustling
street before him. On this cool, bright autumn day, New York was a living,
vibrant thing. Hansom cabs, drawn by patient, uncomplaining horses, wove
their way between clumps of walkers and peddlers handling pushcarts. The
low rumbling voice of the city reached his ears. Doors slamming and shod
hoofs clacking across the cobblestones blended with the hollow clang of tin
pots and a hundred murmuring voices filling the air. The musty odor of
horse sweat mingled with the scent of hot roasted chestnuts. Scarlet-clad
maple trees lined the avenue, sharing their venue with the less boisterous
yellow colors of scattered elm trees. All this deluged his senses, and he felt
at once young again and painfully alive.

Grant straightened his shoulders. Time, he mused. Time is always the enemy of any general, any campaign. You never have enough of it. And there is so much left to do. One last battle to fight. As important as all the others. One last battle, but not for my country this time. This one is for my beloved wife, Julia. He raised his head and jutted his chin forward. One last battle to win.

# THE DEBT

William Henry Vanderbilt slammed his fist onto the polished surface of the table, sending the contents of its inkwell splashing across the leather-rimmed blotter.

"Damn it, Mercer, I thought you were a lawyer! Lawyers are supposed to solve these sorts of things, and you have not!"

In defense, Mercer waved his hands before his face in a gesture of frustration. "I thought I had, sir. The Grants' action is most unexpected. One I hardly anticipated." As an afterthought he added: "You must admit this is quite unusual. Most people would jump at the chance to have their debts erased."

Vanderbilt glared at him. "Are you an idiot? These *are* most unusual people, you fool." He rolled his eyes about in frustration.

To add to his aggravation, the late afternoon sun chose that very instant to emerge from the clouds and enter the room. A shaft of sunlight pierced the drapes and cast an illuminating beam across the massive portrait that hung on the far wall. The light lanced across the painting of his father, Commodore Cornelius Vanderbilt. His stern eyes now flashed down at him with a look of scorn heightened by the light of the sun.

Go ahead, Commodore, Vanderbilt snarled inwardly to the vision of his father, give me that disapproving look of yours. You still think I'm a footloose boy, don't you? You think you'd never have gotten yourself into a situation like this. Hah! That's because you never had friends of this caliber.

The stern portrait continued its mocking gaze.

Agitated, Vanderbilt sprang to his feet and tripped over a large elephant tusk. Uttering an oath, he navigated through the objects that surrounded his desk and filled his foyer until he stood beside his cowering attorney. His hand dropped to a set of worn shoulder straps that sported three worn gold stars. He picked these up and turned them over in his hand, examining them with reverence.

"I go off to Europe, happy in the notion that you would have resolved this issue, and what do I find when I return? My foyer turned into a museum!" Vanderbilt replaced the devices and picked up a decorative sword. His attorney judiciously stepped behind a waist-high porcelain vase. "Read the list again, Mercer," Vanderbilt commanded with a wave of the weapon.

"Elephant tusks from the King of Siam, various jades, teakwood cabinets and porcelain objects of art from General Li Hung Chang of China, gold buttons from uniforms, ornamental presentation swords given to the general, a gold medal from Congress hailing the opening of the Mississippi River, a Coptic Bible belonging to the King of Abyssinia, shoulder straps from uniforms worn during the campaigns against Richmond and Petersburg, the pen used to write orders during the Battle of the Wilderness—"

"Stop!" Vanderbilt sliced the air with Grant's sword to emphasize his point.

"There is more, sir, much more. The deed to his house in Galena, one in Philadelphia, properties in St. Louis and Chicago—"

"And he will take none of it back?" Vanderbilt replaced the sword and ran his fingers across a threadbare greatcoat.

"Not a single thing, sir. He was most insistent."

"You made it clear to him, I hope, that I considered his debt to me to be a debt of honor, with no *immediate* need of repayment? You made that absolutely clear, I hope?" Vanderbilt pointed his sword at his attorney to underscore his point.

"Yes, sir, I did." Mercer eyed the gleaming sword blade. "But General Grant stated that he considered repayment of your personal loan to him to be of the highest priority, taking precedence over all else."

Vanderbilt replaced the weapon on the cluttered table and removed a collection of gold Japanese coins from the nearby chair. He sat down heavily. Taking great care to avoid the vexing gaze of his father's portrait, he dropped his head into his hands. The tycoon clearly recalled that day in May when General Grant had come to him for a loan of $150,000 to cover an overdraft on the Marine Bank of Brooklyn that threatened the brokerage firm of Grant and Ward. Little did Grant imagine that Ward would abscond with the funds.

Vanderbilt raised his head. "I told the general that I didn't give a damn for the Marine Bank, nor for Grant and Ward for that matter. The loan was a personal one. How could he have misunderstood me?"

"Perhaps, you misunderstood the general, sir." Mercer sighed. The attorney reviewed the events in his mind. His research revealed nothing but a trail of financial ruin. The catastrophic fall of the financial house of Grant and Ward was a lesson in human nature as old as the Garden of Eden: Never trust a serpent. Grant was known for his trusting nature, but how he had come to fall under the spell of Fred Ward was an absolute mystery to Mercer. Ward was a complete scoundrel. Perhaps it was because the great man relied upon the judgment of his second son, Ulysses. Buck, as the younger Grant was called, formed a banking and investment house with Ward, with General Grant being a passive partner. Ward must have raised a bundle of cash on the general's good name, Mercer thought.

In any event, Ward fled with Vanderbilt's loan to Grant, leaving the general and his son holding the bag. And this bag contained thousands of dollars in debts. Worse still, the ripples from the sinking of Grant and Ward swamped the closely knit Grant family. Buck, a graduate of Columbia Law School, now hid from creditors in his father's house. Frederick Dent Grant, the oldest son, lost his life's savings and his house in Morristown, New Jersey. He and his wife also clung to the old general for support; Grant's sister, Virginia, was destitute from the loss of her widow's pension. The splash even swamped the boat of Grant's daughter as far away as England.

Vanderbilt interrupted his attorney's train of thought. "That stubborn, proud man even insisted that I place a judgment against him and all his properties, to include the loan interest. Now, he owes me more than $150,000!"

Mercer glanced at his papers. "It is $155,417.20 as of last note."

The tycoon glared at him. "You know what they're saying, don't you? That I'm an old skinflint who doesn't care one whit whether or not the general has a roof over his head. That I'm squeezing the general for every penny he has, and I've snatched all his war trophies as well as his lodgings! Avaricious, money grubbing, they're calling me!" Vanderbilt stared about him in despair. "Heaven knows I tried to give all this back to Grant. You know I tried, Mercer, you know I did."

Mercer nodded. "And you tried your best to deed Grant's properties over to his wife, but once again Grant refused. Does the man wish to be in the poorhouse?"

Vanderbilt shook his head. "Pride, Mercer. You called it correctly. The man's pride will not allow him to accept what he deems is charity. He is one of the most stubborn men I have ever known. Thank God he put his obstinacy to good use against the South. But, by Heavens, I find it trying when used against me!"

One stiff-necked man against another equally as headstrong, Mercer thought.

"Well, I've bested the man this time, Mercer," the millionaire grumbled as he rubbed his neck. This whole affair had taken the edge off whatever rest he had garnered from his trip abroad. "All this ..." He swept his hand over the treasures filling his foyer. "All this will be presented to the United States government to be displayed in Washington as a perpetual memorial to the good general. And I had written to the general that whatever monies I receive from selling his properties, I would place in a trust for the benefit of his wife, so that she might want for nothing during her life. Even Grant could not refuse his wife a roof over her head or food in her mouth."

"And his reply?"

"Hah, I outlasted the master of sieges himself. I bested the general who broke the will of Donelson and Vicksburg. He wrote me that for the sake of his wife he could no longer resist such a generous offer," Vanderbilt crowed. He paused for a moment, ashamed at himself, and cast a wary glance at his father's image. The son winced. He was flying under false colors. "But I took advantage of the great man, Mercer. Have you not heard the rumors that Grant is dying?"

Mercer shook his head, shocked. He had no idea that the general was ill.

"Yes, I fear it is true, Mercer, and my sources are always reliable. They give Grant less than a year to live. A year at most!" Vanderbilt glanced about him in despair. Distractedly, he picked up a carved wooden casket of dark, Irish bogwood bound with four golden bands lacing across its curved top and sporting heavy knoblike gold legs at all four corners. He ran his hand over the engraved plate commemorating Grant's visit to Dublin on January 3, 1879. "How could he refuse my last offer, Mercer? He will leave his wife destitute, penniless, and without even a roof over her head. He could not do that." Vanderbilt felt soiled and unclean. His efforts to force Grant to acquiesce, while clearly for the general's own good, still felt wrong. It was like yoking a lion to a plow.

Mercer recognized his employer's gloom and strove to put the best light on this hollow triumph. "Thank goodness, Mr. Vanderbilt. An end to this affair." Mercer felt the knot of tension somewhere behind his eyes lessen for the first time that morning. He was about to offer further congratulations when a clerk rapped on the frame of the open door. When his employer failed to notice, the scribe coughed politely and knocked more forcefully a second time.

Vanderbilt looked up. For the life of him he could not remember the man's name, although the clerk had been with him for over ten years. "Uh, yes? What is it?" he asked puckishly. The man had interrupted him, further detracting from what should have been his moment of triumph.

"Mr. Vanderbilt …" The clerk approached cautiously, shuffling his feet across the Persian carpet with the utmost care, like a man expecting at any moment to drop into a tiger trap.

"Yes. What is it?" Vanderbilt glared at the letter in the man's hand. A feeling of uneasiness welled up from behind his brocade vest.

"I'm sorry to disturb you, sir, but this letter has just arrived from Mrs. Grant."

"From Mrs. Grant?" the tycoon questioned. "Mrs. Grant, you say?" Vanderbilt's face clouded and he chewed his lip. After a second's reflection, he snatched the letter away. The sunlight moved off the painting, and his father's face darkened into a reproachful scowl. Hastily, Vanderbilt tore open the envelope and read aloud:

> "Upon reading your letter this afternoon General Grant and myself felt it would be ungracious to refuse your princely and generous offer. Hence his note to you. But upon reflection I find I cannot, I will not accept your munificence in any form. I beg that you will pardon this apparent vacillation and consider this answer definite and final.
>
> Yours respectfully, Julia Grant."

Vanderbilt crumpled the letter in his hand as he sank back into the chair. *"Damn her, now she's refused my offer!"*

Unwittingly, he rolled his eyes upward to where his father's specter waited. The face was definitely smirking down at him. Vanderbilt crushed the letter more tightly in his hand.

"Damn both of them," he muttered.

# THE ANGEL,

# MARK TWAIN

Ulysses S. Grant, eighteenth President of the United States, slumped in his worn wicker chair and squinted along the peeling porch railing into the setting sun while he planned his last campaign.

His three articles for *Century Magazine* had earned three thousand dollars, enough to put food on the table. It was a meager start.

Not surprisingly, Grant's lucid description coupled with his uncanny ability to remember the fields of battle with all the precision of a mapmaker's eye brought praise and demand for more of his writing. Now the *Century* wanted him to write his memoirs. With Lee and Lincoln dead, Grant was the only surviving combatant with the breadth and depth of knowledge and command experiences from the War Between the States, which the public so desperately desired to read about.

He didn't mind being buried in potter's field, he reasoned. But Julia's future was another matter. His dear wife had stood by him through thick and thin. She deserved better.

*By God, I won't leave her penniless. I don't know how, but I won't.*

Grant turned his head toward the road to his front gate. A carriage stopped and a man stepped down. There was no mistaking the white linen suit that peeked from beneath the dark overcoat, and the exuberant shock of white hair backlit by the slanting rays of the sun.

Mark Twain galloped up the path with an unconcealed energy that belied his fifty years. He paused at the foot of the steps, drew to attention, and cast a raffish salute at the former commander of the Army of the Potomac.

"Mr. President, I hope I am not intruding." The writer extended his salute into a broad sweeping bow. "I just happened to be in the vicinity, and I hoped I might pay my respects."

"I was not aware Hartford, Connecticut, was so near to New York geographically, Mr. Twain," Grant replied with a smile. "But it is always a pleasure to see you. Julia, I'm sure, will be as delighted as I am. It's late. Will you stay for supper?" Grant made the offer, knowing their fare would be only soup. Julia would scold him, but he didn't care. Twain always brightened their days.

"That's most kind of you, Mr. President." Twain shook his head as he replied. He was well aware of the Grants' dire straits and had no wish to tax their already strained resources. "Normally I'd be honored, sir, but I must catch the train back to Connecticut within the hour." He nodded toward the waiting carriage while his hand searched inside the folds of his white coat. His hand withdrew two cigars. He waved these with a flourish. "I do have time for a smoke with the most famous general since ... since Hannibal."

"Hannibal?" Grant frowned.

Twain's tangled eyebrows shot skyward. "Perhaps Hannibal is not a sufficient comparison? His name just popped into my mouth because of my long association with the town of Hannibal, Missouri. Would you prefer Julius Caesar or Napoleon, instead?"

Grant leaned forward in his chair. His eyes glinted, flinty and sharp like the hard stone found near his birthplace in Galena. "I thought you were going to say since ... *Bobby Lee*...."

Twain's hand froze in midair, still grasping the cigars. His bushy eyebrows rose even farther. For this rare moment, the literary genius was speech-less, caught off guard by Grant's remark.

A dry rasp erupted from the general. It rolled up from somewhere within the depths of the shawl covering his shoulders and slipped through his beard, more like a bark at first, until it grew into a definite chortle. Mark Twain blinked in amazement. Grant was laughing.

The laughter grew as Twain joined in. Tears filled his eyes, and the author grasped the corner railing to steady his shaking body.

"By God, Mr. President, you got me with that one!" Twain gasped. "By Heavens, Bobby Lee! Few people have sampled your wit, sir."

Grant stopped to wipe his own eyes. He blew his nose on a tattered handkerchief. "Well," he said philosophically, "I never was paid to be hu-morous. Soldiers are not employed to that end. But I owed you that since the first time you brought tears to my eyes. Do you remember, Mr. Twain?"

"How could I ever forget, Mr. President. I remember the date pre-cisely. It was November thirteenth, 1879, in Chicago, at the reunion of the Grand Army of the Republic. I must confess I was a bit nervous sitting on the podium before all those old soldiers."

"You did look out of place."

"All those splendid dark uniforms," Twain continued, "bedecked with medals, hundreds of seasoned warriors, and here I was an irregular Confed-erate, a lone Johnny Reb, facing the likes of Sherman and Sheridan. I felt like a hen in a foxhouse."

Grant nodded. "A Confederate only for a very short time as I recall."

"Yes, sir. I did desert within two weeks of joining. Soldiering was not my cup of tea. All that advancing and retreating. Although I believe I could have become a good soldier if I had waited. I got part of soldiering learned, that much is true. I knew more about retreating than the man who invented retreating." Twain clutched the cigars like he was holding the handle of a saber. "It was your fault after all, Mr. President. We were in dan-ger of being flushed from our hiding place by the 21st Illinois Volunteers—commanded by none other than an unknown colonel of volunteers named Ulysses S. Grant."

"You showed admirable good sense."

"But still I was a deserter, Mr. President, surrounded by hundreds of battle-hardened veterans." Twain paused to inspect his cigars. "As I recall, both sides, Federals and secessionists, shot deserters. I had no idea how I might be received."

Grant smiled. "I suspect most there felt you had regained your sense of loyalty to the National cause a mite sooner than did those who fought longer. I know I did."

"You were so stone-faced, sir, sitting there on the dais. As the guest of honor, I expected you to make a speech, and when you did not, I was perturbed to no end. And when I began my speech, I had no idea how you might receive it. After all, it was a bit impertinent."

"Comparing me to a babe, sucking his big toe and wearing diapers?"

"I don't mind telling you, Mr. President, when I looked over and saw you laughing with the tears rolling down your cheeks, I was the most gratified man in that entire assembly."

"I think Sherman enjoyed it as much as the both of us."

"Ah, yes, General Sherman, another man who frightened me."

"Cump is a man of great paradoxes. He loves the South. Did you know he was superintendent of a military academy in Louisiana before the war?"

"And yet his name is synonymous with destruction of that region."

"Cump is a soldier who hates war. Pure hell, he called it. He is also a brilliant general who realized the quickest way to end that hell was to create what he called total war, to destroy the economic strength and the South's will to resist by the massive destruction he employed. I know he took no pleasure in it."

"To be sure, to be sure." This conversation was not following the route that Twain had planned. He needed to put it back on course. The cigars in Twain's hand caught his attention. He handed one to Grant, placed one in his own mouth, and struck a match.

Both men puffed on their cigars in silence. Grant studied his friend. Twain was desperately trying to create a screen of smoke with his cigar while he struggled for the right words to broach the real reason for his visit. Finally, Grant spoke.

"I am not fool enough to believe you drove all the way out here just to see my ugly face," he said slowly. His voice hardened. "I trust you would not be rash enough to endanger our long friendship by offering charity."

Twain shook his head vigorously. The fading light danced among the disorderly curls, giving even more emphasis to his denial. "Charity! No, sir, never! But I do have a business proposal—a *very* serious business proposal." He emphasized his statement with the glowing tip of his smoke.

"Go on." Grant studied Twain with the same intensity he had studied the hills and roads of a future battlefield.

"Well, General ..." Twain purposefully used that address. "General, I know that since your articles for them were so well-received, you have been approached by Robert Johnson and Richard Gilder, editors of the *Century Magazine*, to write your account of the last war."

"I have."

"Have you signed a contract with them?"

"No. Not yet."

Twain sprang into the air. "Thank God!" he exclaimed. "I have not arrived too late."

Grant watched his friend with undisguised amusement. For a grown man, Mark Twain still retained his childish nature.

Twain continued. "I assume the *Century* offered you the usual ten percent royalties *and no advance on your writing.*"

Grant nodded.

"Disgraceful," Twain sputtered. "There is no other word for it but disgraceful. That is the usual, undisguised highway robbery the publishing houses foist on me and other authors." He waved his cigar in a wide arc to emphasize his point. "To offer you that has got to be the monumental injustice of the nineteenth century. I know from personal experience that your articles boosted the magazine's sales by tenfold. My advertisements for one-fifth of a page in the *Century* jumped from seven hundred dollars to eighteen hundred dollars during that time.

"May I ask, General, whether you asked the *Century*'s publisher for a guarantee? You know, of course, that Scribner's paid Sherman twenty-five thousand for his memoirs." Twain already knew the answer, but he wanted to drive that extra wedge between Grant and his publishers. He struggled to keep his best poker face.

"I did, Mr. Twain. He replied that he would not risk such a guarantee on any book ever published."

Thank you, Roswell Smith, Twain crowed silently, for being so hidebound. You've made my work easy. I can offer Grant a better deal.

Grant studied his own cigar. Julia and the doctor would be displeased, but he did enjoy the smoke. "It cannot be helped, I suppose," he said at length.

"But it can, sir! It can be helped. Something must be done about their stranglehold. It must be broken so that authors will receive a decent fee for their efforts, and I propose to do that something myself. I intend to do my own publishing!" Mark Twain smashed his fist into the palm of the hand holding his cigar. The glowing ash sailed into the air.

Grant smiled at this volatile display. If half my generals had showed this spirit, I could have shortened the war by two years, he reflected. Only Sherman showed this much animation. The others, save for a handful, worried more about how they looked or how their actions would appear to the press than about the actual conduct of the war.

That thought sobered the general.

"Mr. Twain, it is no secret that I am deeply in debt, and that I am dying. All my doctors give me less than a year to live." The ailing former President paused to watch the cloud of smoke from his cigar hang in the still air.

"Mr. President!" Mark Twain looked genuinely distressed.

Grant waved away the protest. "It is all too true," he said flatly. "Oh, they don't say that directly to my face, but I've overheard them in the parlor whispering with their graveyard faces. A year at most, they say."

Twain's shoulders sagged, and his white suit now looked too large and ill-pressed. To Grant, the man appeared to shrink like a punctured balloon. Only his shock of white hair and his mustache remained unchanged.

"Surely, there is some hope?" Twain pressed. "There is always hope, sir. Some new cure, perhaps? Or—"

"Or a miracle, Mr. Twain?" Grant chuckled, but the action caused him to cough, and his laugh turned into a rasping bark.

Twain hung his head. "At times like this, I wished I believed in an Almighty. For your sake, I wish I could."

Grant shook his head, feeling the tightness in the right side of his neck. "Don't alter your beliefs for me, Mr. Twain. Providence has gifted me with more prodigies than I deserve."

Twain looked bleakly at the man in the chair. Here was the former President of the United States, the greatest hero of the Great War, the savior of the nation, calmly discussing his own demise as if it were nothing more than a footnote on a page. Twain marveled at the man's detachment.

Grant continued, his voice flat and level, as if he were issuing orders to his staff for the next battle. "Twain, my death will be just the tidying up of one more loose end in that fateful chapter of our nation's history. My passing will simply add another old soldier to the casualty lists. Lee has gone to join his men. It appears I am to be next."

Twain emitted an audible sigh.

"Still," the general continued, "there are two things I had hoped to do before my end. I detect a lingering division of our nation. I would like to do something to bring the two regions closer together. We must go forward as a united country."

A slow smile crept onto Twain's face. His white suit appeared to rein-flate as the glint returned to his eyes. "And the other?"

Grant's eyes turned to fix his friend with the same level gaze that marked his coolness in the height of battle. "To leave my wife, Julia, penniless after my death is too painful a situation to contemplate. I had hoped to earn enough money from my writing to ensure my wife can keep the roof overhead and live a comfortable life. But I do not see that as a possibility. What I receive from my writing is not enough. And time is running out for me."

Mark Twain spun on his heel, reanimated by his sole purpose in coming to Mount MacGregor. "Mr. President, I believe both your wishes can be attained," he urged.

"How so?"

"By writing your personal account of the war. The country is crying for your thoughts on this most important subject. *And you can dedicate it to both sides.* That should go a long way to healing the wounds."

Grant ran his hand along his coarse beard. His hand scraping across the bristling stubble focused his mind on the idea. "I could dedicate the book to the *American* soldier and sailor. Not to National and Confederate, not to North and South, but to the Americans, for they are both Americans now."

Remarkably, Twain found that simple idea deeply touching. He forced back a lump in his throat. "That would go a long, long way to healing the breach, Mr. President," he said. "To the American fighting men! It is an elegant thought."

Grant dropped both his hands into his lap. He studied the gnarled fingers. More the hands of the woodcutter, which I used to be, than of a general, he mused. Shrewdly, he kept his gaze fixed on his hands as he asked: "You stated that both my wishes could be attained, Mr. Twain. We both know that what the *Century* will pay cannot absolve Julia of my debts."

"Let me publish your memoirs." Twain could hardly contain himself, but he mustered all his reserve to present his proposal with a level, matter-of-fact tone. "I know I mentioned doing just that during our last meeting at your house on East Sixty-sixth Street. I feel you did not take my offer seriously then; but I am quite serious, and I am once more extending that offer."

"You, Mr. Twain? Is that possible?"

"It is. Charles Webster and I have formed a publishing company to sell my latest book, *The Adventures of Huckleberry Finn.* Have you heard of it?"

Grant shook his head. "Can't say as I have."

"No matter. It's about a boy growing up on the Mississippi. I suspect it might have some limited appeal. But the important thing is, I can be your publisher."

"But you have no connections, Mr. Twain. How will you sell your books?"

Twain spread his arms and beat the air like a giant bird. "By subscription, Mr. President!" he chortled. "I have hit upon the idea of selling books by direct subscription. I will advertise and canvass my book all across the nation in advance of its printing. I know the method has fallen into disfavor, but I believe it can be done successfully." Twain ceased his fluttering. "So, I can give you a much better deal than the *Century*. I am prepared to offer you *seventy percent* of the profits on the sales of your memoirs, Mr. President."

"Seventy percent!" Grant carefully put down his cigar and scowled at the would-be publisher. "I warned you about charity. I will not accept it."

Twain's eyebrows dropped to hood his eyes in a deep frown. He spread his fingers in defense. "This is most definitely not charity, sir. It's damned good business. I intend to make a profit on your writings, just as you will—only not as much as that avaricious Roswell Smith planned on earning."

"But seventy percent of the royalties? Why, that's unheard of. It's most extraordinary."

"Extraordinary." Twain repeated the word. He could not have thought of a better word himself had he tried. He bent over the sitting man, and a broad smile spread across his face, lifting the corners of his thick, white mustache until they almost touched his ears. His eyes glittered like those of a man who was sharing a great treasure with a long trusted friend. The author spoke slowly and carefully so as to keep the emotion that coursed through his body out of his voice. "Seventy percent *is* unprecedented. Extraordinary, indeed. But believe me, General, so will your recounting of this last terrible war...."

# SHILOH,
# THE FIRST DAY

*When I reassumed command on the 17th of March I found the army divided, about half being on the east bank of the Tennessee at Savannah, while one division was at Crump Landing on the west bank about four miles higher up, and the remainder at Pittsburg Landing...*

Grant paused and studied the worn nub of his pencil.

*When I reassumed command...*

That says a lot to those who can read between the lines, he mused. But not everything. What I won't write is that Halleck was a thorn in my side, using any opportunity to pick a fight with me. What a sigh of relief I breathed when he was promoted to General-in-Chief of the Armies. He was out of my hair then. In Washington, Lincoln kept him on a close rein. And I won't write that if that fool Halleck had ordered coordinated attacks on Corinth and Memphis and Vicksburg while the rebel forces were still reeling after the fall of Forts Henry and Donelson, we could have driven them back to the Alleghenies ... in 1862. But he did not. Many more men would die before that happened.

The wind ruffled the edges of the foolscap beneath his hand, and the tired man looked across the fields to his right at the summer fields, ripe with wheat, flowing in sections. The late sun shadowed the golden shocks into battalions that wavered and wheeled in the wind. The shimmering haze overhanging the heated field recalled to his mind the smoke obscuring a battlefield. So long ago, and yet he could see it now, could hear the distant din, the shouts, the cries, and the low rumble of cannon like the roll of far-off waves breaking on rocks. He thought back to that day twenty years ago.

Pittsburg Landing. Shiloh. I blundered badly on that one, Grant thought. And Albert Sidney Johnston caught me unawares. I thought the Confederates were on the defensive. I never thought they would leave their strong entrenchments to attack Pittsburg Landing. If anything, I expected they might attack my lone division at Crump Landing, where our supply depot was.

I was so sure then. The confident victor of Fort Henry and Fort Donelson, and I got caught with my forces divided like a wet-nosed lieutenant. Johnston nearly beat me and almost ended my career that day.

Grant rubbed his eyes and leaned back in his wicker chair. He swallowed, feeling the constant ache in the back of his throat turn into a liquid fire that ran down his neck. So many died that day at Shiloh, he recalled. No one had ever seen killing on such a grand scale before. But it was just the beginning ... just the beginning.

Grant closed his eyes, and his mind drifted back in time.

APRIL 6, 1862

The smoke of a thousand cooking fires pierced the early morning mist that enfolded the army encampment. Row upon row of pointed, white, Sibley tents bit through the ground fog like dragon's teeth; where the haze relented, the scattered fires shone like unblinking, angry eyes. Muted voices melded with the clank of tin cups and shuffling feet into a low hum.

The raw recruits of Sherman's and Prentiss's divisions prepared their breakfast, huddled around the cook fires to ward off the dampness arising from the rain-soaked ground. Days of torrential downpouring had saturated the ground and all their gear.

A light breeze off the Tennessee River three miles northeast of the camps carried the fresh scent of peach blossoms from the nearby orchard across the crouching men. The fragrance soon vanished, overwhelmed by the mixed odors of sweaty men, musty leaves, and smoking wood.

A rough-hewn log meetinghouse called Shiloh topped a low ridge between both camps and overlooked the meandering of the muddy waters of Snake and Lick creeks, which encircled the base of the ridge. Far to the southwest a plateau of scrub pine and brush rose above dense thickets and patchwork fields of newly planted cotton and corn.

An air of victory and confidence rose alongside the wood smoke this morning. Drowsy soldiers joked and laughed as they tended to the bubbling pots of chicory and slabs of frying bacon or crowded around the cook tents. In the West the Southern armies were holed up in Corinth under Albert Sidney Johnston, guarding the junction of their two important railroad lines between Nashville and Vicksburg. But Grant, their new commander, would drag Johnston out of his hole just as he had at Fort Donelson. A regular terrier that Grant was, the men boasted.

Besides, it was Sunday, April 6, a day to rest, attend prayers around this Quaker meetinghouse, and enjoy the fine spring warmth.

Newly appointed commander of the Army of the Tennessee, Ulysses Grant studied the inside of his tin coffee cup while he tested his weight on his swollen right ankle. He winced as the injured limb protested. He frowned down at his boot, which was split from strap to toe to accommodate his injury.

Gingerly, he shifted back onto his left leg. Foolish of me to be riding about in the dark last night, especially with all that rain, he thought. But I needed to see Colonel McPherson and General Wallace. I needed to find out what that firing was along their line. I never expected my horse to lose its footing and roll on me.

He studied his right boot, and his frown deepened. At least it was not broken, he consoled himself, but these were his best pair of boots. His free hand patted the inside pocket of his field coat, searching for his cigars. Streaked with mud and rumpled from being used as a blanket or a pillow, the wool coat gave little hint that its wearer commanded this army. Save for the tattered shoulder straps with their gold stars, it carried no other sign of rank.

His fingers found the familiar bundle of cigars tucked in the inside pocket. Grant sighed while the perpetual frown on his face lessened. Good thing my cigars stayed in my pocket during the fall, he reflected. The way this army is foraging, I doubt if a good smoke is to be found within fifty miles in any direction. He recalled the frenetic scene yesterday as men from Prentiss's division stripped a farmhouse of its chickens and geese while the woman who owned them stood in her doorway and cried. Somehow, that woman reminded him of Julia, his wife. He shook his head to clear the image.

Grant placed his cup down, withdrew one of his precious cigars and lighted it. He puffed away until a cloud of smoke surrounded him, before he picked up his coffee. Off to his left, his staff lounged against a Rucker ambulance wagon and ate their breakfast. John Rawlins, his chief of staff, sorted the mail which had just arrived at their headquarters at the town of Savannah, in Mississippi.

Grant wondered why his staff worked so hard to appear nonchalant and relaxed. He knew each one of them kept their eye on him. All he had to do was twitch and a dozen tin plates and cups would rattle to the ground as his aides rushed to his side. It was both reassuring and embarrassing.

Absentmindedly, Grant stirred the mud with the toe of his ruined boot. The sticky mud clung to his boot. Rich soil, the failed farmer in him noted. But the soldier noted this sodden ground would bog down his wagons and artillery. He looked up to confirm his judgment. All around him battery wagons, caissons, and field pieces lay mired to their axles in the muck. The lighter Rucker wagons fared better, but he realized that loaded with wounded, they too would sink. He pictured the overloaded springs of the hospital wagons lurching and jarring the bullet-shattered limbs of his wounded men. He hoped Flag Officer Foote's naval flotilla included one of the new hospital steamers among its gunboats. He made a mental note to ask for one. Transporting the wounded by steamer would be best.

And he knew they had to secure the roads. You couldn't move any sizable force through that broken ground and underbrush. Certainly, no amount of cannon could be moved except on the roads, poor as they are. Good thing Sherman is guarding the road to Crump Landing, he thought.

Otherwise, my forces are split with General Lew Wallace at the landing and me here. When Buell gets here with his forty thousand men, we can move on Corinth. Yet, if the road should fall ...

It won't happen, he assured himself. Johnston is in Corinth awaiting my attack.

Grant surveyed the men around him as they cooked breakfast. Raw recruits, he mused, some having just received their rifles on the march down here. He had watched them drilling with their newly issued Springfield rifles. Some looked like they'd never held a gun in their lives. Those with the lever-action Spencers will prove useful if they can get the hang of them, he thought. But I wonder how they'll fight? They'll do well with the proper training. But they need more time.

He sipped his coffee and thought of the piles of supplies and disorderly clumps of men surrounding their campfires at Pittsburg Landing. The steep-cut banks to either side of the landing crowded the Union forces into the only level plain for miles on either side of the swollen Tennessee River. Crump Landing was the only other place level enough for an army to use as a staging area along the river. Down at Pittsburg Landing, a white frame house and a rough-hewn log building with imposing stone chimneys on either end marked what must have been a quiet levee.

Far from quiet now, Grant noted. He thought how strange it was that the fortunes of war and the vagaries of geography doom a place. He tried to imagine his hometown of Galena overrun by enemy forces, the homes occupied, the farms ransacked, the men run off, and the women left to fend for themselves. After all, Galena was not so different from this place. Surprisingly, he found it easy to make the comparison.

No, he corrected his thoughts, this place is rebel land, not at all like Galena. The people here have brought this discomfort on themselves.

Grant watched a mobile forge, drawn by six mules, tilt precariously to one side as its wheels slipped beneath the soil. Already the banks of the river bluff lay churned into a field of boot-sucking mud, scarred and broken until the very army that defiled the soil now seemed a part of it.

Blue-coated men rushed around the forge to right it. His gaze passed them to rest on the square sides of the hospital tents. More men sat around the tents, oblivious to the mud. Many of his recruits had thrown away their wool greatcoats before Fort Henry, only to suffer in the freezing rain and sleet that followed the next night. Pneumonia and dysentery were causing more losses than rebel bullets.

His thoughts returned to the disposition of his forces. Best to keep General Lew Wallace at Crump Landing to protect our transports and stores. I fear Johnston might send a raid there to hamper our advance.

Might Johnston attack us here at Pittsburg Landing instead? Should I have given the order to entrench, to prepare breastworks for just such an eventuality?

No. Grant stood by his decision not to prepare defenses. These men need training, but not that kind, he thought. They need practice reloading and firing their new rifles, practice drilling, wheeling, and close-order marches to weld them into an effective fighting force. What was it General Smith said yesterday? "By God, I want nothing better than to have the rebels attack us! We can whip them to hell. Our men suppose we came here to fight, and if we begin to spade, it will make them think we fear the enemy."

Well, Grant thought, when Buell arrives with his forty thousand veterans, we'll see how much Smith's men like to fight. I propose to move on Corinth forthwith.

A chilling roar abruptly sundered the morning calm. The dull thumps of cannon fire rolled along the river and over the trees from upstream.

At Pittsburg Landing battle lines of Confederate soldiers, three deep, broke from the trees and boiled out of the brush lining the creeks. What moments before had been torpid thickets, covered with buds and emerging spring leaves, now vanished beneath heavy boots as butternut-gray-coated soldiers crashed from the underbrush. Their deep-throated rebel yell filled the air just as the first line of attackers loosed a volley of musket fire. Without stopping, the gray line charged through the curtain of gun smoke and out of the creek beds.

Minié balls crackled through the air like a thousand angry hornets. A shower of leaves, twigs, and branches, clipped from the trees by the bullets, rained down upon the astonished Federals. Men froze over their skillets or sprang to their feet to stare at the onrushing tide of butternut-gray.

A second volley exploded—this one better aimed.

Union soldiers gasped and grunted from the impact of heavy lead slugs striking flesh and splintering bone. Some pitched forward into their own fires while others grasped reflexively at the spreading patches of red that stained their uniforms. Acrid smoke obliterated all smell of food as a cloud of burnt powder ballooned over the camps.

Then pandemonium struck. Galvanized by the bullets, the untrained soldiers dropped their breakfasts and ran for their stacked arms. Many simply ran, seeking safety with the gunboats moored at Pittsburg Landing. Several fired back at the charging lines. But the wave of gray swept on unabated, like a fateful tidal wave wreaking mayhem and death.

The distant explosion of heavy gunfire caused Grant to pause. He set his cup down and cocked his ear.

A panicked soldier ran past. "Good God," he cried, "we are being attacked!"

Grant rose on his sore ankle. He turned to his wide-eyed staff. "Gentlemen, the wheels are in motion," he said. "Let's be off." Grant's luck, he thought as he hobbled down to the levee. A good thing I planned to move upstream today instead of waiting here for Buell to arrive. Consequently, his steamer, the *Tigress*, lay ready to go with a full head of steam up and the horses already loaded. Within minutes Grant and his entire staff sped upriver at full steam in the direction of the battle.

No sooner had the *Tigress* ground her bow into the mud of the landing than Grant raced for his horse. Ignoring the pain in his ankle, he sprang into the saddle and spurred his mount down the ramp and toward the firing. His staff scrambled to find their own mounts and follow their commander. The massed soldiers at the landing stood in frozen amazement as Grant and his staff galloped past.

More sounds of firing reached his ears, this time different from the Confederates' explosive volley by ranks. A ruffling staccato sound grew in intensity directly ahead and off to the right. Sherman's and McClernand's men were returning fire. Grant dug his right heel into his horse's flank, spurring him on. He scarcely noticed the pain in his ankle.

Already, panicked soldiers clogged the road ahead, stumbling and running in blind terror from the sound of fire. Few carried their rifles. Many were half dressed. Grant forced his horse through the swelling river of blue coats. The animal lurched and shouldered against the oncoming tide.

Moments later a wide-eyed captain galloped past Grant. The man was hatless, his tunic unbuttoned, and the stitching of the left shoulder was cut from a bullet's passage, revealing a trace of fresh blood on the blue wool and an angry red furrow in the flesh of his shoulder. The general snatched the man's reins and jerked his horse around. The captain lurched in the saddle and almost pitched over his horse's neck before regaining control. His eyes rolled while his lips mouthed incoherent sounds.

"What's happening, Captain?" Grant snapped. "Give me a report!" The hard edge to his words struck the officer with the impact of a bullet.

The frightened officer forgot his salute and babbled, "The rebels are out there thicker than fleas on a dog's back!" His eyes focused on the shoulder straps of Grant's mud-streaked coat. The morning light glittered off the general's stars. "Sir!" The captain saluted awkwardly. "We've got to run. There're thousands of them. We've got no chance. No chance at all!"

Grant gave the man's reins a hard snap. He fixed the captain with a cold stare. "Get back to your men, Captain," he ordered, but his voice was level and calm, devoid of any excitement. "We have to fight. The river's at our backs, so there is no place to run."

His tone caused the officer to straighten. The man pulled down on the front of his tunic to rectify the disordered row of brass buttons. "Sir?"

"Back to your men, Captain. They need your leadership. Form them into a line and hold your ground. Do you understand?" Grant leaned forward in his saddle so that his stubbly beard was just inches from the man's face. "Hold your ground!" he hissed.

The light of understanding suffused the young officer's eyes. He nodded his head rapidly. "Yes, sir! Form up and hold. I understand."

"Good, son. Now git."

The captain set spurs to his horse and plunged off to the left. The scattered fire of the Union solders ahead of him was met with an eruption of rifle fire and the sharp crack of a cannon. Flying balls of canister filled the air with frightening whines. Bark flew from the trees while the captain's head dissolved in a red mist. Slowly, his headless body slid backward over the rump of his animal to vanish beneath the feet of the retreating men.

*They're turning our own cannon against us!*

Grant's horse shied as the smell of blood assailed its nostrils. A blue sea of men, mostly without weapons, swelled past him while blast upon blast of grapeshot cut bloody swaths in their ranks.

The general spurred his horse ahead, forcing the animal through the welling mob that moments before had been his overconfident army. Within minutes he reached a confused throng of soldiers crouching behind a clump of trees. He was relieved to see the men were firing and reloading in orderly fashion. Bullets snapped through the air around him, and a cannonball exploding off to the left uprooted a tree and peppered his face with burning dirt. Smoking shards of debris clung to his uniform, but Grant took no notice. Everywhere men were shouting and firing into the roiling clouds of stinging smoke that engulfed the field. Nothing could be seen but tongues of flame piercing the smoke as battalion after battalion engaged one another. The noise rose to almost mask the shouted word, and the roar of cannon threatened to split his eardrums. By the sound of the fire, Grant estimated two divisions imperiled McClernand's and Sherman's front.

*But where is Sherman? Is he down? God, I hope not.*

As if in response to Grant's plea, Sherman emerged out of the smoke on a lathered horse. Blood streaked the horse's flanks, while Sherman's hat was missing and his coat was torn in several places. He spotted Grant and coaxed his stricken mount over to his commanding officer's side. Sherman—his face ashen, and his eyes nearly starting from smoke-streaked sockets—was shaken, something Grant had never seen before in his division commander.

"What's the situation, Cump?" Grant asked, purposefully using his friend's nickname. He kept his voice level, as if the hell around them did not exist. If Sherman fails me, we're lost, Grant realized.

"Sam, by God, they caught us napping!" Sherman stammered. "It's a full-scale attack, that's for goddamned sure. My guess is four, maybe five divisions. They rolled right over my camp, and Prentiss's on the left over there—well, he's getting just as bad a whupping. I've got my boys placing fire on them now, but they're pushing us steadily back."

Grant leaned forward in his saddle while his ear sought the heaviest fighting. With studied deliberation he withdrew a cigar from his inner pocket and jammed it between his lips. It took all his self-control to keep from biting the cigar in two. "Don't think they stopped to eat your breakfast, do you?" he drawled.

"Hell, no!" Sherman swore. He stared, mesmerized, at the glowing tip as Grant lighted the cigar. He could detect no trace of tremor in Grant's hands. Goddamn, Sherman thought, the rebs are kicking hell out of our butts, and Sam still wants to smoke one of his damned cigars. Son of a bitch, but he's a cool one.

Seeing Grant's action seemed to steady Sherman. His staccato speech slowed a bit while color returned to his seamed face. "I've got my men stabilized for now. This brush is hindering them as much as it is us. But they're slowly pushing us back toward the river. Lord, the rebs are coming on strong. We're inflicting heavy damage on them, but my men are taking just as heavy casualties. But they keep on attacking. From the few prisoners we've taken, we appear to be facing Polk's and Hardee's divisions. I sent a messenger over to Prentiss. Haven't seen him back yet."

Grant turned as a rider collided with his horse. The sergeant blinked to see Grant at the front. Halleck, whom the soldier had served before, never got this close. Bewildered by the presence of two generals, the sergeant saluted them both while looking back and forth from one to the other. He seemed unsure which one ought to receive his report.

Sherman solved his dilemma. "Well, damn it, Sergeant, let's have your report!"

"Yessir, sir!" The man fought to control his horse. "General Prentiss's compliments, sir. He wishes to inform you that he is heavily engaged on his front by at least a division."

"Does he know who leads them, Sergeant?" Grant questioned.

"Sir! He believes the rebs are under command of General Bragg."

"Braxton Bragg!" Sherman snickered. "Well, that's the first good news I've heard today. He'll probably stop to hang a few of his men for insubordination before pressing home his advantage."

The sergeant swallowed hard. He'd never heard one general criticize another in front of an enlisted man during his twelve years in the service. Confederate or not, Bragg was still a general.

Grant nodded. "Thank you, Sergeant. Back to your men. We need every experienced soldier to steady the new recruits."

"Yessir!" The sergeant saluted in the direction of both men and galloped away. If he and his messmates lived to see the end of this day, he had something juicy to tell them.

"Sounds hottest on the left," Grant shouted over the din. He ignored the falling leaves that landed on his shoulders and decorated his slouch hat. "That must be it. Johnston aims to turn our left flank and drive us off Pittsburg Landing. If he does, we'll be cut off from our supply ships and Buell's reinforcements coming downriver by boat." Grant stopped to look at his friend. A dirty, blood-soaked bandage covered the back of Sherman's left hand.

"Are you wounded, Cump?" he asked.

"Just a scratch, Sam. Nicked my shoulder as well." He cocked his head toward the slit in his coat and shrugged. His eyes cast about at the growing pile of wounded men, some limping, some crawling toward the river. The churned mud beneath their horses' hooves glistened with trails of bright red blood—all heading in the direction of the landing. "Could be worse," Sherman muttered.

His eyes fastened on a pile of bodies, torn apart by round shot; missing heads and limbs, the mangled heap of blue uniforms, covered with dark blood and glistening loops of bowel that scarcely resembled men. Whoever called war glorious ought to see this, Sherman thought with a shudder.

Nothing glorious about being ripped apart by a cannonball. Nothing at all. This is pure hell.

"Could be a lot worse," he repeated as he tore his gaze from the carnage.

Just then a bullet punched a path through Sherman's slouch hat. The general reached up, removed his cover, and poked a finger into the half-inch hole. "Goddamnit!" he swore. "Now the bastards shot a hole in my new hat. It's damned hot work today, I'll tell you. I've had two horses shot out from under me since breakfast." He stuffed the battered hat back on his head. His scowl deepened. Maybe I am crazy like they say I am, he thought, but shooting a hole in my hat makes me really angry.

Grant reined in his own nervous horse. The animal had started to prance around in circles. "Can you hold, Cump?" he shouted over the firing. "Lew Wallace should be here within the hour. If you can hold, I'll use him to counterattack the rebels' left flank. Can you hold?"

Sherman screwed his face up as he stood in his stirrup to study the undulating tangle of thickets, trees, and heavy brush behind him. "I'll pull my men back across the River Road."

Grant nodded. He could picture every inch of this tangled terrain. He thanked God for this gift. Once seeing a map or the lay of an area, he never forgot it. He could recall even the smallest detail. "The road's about a mile to the rear. There's high ground beyond it. From there you can shorten your line and still keep the road to Crump Landing open."

"We can give them a damned good run for their money there, Sam. The ground's too broken across the road for the rebs to make a concerted rush. But I'll need my flanks looked after."

"Do it!" Grant commanded. "McClernand will support your left. His men fought well at Donelson, so I consider them veterans. Snake Creek is still swollen from the rains last night. It will protect your right flank until General Wallace comes over its bridge."

Sherman saluted and wheeled his horse. A half-dozen steps carried horse and rider into the bitter smoke. Grant motioned to his quartermaster, Captain Baxter, who had raced after his commander with several of Grant's staff.

"Ride to General Lew Wallace and direct him to come immediately to Pittsburg by the road nearest the river. Tell him to come at all haste as we are under heavy attack."

"Yes, sir!" Baxter scribbled down the order on a sheet of foolscap, stuffed the note into his tunic, saluted, and galloped off to the right. Despite himself, the captain hugged the back of his horse in fear as another hail of bullets filled the air. A rebel cheer rose behind him. As he looked back over his shoulder, he saw Grant drive his right knee into his horse's ribs, spurring his mount off to the left and riding to the sound of the most intense firing.

Grant, forcing his horse closer to the battle line, studied what little he could see of the jumbled landscape. Smoke, spurts of flame from cannon fire, and heavy brush revealed only tantalizing glimpses of the battle. As soon as he caught sight of a battle line, roiling fumes masked his view within minutes.

Thank God I rode all over this ground yesterday, he thought. His mind's eye roved across the geography that he could not see. Behind me is a sunken road that runs from a peach orchard through dense trees to connect with Purdy Road off to the right. There's a wide pond anchoring the left side of that sunken road. If Prentiss can hold the center there, we'll be all right. We must hold until Don Carlos Buell arrives by steamboat from across the Tennessee. Then, with Sherman holding open the bridge across the Snake for Lew Wallace, we'll have them. But Prentiss must hold! If the landing is overrun, Buell's reinforcements will be unable to land.

Grant chomped down hard on his cigar. Johnston knows that as well as I do. I underestimated the pluck of that man. He'll throw everything at Prentiss and try to roll around his left flank to overrun the landing.

A round shot split a gum tree five yards to Grant's right. The ball transformed the trunk into a mass of stinging splinters before screaming off at an angle into a row of Union men who were firing and reloading under the direction of a thin sergeant with a wiry mustache and a green scarf tied around his neck. Like ninepins, the orderly array of men disappeared into parts of flesh. The sergeant simply vanished while his men flew apart into torn legs and torsos.

Grant blinked away the blood that covered his face. His gaze fixed on a scrap of blood-soaked green cloth—all that was left of the brave sergeant—fluttering from a burning bush like some forlorn guidon.

"General! General Grant! You must go back!" General Benjamin Prentiss rushed on foot to the general's horse and grasped the bridle. "It is too dangerous here."

Grant looked down at the officer. Prentiss seemed surprisingly calm for all the combat surrounding him. Where has he been? Grant wondered. He looks ready for dress parade. Prentiss's hat sat squarely on his head, and his field jacket was buttoned and still pressed; however, when he turned to look to his left, Grant noticed the man's entire side was caked with mud. "I can't command from the rear," Grant snapped as he pulled his reins free. "Where is W.H.L. Wallace's command?"

The mud-stained officer looked about. He removed his hat and ran his left hand through his hair. Blood caked his dark hair, and his right hand clutched his sword although the blade was broken mere inches from the hilt. "This is it, sir. Mixed with my own division. General Wallace is dead, mortally wounded at the onset of the attack."

W.H.L. Wallace's youthful appearance entered Grant's mind: clean-shaven with a long, thin, earnest face and the hint of a receding hairline. From Ottawa, Illinois, Grant recalled. He was so proud of that horse of his. Was it a bay or a roan? He couldn't remember. He did recall how Wallace thanked him when he handed Wallace temporary command of C. F. Smith's division. Well, Grant thought, he can thank me for his death, I suppose.

"What is your situation, General Prentiss?"

"The rebs are pushing us sorely. I face the combined troops of Braxton Bragg and Breckinridge, General. Two divisions, at least. First Louisiana Regulars among them. They're fighting like tigers. We must fall back or be overrun!"

Grant jerked his horse around so his back was exposed to the battle line. "Whose men support your rear, General Prentiss?" Grant's finger stabbed at a line of blue, bristling with bayonets and flanked by waving battle flags.

"Hurlbut, sir. His division is still intact. They are the reserve."

Grant sprang from his saddle, landing on his swollen ankle. Pain shot up his leg from the jarring impact on the injured limb, but he ignored it. He hopped to Prentiss's side and grasped the man's coat lapels. Drawing the officer to within inches of his own face, Grant spoke slowly and carefully so there could be no misunderstanding.

"General Prentiss, you must hold at all costs," he ordered. "All costs, is that clear? If you collapse, Pittsburg Landing will fall. That must not happen."

Prentiss looked forlornly at his fractured sword. To him it symbolized his equally shattered command. His head hung in shame. "I don't think we can, General. They're pushing us back with each attack. My men ... well, they're ... doing the best they—"

Sensing the despair in the general's voice, Grant squeezed the man's trembling arm. "I've got a good piece of ground for you to hold on to, Ben. The best in this whole damned swamp. It's just a ways back. There's a sunken road that runs roughly parallel to the river. Do you remember it, Ben?"

Prentiss nodded.

"Good. The north side of the road is good ground, raised with trees for cover. There's a peach orchard off to the east and a pond."

Prentiss recalled his men filling their canteens in the quiet pond the night before. The tranquil waters and scented peach blossoms belonged to another world, not this nightmare of shot and steel.

"Withdraw slowly to behind the sunken road at your rear. An orderly withdrawal, do you hear? Not a rout. You'll get better cover there, and the pond will protect your left flank. You will be our center. You must hold that ground at all hazards. Is that clear?"

Benjamin Prentiss straightened. He had not remembered Grant ever using his first name before this. His head bobbed in agreement. "Yes, sir. Hold the center at the sunken road ... no matter what. Yes, sir, I will."

"Good." Grant patted his shoulder. "Now see to your command. This army depends on you today."

Prentiss stumbled back to his company commanders to issue orders before he realized he had forgotten to salute his commanding officer. He turned around, but Grant was gone.

Grant drove his horse along the front line until he reached Colonel David Stuart, anchoring the extreme left flank of his battered forces. Stuart's brigade, from Sherman's division, abutted a tangled swamp just south of the Tennessee River.

"General." Stuart saluted Grant. "A hot day, is it not, sir? The rebs are testing my line, but I think I can hold."

Grant looked about. Stuart's line faced the road on the other side of the peach orchard and the pond. The road to his front headed northwest in a wide arc leading directly to the vital bridge across Snake Creek. Confederate troops charging down the road would hit Sherman's left flank and roll it up. Even more worrisome was the open field directly behind Stuart's line. Flat and clear, it led directly to Pittsburg Landing like a spear point aimed at the heart of Grant's command.

Grant squinted over Stuart's line. Johnston has not yet discovered this weak point, he realized. Maybe it's because I have *so many* weak points that he can't exploit them all. His senses warned him that the fire on this section of his perimeter was steadily increasing. They're probing here, he thought. I can't believe Johnston doesn't have at least one farmer in his army from Tennessee who doesn't know this ground like the face of his mother, hasn't told him that this flat ground extends all the way to the landing. He'll be coming.

"Son, I think your line is about to be tested beyond all your expectations," he said slowly. "Behind you is an open road to the landing. Any fool of a general can see that."

"Sir?" Stuart's face paled.

Grant searched inside his coat pocket for his memo book. With the stub of a pencil he scribbled down an order, tore the page from his book, and handed it to one of his aides. The man saluted before riding off. "I'm going to give you some of General Wallace's men, Colonel."

"General Lew Wallace, sir?"

Grant shook his head. "No. W.H.L. Wallace. He was killed in the first attack. Lew Wallace is marching down from Crump Landing with his division. When Lew arrives, he will reinforce Sherman on the right. I'll put Buell's men into your line when he crosses the river. Then we should be able to beat back this attack."

Stuart studied Grant's face. "When will that be, sir?"

"Damned soon, I hope, son. Damned soon."

But an hour passed with no sign of either Wallace or Buell. Then another hour, and another.

And still the Confederate attacks continued with unabated fury. Fearsome fighting, hand-to-hand at times, accompanied the unending assault. Madness and blood lust consumed the soldiers of both sides, driving all thoughts of safety from their minds. Line after line of men stood so close that their rifle muzzles touched as they poured round after round of fire into the densely packed ranks. Panting from the heat and from exertion, their parched throats continued to utter cries that the blast of cannon buried.

Men leaned forward into this deadly wind of lead. As one soldier fell, another brave man stepped up to fill the gap. Feet planted in the face of destruction, they loaded and fired until their rifle barrels glowed red. Bodies piling about the lines acted as impediments to advancement and marked the field of battle as ghastly barricades, the dead still serving their commanders.

Throughout the day, Grant raced his horse back and forth along the front with little regard for the bullets that passed within inches of him. Time after time he paused to encourage his troops when it looked as if they might break and run. But each hour saw his lines pushed slowly back toward the river.

Colonel Rawlins and the paymaster finally located their general by riding to where the fighting was hottest. The paymaster cast a quizzical look up into the steady shower of leaves. "Is it raining?" he asked Rawlins.

"No, Douglas," Rawlins replied, "those are bullets."

To both men's astonishment, they could actually see the volleys of musket balls passing through the air, looking and sounding like swarms of hornets.

By afternoon Grant had ridden to the Union's right flank where Sherman stubbornly held the pontoon crossing of Snake Creek constructed earlier by Federal engineers. The rumpled officer who met Grant bore no resemblance to the shaken man of that morning. Instead, Sherman appeared a grim and resolute warrior firmly in command of his men. His brigades, no longer green since their early morning baptism by fire, reflected his tenacity. Every clearing in the heavy forest to their front was carpeted with gray bodies.

Like Grant, Sherman had constantly traveled the length of his line to shore up his men's morale. And with telling effect. Despite desperate attempts by Hardee to cut through the Union's defenses, Sherman's men had held. The road to Crump Landing remained firmly in Federal hands.

"Any sign of Lew Wallace's division?" Grant asked anxiously. His eyes followed the empty road to his right.

"Nary hide nor hair of them, Sam," Sherman snarled as he hawked thick phlegm from his throat. "I'm calling them 'the Lost Division,'" he added bitterly. "But how the hell they can get lost on a road that leads directly here is beyond my comprehension—unless Wallace is marching backward!"

Grant shook his head. He motioned to two riders on his staff. "Colonel McPherson and Captain Rawley, ride to General Wallace and bid him bring up his division without delay."

Both men saluted and wheeled away over the precious bridge. An artillery round struck the water near the crossing with a loud slap and a geyser of muddy steam.

Both Grant and Sherman blinked at the steam settling back into the disturbed water.

"Can you hold this road, Cump?" Grant asked earnestly. Of all his division commanders, Sherman was the one he depended upon most, trusted the most.

Sherman spit again. His face fractured into a series of furrows like contour lines on a map, they surrounded his forehead and his grimacing mouth. "I'll hold this damned bridge for you until Christmas if need be, Sam. As long as I'm still alive and kicking."

Grant nodded. "Can't ask for more than that, Cump."

"That's for goddamned sure," Sherman swore.

They shook hands, neither knowing if this might be the last time they saw the other alive, then Grant galloped back to the shrinking center of his command at Pittsburg Landing.

The day progressed with no sign of Lew Wallace and no letup in the relentless attack by the Confederates. All the while, Grant watched his left flank collapse inch by inch, pushing his army closer and closer to the precious landing, each bloody foot of clinging mud paid for by the lives and hopes of youths from both sides. The steep banks of the Tennessee River above and below made Pittsburg Landing the only site capable of resupply, yet the constant attacks threatened his hold on that precious base.

Worse still, thousands of frightened stragglers now packed the narrow perimeter of his defense, huddling against the banks and bluffs of the river with no more than a handful of rifles between the thousands. Should his line break, Grant realized, these demoralized men would be shot where they crouched or be driven into the swift river to drown. It would be a massacre of unmatched proportions.

Skillfully, Grant handled his ever-diminishing line. By late that day he had withdrawn McClernand's division to the left of the road that Sherman held. McClernand's troops formed a chevron bending back to link with Hurlbut's soldiers holding the high ridge that protected the landing itself. On Hurlbut's left the Union line followed the curve of the high ground with cannon and siege mortar placed wheel-to-wheel.

Grant glanced at the setting sun as it cast mournful shadows over the killing ground and tinted the sky an appropriately bloody red. Dusk would come soon. Would the attack break off then? he wondered. Surely Johnston's men must be as exhausted as my own.

"General."

Grant lowered his field glasses and turned to Major Hawkins, his chief commissary officer. The major shook his head and fought to control his voice. Tear stains streaked his grimy face.

"General, a courier just brought news. General Prentiss has been surrounded and forced to surrender. His men valiantly repulsed twelve assaults, but when the rest of our line withdrew toward the river, the rebels flanked Prentiss on both sides. He could hold out no longer. Twenty-two hundred men, half his command—" Hawkins paused to control the sob that escaped his lips. "—that's all that were left...."

Grant nodded. But Prentiss held his ground just as I asked him to do, he thought. He did what I needed him to do. God bless him and all his men for that. And God help him, as well. His stand bought me what time I have now. For some reason the Southern attack seemed to center on Prentiss's sector. Instead of pushing past him on both flanks, they concentrated their fire mainly on him. And that held up their advance. That gave me a chance to form a stronger line behind him.

Strange, Grant mused, I would not have expected General Albert Sidney Johnston to allow his attack to bog down like that. I would not have....

Grant looked about at the once serene hillside. The trees that yesterday sported spring green leaves and blue and pink blossoms now stood stripped of foliage by the day's murderous gunfire. The peach orchard lay in smoldering ruins, the mossy riverbank and verdant glades now reduced to bloodied mud.

A corporal approached with a captured Confederate private. The soldier presented his musket and nudged his captive forward. Grant studied the prisoner. He can't be more than sixteen, if that, Grant surmised. Neither is my soldier. With his towhead, he ought to be carrying a fishing pole rather than a musket. Both boys. So young—on both sides.

The Confederate's butternut uniform was so caked with mud as to resemble a mound of moving dirt more than a suit of clothing. His left boot was missing, and an ugly gash crossed the boy's right cheek. His right eye was swollen shut, but he stood erect and proud.

"This reb's from Johnston's command, sir," the Union soldier said sternly. "My captain told me to bring him to you, sir. Said he had important information you might find helpful." With that the young corporal nodded to his prisoner. "Go on, Johnny Reb, you tell the general what you told the captain and me."

The Confederate regarded Grant suspiciously with his one open eye, but said nothing.

"Go on," the corporal urged. "You said you'd talk to the general."

"He don't look like no general to me," the boy replied. "Ain't got no gold braid, nor nothin'."

"Well, he is," the corporal said defensively. "And a damned fine one at that. He's gonna whip your General Johnston by this day's end."

"That ain't hard," the captured lad replied. "General Johnston is dead. But Beauregard is leading us now, and he's planning a whopping attack just afore sundown."

"General Johnston is dead?" Grant asked softly. He had known the man from the Mexican War.

"Yessir. He got shot around two o'clock over there in that damned peach orchard. I was within spitting distance of him when he done fell off his horse. Hit in the leg while he was leading us against the Hornet's Nest. He bled to death afore his surgeon could get to him. His own doctor was off tending to wounded Yanks. Ain't that a joke."

"The Hornet's Nest, what's that?" Major Hawkins asked.

The reb jerked his head toward where Prentiss made his fateful stand. "That sunken road by the peach orchard. We call it the Hornet's Nest 'cause so many of us got stung by your bullets and 'cause the air fairly buzzed with the sound of minié balls."

"I see," Hawkins replied. "The Hornet's Nest..."

"Who was that we was fightin'?" the boy asked.

"That was General Prentiss's division, son," Grant replied. "He was doing what I asked him to do."

"He did it damned well," the youth snorted. "It took Dan Ruggles and his sixty-two field guns to blast them at close range before he surrendered. Lord Almighty, I ain't never seen such killing in all my born days. This here is butchery on a grand scale. You can't walk over the ground without stepping on dead and dying—both blue and gray."

Grant nodded. Prentiss's sacrifice had bought him time. Now he must use it wisely, or all those men had died for nothing.

"What's to become of me?" the young rebel asked. "You ain't gonna hang me, nor nothing like that, are you? I ain't scared of dying, but it don't sit right my surviving all them Yanks shooting at me jus' to have you string me up like some runaway nigger."

Grant studied the prisoner. "No, son, we don't hang prisoners of war. One of our doctors will see to your wounds, and then I suspect you'll be exchanged for one of our men."

"Good, 'cause I may be scuffed a bit, but I'll mend. And I want to git back to my regiment. I ain't done fighting you Johnny Yanks—not by a long shot."

Grant's eyes narrowed as the lad's words sunk in. "Corporal, take your prisoner over to the field kitchen and give him something to eat. Grab a bite for yourself. You both look like you could stand a square meal."

"Yes, sir!" The soldier's face broke into a tired grin. He shouldered his rifle and led his charge toward the river.

Grant and Hawkins both heard the Southerner complain to his captor as they trod tiredly away, "Are you sure he's a general? He don't look like no general I ever did see."

Grant looked at his aide. "So Beauregard is planning a 'whopping' attack, eh?"

Hawkins's shoulders sagged. In his heart he knew they were beaten. Lee and Jackson were thrashing George McClellan in Virginia, now it was their turn here in the West. It was inevitable, he guessed. Grant's success at Donelson had been a fluke. Never in his life had Hawkins seen fighting like this. One more big push would drive them into the river. A lump rose in his throat. They had come so far, only to have this happen. It would be the end of Grant, he knew. Halleck was only looking for another excuse to sack him. Hawkins swallowed hard as he fought back tears.

"Shall I order a flag of truce, General—to arrange terms of surrender?"

But his commanding officer was patting his pockets as he searched for something. He appeared not to hear.

"Sir? Shall I make plans for a surrender?"

The general looked up. "Surrender?" he sighed. "Major, you heard what that boy said. They're not going to surrender to us, Hawkins. I thought if we won a major victory, maybe even two or three, the Confederacy would sue for peace and this war would be over."

"Sir?" Hawkins looked bewildered. With all this noise from the rifle fire and cannon, had Grant misunderstood? They, the National troops, were licked, not the Confederates.

"But I was wrong," Grant continued. "There is no thought of surrender in the rebels' minds. They plan on driving us back and recapturing what they lost." His jaws clamped on his cigar and he shook his head grimly. "Hawkins, we're going to have to knock them to their knees before this war will end. It's not going to be over soon."

"You ... you don't want to surrender, sir?"

Grant's face darkened in a scowl. "Surrender? Surrender? The Confederates won't surrender to me, and I certainly don't propose to surrender to them. What were you thinking, Major? Surrender!" He spit out the soggy remnants of his cigar and lighted another one. "We're going to repulse their 'whopping' attack and hold our line until Buell and Wallace arrive. Then we're going to counterattack. Now, where will the attack come from? Let me think. Beauregard is in command now. He tends to be impetuous, I think. He'll want a single massive blow, one that will cut us off from relief and resupply. A *coup de main.*"

A percussion charge exploded over the lines to their rear with an ear-shattering crack. Smudges of smoke spread out from the center of the blast like dirty fingers grasping in the mustard haze that long ago replaced the blue sky. Hawkins ducked involuntarily, but Grant never noticed. Chagrined, the major resolved not to let his fear show again.

"Most of his forces are concentrated facing our left flank. His preoccupation with Prentiss in our center led to that. The terrain funneled them across to our left." Grant paused to relight his cigar.

"Sir?"

Grant continued his thoughts out loud. "Beauregard could attack our right flank. But I do not think he will attack us on Sherman's side of the line. Sherman has good ground there and is firmly fortified now. To attack

Sherman would require a left-wheeling deployment of his divisions across the front of our line. If his lines of communication are as bad as ours, he won't try that with green troops. Besides, he knows Sherman must hold the road to Crump Landing and will not counterattack the rebels' left flank if Beauregard weakens it to strengthen an attack on the other side of our line."

Hawkins watched in fascination. *Grant had never even considered the possibility of surrendering his forces.*

"So that leaves only our left, eh, Major. If I were Beauregard, I should attack our left flank. But where exactly would I attack ... ?"

Grant withdrew a crumpled map from his pocket and laid it across his horse's saddle. Thankfully, he leaned against the animal and shifted the weight from his throbbing ankle. He pored over the pencil marks. His finger jabbed at the map. "See this ravine on our left? The one that drains into the Tennessee?"

Hawkins craned his neck to follow. As always, the lines on a map never translated well in his mind.

"Over there, Major." Grant pointed with his pencil. "Beauregard will attack through that gully."

Hawkins followed his commander's arm. He let his gaze run from the battered log house with its stone chimneys that stood at Pittsburg Landing to the bluff that rose just south of it. The once grand house now sported gaping holes in its walls, and the south corner of the structure was blown away to reveal splintered cross beams poking from the opening like exposed ribs.

The rise itself bristled with Webster's cannon and hastily prepared defenses of split rails and piles of dirt and rock. Desperate men had thrown up whatever protection they could find to stop the incessant flight of bullets. Their frantic efforts turned a gentle wooded slope into a refuse pile of stumps and rock. Fire and smoke spurted from the tree line less than fifty yards away, where the Confederate line huddled behind similar defenses. Return fire of equal ferocity emanated from the Union line.

Behind that rise lay the river, with its landing alive with a flowing mass of blue uniforms, overturned wagons, and panic-stricken horses.

Frightened men pushed and shoved in all directions, without leadership, without order.

My God, Hawkins thought, if our line is breached, the men down there will be slaughtered. It'll be like shooting fish in a barrel.

"Do you see the ravine?" Grant asked impatiently. He shook his head to dislodge a tree branch that fell across his hat. Bullets had long since shot away the last vestiges of every spring leaf. Now the rifle fire pruned the trees themselves so that a constant hail of limbs and branches rained upon the soldiers.

"Yes ... yes, sir, connecting to the river by our left flank. It's partially filled with water from the rain."

"I think they'll come at us from the ravine, Major. Our line is weakest there. It is also closest to the landing. Have Colonel Webster direct as many of his artillery pieces along that ravine as possible. And order Captains Gwin and Shirk to be ready to steam upriver with their gunboats, *Lexington* and *Tyler*."

"Sir?"

"I want those two gunboats ready to bring their twenty-pounders to bear on that ravine if need be. From the river they will be able to fire the length of that gully."

Suddenly, Hawkins understood. The image of twenty-pound shot and canister raking the length of the swampy ravine and their devastating effect on troops packed within those narrow confines chilled his blood. "God help the rebs if they do attack across that ravine," he whispered.

Ulysses Grant studied his aide. "Let us hope for all our sakes that General Beauregard does not launch another attack. Yet, I believe he will come."

When the sun dipped beneath the ridge to the west as if to hide its rays from the carnage it had witnessed, the rebel cry, heard so often that day, sprang once more from a thousand parched and rasping throats. Bone-weary men reached into their last reserves and rose from their meager protection.

Bending forward against the deadly wind of bullets, the Confederates advanced toward the Union line. Red and blue battle flags waved above the smoke, faltered and fell, only to arise in another set of animate hands. The shouts and screams of battle-crazed men merged with the roar of cannon fire and the crackle of muskets into another thunderous din that deafened the ear and drove all reason from the minds of both sides.

Amidst this attack that would decide the fate of his command, General Grant sat astride his horse on a small rise overlooking his line and chewed on the soggy stub of his last cigar. Couriers with dispatches raced to and from his small cluster of remaining staff. Most of his followers lay killed or wounded or had been sent to bolster the sagging lines. Fighting men counted more at this desperate time than anyone else. Every hand was needed to man a gun or wield a bayonet.

Grant scribbled all his orders himself. Short, to the point, and clearly written, his messages left no room for misinterpretation. *Hold the line at all costs!*

Grant watched the sea of gray attackers pour into the ravine as he had predicted. Funneled by the folds of land and the pressure of Union fire, the Confederate attack flowed into the sodden gully in a packed mass of humanity. Crammed together, the men in the center stumbled over their fallen comrades while those on the outside slipped and fell down the treacherous slopes. Wading in water up to their knees, the rebels pressed grimly onward.

To his left Grant followed the dark shapes of the *Lexington* and *Tyler*, glistening like malignant, armored beetles, sliding into position.

Without warning, the gunboats unleashed a coordinated barrage. As if a single hand pulled the lanyard, the *Tyler* and *Lexington* fired as one. Their broadside wrought shocking havoc on the tightly packed Southerners.

The rebel charge faltered and a terrible groan rose from the gully as the shot and steel struck. The gunboats continued to pour their relentless fire into the attackers, adding their weight to that of the cannons that stood wheel-to-wheel on the ridge. Paddle wheels thrashing the leaden waters while tongues of flame spurted from their ugly sides, the gunboats plied a deadly trade as they coursed back and forth along the river's edge.

The deafening roar suddenly ceased. Like tiny ants who had lost their queen, the gray men in the gully broke into aimless clusters and clumps, stopped their fatal climb toward the Federal line and fell back. The attack was broken.

No cheers erupted from the Union line. The surviving men were too exhausted, too numb to react. Like their counterparts, they simply sought shelter or pressed themselves deeper into the damp ground in search of safety.

"General Grant!" A rider spurred his wide-eyed horse past the ruins of battle to the general's side. He gestured with his arm toward the Tennessee River. A string of barges and riverboats clogged the darkening waters. The last rays of the setting sun glinted on the steel bayonets of hundreds of troops packed inside the boats. "General Buell's men have arrived! They are crossing the river now! Twenty thousand strong!"

"God be praised!" the red-eyed Hawkins cheered. "They have saved us!"

"No." Grant shook his head. "Those men come too late to affect the outcome of this battle. Only the gallant service of our men have won this day. No one else can take the credit."

Grant looked about him. It was over, at least for today. The slaughter was ended. He would not counterattack tonight. His own men could not muster the energy. They lay among their dead comrades gasping for breath and staring into space with eyes that saw little more than their deceased companions.

Slowly and with infinite care, Grant guided his horse among his exhausted troops and down to the landing. Already his mind turned to plan tomorrow's attack.

# SHILOH,
# THE SECOND DAY

Night brought sheets of torrential rain. Thunder and lightning split the darkness with a ferocity exceeding the battle that day. Nature seemed resolved to demonstrate its own power over the puny armies that had shattered the previous day with their sound and fury.

Wounded and dying suffered beneath the chilling rain. Those too weak to move from shell hollows and streambeds drowned as the water rose. Unfortunate Confederate and Federal injured were swept into the swollen Tennessee River, to wash up downstream.

All through the night, feeble pinpoints of lantern light pricked the black curtain of the falling rain as men from both sides searched the battlefield for missing comrades. Groans and cries for help rose and fell on the howling wind while a constant stream of litter bearers picked their way to the field hospitals. This night the demons of the dark carried the field.

Feeling less than victorious, Ulysses S. Grant huddled beneath a shattered tree a short way from the riverbank. Cold, drenched to the skin by the constant rain, he tried to grab a few hours of sleep. But the throbbing of his twisted ankle kept him awake. Turn as he might, he could not find a comfortable position, let alone a dry one. Finally, around midnight, he rose from his wet blanket and made his way toward the inviting light from the log cabin that had been the center of his defense. Splintered and holed by musket and cannon, the log house had refused to catch fire and now stood leaking light from its many gaps.

Hobbling to the house, Grant drew back the blanket that had replaced the door. Instantly, the odor of sweat and blood assailed his nose. Grant blinked at the scene before him. He cursed himself for forgetting that the cabin was being used as a hospital.

Even the dim yellow light of the few lanterns failed to disguise the dark stains of blood that covered the floor and the plank doors that served as operating tables. The four exhausted surgeons did not look up as the general entered, remaining intent on their task of sawing off shattered arms and legs. In his mud-stained coat, no one recognized him.

In one corner a wooden tub sat filled with amputated limbs. Wounded men occupied every inch of floor. Low moans issued from the living floor. Here and there among the drawn faces, Grant recognized the peaceful countenance of those who had died.

A medical officer, Captain Hyde, looked up from the pile of bandages he was stacking and saw the little man standing in the doorway. He was about to yell at him to close the blanket when his words died in his throat. It was General Grant!

Hyde made his way to his commander's side. "General, are you wounded? Do you need medical attention?"

Grant continued to stare at the pile of body parts. Off to his right, one of the surgeons paused to wipe his bloody hands on his apron while an assistant administered more chloroform to the sallow lad with a bullet wound in his groin. With a sigh of resignation, the surgeon picked up a slippery probe. Using it to lever a burnt patch of the man's uniform out of the ragged hole, he continued his search for the elusive bullet.

"General?"

Grant noticed the officer, but his eyes remained fixed on the pile of shattered limbs. "Do they always have to cut off the limb?" he asked slowly.

Hyde glanced at the amputated extremities. "Not always," he replied softly. "We try to conserve whatever we can. I know the army thinks we're a bunch of butchers. Sawbones, they call us, but when possible we favor excision of the wound and not amputation." He paused to let his words soak in. "It's ... it's just that this minié ball has such a high velocity, it shatters any bone it strikes. A direct wounding of a long bone splinters that bone beyond repair, not to mention the damage to the artery and the nerves."

"Yes, I see, Doctor," Grant mumbled. "Thank you. I won't take you away from your duties. I can see you are sorely needed."

The general backed into the night and let the rain wash over him. So much death, so much suffering, he thought. Am I to blame? Am I solely to blame? He wiped his hand over his face and down his beard. Should I have entrenched my camp? I doubt that would have thwarted Johnston's attack. They would have overrun our lines anyway.

A hand reached out in the darkness to rest upon his shoulder.

Grant turned to gaze at his friend. Sherman's eyes appeared flat and faded, and his face twitched from nervous exhaustion. Even in the darkness the disarray of his uniform was evident. One wing of his collar poked tiredly into his grizzled beard. The black string tie that bound his collar hung undone like a child's shoelace.

"Lew Wallace finally showed up," Grant said.

"He took his damned sweet time doing so!" Sherman stammered. His breath carried the odor of sour mash whiskey.

"Are you drunk, Cump?" Grant asked.

"Hell, no! But I wish I were, Sam. I dearly wish I were. I had to wade through a whole hell of my men's mangled bodies to find you. Half of them didn't have heads or limbs." Sherman's eyes regained the wild light that led so many to proclaim him mad. He searched about him as if the force of the storm could explain the reason for the day's slaughter. His only answer came in the form of a bolt of lightning that lit up the sky momentarily and left him with a stark image of black and white bodies. With a shiver, Sherman took another long drink from his hip flask. He offered it to his friend.

Grant shook his head. "I better not, Cump. I need a clear head."

Sherman emitted a ghastly laugh. "If any of us keep a clear head, we surely *will* go insane." His hand still held out the bottle.

Grant nodded. He took the flask and drank. The Tennessee sour mash burned as it rolled down the back of his throat. A part of him cried out to empty the bottle, to drink it all, but he handed it back to Sherman. An awkward silence followed.

Grant studied his muddied boots, with the split one half exposing his bandaged ankle. The brush at his feet was neatly clipped at ground level, as if recently mowed. Strange, he thought, at breakfast this area was covered with brush, some of it eight feet high. Hard to imagine bullets cutting down this covering and leaving anyone still alive.

Grant rubbed his beard. "I've read our casualty reports, Cump. Over seven thousand killed or wounded."

"Seven thousand!" Sherman blinked. "There must be just as many Confederates killed before my position alone. My front lines are carpeted with dead rebels. This is pure hell, Sam. I think we won today, but I don't know for sure. I do know I don't feel victorious. I feel ... dirty inside."

Grant nodded. Sadness filled his naturally frowning face. "I was wrong about something, Cump," he said slowly. "Today changed my thinking."

"Wrong?"

"I thought the rebellion against the government would collapse if the South were dealt a decisive defeat. I beat them at Henry—conclusively—and again at Donelson. I forced my old friend, Simon Buckner, to surrender without condition, but today the rebels came at us as if none of those losses had ever happened. They planned to whip us and drive us back to Ohio."

Sherman looked at his commander. "Like I said, Sam, the South won't quit until they're beaten into submission. We're going to have to destroy the whole region down to the last stubborn mule."

Grant watched his friend closely. He knew how much Sherman loved the South and its courtly ways. Sherman's years as superintendent of a military academy in Louisiana left him with a deep fondness for their lifestyle. To say what he had must have pained him greatly. "I'm afraid you're right, Cump. It's going to take complete conquest to save the Union."

A heavy silence hung over the two men as they stood by the shattered tree. The rain continued.

"But, my God, Sam, they tore into us something fierce today!" Sherman said, finally breaking the silence. "They gave us a capital licking."

Grant's resolve returned. He smiled grimly at his division commander. "That's all right, Cump," he said. "We'll beat them tomorrow."

Throughout the night the barges ferried Buell's Army of the Ohio to the aid of Grant's stricken forces. Like slick-backed death beetles, bristling with muskets and bayonets, the boats crossed and recrossed the swollen river. All the while, the thunder and lightning continued unabated, supplemented by the roar of the gunboats' siege mortars. Without regard for the wounded and spent men of either side, the vessels vied with the storm as to which could deliver the most misery. In the end they tied.

Grant continued to direct the insertion of these fresh troops among his battle-weary soldiers. All night long he rode his horse up and down the lines, issuing orders and assessing the strength of each unit. The slightest suggestion of the coming morning light appeared in the east before the general had satisfied himself that Buell's men as well as Lew Wallace's division were in place.

Only then did he close his eyes. Just for a moment, he told himself, to rest them.

"General Grant!"

Grant awoke, suddenly realizing he had fallen asleep in the saddle. Disoriented, he glanced about. Mounted men surrounded him. He focused on the horsemen. For a terrible moment he feared he had been captured by rebel cavalry. The dark blue of the sodden uniforms reassured him.

"General Grant." Lew Wallace saluted. The bearded general leaned forward in his saddle, the wet leather groaning. He studied his commanding officer. The sweet smell of stale liquor reached his nostrils. By God, the man is drunk, Wallace thought. Disgraceful! He ought to be stripped of his command, here and now. Instead, the savvy politician hid his thoughts and asked solicitously. "Are you ill, sir? My personal surgeon is nearby. He is at your disposal."

Grant recognized the tone instantly. Damn him. He thinks I'm drunk. No doubt he will drop word of his impression to the first newspaper reporter he encounters. And why not? What better way to deflect the cowardly way he failed us yesterday than to raise the specter of my drinking? No wonder the South whips us at every turn, when our generals would rather stab each other in the back than advance against the enemy.

"You are late, sir!" Grant replied sharply. "The battle was yesterday, and we had great need of your services then."

Instantly put on the defense, Wallace became solicitous. He saluted again, this time holding his salute until he received Grant's halfhearted wave in return. Behind him, his staff saluted as well. "General Grant, sir!" Wallace protested. "I have sought you out for the very purpose of explaining my unfortunate delay. Please do me the courtesy of hearing me out!"

"Unfortunate, indeed!" Grant hissed. "Your 'delay,' as you so offhandedly call it, nearly cost us the day. General Sherman has suggested that your men are proficient in marching in reverse."

Even in the predawn darkness, Grant could see the pained look on Wallace's face. The stricken general's horse recognized his rider's unease and responded by pawing the sodden ground. The sucking sound of his hooves were all that followed Grant's rebuke. At a loss for words, Wallace turned to his staff for help.

"Sir," a colonel from Wallace's staff said, urging his mount abreast of the angry Grant. "Yesterday, our First Brigade was stationed at Crump Landing, but the Second and Third were some miles along the road from Adamsville to here. When we first heard firing, General Wallace ordered the First and Third to concentrate on the Second Brigade."

"That is true." Wallace found his voice. "We then marched to the sound of the fighting. Toward Purdy Road. Where our last knowledge of your front lines directed us."

"But—" the colonel continued.

"But then," Wallace interrupted, "we found the sound of battle had shifted so that it was far to our rear."

Because my men were being pushed back, Grant thought, fighting every inch of the way while your men dragged their feet.

When he heard no protest from Grant, Wallace, emboldened by this silence, continued. "Naturally, I feared for the worst—that your command had fallen back and I had passed too far to the rear...."

"Naturally," Grant echoed hollowly.

"I wheeled my columns about face and we retraced our steps to avoid my men engaging the enemy far behind their lines."

Engaging the rebels far in their rear would have been most helpful to me, Grant thought. It would have thrown them into disorder. But then you'd have had the fight of your life on your hands—like I had.

"And then I received your verbal order to proceed by the road nearest the river.... Well, sir, we had passed the juncture of the road crossing Snake Creek, so we had to retrace our steps a second time."

Grant cursed himself for giving that command as a verbal order. It allowed Wallace room to equivocate, room for doubt as to what his actual order was. Too many good men fell from misunderstood orders. In war there was no room for such mistakes. Never again, he vowed, would he issue anything but clear-cut *written* orders. Henceforth, even the most thick-witted officer under his command would know *precisely* what he wanted done. He would see to that.

Grown suddenly weary with this parrying, Grant waved his hand in a gesture of dismissal. "We must look to this morning, General Wallace. We have great need of your fresh troops on our right flank."

Wallace smiled inwardly. After this fiasco, Halleck would remove Grant for certain. Yesterday's slaughter was unprecedented. The Army of the Tennessee would need another commander, and who better to fill that post than the general whose men saved the army that Grant had led into this debacle? *Major* General Lew Wallace. The title had a crisp ring to it. Already Wallace could feel the extra weight of an added gold star on his shoulders. "My men are ready to cover your retreat, General Grant," he said solicitously.

"Retreat?" Grant frowned. "Retreat? No. I propose to attack at daylight and whip them."

The break of day saw the strengthened Union Army advancing over the ground they had relinquished so stubbornly the previous day. Grant's old command, reinforced by Lew Wallace's fresh division, now occupied the right half of the attack, with Sherman, McClernand, and Hurlbut extending their line until it linked with the men under Buell's Army of the Ohio. That army, with its four divisions led by Nelson, McCook, Crittenden, and Wood, attacked the battered remnants of Hardee and Breckinridge along the left. By noon the Union forces had recaptured all they had lost the day before.

Riding with the advance of his forces, Grant spurred his horse back and forth, keeping contact with his commanders and urging his men onward. At noon he and his staff, now reduced to Major Hawkins and Colonel McPherson, directed their tired horses past a clearing. Without warning, the woods beyond the opening erupted in smoke and fire. McPherson's horse reared, nearly throwing its rider, and Hawkins's hat flew from his head as a bullet struck it.

"Ride for it!" Grant yelled just as a cannon fired from within the smoke-filled thicket.

An evil wind of grapeshot scythed limbs from a clump of gum trees directly behind the startled riders, miraculously sparing the three Union officers. Staccato bursts of rifle fire followed the deafening blast.

Galloping away as bullets whizzed through the air, Grant drew up when they were out of range. With a sigh of relief he saw two companies of Sherman's division charge the thicket and drive the attackers back.

"General, are you wounded?" a concerned McPherson asked. "Is it your leg?"

Grant followed his aide's worried gaze to his left leg. The scabbard of his sword dangled at an acute angle, almost severed by the impact of a minié ball. As he raised the scabbard to inspect it, the shattered metal covering broke off at the hilt along with his sword.

Grant grunted in surprise. "They shot away my sword. Well, better that than my leg." His mind recalled the piles of limbs stacked outside the makeshift hospital he had entered last night. Uncontrollably, he shivered.

Would Julia still love me with a missing leg? he wondered. He shook off those thoughts with a shrug. "Nothing of less use in a battle to a general than his sword," he quipped while he turned the abbreviated hilt over in his hand and inspected it.

"Take mine, General," the colonel urged. McPherson withdrew his own sword, intending to hand it to Grant, but before he could, his horse ceased its labored panting and dropped dead in its tracks. McPherson leapt from his saddle a moment before the dead animal rolled onto its side. Dark blood poured from a bullet hole less than an inch behind the saddle.

McPherson rose with his sword still clutched in his hand.

"No, Colonel." Grant shook his head. "You keep your sword. What a fine sight we are! Of the three of us, one has lost his hat, one his horse, and one his sword." He scratched at his beard while a slow grin spread over his face. "Thank God, it is no worse."

Then General Sherman, looking as wild-eyed and disheveled as ever, rode over. He reined in his lathered mount, looked down at the dead horse, then at Grant's broken sword. Sherman started to speak, thought better of it, then stood in his stirrups and pointed to their left flank.

"Sam, we're pushing them back smartly . . . so smartly that they're abandoning their artillery and supply trains. In fact, we've recaptured all the cannon we lost yesterday. And you know what? A captured rebel captain told me Beauregard actually slept in my tent last night. What cheek! My captured tent, would you believe it?"

Sherman's face turned somber. He jerked his head toward the rolling wall of smoke ahead of them. His eyes seemed to lose some of their wildness as tears filled them. "We're passing over the bodies of our men who died yesterday, too," he said in a hushed voice. "God Almighty, but there are piles and piles of them. Some of the poor devils are still alive. I can't imagine their torment, lying all night in the rain like that. God help them." He sniffed loudly and drew himself upright in his saddle. "It's a hell of a trade, Sam."

"A hell of a trade," Grant echoed. "Keep pushing them, Cump. The quicker we destroy their armies, the sooner this will end."

Sherman nodded gravely. "Buell's front is slowing down. You need to tell him to push forward. Nelson on my left has all but stopped his advance."

Grant flung his shattered hilt away in disgust. "I was afraid of that!"

"Order them to advance, Sam."

"General Sherman!" Colonel McPherson protested. As Grant's staff officer, McPherson well knew the intricate protocol that dictated orders in the Union Army and ensnared all those who sought to bypass it.

"Colonel McPherson is right." Grant looked down at his grounded colonel and smiled ruefully. The head of one army never ordered the head of another, a weakness that raised its ugly head all too often when the War Department insisted on compartmentalizing their forces and naming them after the river or region where they fought. "I ... I can't issue that order, Cump. Protocol. I know I'm senior to General Buell, but the Army of the Ohio is his command, not mine. I only command the Tennessee. I can't rightfully place him under my command."

"Damn protocol!" Sherman slapped his thigh in disgust. "If Buell's men do not advance and seize the junction of the eastern and western Corinth roads, Beauregard's troops will slip through our fingers."

"I know," Grant sighed. He fished inside his coat pocket and withdrew two abraded cigars. He offered one to his friend. It was his way of saying: I agree with you; there's nothing I can do about it, so let it pass. "Have a cigar, Cump," he said. "Your men again fought well today, and you have done all that you could possibly have done."

Sherman accepted the gift, but held it in his hand. He rubbed the back of his neck while he grimaced. "Well, then, we're not going to get the whole pie, are we? Only part of it. The rebs will retreat to Corinth with a good deal of their army intact."

Well past sundown, a weary Grant directed his horse to the rectangular command tent his men had erected. The day's end saw his exhausted men entrenched along the road to Corinth. While the Union forces held the field, Sherman's prophecy was fulfilled. Beauregard's soldiers had slipped past the Union's closing jaws; but in their haste, they left behind a trail of wounded men, overturned supply wagons, and artillery caissons mired to their hubs in the sunken road.

Grant slid from his saddle, carefully landing on his good leg, and limped toward the tent. Outside the opening, two immaculately attired privates snapped to attention. Instantly, misgivings flooded over the general's tired mind. Where did these fresh troops come from? he wondered. He eyed the spotless uniforms and polished brass buckles uneasily. All his men had been committed during the two days' fighting. I'll wager there's not a clean cross belt to be found among all my soldiers, Grant thought. He returned the salute and ducked beneath the closed flap.

Lieutenant General Henry W. Halleck, Commander of the Union Armies of the West, glared up at Grant as he entered.

Sweat glistened on Halleck's balding forehead and ran in rivulets down to his eyebrows, which seemed locked in a perpetual frown. The dark circles beneath Halleck's eyes only accentuated their bloodshot appearance. To Grant, Halleck's eyes appeared ready to start from his head.

Old Brains, Grant thought. I should have guessed it from the guard. He drew himself upright and saluted. Why does Halleck always look like he has just ingested a rotten egg?

Halleck's face twitched and his lips pursed into a tight line, but he returned the salute. Then his head dropped to the sheaf of papers in his lap. In doing so, Halleck's chin vanished beneath the raised blue collar of his double-buttoned dress coat, his jowls flowing over the constricting neck piece. Grant noticed that Halleck's sizable belly heaved and that his hands twitched, causing the papers he was holding to rattle. Newspapers, Grant noted ominously.

"By God, Grant!" Halleck sputtered. "Have you seen this! Have you read what the papers have written!" He waved the newspapers in Grant's face.

"No, sir," Grant answered. "I have been preoccupied with conducting a battle."

"Watch your tone with me, sir!" Halleck warned. "You may be a major general, sir, but I need not remind you that you are a general of volunteers—not a general of the Regular Army!"

Grant remained silent.

Satisfied that he had put this upstart in his place, Halleck continued. He blinked at the glaring headlines that he held in his hands. "'Soldiers Bayoneted in Their Tents! Grant's Army Cut to Ribbons!'" he read. "'Ten Thousand Fall!'

"By God." Halleck crumpled the papers between his plump fingers. "Ten thousand! That exceeds the casualties of Bull Run and Pea Ridge together. The papers are saying that only the timely arrival of General Buell saved your army from total annihilation."

"General Buell's forces in no way contributed to the army's victory on April sixth," Grant protested. "His men did not cross the river until *after* the battle had ended. Who gave these rumors to the reporters? Surely, not my staff. They have been too preoccupied with fighting."

"Apparently from General Buell's staff," Halleck added darkly.

"Self-serving bastards," Grant muttered.

"That may be," Halleck conceded. "But the North is up in arms over the casualties, sir! Congress is calling for a full investigation. And you, General Grant, are in disgrace. Your incompetence has cost us dearly. Your star is tarnished." Halleck paused in his tirade to study Grant closely. "Are you drunk, sir?" he demanded abruptly. "They say you were?"

Grant's face darkened. "I was not drunk." Will they never let go of my past? he brooded. The captain of 1854 might have been drunk, but I am no longer that man. Sherman was right. The newspapers love crucifying their heroes even more than creating them.

"I will accept your word," Halleck replied magnanimously. "Still, the rumors persist."

"I cannot fight rumors, sir. My task is to fight the Confederates."

"You were told to wait for me, Grant." Halleck tried a different tack. "With Buell's Army of the Ohio and your Army of the Tennessee, I planned to advance on Corinth."

At a snail's pace, Grant thought.

"You disobeyed my orders!"

"I did not, sir. I was concentrating my forces at Pittsburg Landing in anticipation of your arrival *when I was attacked.*"

"Grant! Grant!" Halleck shook his head and his jowls flapped about his collar. "What am I to do with you?" The commander pressed his index finger into the cleft in his chin as he pondered his own question. He would have loved to send Grant packing, and had already tried that, but Lincoln had jumped down his throat. One Illinois roughneck looking out for another, Halleck thought. Grant had not heard about Pope yet, he suddenly realized. That should take the wind out of his sails.

"Do you know that General Pope's Army of the Mississippi captured Island Number Ten this very day?"

Island Number 10, Grant recalled, was the fortified Confederate island fifty miles below Columbus that blocked the Mississippi.

"Pope took the place with only a handful of casualties. Captured seven thousand men and over fifty coast howitzers."

"That is wonderful news, sir."

Halleck took care to shake his head with his best imitation of sadness. "Not for you, I am afraid, Grant. Now the papers have a new hero, General Pope—not you. You are their latest goat." Halleck spread his fingers and studied his nails carefully. *"Sic transit gloria mundi."*

"Your Latin is better than mine, General Halleck, but I get your meaning. However, I have never sought notoriety. I simply wish to do my duty."

"And you will, Grant. You will," Halleck added smugly. "I have ordered the victorious General Pope to march here with his army. Then I will assume command of all three armies and move on Corinth as I originally intended."

"And me?" Grant had to ask what his sentence was to be.

"You, General Grant, will assume the post of second in command of my combined forces," Halleck replied with ill-concealed glee. "Under me."

A feckless position, Grant realized. One with neither power nor real authority. "I would like to request a transfer, sir."

Halleck sighed. "That is your right, Grant, of course. But it must be approved by your commanding officer, me, and I must tell you that with all the paperwork I already have, there will be some considerable delay in obtaining my approval."

"I understand, sir." Grant saluted and stepped outside of the tent. He inhaled the moist air to clear his mind. A full moon hung balefully above the splintered tree trunks. Its yellow light cast eerie shadows across the companies of marching men and illuminated the yellow hospital flags that hung limply in the heavy air that surrounded the operating tents. The surgeons' work continued, even as fresh troops deployed at the landing.

With cautious men like Halleck in command, this war will go on for years, Grant realized as he watched the new arrivals. Disheartened, he shut his eyes against the grim reality that he knew lay ahead. Advancing by inches will only prolong this conflict, and thousands upon thousands more will die.

Disheartened, Grant sought the one avenue of escape that always brought him solace. Wandering through the camp, he found a campfire bright enough for his purpose. The drained soldiers huddled around the blaze for warmth paid little mind to what passed to them as another miserable soul. Finding a shattered stump to rest against, Grant produced a worn stub of a pencil and a sheet of torn paper. Using his knee as a writing desk, he began to scribble.

> DEAR JULIA,
>
> Again another terrible battle has occurred in which our arms have been victorious. For the number engaged and the tenacity with which both parties held on for two days, during an incessant fire of musketry and artillery, it has no equal on this continent.

He stopped as his mind balked at the slaughter of the last days. Best say little more, he reasoned. He could not, would not, subject his wife to the terrible details, men butchered and dismembered like something less than animals.

The best of the rebel troops were engaged to the number of 162 regiments as stated by a deserter from their camp, and their ablest generals. Beauregard commanded in person aided by A. S. Johnston, Bragg, Breckinridge and hosts of other generals of less note but possibly of quite as much merit. Gen. Johnston was killed and Bragg wounded. The loss on both sides was heavy, probably not less than 20,000 killed and wounded together. The greatest loss was sustained by the enemy. They suffered immensely by demoralization also many of their men leaving the field who will not again be of value on the field.

I got through all safe having but one shot which struck my sword but did not touch me.

I am detaining a steamer to carry this and must cut it short.

Give my love to all at home. Kiss the children for me. The same for yourself.

Good night dear Julia.
ULYS.

The heavy burden lifted from his heart for the moment, his head drooped and he fell asleep.

Grant opened his eyes with a start. It was still dark. He must have dozed off, he realized. He blinked, forcing his eyes to focus. The full moon still divided the landscape into stark lines of light and shadow, but the rows of Sibley tents and the columns of marching soldiers were gone. He was on his porch at Mount MacGregor. The shocks of wheat were just that—wheat. The marching soldiers had vanished.

# JULIA

Crouching as much as the whalebone stays in her corset would allow, Julia Grant cautiously opened the front door and tiptoed onto the porch. Try as she might, the wooden boards creaked beneath her shoes, betraying her presence. The pile of blankets in the high-backed wicker chair stirred and turned to greet her.

"Trying to outflank me, were you, my dear?" Grant peered over the rims of his glasses and grunted. "Well, it won't work. I heard you the instant you cracked the door, and I am prepared to refuse my left." He put down the pencil and sheaf of papers in hand. The wind tried to scatter the pages, but Grant secured them with a rock he had borrowed from the garden.

Julia drew herself upright and moved briskly to his side. She looked down at her husband. A cloth napkin rested against the right side of his face; the sharp spring wind played havoc with his swollen neck. Half buried in his blankets and shawl, with his head covered by a soft smoking cap, he bore little resemblance to the sturdy young soldier she had married so long

ago. Nor do I, Julia reminded herself. My figure is certainly not that of a
young girl.

Still, as she gazed lovingly at her husband, her heart warmed, and she
smiled inwardly. His grim determination remained. His face, thinner now
and graced with a thicker, grayer beard, still bore the resolute look that
knitted his forehead into a series of wrinkles that reminded her of breakers
along the Pacific coast.

Grant watched her closely with one eye partly closed. "What are you
looking at?" he asked half jokingly.

Julia glanced about, assuring herself that they were alone. "My dear,
dear Victor," she said, using the private name she gave him after the fall of
Vicksburg. Her beloved husband was a hero to the defeat-weary North
then, a victor whose name graced everyone's lips. But she already knew
what he was. She always had. "I was just recalling what Colonel Lyman
wrote about you: 'Grant is a man of a good deal of rough dignity, rather
taciturn; quick and decided in speech.' Did he not?"

Grant frowned. "Lyman also said I bore the habitual expression of a
man determined to drive his head through a brick wall and about to do so."
He shifted in his chair, pulling himself more upright. "But I have been
called far worse. Nothing that might compare with the epitaphs laid on
Sherman, though."

Julia settled onto a bench beside him. She arranged her skirts, folded
her hands in her lap, and gazed fondly at her husband. While she knew she
was interrupting his writing, just now she felt the need to be close to him.
All the trouble that had happened to them in so short a time frightened her.
Her husband was the only rock upon which she founded her life, that of
their family, their happiness and personal security. In all their years together, lean as well as fat ones, he had never failed her.

"Yes, poor General Sherman," she agreed. Her hands busied themselves tucking in the blanket around his legs. "To be pilloried by the South
for his campaign in Georgia, and then treated just as badly by the politicians in Washington over the surrender terms he granted General Johnston. He has every right to be embittered."

"Embittered, Sherman? Not embittered, my dear. Sour, maybe. Cump has always been soured about some thing or another, at least as long as I have known him. The only times he wasn't, people were saying he was crazy." Grant dropped his pencil and chopped the air with his right hand in the familiar way he did when he emphasized a point. His arm remained frozen in midair.

Julia craned her neck to see what he had been writing. Her eyes followed his scrawls with little understanding. Military terms, she thought. He's working so hard on his book. She reached over and patted his hand affectionately. His hand felt dry and bony, almost skeletal in its thinness, no longer strong and callused as it once was. He was losing so much weight. He wouldn't tell her, but she knew he weighed less than the sparse 145 pounds he carried at the end of the war. Julia thought he was too thin then, worn down from stress and worry over the war, and she promptly fattened him up to 185 pounds.

Suddenly she was afraid. But she hid her fears. "Are you almost finished, Ulys? I mean with your writings."

He deflected her question. "I am for today, my dear." He dared not tell her he was less than halfway through his rough draft. There was so much left to do, so much more to write; yet each day he felt weaker. Just as he had dogged Lee and worn him down, the growth in his throat was sapping his strength.

Julia brushed her hand across her eyes to hide her tears. She raised her chin and looked longingly at the tree line that marked the boundary of Central Park while she wrung her hands together. Myriad buds knotted the bare branches and turned them into parodies of cruel cat-o'-nine-tail lashes. Warmer weather would split these knobs into clusters of soft, green leaves, Nature's way of transforming ugliness into beauty. But that was some time off.

"It's just like the old days isn't it, Ulys? Like when we were cold and hungry in St. Louis. After you left the army."

Grant reached out and grasped her hands in his. "One cold, hungry day with you, Julia, was far better than any day I've spent in the army away from you and my family." He shook his head in disgust. "I've never done well being separated from you, Julia." He stopped short of describing the fits of depression and drunkenness that led to his leaving the army then. Julia knew all that.

Posted to the Northwest after the Mexican War, the young hero of the war found himself adrift and lonely. Heroes were a dime a dozen, and the drizzly Pacific coast only accentuated the ache Grant felt for his wife. Taking refuge in the bottle, one drink led to another.

One day his superior officer found Grant too drunk to complete his duties. Resign or face a court-martial, he was told. Grant chose the lesser of these two ills. He resigned. Despite pleas from Congressman Andrew Ellison and Grant's father, Jesse, the Secretary of War refused to cancel the young officer's resignation.

Grant noted the irony of that. The Secretary of War was Jefferson Davis. Had Davis reversed that order, Grant might have remained posted to some backwater fort out West, bypassed during the great conflict to come like so many of his colleagues. What would have happened then? he often wondered. And how many times during the Civil War, while he battered away at the walls of the Confederacy, did Jefferson Davis rue that decision?

Leaving the army left him so broke he could not get back to his wife without help from his friends. Grant rubbed his beard as he remembered wandering the backstreets of San Francisco without the price of a hot meal in his pocket, let alone the money for a steamship ticket. His friend, Major Robert Allen, found him in the attic of a flophouse, called the What Cheer House, and wrangled a free ticket for him using his clout as quartermaster.

That got Grant as far as New York. Again, help came from an old classmate from West Point, Captain Simon Bolivar Buckner, who paid his hotel bill and loaned him money to get home.

But harder times awaited him in Missouri. Still, he was reunited with his beloved, Julia.

Julia squeezed his hands and leaned closer to her husband. She, too, was reliving those lean times in her mind, and a lump rose in her throat as she recalled how tattered he looked slumped in that wagon seat. "I thought my heart would break when I would see you hauling wood, Ulys, for I knew you were doing it for us. Ragged, dirty, pitied by the townsfolk, you never once complained. I remember the faded blue greatcoat and the old army hat that you wore. Threadbare and frayed, they were all you had to show for being a hero in the Mexican War. It was so sad."

Grant looked at her questioningly. "I was happy being reunited with you and the children. Besides, that was the best job I could find at the time."

Julia pulled one hand free to dab at her eyes. "Four dollars a cord for that wood, and ten miles each trip to the city!" she cried bitterly.

"It kept us fed, Julia. And we did have a roof over our heads. Many did not have even that much. 'Fifty-seven was a bad year, what with the bank panic."

"That panic made your crops worthless that year. And the frost killed off your crops of oats and corn the next year." Julia shook her head sadly. "Two bad years! You were the hardest working, most unsuccessful farmer I ever knew." She smiled at him while her eyes studied every inch of his seamed face. Those bad years lined his face and bent his shoulders, she told herself, but nowhere near what the war years did.

Grant scratched the left side of his beard. Scratching his beard was a habit he had for so long, and now had to modify. The tenderness of his swollen right neck forced him to rub only the other side. "I wasn't the only one, Julia. Look at Sherman. His career as a banker was less than stellar. What was it he said when he passed through St. Louis that year? 'West Point and the Regular Army are not good schools for bankers and farmers!' He was worse off than we were. He'd lost his entire fortune with the bank collapse."

Grant cursed his careless words. Now they were destitute as well, deep in debt, and far worse off than the young Sherman was then. Fearing his remark might unsettle his wife, he changed the subject. "We did have Hardscrabble, though," he beamed. "A fine house."

"Which you built every inch of! You cleared the land, cut the trees, split the shingles, dug the root cellar, and even built the stone fireplace with rocks you carried from the creek bed. When I think of all the fuss they made over Mr. Lincoln splitting logs, and not a word of your own accomplishments, I am much distressed." Julia drew herself up and squared her shoulders.

Grant chuckled. "It's hard to run a political campaign on a log house named Hardscrabble, my dear. Besides, I did have to get help with the door and the window frames." He turned serious. "It was a generous gift from your father, Colonel Dent, Julia. I just wish he had not given us that slave along with the property."

Julia frowned. "You gave the poor soul his freedom the next year; what more could they ask for?"

"I know, but technically we *were* slave owners. That caused a great deal of unrest when I first took command of the 21st Illinois Volunteers. You can hardly imagine the disputation that fact caused. Here were these Illinois farm boys, especially those from upstate, all set on freeing the slaves at the risk of their lives, only to discover their new colonel once owned a slave himself."

Julia stared at the papers flipping under their stone paperweight. "Well, don't say too much about that in your memoirs," she instructed him sternly. "People still might not understand."

Grant nodded his head, ignoring the sharp pain it caused. He cleared his throat and swallowed. That act by itself produced more discomfort than anything else. The cancer is encircling my throat, closing it off, just like I surrounded Vicksburg, he realized. The metallic taste of blood followed his swallowing. Bleeding from the ulcerations came and went at its own pleasure. He looked over the tops of his spectacles at the fields. Spring is trying to come early this year, he thought. Summer will be hot. Will I live to see it?

A grim determination settled itself about him. Like the iron in his nature that supported him during four terrible years of bloody slaughter, it invested every inch of his body, ingrained into the very marrow of his bones. Come what may, he would finish his book.

Julia sensed this conflict within him. "But Galena was better, wasn't it Ulys? The house on High Street was better than Hardscrabble."

Grant chuckled. "No one else would pay $125 a year to climb all those steps to the front door. Nothing did more to get my legs in shape for all the riding I did during the war than climbing all those steps. There were two hundred as I recall."

Julia patted her midriff. "At times I wish I had those steps now. All that climbing kept my figure. Do you recall little Jesse waiting for you at the top of those stairs each night?"

Grant nodded. His thin lips twisted into a wry grin. "Of course I do, Julia. How could I ever forget? He met me every night after I was winded from climbing those two hundred stairs. 'Do you want to fight, mister?' he'd say."

Julia stood up, bent into a crouch, jutted her chin out and placed her hands on her hips to mimic her husband. " 'Even though I am a man of peace, I will not be hectored by a person your size,' " she said, imitating Grant's deep voice. "And then the two of you would wrestle on the floor until I called you to supper." She laughed at the memory, caught up in the days of their youth. "We had some happy times in Galena when you worked for your father. The work was better than cutting firewood."

Except for the rawhides, Grant thought. That part I hated, tanning those bloody, raw cowhides. I can still smell the stench, even now after all these years. And the red flesh. That's why he couldn't stand his meat unless it was cooked to a blackened cinder. Even bloody juices turned his stomach. The 21st Illinois snickered about his distaste for bloody meat when he first assumed command. They thought I wouldn't have the stomach for fighting if red meat made me sick, Grant paused to reflect. I never heard that comment again after Shiloh and Vicksburg.

Julia rose and kissed him softly on his cheek. "Then the war came and changed everything," she added wistfully. "Look where we've been and all the things we've done since then."

Grant looked at her without pretension. "I guess I've almost come full circle."

A deep shadow filled Julia's face. Poverty meant nothing to her. She had been there before, and hardships were familiar to her. Hadn't she followed her Ulysses on his campaigns in the East, living in tents and run-down cabins like the commonest camp followers? Always she had tried her best to provide him with a home, a small island of refuge, amidst the horror of his work. She would do it again without complaint.

But her husband deserved so much more than this. That distressed her the most. He did not warrant this hardship; not after all he had given to his country. He had spent his life in that service. Surely he merited better.

What cut her heart to the quick was the way he accepted his fate— like he did everything that life handed him—good or bad, without complaint, without self-pity, and with clear understanding. A lump grew in her throat. Try as hard as she might, she could not keep tears from filling her eyes.

"What is this?" he questioned gently. "My gallant soldier worried before the battle has begun? I allow none of that in my army." He raised his emaciated hand and wiped away her tears.

His eyes sparkled as he studied the droop of her right eyelid. A childhood illness left Julia with a permanent squint in that eye, which worsened with age. Julia, always sensitive to her deformity, immediately recognized what he was looking at. She drew back.

"Are you looking at my squint, Ulys? You shouldn't make light of my affliction."

"No, my dear, I was just recalling that day in the White House when I came home to find you with your bags packed. You had screwed up your courage to go and have surgery on your poor drooping lid."

Julia nodded sadly. "I always felt uncomfortable with my squint. It appears so prominently in photographs, and I hoped to have it fixed."

"You planned on slipping out without my knowledge."

Julia looked down at her skirt. Her hands smoothed the yards of brocade. "I wanted to improve myself. I thought that I would be less reluctant about having my photograph taken, and then that might help your presidency. The papers place great stock in family photographs of the President."

"I told you then I liked your squint just the way it was. I would miss it if it were gone. And I would miss it now."

"Yes," Julia agreed. "And you asked me to please unpack my bags and not have the operation. You could have ordered me, but you didn't. You asked me instead. You, the Commander-in-Chief, who gave orders to thousands of men, yet you simply asked me. How could I refuse?"

"My dear Julia," Grant said as he studied her, "a good soldier knows *never to give an order to his superior.*"

# SHERMAN'S VISIT

Grant set his pencil carefully down and rubbed his chin thoughtfully. His eyes darted across the piles of correspondence stacked about him like artillery revetments. Where was that report from Sherman? he wondered. His fingers stirred the sheaf of papers by his right elbow.

With his eyes closed he could still recall each and every twisted and rutted road that lay before his troops on each and every campaign. The lay of the land that he used so often to his advantage was forever etched in his mind. So, too, were his orders to his generals. Written so clearly that there was no room for misunderstanding, he rarely needed to refer to them while he wrote his memoirs.

I learned that lesson the hard way, Grant mused. Learned it once at the side of General Zachary Taylor, forgot it, and relearned it the hard way at Shiloh. Old Rough and Ready dressed plainly and spoke simply, and I patterned myself after him rather than Scott. At Shiloh, however, I issued too many verbal messages, and that allowed Buell and Lew Wallace to muddle my plans. After that I wrote my orders myself, clearly and plainly so that even a drummer boy could understand them. Just like General Taylor taught me.

Not that they still couldn't confound my plans, he admitted. As clearly as I could spell out my orders, some of my officers could stretch and bend my intentions to an extreme that would make a barroom lawyer blush. Meade especially could drag his feet and procrastinate like no one I ever saw. I suppose that's why his men called him an old snapping turtle. Besides looking like a turtle, he could move as slowly as one. General Nathaniel P. Banks was another. His men caught his measure quickly. Nothing Positive Banks, they tagged him. And Major General John Alexander McClernand, former congressman from Illinois.

What a thorn in my side McClernand was! Proud, vain, ambitious, he operated as if Lincoln himself had given him independent command. For so stubborn and haughty a fellow, he sure took offense quickly, Grant recalled, especially when reprimanded. At Donelson, McClernand recklessly launched an attack on a rebel artillery battery without orders, without asking my permission, and with no thought of the consequences. His attack was a failure, as anyone with an ounce of brains could predict. Too many good men died because of that attack—far too many. It weakened his forces and needlessly spent their ammunition.

His blunder almost cost the Union its victory at Fort Donelson. As expected, the Confederates counterattacked and almost cut their way free to the Nashville road. McClernand's division broke and ran, in full retreat because they ran out of bullets. McClernand did not take kindly to Grant reminding him that a general's task—besides ordering attacks—was to see that his men were constantly supplied with the wherewithal to fire their muskets. Grant could still see his face flushing with anger.

But the fool never stopped to consider that an abundance of ammunition lay at his very feet, among the dead and wounded. Had he detailed a party to collect the cartridges, he could have resupplied his men. Instead, he chose to skip and scamper over the means of his salvation as he led the retreat. After that I had to watch my back until after Vicksburg. I wasn't entirely proven until then. McClernand had Lincoln's ear, and whenever he could, he was inveigling to take the Army of the Tennessee away from me. Writing letters behind my back to Halleck and traveling to Washington, he made my life almost as hard as the swollen swamps around Vicksburg.

Lord save us from political generals. They've killed more good men than typhus.

Grant paused to squint at the icy rain spattering against the window-panes of his study. Through the lace curtains the rain looked like a hail of bullets. A cold and gray day had forced him from his favorite wicker chair on the front porch, where he loved to write, to his fallback position in the study. Cramped and cluttered with books and maps and folios of official documents from the War Department, the place reminded him of the rabbit warrens and foxholes that pockmarked the hills during the investment of Vicksburg. There, his men had been transformed from freely marching and maneuvering brigades into moles and sappers who spent more time belowground than above it.

A gust of wind rattled the casement and drew his attention back to his search. Where was Sherman's dispatch? While the marches and battles and the land remained clear to him, his memory of the reports and notes scribbled by his officers often grew fuzzy with time. Both Charles Webster and Mark Twain gently but firmly insisted that accuracy of the military transcripts was essential. Grant grunted as he recalled an apologetic Twain relaying his publisher's dictum.

"It's the damned lawyers, you see, General," Twain sputtered as the two mingled their cigar smoke that evening. "Those buzzards have probably got the original contract between God and Adam locked up in one of their file boxes, and they'll be the first to make a fuss if you publish what you think is the correct correspondence and don't have all the i's dotted or the t's crossed. Why, some offended general who fought the war from the bar in Willard's Hotel in Washington will reach into his hatbox and produce the very scrap of paper and claim his feelings were hurt forever.

"Personally," Twain blew a perfect smoke ring, then paused to watch it dissipate above his head, "I'd tell 'em to go to hell, but even the *thought* of litigation makes Webster break out in a bad case of the shivers. So we best be prepared for a counterattack, General." Secretly, Twain worried that litigation might tie up proceeds from the book, which he knew Julia Grant would so desperately need. The general knew that as well.

Grant broke into a spasmodic cough as he laughed at the thought of Twain's last visit. While the white-suited author's obvious infatuation of Grant embarrassed the general, Twain's biting humor never ceased to brighten their meetings. The cough grew to a rasping, rattling hack that racked his entire frame.

The general's oldest son, Fred, ever attentive to the needs of his ailing father, dropped the box of papers he was carrying into the room and reached for a carafe of water on the cluttered table. He poured a glass and brought it over. Grant gave his son an appreciative nod and accepted the drink. He sipped tentatively.

Swallowing grew more painful and more difficult with each passing week, so much so that Grant ate very little these days. Never a slave to his palate, the general now nibbled from his plate, leaving most of his food untouched. To hide his dropping weight, Grant let his beard, always closely cropped even during the height of the war, grow fuller. The grizzled whiskers masked his hollow cheeks and gaunt appearance.

Like molten lava, some of the water ran across the raw surface of his throat. He gasped. A stream of water slipped from Grant's lips to dribble down his loosely knotted tie. Peeved by this, Grant pawed at his jacket until he had turned the droplets into splotches.

"Dribbling all over myself like a newborn babe," he mumbled as he studied the stain on his coat. His eyes darted back to his son. "Best be more careful, or people will be saying I've fallen off the wagon."

Fred stood waiting with ill-concealed anguish. But when his father looked up at him, he flashed a brave smile.

Grant smiled back. How proud he was of the way Frederick Dent Grant had turned out. How all of his children had, for that matter. But Fred was special.

At six feet tall, Fred towered over his father, inheriting his stature from his grandfather, Jesse Grant. Born in 1850, the lad's early childhood saw poverty followed closely by the terrors of war. Whenever circumstances permitted, Fred followed his father throughout the war, as Julia used every opportunity to be by her husband's side. From battle to battle, one campaign after the next, Julia and her brood endured the hardships with the general. Always remembering the biting loneliness that came with their separation and how it drove Grant to the bottle, both Julia and the general strove to be together—no matter where.

While Grant made every effort to ensure the safety of his family in camp, often the tides of battle washed perilously close to their field tent or river steamer and exposed them to shot and shell. At age thirteen, young Fred suffered a leg wound at the battle of Shiloh. There, as in the Wilderness, battle lines swirled and flowed so that no piece of ground went untouched.

Fred had borne his wound with stoic reserve while the surgeon probed the tract. Grant, of course, had been preoccupied with saving his command. Only later did he find his son among the wounded. Fortunately, no bone was struck, so Fred attended West Point later on two legs. Serving out West with the Fourth Infantry Division, Fred fought Indians, and even found time to write about his travels through the Yellowstone.

But Fred had resigned his commission to work for Grant and Ward, a move that left him vulnerable. All the Grants' eggs broke in that one basket. His fortunes tumbled with his father's. Now, as impoverished as his father, he lived with the man.

But never had a father a more dutiful son, nor an author a more devoted secretary. Hour after hour, Fred worked tirelessly, retrieving dispatches, correspondence, and maps, and answering letters, while his father fought his great battles again on paper.

On paper or in the field, to the general it made little difference. In writing about the war, Grant relived each fateful battle. Day by bloody day, mile by dreadful mile, Grant's pencil fought his way down the Mississippi and across Virginia with a determination that frightened his son.

At times Fred wondered which of the two was actually dragging his father to an early grave: the cancer in his throat or the strain of reliving the conflict. He decided it was both.

A polite cough interrupted their work.

Grant looked up to see Ida Honore Grant, Fred's charming wife, standing at the entrance to the study. The sister of the famed Mrs. Potter Palmer, who ruled Chicago Society, Ida's own position in society shattered with the fall of Grant and Ward, but she bore this indignity bravely. Perhaps she had little choice but to follow the example of Julia, who never lost faith that her husband would batter his way to one more victory.

Ida held a calling card in her hand. Water dripped from the sodden card. Behind her stood a black man, equally as wet as the *carte de visite*. Rainwater ran from the man's face and soaked jacket in rivulets. As Ida was dry, Grant deduced that Harrison, ever on the job, had received the card and passed it on to the young Mrs. Grant.

Tyrell Harrison, the general's valet of many years, was the only one left from the once numerous household staff. Of all the servants, only Harrison remained. All were let go, as the Grants could no longer pay them. Harrison refused to be sacked.

Whenever Grant saw Tyrell Harrison, their conversation came vividly to mind as if it were yesterday.

"But Harrison," Grant had pleaded, "we are penniless. Mrs. Grant and I have had to let every last one of our servants go. The cooks, the livery boys, all Mrs. Grant's maids—everyone. We cannot afford a single servant. In fact, our entire worth is now less than two hundred dollars—most of which is in Mrs. Grant's cookie jar. It is doubtful whether we shall be able to feed ourselves, let alone you, Harrison."

"Haven't I been a good servant to you, General?" Harrison asked.

"The finest. No one could ask for a better valet—for all these years. I intend to provide you with the highest letters of reference. You will have no difficulty finding another employer, I am sure."

"No, sir." Harrison shook his head vehemently. "I ain't going. With all your servants gone, you need me more than ever."

"We cannot pay you," Grant emphasized.

Harrison straightened his shoulders. Talking back to Grant was terribly hard for him. For most of his tenure, he functioned as Grant's shadow, being seen and not heard, doing his best to smooth the way for this man he loved and admired as much as Mister Linkum, who freed the slaves. But Harrison knew in his heart the martyred Emancipator's work would never have succeeded without this little general who whipped the South. He could not desert him in his time of need.

"If you can't pay me my wages, I'll work for nothing."

Grant shifted in his chair. He shook his head. "That would be slavery, Harrison. We have just fought a terrible war to abolish that abhorrent institution."

"I know that, and I am a free man because of you and Mister Linkum," Harrison argued shrewdly, "God bless him. Just like Jesus, he died so that all men could be free."

"Many thousands of brave men gave their lives in that struggle," Grant added. "But you are correct. You are a free man, and you have freedom of choice."

"So, I can say what I want to do or don't want to do? Isn't that right, General?"

"Yes," Grant said slowly. He knew he was being outflanked.

"Well, then, I want to work for you—for nothing."

"That is not possible, Harrison. I would consider that slavery."

"Not if I want to work for nothing." Harrison insisted.

Grant rubbed his beard. He squinted up at his faithful friend, for Harrison was more a part of the family than an employee. Still, he was officially a hired servant, and as such could not be asked to bear their hardships as a family member could. Perhaps a compromise could be reached.

Harrison beat Grant to the punch. "I'll just keep on working for you, General, and you can pay me when you get the money," he concluded.

"I may not ever have that money, Harrison. You must know that. You are taking a gamble."

"I'm willing to bet on you, General. You ain't never lost a battle yet, and I think you're gonna beat this thing, too." Harrison beamed.

"All right." Grant offered his hand to seal the bargain. "But you must charge me interest on your unpaid wages."

"Okay," Harrison had said as the two men shook on their bargain.

Ida coughed again, politely, as Grant stared at them. He blinked, and his mind returned to the present.

"Ah, Ida and my faithful Harrison," Grant greeted them. "What have the two of you been up to?" He studied the smiles on both their faces. Obviously, they felt he would be pleased with their interruption.

"You have a visitor, Father," Ida blurted out. But before she could complete her revelation, a tall intruder appeared in the hallway behind them and pushed past the two.

From the quick, nervous energy directing the steps, and the impulsive way the man burst into the room, Grant had no need of an introduction.

"Sherman," he exclaimed, rising from his chair, "what a welcome surprise!"

William Tecumseh Sherman strode to his friend's side and pumped his outstretched hand. "By God, Grant, some scoundrel keeps spreading the rumor you are ailing, but you look fit to me," he lied. Sherman's eyes probed past the screen of Grant's beard while his hand sensed the thinness of the hand he shook, and his heart dropped. But the clasp was strong and direct—just like his commander of old.

Thank God, his spirit is undimmed, Sherman thought. But then, why shouldn't it continue to burn brightly even under this adversity? Grant was made of the strongest steel. He would not twist or bend under any circumstance. Sherman smiled broadly at his shorter friend, noting the familiar stoop of Grant's shoulders, while he swallowed the lump in his throat. Grant will resist to the end, he thought. Then he will simply break.

"It *is* good to see you, Sherman," Grant continued. Gazing up at the lean six-foot figure dripping rainwater on him, Grant's eyes sparkled and he smiled excitedly. "Don't tell me that you were just in the vicinity and you thought you'd drop by. I've had too much of that excuse lately. Mark Twain uses it a lot." He paused to watch the effect of his words. Sherman's hatred of politicians was so great that as Commander-in-Chief of the Army he had purposely moved the army's headquarters to St. Louis, as far from Washington as he possibly could. Grant continued, "I know for a fact that Mount MacGregor is nowhere near St. Louis."

"Hell, no, Grant," Sherman snapped. "But the capital is, so I have an honest excuse."

Grant snorted and his eyebrows arched. Washington? What mischief led his old friend to Washington? He studied Sherman.

The excitable energy and intensity that galvanized Sherman and made his speech so staccato and his movements rapid and jerky had not diminished. Though gray streaks now laced his red hair, he still looked like he had cropped his own hair with a dull scissors without benefit of either comb or mirror. Yet, that familiar feral glint still filled Sherman's eyes, and the additional seams etched into his lined face by time only accentuated his wild look.

But Sherman's presence pleased Grant. Watching his friend drip water on the carpet, Grant marveled at their friendship.

Like wind and water, the two men complemented and bolstered each other, as they had from their very first encounter. Although the seeds of their latent greatness passed unnoticed at West Point, the blood-soaked fields of the Civil War nurtured their talents at war to the fullest.

Brilliant, erratic, dynamic, but initially unsure and easily deflected from his purpose, Sherman found the stability that he needed in Grant. If Sherman was that rare plant that only blooms during times of disaster, Grant was his patient gardener, who nurtured him until he blossomed.

Both men hailed from Ohio, but never were two men more different.

Orphaned at an early age, Sherman needed a father figure, someone who believed in him, who took him at face value and appreciated his true worth. Only that certification enabled Sherman to believe in himself.

And Sherman set high standards for his father figure. As a soldier, he had to be cool under fire, pugnacious in combat, and flexible to fit the changing face of battle. As a man, he had to stand for the rightful order of things. Above all, he had to represent stability, especially in a war that tore the country and its core beliefs asunder.

The stolid, plodding Grant fit the bill. Constant, stubborn, and persistent as the Midwestern soil that shaped him, he became that father figure to Sherman, that block and tackle to Sherman, the loose cannon. Under Grant's direction, William Tecumseh Sherman, "Crazy Uncle Billy" to his men, became a deadly fighting force.

Sherman loved the Southern manner of living. But when they rebelled against what he considered their rightful government, he felt no qualms at destroying them. Secretly, Sherman knew many of his fellow general officers harbored doubts about the Union's cause, and that affected their resolve to win. Sherman had no such doubts, especially after fighting under Grant.

And Grant, too, gained immeasurably from his friendship with Sherman. Where Sherman learned from Grant the need to power his flights of inventiveness with persistence and determination, Grant learned from Sherman to flavor his drive with imagination. Together as left hand and right hand, they smote their enemy with deadly combinations of punches.

Both men knew what they meant to each other. Both felt it with their hearts rather than with their minds, so they would never reduce it to words.

Now, when his friend failed to illuminate on his reason for being in a city he despised, Grant prompted him. He pointed to the scattered chairs, most of them filled with maps and portfolios. "Washington, Sherman? It must have been something important to get you there. Care to take a pew and tell me about it?"

Sherman shed his wet coat, thrust it at the startled Harrison, and dropped into the first empty chair he spied. "Washington!" he spat. "I told you years ago it was a nest of vipers, Grant, and it still is. If anything, it's gotten worse, if such a thing is possible! We should have let Dick Ewell capture the damned place when he wanted to. He might have hanged half the politicians there and done us a huge favor."

"Including Lincoln and your brother?" Grant questioned good-naturedly.

Sherman pondered that dilemma. He grunted at his checkmate and sank back into his chair with a great sigh. "No, I guess you were right to send the Sixth Michigan to stop Baldy Dick." He snapped back onto the edge of his chair an instant later and jabbed his finger at Grant. "Not that hanging the rascals isn't a good idea. It's just that new ones would spring up faster than weeds to take the place of those dancing in the air. There's no end to these scoundrels."

Abruptly, Sherman stopped and looked hard at Harrison and Ida Grant, standing behind the general. Although he knew the two quite well, his eyes narrowed mistrustfully.

Years of discussing their battle plans only with each other caused Sherman to distrust any unnecessary presence. Extra minds and extra mouths only led to rumors, confusion, and bungled orders. Their greatest strategies were hatched between themselves alone. Old habits died hard, so whenever Sherman visited Grant, he lapsed into battle-planning mode. With a wave of his hand he dismissed the young Mrs. Grant and the scowling servant.

"Leave us," Sherman ordered. "At once!"

Ida blinked at this astonishing breach of etiquette. While Julia had always been regarded as the acknowledged mistress of Mount MacGregor, Ida played no small part in keeping the struggling family's heads above the turbulent seas that engulfed them. Therefore, she felt that she, too, ought to be accorded all due respect.

Her husband, Fred, moved to her side and gently held her arm. His years in the military made these blunt orders easy to obey. But Harrison stood his ground, looking to Grant for his instructions. When his commander nodded, Harrison stomped out, followed by Ida with a swish of her skirts, Fred by her side. The study door closed behind them.

Sherman waited until the door latch clicked. His careful eye noted the vast difference in the Grant household since their last meeting. So the rumors were true, he realized, and they didn't tell the half of it. Grant was far worse off than the papers reported.

Sherman's heart sank as he looked about him. Gone were the servants. Gone as well were the trappings of wealth that once graced the Grant home. But most distressing was the absence of all his old friend's mementos. The swords, the faded uniforms, the battle honors, all missing.

Sherman knew well that these shopworn pieces of a glorious history were as integral a part of his friend as his stooped carriage or the limp he had from all those times his horse fell and rolled on him. Those things mattered to Sherman, too. His home in St. Louis bulged with his own war trophies.

It is worse than I suspected, he thought. Grant is destitute. Only such a heavy financial burden could induce him to pawn these important symbols. Indeed, Sherman knew that Grant's honor would require him to settle his debts—at all costs.

Gravely, Sherman turned his head back to his friend and fixed him with narrowed eyes. "You should never have gone to Washington, Grant," he pronounced slowly. "I warned you not to, didn't I?"

"Yes, you did. But you also warned me not to attack Vicksburg from the east. At least I was right about my campaign to take that city." Grant leaned forward and put his hands on his knees. "In fact, Cump, as I recall, you were doubtful about every one of my campaigns at first. It wasn't until you captured Atlanta that you really took the bit in your teeth and showed the world what I knew you had inside you. Then, you made us all proud."

"Cump." Sherman mouthed the word like a questionable vegetable. "The seniors at West Point hung that moniker on me from the very first day our names were posted on the freshman roster. 'Cump.' Never cared much for that name, one way or the other. Just got used to it, I suppose. Like Uncle Billy, as my men liked to call me."

"Or Uncle Sam as they called me," Grant replied.

Sherman chuckled. "That was an easy one. I volunteered 'Uncle Sam' for you when I first saw your initials posted with the freshman class."

"Yes, I know I have you to thank for that, Cump. A general has power over many things, but not over what his men call him. Look at me. I even had to take an entirely different name from my baptized one. Hiram Ulysses Grant. H.U.G. I just knew the seniors would call me Hug. In fact, I greatly feared that."

"You, fear anything?" Sherman scoffed. "My ass." He stopped abruptly and looked over his shoulder at the closed door.

Grant read his friend's mind. "Julia's off shopping. She insists on doing all the buying herself. Looks for the best buys, says it keeps the costs down."

Sherman relaxed somewhat. For him that only represented a slightly lower state of agitation. "Would she mind if we smoked?" he asked. "My wife, bless her soul, raises an almighty fuss if I light up inside. But I'd desperately love one of my *seegars* right now."

Grant answered by extracting a cigar from his inside coat pocket. With a quick movement, Sherman stuffed the thin, black cheroot that he favored into his mouth, struck a match, and lighted Grant's cigar before lighting his own.

Both men puffed in silence, savoring the moment. Dr. Shrady had hinted darkly that these days of smoking were numbered, Grant recalled. Like so many things, he would cross that bridge when he needed to.

"So, tell me. How did that happen? How did you manage to change your name?" Sherman prompted. "I never got the straight story on that one."

Grant leaned back in his chair and shifted his right hip to relieve the sciatica that plagued him. Unconsciously, he switched his cigar to his left hand so he could rub the burning path along the back of his leg.

"Well," Grant began slowly. Like some storyteller of old, his eyes remained fixed on the glowing tip of his cigar. "I got my appointment to the Point through Congressman Thomas Hamer of Ohio, who owed my father, Jesse, a favor." Grant paused. Father always planned on my going to the academy, he thought silently. Mostly, I still believe, because he wouldn't have to pay for my education then.

Sherman puffed away rapidly while remaining attentive.

"Hamer only remembered me as Ulysses, believing that to be my Christian name, and he knew my mother's maiden name was Simpson. So he filed my appointment under Ulysses Simpson Grant. When I got to the academy, the registrar said: 'I have no appointment for a Hiram Ulysses Grant. I do have an appointment for one Ulysses Simpson Grant. If you are not he, then there is a problem. Any changes will require corresponding with Washington, which will take two weeks at the best.'"

Grant paused for effect. He loved telling stories, although he knew he could never equal Lincoln's dry wit and clever timing.

"And?" Sherman prompted.

"Well, I thought about that two-week delay and all the fuss. It was more than I cared to have. So I straightened my shoulders and stepped forward and said: 'Here I am, sir. I am that man that you have the appointment for. I am Ulysses Simpson Grant.' And that was that. I've been Ulysses Simpson Grant ever since."

Sherman slapped his knee in glee. He let loose a hearty guffaw that filled the room. "Best goddamned mistake the army ever made," he chortled. "We're damned lucky they didn't insist on you calling yourself Pete Longstreet, aren't we, Grant? You would have done it, and you might have ended up as a Southern general. That might have cost us the Union!"

Both men laughed.

Then Sherman turned serious. He chewed on his lower lip for a moment before leaning forward until his face was inches from Grant. "I never voted for you for President. You know that?" he said in a rough whisper.

Grant stroked his beard. While he had heard rumors to that effect and believed them, this was the first time Sherman had mentioned the subject directly to him. "Not even for my first term, Sherman? I was untested then. I *might* have been a good President, you know," Grant said with his usual candor.

"Nope, not even the first time."

"Well, the second term, I could expect. Why I ever let them talk me into another four years is beyond me."

"Sam, you never had a chance, even from the very start."

Grant ran his hand through his hair. His abysmal tenure in the only public office he ever held, albeit the highest one in the land, weighed heavily on him at times. He spoke little about that sadness, and only in private to Julia. To her, he admitted that he was lucky to emerge with his personal honor intact. Now, the fall of Grant and Ward, besides bankrupting him, also posed another assault on his good name.

"Why the public reelected me is an even greater mystery. Cump."

"Because they love you, Grant. And they know you're an honest and decent man."

"One who couldn't see all the corruption around him."

"Hell, Grant, you're a soldier, probably one of the best ever. But you're no politician. Jesus Christ himself couldn't ride herd on those men. Those thieves would winkle Adam out of his fig leaf and sell it back to God for a profit. In the army we could shoot the bastards, but not in Washington. It's the only place on this earth where a bill of legislation is more powerful than a bullet! You're just too honest, Grant. You believe everyone else is like you, and it goddamned ain't so."

Grant chuckled at Sherman's blunt words. "Not even for my first term?" he asked sadly.

"Not once," Sherman answered defiantly. "And I was doing you a favor."

"I believe you were." Grant shifted in his chair.

"The bastards tried to snare me in after they'd done for you. You know that? Hell, I told them if they nominated me, I wouldn't run, and if they elected me, I wouldn't serve. That got them off my back in a hurry."

"Well, what were you doing in that nest of thieves?"

"I was there on your behalf."

Grant stiffened. Sherman's efforts on his behalf could only cause more embarrassment. Only months before, Sherman had started a subscription among the millionaires who counted themselves friends of General Grant. Thousands were raised to aid their friend. When Grant learned of their enterprise, he wrote asking the men to stop. To bail him out personally when so many others had lost their money by trusting his name was unacceptable. As added insurance, he had his letter published in the papers.

"I wish you wouldn't, Sherman," he cautioned. He paused when a hurt look filled his friend's eyes. To soften his admonishment, Grant joked, "Ah well, Sherman, I suppose I am safe from the workings of the Washington mob. After all, I don't have so much as a fig leaf for them to take from me."

"Damnit, Grant, you sank my efforts to raise to raise a subscription on your behalf. I would have got the thing done, too, if the damned newspapers hadn't got hold of it and printed the story. That, I believe, is where you first got wind of it, am I right?"

"Yes, and I immediately wrote to George Childs to refuse their generous offer."

"And you cunningly sent a copy of your refusal to the *Tribune*, so we could not outmaneuver your counterattack. Hell, Grant, those men— Childs, Cyrus Field, and A. J. Drexel—were all too happy to help. It's not as if they would miss their contributions."

"It would weigh too heavily on my conscience." Grant smiled.

Sherman bobbed his head. "Hell, I understand, Sam. But I do have something that even you couldn't object to. And you might even term it as my returning a favor," he said mysteriously.

"Such as?"

"You remember James Blaine as Speaker of the House proposed a special bill when you were elected in 1868 that would allow you to take a leave of absence from the army while you served out your term as President?"

Grant puffed thoughtfully on his cigar. Where was Sherman going on this? he wondered.

"That bill would have kept your rank of General-in-Chief of the Army intact. Which you refused to do, and you resigned your commission when you became President."

"Because it would have blocked the promotions of you and Sheridan, and all the other generals. I said then that it rightfully would keep me from sleeping, knowing that I was interfering with the advancement of those who had won their promotions just as I had."

"And you appointed me to fill your place as four-star general."

"And you wisely moved the army headquarters out of Washington to St. Louis—away from that nest of thieves." Grant chuckled.

"Well, now, I'm working to return that favor," Sherman said, grinning. "There is a bill circulating in Congress to reinstate you to your old rank of four-star general...."

"I will not displace a good man just to resolve a difficulty I got myself into," Grant protested. "I refused to replace John Logan as senator from Illinois when that was suggested, and I won't do that to a general of the army."

"Retired," Sherman completed his sentence.

"What?"

"*Retired,*" Sherman emphasized. "You will be restored to the rank of General-in-Chief, *retired,* Sam. No one on active duty will suffer for it. Then you can receive retired pay. Think about it, Sam. You would have stayed in the army anyway and retired at that rank if you hadn't been fool enough to let them talk you into being President. You're entitled to that retirement pay! God knows, you earned it!"

"Well ..." Grant paused. He was less than halfway through his memoirs, and his strength weakened with each passing day. If he failed to complete his writings, his retirement pension would help Julia.

Sherman's face flushed dangerously. "Don't tell me you're thinking about refusing that, too, Grant!"

"Has it passed yet?"

"No, that's why I went to Washington—to lobby for its passage. Some Democrat who just wants to be peevish is holding it up in his damned committee. I told him in private that if this bill failed because of him, I'd show up on his front step with a battery of six-pounders and blow his house into matchsticks. And he knew I meant it." In his exuberance for this cause, Sherman forgot where he was. Scarcely able to keep his seat, he waved his arms through the air as if directing his army corps, and scattered his cigar ash across the study carpet.

"So you can't be against this, Sam. Say you'll not refuse it if it passes," Sherman pleaded.

But he never received his answer. The door to the study swung open and Julia Grant stood in the entrance, backed by the still smoldering Tyrell Harrison. Sherman swiveled in his seat to meet this unexpected maneuver on his flank. His cigar hung in midair.

"General Sherman, what a pleasant surprise," Julia exclaimed as Harrison closed the sliding doors. Her eyes followed the last cloud of Sherman's cigar ash as it floated down onto her carpet. A Persian rug received as a gift from some sultan during their travels abroad, Julia loved its subtle colors and intricate patterns, and she insisted on keeping it, over her husband's objections. He might well place all his gifts in trust to Vanderbilt, she argued, but this rug had been a gift to her.

With no attempt to disguise her concern, Julia perused the trail of ash across her precious carpet. Satisfied that no holes were burnt in the rug, she marched forward and gave Sherman a perfunctory kiss on his scruffy cheek. Sherman awkwardly accepted the token, springing from his chair and shuffling his feet while in Julia's grasp.

Julia sniffed, and her eyes widened in mock surprise. "Why, General Sherman, what is that fragrance I detect? Are you wearing a cologne?"

Sherman's face turned bright scarlet. "It is not of my choosing, Julia," he sputtered defensively. "Some dandy riding in the same parlor car with me was spraying the stuff around like he wished to fumigate the world. I could not avoid being hit by the spray, I'm sorry to say."

Julia tweaked him. "I rather like it, General. I might write to your wife and recommend she buy you some on your return to St. Louis."

Sherman scowled. "Good God, Julia, I beg you not to!" Anxious to change the subject, Sherman glanced about the room for something to comment on. But the room, stripped of its trophies, depressed him.

Grant, however, noted his friend's discomfort. "Cologne is not for you, Cump. You are a man of basic and simple tastes, as I am. Perhaps it is our Ohio roots. Rumpled clothes and unkempt hair suit us better than pomade and fancy perfumes. And why not? We were soldiers, not dandies. Did I mention I had the opportunity to view that painting of you when it was unveiled? What was it called?"

*"The March to the Sea,"* Julia prompted, "by the famous Theodor Kauffman."

"An utter embarrassment to me," Sherman added. "I hope you told that Kauffman as much."

Grant gave a short laugh. "It was highly dramatic, moonlight, flames from the campfire and all. You looked mighty fine sitting by the fire in that clean white shirt."

"Oh, God," Sherman moaned. "What did you say to that, Grant?"

With a straight face his friend answered, "Well, I told Kauffman that it looked like you, all right, but that I never knew you to wear a boiled shirt."

The three of them laughed at that story until Sherman motioned to the stark room. "It pains me, Sam, to see your honors gone, but I understand your reasoning."

Grant leaned forward. "Did you know I recently received an offer from that showman, P.T. Barnum? He offered me one hundred thousand dollars for my things. Wanted to exhibit them in his traveling circus."

"Christ Almighty!" Sherman stamped his foot. "I hope you caned the bastard. Place your trophies on display with his freaks? Why, the cheek of that man."

Grant's mind followed the association with Barnum. He was preparing to write about his campaign against the Confederate stronghold of Vicksburg, and Barnum's name sparked a link to that time. "Sherman, wasn't Barnum's circus all the rage when we were slogging our way around Vicksburg? Didn't he have something going on?"

Sherman thought for a moment, then snapped his fingers. "Of course! The papers were full of it. Tom Thumb, his midget, was getting married, as I recall. The little fellow had found a girl his size and was smitten by her."

"That's right. Tom Thumb's marriage." Grant shook his head in amazement. "Here we were about to take Vicksburg and split the South right in half, a move that decided the fate of the Confederacy, and all the papers could talk about was the little Tom Thumb."

"Well," Sherman sniffed, "they couldn't print much about us, as I kept arresting their reporters."

"You were a bit hard on them."

"Nonsense, Sam. I should have shot them, snooping about the camp like hungry hogs. They cared not a whit about our conduct of the war. All they wanted was evidence that I was stark raving mad and that you were roaring drunk. I believe to this day that half of them were in the pay of General McClernand solely to spy on us. He used every conceivable trick to wrest your command away from you. Secret dispatches to Halleck, leaking lies about us, and even snitching to Lincoln and Stanton. He was as dangerous as an extra corps of rebels."

"McClernand was a thorn in our side," Grant admitted to his friend. "His actions caused us no end of grief." Soberly, he added, "And he cost the lives of many a good man."

Julia rose from her chair. She looked at the watch pinned to her blouse. "All this talk has caused me to forget my manners. It is time for dinner. You will stay, of course, General Sherman. I will not take a refusal. You are an old friend and have traveled all this way. You must dine with us. I have already instructed Ida to set a place for you."

As if on cue, the sliding doors leading from the study to the hall opened. Ida and Fred stood in the hall behind Harrison.

"Dinner is served," Harrison announced gravely. He had changed into a dark velvet jacket that formerly belonged to the butler. Harrison would do his best to maintain the decorum of his friend and employer. The task of announcing the noon meal once belonged to the butler or the chief cook, but these days Harrison was the entire household staff.

Grant rose and offered his arm to his wife. Sherman unfolded from his chair and followed his commander. Beyond them he saw the table, plainly set. The meal would be Spartan, just bread and soup.

# THE LAST CAMPAIGN

"The cannon did it!" Grant suddenly cried out. With a start he jerked upright in bed, awake and coughing in the darkened room. One minute before, he tossed fitfully under the deep embrace of the opiates administered by Dr. Shrady. Now, he fought for air and struggled to clear a throat that felt stuffed with sandpaper. His limbs shook convulsively while his hands tore at the muffler around his neck.

Instantly, light flooded his bedroom, and Julia and Fred were by his side. A gush of fresh air followed them inside, to replace the stale air of his tightly closed bedroom. Julia cradled Grant's trembling shoulders while his son poured a glass of water from the bedside carafe. But sipping only provoked another coughing spell. Helplessly, Fred held the glass while water and phlegm spewed from his father's lips.

By a supreme act of control, Grant leaned forward and grasped the foot of his bed with both hands. While his fingers clutched the footboard so firmly his nails dug into the wood, he willed his breathing to slow. Slowly, ever so slowly, his throat loosened and his shoulders relaxed.

One hand released its hold to wipe the tears from his eyes, and he turned to smile wanly at Julia. She smiled bravely back.

"Sorry to disturb you, my dear," he whispered painfully. "I must have been dreaming." His voice was so thin and weak that Fred strained to catch the words. Grant tried to laugh, but the effort simply doubled the pain in his throat.

Julia squeezed his shoulders in response, forcing herself to ignore the gaunt frame that once held solid muscle. Her husband was dissolving before her very own eyes, shrinking into a skeletal image of the stocky, robust man she loved. Mostly, he camouflaged his weight loss with his clothes, the blanket he kept over his legs, and his full beard. But in his nightshirt, his affliction was plain for her to see. Her heart sank whenever she saw how thin he was. Worst of all, he continued to lose weight.

Grant patted her hand. "I'm better now, thank you." His eyes turned to his son. "You'd best get some sleep, Fred. Thank you for coming."

Fred nodded and backed out of the room, but he left the door ajar.

Grant watched his son leave. Sleep, he told himself, we all need sleep. Yet, it is the most difficult time for me. I am exhausted, weary to the bone, but I cannot sleep except fitfully. Shrady has reassured me that I will not choke to death in my sleep; still I fear I might. A giant hand presses on my throat at all times, threatening to cut off my breath. And night is the worst.

Grant studied his wife. The darkened room hid the lines of concern about her eyes, masked the loose folds at her jaw and neck. The smell of her hair had not changed after all these years, he realized. Here in this darkened room, she was still the young girl who had captured his heart.

Dear God, he thought, I am nowhere near done. I need to sleep. I cannot write, I cannot complete my memoirs, as tired as I am. And I have so much left to finish.

"Julia, do you remember how easily I once could fall asleep?" he rasped. "At the height of the Battle of the Wilderness, I took a nap. Now, it is my most difficult task."

"Do you want me to fetch Dr. Shrady's medicine?" she asked.

"No." He shook his head slowly. "I do not wish to be drugged."

"Well, then I will stay by your side, Ulys, until you fall asleep. If you can't sleep, I won't either. We will share the sunrise." She smoothed his hair. "With all the times you were away, Mexico, Fort Vancouver, and the last war, we have missed too many sunrises. Far more than we ought to have missed."

Grant sighed. "Where did our life go, Julia? I seem to have frittered it away."

"No, Ulys," she gently rebuked him. "You have given your life in the service of your country, and I am more proud of you than any woman has a right to be." She cocked her head to listen to the rain against the window. She hated rain. "Still, some would say it was a hard life."

"Not a hard life, my dear. One just beset with difficulties."

They sat for a long while in the dark, savoring each other's company. Outside, the storm worsened. Wind rattled the shutters and drove the droplets of rain against the glass panes like volleys of shot.

Finally, Grant reached his decision. If I cannot sleep, I will write. "Julia, I am much better now. I think I can rest, so you must go back to bed. It would not do for you to lose your beauty sleep."

She protested, but he insisted, promising to ring the bell by his bedside table if he needed her. Reluctantly, she left.

Grant waited until she closed the door before switching on the electric light. Sliding from bed, he donned his bathrobe and moved to a writing table Fred had placed in the corner. Carefully ordered notes piled one side of his desk like counters for divisions on a military map. To his right, a card table with folding legs held a large map of Vicksburg. Thick crayon marks laced across the map, marking the Confederate and Union positions.

Grant cinched his robe and eased his tired frame into the chair. He pored over the map, shoulders hunched, as he had done so many thousands of times in the past. A spark of determination grew in his breast, and with it came the realization that this would be his last campaign—and his most important: his campaign to help Julia.

He would fight through to victory just as he had in that terrible war, mile by mile, battle by battle, day by day. He would endure and claw forward until the thing was finished. Nothing else mattered now save completing his task. Only then would his work be done. Then, he could rest.

Grant's jaw clenched in grim resolve. Focus on the task at hand, he ordered himself: one battle at a time, one step at a time. His fingers traced across the snakelike path of the Mississippi River and came to rest on the tight hairpin bend where Vicksburg, the rebel stronghold, rested.

Vicksburg, that was a tough nut to crack, he thought, a very tough nut. That was really the turning point—for the war and for me. Vicksburg was where Sherman and I stumbled across our change of tactics. Although neither of us realized it at the time, Vicksburg was where the two of us truly came of age.

Until then I was a general on trial like so many of Lincoln's generals. I was teetering on a seesaw, with Donelson and Henry to my credit and Shiloh against me. Halleck wanted me sacked, and Stanton tended to agree with him. But Lincoln remained undecided. I had won battles for him, something he desperately needed. Every day the Peace party in the North grew stronger as Lee in the East confounded one Union general after another.

Grant smiled grimly. Lee did me a favor, though. He kept Washington and Richmond frightened of their own defenses, fixed on the battles along the coast, and he kept their minds off of the West, *and off of me.*

Only old Winfield Scott and a handful of us realized the West was the key. Control the Mississippi and you split the Confederacy in half, separating East from West. Then you could drive east to the rising sun across Tennessee and Georgia, far below Bobby Lee's fortifications, to quarter the South. But Vicksburg stood in the way.

At once his mind began to work, to recall, and to relive that struggle. His hands traced across the lines on his map. Only paper now, he thought, but back then these lines were mud and water, thickets and swamp, miles of painful progress written in misery and blood. The tightness at his throat loosened as the map transported him back.

The rain spattered his window, and the shadows from his single incandescent lamp deepened with his thoughts. His fingers clutched the stubby pencil and began the incessant tapping that marked his mind at work.

# FIRE ON THE BAYOU

Ulysses Grant waited in the darkness. Hunched toward the inky expanse of the Mississippi River, the customary crouch of his body seemed to defy gravity, threatening to tumble him into the dark water that swirled inches from his feet.

Behind him other figures waited silently. Unlike Grant, his staff stood nervously in tight groups. Hardly daring to breathe, their tense postures added fuel to the charged night air. The soft scuff of a foot tripping over a root led to the tin rattle of a saber. The moon chose that moment to shed the incessant clouds that plagued the night, casting its light on the assembled party.

Grant looked back at his son, young Freddy, rising to his feet while untangling his legs from his father's dress sword, which hung from a wide yellow sash encircling his waist. Fred grinned with embarrassment. His mother shot him a stern look, hoping to convey to the child some of the tension that filled the air. But Fred cared little for the anxiety of the grown-ups and continued to prance about in the dark, clanking his oversized sword and weaving between the tight knot of officers. Stumbling again, he fell into the arms of a civilian.

Grant watched the man catch his cavorting son. Charles Anderson Dana, Grant noted, former editor of Horace Greeley's *New York Tribune*, had recently joined his staff. His broad, high forehead, receding, backswept dark hair, drooping nose, and full square beard which hid his tie, made Dana appear older than he was and gave him the look of a patent medicine salesman. But he was far more dangerous. As special commissioner of the War Department, he had been ordered there to investigate the paymasters of Grant's Army of the Tennessee.

But everyone knew Dana was an outright spy: for Secretary of War Stanton. The "Black Terrier," as Stanton was called in Washington, sniffed trouble along the winding Union advance down the Mississippi. He mistrusted Grant and wanted him closely watched.

Perhaps I should have taken the advice of Colonel Duff, my chief of artillery, and thrown Dana in the river the moment he arrived, Grant mused. But he's a likable fellow, and Freddy likes to play with him. After all, Dana's secret messages save me the tiresome chore of informing Stanton of my intentions. Dana's rather good at that. Besides, I have a surprise up my sleeve for both of them.

Grant knew that whether Stanton kept him in command or sacked him would depend on what happened that night, not on what Dana wrote. All Dana's fancy words, good or bad, would count for naught if Grant had miscalculated. He turned back to survey the dark expanse.

As if he had read Grant's thoughts, Dana smiled apologetically at the back of Grant's head. He was a spy, and Grant and his staff knew it. Still, Dana found himself beginning to like Grant. But being a general was a slippery slope—more uncertain than writing for Horace Greeley. All it took was one misstep to send him tumbling down.

Stanton keeps pressing about Grant's drinking, Dana reminded himself. Where was the secretary getting those reports—from General McClernand? Dana grunted out loud. A few heads turned in the dark to look at him, but Dana pursed his lips and continued his musing. McClernand was one incompetent general, for certain. He deserved to be canned if anyone did, not Grant. But for some reason, McClernand had Stanton's ear. Perhaps because they both were politicians, Dana speculated. However, that made McClernand doubly dangerous.

Dana shivered involuntarily. The thought of McClernand succeeding the little general in front of him frightened the former journalist. McClernand in charge would be disastrous.

Grant hadn't touched a drop, to his knowledge. Still, Dana thought, where there's smoke, there's fire. Why else would Grant's close friend, Colonel Rawlins, scour the camp and each new arrival for even the smallest whiskey bottle? It couldn't be from religious fervor that Rawlins smashed all that he found. He must be protecting his commander.

At Dana's right stood the bulky shadow of Sylvanus Cadwallader, official reporter in the field to the *Chicago Times*. Corpulent, loud, hard drinking, and opinionated, Cadwallader pranced about the camp like Falstaff to Grant's Prince Hal.

But, behind the *Times* reporter's facade hid a sharp and discerning mind. Dispatched officially to follow the war in the West, the reporter represented a paper with distinctively copperhead proclivities. On his train ride to the front lines, Cadwallader had heard many stories of Grant's drinking.

Despite that, Cadwallader also had fallen under the spell of the plain-speaking, hardworking Grant. But as much as he liked Grant, the reporter knew he would readily sacrifice his general for a juicy story. So far, Grant's desperate maneuvering to take Vicksburg provided plenty of interesting copy.

Sylvanus tugged at the cravat around his neck and squirmed inside his waistcoat as a trickle of sweat ran down his armpit. He'd been sweating like a pig before the sun sank. Now he felt chilled. The humid air turned cold along the river, and a thin fog rose from the swirling water.

This flooded canebrake is a devil of a place to make war, the reporter thought. Only a fool or a very brave man would lead his army into this morass. The bayous and swamps could swallow an entire corps. Swamp fever and typhoid already are thinning the ranks of fighting men. Grant better produce a miracle this time. Washington is getting restless. One more failure will cost Grant his head. The thick man shrugged unseen in the dark. Oh, well, I'll get a good story one way or another.

On several occasions Cadwallader had slaked the general's thirst from his own secret cache of whiskey. However, he had to be careful, he reminded himself, Colonel Rawlins suspected him.

Cadwallader glanced furtively at the object of his anxiety. John G. Rawlins stood beneath the shadow of a twisted white oak just behind the newspaperman and less than two strides from his commander. Dark eyes flicked out from Rawlins's thin, bearded face, as pale as the moon, glaring back at Cadwallader. Sylvanus realized Rawlins had placed himself where he could watch them both.

Faithful and ever present, Rawlins served as much as the general's alter ego as his chief of staff. Even though both men came from the sleepy river town of Galena, Illinois, no two men were less alike.

Where Grant was slow, thoughtful, and easy as a well-worn pair of shoes, Rawlins was quick-tempered, sharp of tongue, and tireless in his protection of his commander. Grant, out of shyness or modesty, never exposed his body in camp. Privacy was a rarity during a campaign. Still, Grant had his tent flap tightly tied whenever he took a bath. One time, Cadwallader was shocked to find Rawlins, naked as a jaybird save for his hat and boots, sitting atop a table and sawing away on his fiddle for the benefit of a group of dancing colored contrabands. A teacup and a bottle of whiskey rested beside the fiddling colonel. Paradoxically, though, it was Rawlins who destroyed whatever spirits he found in camp.

Just then, a cloud extinguished the moonlight, and the group stood again in total darkness, waiting. Julia stepped forward and slipped her thin hand inside her husband's. He squeezed her fingers gently but made no other sign of recognition.

Puffing intently on the stub of a cigar, Grant worked the lighted end into a fiery red glow, then fished inside his coat for his pocket watch. By the glowing tip of the cigar, he read the hands on the dial. Ten o'clock. Time to open the ball, he thought, borrowing a phrase used commonly by his infantry for the opening of an engagement.

As if by signal, dark shapes separated from the shadows of the steep-cut banks of the Mississippi, moving silently away from the protection of the bluff and into the mainstream.

Grant watched the gunboats drift into the current. They will have to get up steam shortly, he thought, or else the pull of the current will spin them downstream and run them aground on the waiting sandbars. He could imagine the pilots inside each vessel peering through their view ports at the expanse of ink ahead.

Grant could picture Flag Officer David Dixon Porter, aboard his flagship, the ironclad *Benton*, his face pressed so tightly against the cold metal of his port light that his wiry black beard threatened to fuse with the iron. Porter possessed a hardened resolve, but this river campaign tested skills than no one in the blue-water navy had.

Steaming up and down bayous and across flooded forests, Porter's fleet went where no rivers existed and where no ironclads were meant to sail. Incessant rain, while forcing Grant's foot soldiers to become river rats, afforded Porter the opportunity to steam over submerged canebrakes and cypress swamps. Time after time his ships rumbled like darkened wraiths among ancient trees that had not witnessed the passage of vessels in all their hundreds of years in existence.

While Grant's men battled the waters in an attempt to reach the same side of the Mississippi as Vicksburg, Porter's fleet battled the sunken land, grounding on sandbars, suffering in silence as great limbs toppled their smokestacks, and enduring incessant gunfire from rebel sharpshooters.

He ought to make steam soon, Grant thought. What was Porter waiting for?

A shower of sparks answered Grant's question. With a low rumble, the fleet came alive. Seven slope-backed ironclads, looking in the dark like turtles, belched forth fire and smoke from their stacks, while their screws churned the waters.

Under this fleeting illumination, Grant could just make out the shapes of one stern-wheeler and two side-wheelers, followed closely by an armor-plated ram. Each paddle wheel packed cotton bales along their port side, and iron plate for protection, while their starboard side held a tightly lashed supply barge. A string of twelve barges silently followed the riverboats.

Grant searched for the lone gunboat somewhere out there in the darkness. The *Tuscumbia* lagged behind the fleet, valiantly pulling the transport *Forest Queen*. He held his breath as he watched her approach the looming bluffs of the rebel stronghold. The *Queen* carried all of his army's ammunition in her poorly protected hold. If the *Queen* made it through that gauntlet of four miles of close-range artillery fire without exploding or catching fire, it would be a miracle.

Grant wondered if Porter was recalling what happened when Flag Officer David Farragut crossed these same deadly waters less than a year ago. Flush with successes at New Orleans and Baton Rouge, Farragut forced Natchez to capitulate before steaming up the Mississippi to Vicksburg. "Surrender," he demanded, only to be told that Mississippians didn't know how to surrender and refused to learn. Riddled by Vicksburg's cannon, Farragut retreated in haste.

Or is he like me? Grant wondered. Thinking only about what has to be done. Trying to cover all the details, wondering what he forgot, and waiting for those myriad turns in the battle that could shatter even the most carefully planned attacks.

Suddenly, pinpoints of fire winked along the high bluffs commanding the hairpin bend of the river. One after another, barrels of pitch and pine tar ignited to illuminate the river below. A frame building, perhaps deserted because it was outside the fortifications, burst into flames as the rebels fired its wooden frame for added light.

In a nightmarish scene, the entire bluff blazed into life. All hope of surprise vanished along with the cloak of darkness that the ships so desperately sought. The fires cast lurid shadows across the broken water, down the craggy slopes of the commanding heights, pinpointing every ship for the enemy gunners to see. Strung out in line like a disjoined snake, the ironclads, ram, and armored gunboats kept their prescribed distance of two hundred yards apart and hugged close to the enemy shore. By doing so they hoped to use whatever protection the steep bluffs could afford. Stray too close and they would run aground, but too far away, and stranded within clear sight of the rebel batteries, they would be destroyed.

For an instant only the sound of the ships' engines attended this unwanted display of light. Then a sharp crack split the night, echoing along the steep bluffs, and a waterspout rose a hundred feet short of the lead vessel.

As if animated by that signal, tongues of flame spurted from the clusters of cannons as each battery opened fire. The sharp report of the ten- and twenty-pound Parrott guns mingled with the deep thump of six- and twelve-pound howitzers until the night thundered like a violent storm.

Men ashore and on the plodding ships watched the flashes and waited for the concussion to strike their faces at the same time the sound assaulted their ears. The lucky men afloat felt only that. The luckless others felt the sting of flying splinters and the numbing shock that erased limbs or ended lives.

The flaming fuses of the shot crossed and arched down into the river gorge, leaving sparkling trails before the shot exploded like crimson stars or burst into fiery fragments. Here and there a shower of sparks erupted as a shot struck home. Soon, tongues of flame sprouted among the stricken vessels. As expected, the fleet returned fire, but most passed over the Confederate batteries or struck the soft dirt of the riverbanks.

Grant well knew that Porter could not elevate most of his cannon to effectively return fire. The city stood too high. Only the few siege mortars bolted to the decks of the gunboats could lob their shells high enough. It would be an insufficient response: a scattering of mortar bombs against hundreds of aimed, round-shot and red-hot cannonballs. Porter's only hope was to grit his teeth and press on.

His task is not to fight, Grant thought. I hope he remembers that. Too often the blood becomes hot in the midst of battle, and a man's passions overcome his reason, causing him to turn and fight back when he should obey his orders. Porter's task is to run the blockade. He must get his fleet safely below Vicksburg, or my plan will fail.

Fail? Grant knew that thought was in the back of his generals' minds, all of them. No one believes we can do this, he thought. McClernand would love to pick up the pieces. I'd gladly give my command to him if I thought he could do a better job, but I *know* he can't. No one else can do this job as well as I can.

The general grunted in disgust, causing Julia to glance at him with concern and Rawlins to take one step toward his chief. Grant saw their anxiety and waved his glowing cigar in dismissal. He smiled wanly, as if to say, "I'm all right, just thinking out loud." Rawlins nodded silently and moved back to his post by the tree.

Grant studied the remnants of his cigar. Little more than a smoldering inch and a half were left. His fingers plucked another cigar from his coat. He lighted this with the stub of his last smoke, and resumed his puffing away like a steam engine.

Not even Sherman can do this, Grant thought, returning to his brooding. Last night Cump had clamored aboard his headquarters ship and burst into his quarters waving his dog-eared copy of Baron Jomini's *The Political and Military Life of Napoleon.* It was thoughtless of him to quote that book. My nemesis, General Henry Halleck, translated it from the French, a language that is still a mystery to me, but for all Halleck's translating skills, how to fight this war is a mystery to him, too. Grant smiled in the dark at that thought.

Secure the road to Memphis before sending the gunboats below Vicksburg, Sherman argued. Try another route through Yazoo Pass again or Lake Providence or Haines' Bluff, but not this crazy thing. What you are attempting is against all of Napoleon's principles, he had cried, almost frothing at the mouth and slapping the book on my desk. "An army travels on its stomach," he said, quoting Napoleon. One cannot move without securing their supply lines. Any fool knows that.

But do they? This is a far different war from the ones Bonaparte fought, and it demands a different approach. Grant sniffed and dug the toe of his boot into the soft mud. His right hand thrust deep into his pants pocket and he rattled a box of matches. Julia squeezed his other hand even more firmly as the thunderous barrage doubled in intensity.

The first traces of burnt powder wafted over the party. Blowing upriver, the clouds of white and gray smoke from the battle now reached them. Shells bursting within the clouds illuminated them momentarily like enormous incandescent lamps. The biting, bitter stench of cordite mixed strangely with the soft fragrance of the magnolias, Osage oranges, and myrtle blooming along the river.

We must take Vicksburg to win this war, Grant thought, reminding himself of the obvious. Sited atop a three-mile hairpin bend in the Mississippi where its batteries commanded the river, Vicksburg dominated the eastern bank of the Mississippi, whose sheer-walled bluffs rose like ramparts for over two hundred miles. Never was a natural barrier so formidable, or so unfortunately placed to block the Union's attack from the west.

Over a year of maneuvering and four frustrating failures under my orders to get to this night, Grant thought. A cat may have nine lives, but I think I only have five, and I've used up four already. Battling south by land, cutting canals, and steaming up and down the twisted creeks and bayous of the Mississippi have all failed. This is my final chance. So we make this last, desperate attempt. The last one Halleck and Stanton will allow me to have. Porter will run past Vicksburg while I march my army south along Roundaway Bayou across the river from Vicksburg. If all goes well, we will meet at New Carthage, below Vicksburg, and Porter will ferry my troops across.

I'll be on the same side of the river then, on solid ground with my army, and behind the rebel defenses up north.

A violent explosion rocked the night and echoed along the bluffs, drawing Grant's attention back to his gamble. Sparks and rocket trails scattered from a stricken vessel, and the people standing beside Grant murmured in concern. Rawlins jammed a telescope to his eye and studied the blazing ship. To his relief, he saw tiny figures rushing aft to cut loose burning cotton bales. "It's not the ammunition ship!" he cried out. "It's the *Henry Clay*. She's burning and adrift in midstream." Those around him relaxed visibly. Loss of the *Clay* was serious but would not be fatal, as the loss of all the expedition's gunpowder would be.

Rawlins stepped close to Grant and shouted over the din, "General, what is to prevent Pemberton from suspecting the purpose of Porter running past his guns?"

Grant shifted his cigar to one corner of his mouth and replied. "I'm hoping he'll think we're giving up after four tries, and Porter is running downstream to Natchez to refit." Grant paused to let his words sink in. Craftily, he watched the ill-concealed doubt in Rawlins's face. John Rawlins was Grant's dear and trusted friend, but he was no fool. Grant let his other shoe drop. "And this morning, I secretly met on my boat with Colonel Grierson."

"Ben Grierson." Rawlins nodded. He could picture Grierson from their days back in Illinois, where the man taught music and sold farm produce. With fiery eyes glaring above a woolly beard, Grierson's short temper matched his own. Rawlins liked Grierson and thought his long, aquiline nose gave him a horsey look well-suited for a cavalry leader. But what had Grierson to do with their crossing? he wondered.

"Grierson is to lead a thousand of his Illinois cavalry out of La Grange today. They are to ride directly south, straight through to Baton Rouge, raising all the hell they can—burning warehouses, wrecking train tracks, and disrupting commerce."

"Baton Rouge!" The logic of Grierson's raid dawned on Rawlins. He snapped his telescope shut and slapped his thigh. "Pemberton can't ignore Union cavalry rampaging to the east of him. Even if he would like to, the citizens of Mississippi will be clamoring for protection. He'll have to send his forces out in search of Grierson. And he won't expect Ben to go through to Baton Rouge. That would be like heading deeper into the bear's den. Pemberton will deploy north and east of Vicksburg in wait for Ben to return to La Grange. But Grierson won't be returning. And—"

"And that will give us time to ferry our troops ashore."

Another flurry of cannonade lit up the sky and set their ears to ringing.

"Looks like half of Porter's fleet is past the Vicksburg batteries," Grant mentioned. "Now he has to pass the guns at Warrenton."

One by one, Grant watched the string of vessels crawl down the river. With the light of the burning *Clay* amid the flares and rockets, he could identify many of the ships: the transport, *Tigress*, the gunboat, *Tuscumbia*, towing the *Forest Queen*, all valiantly followed Porter's lead into the gauntlet of raining iron.

The bombardment continued for over an hour and a half. All that time, Grant stood watching, with Julia holding his hand. Couriers came and went with dispatches for his staff, but none brought important news or a single message for Grant.

As the last gun sputtered to a halt, Grant still waited. Rawlins and his staff waited in the dark as well. Fred fell asleep in Dana's arms, while Cadwallader retired to a sawn stump where he could watch both Grant and Dana.

Where is the message from Sherman? Grant wondered. After all of Sherman's protesting yesterday, he practically begged me for a council of war, hoping I might change my mind and retreat to something that Napoleon might approve. But when I told him my mind was set, he offered to wait at New Carthage and report back to me upon Porter's arrival.

All night, Sherman's men had dragged four shallow boats through the bayou and over the swamps to be ready to meet Porter. Grant believed that Sherman secretly feared he would have to use his tiny fleet to salvage the disabled and burning wrecks of Porter's once proud flotilla.

Around three in the morning, wind cleared the last traces of smoke, and the disrupted fog thickened over the river. The fires on the high bluffs now burned low or sputtered into embers. Anyone with a good imagination could sense the glow in the east, behind the stark and deadly bluffs, that foretold the coming of a new day.

I wonder what will this day bring? Grant wondered. Success or failure? The relief of all these months of fruitless toil, or disaster and the loss of my command? Whatever happens, I must appear unruffled. Each successful general has an image, not often one he picks for himself, but his soldiers' impression of him. A good image is worth ten regiments, a bad one the loss of an equal number of men in a fight. It is that tenuous bond that enables men to march into the face of death on another man's orders.

My men expect me to be unflappable. A soldier of the Fifth Wisconsin established that image when he saw me writing out a dispatch. A shell had exploded nearby, and Grant looked up only momentarily before returning to his work. The man exclaimed to his comrade as they passed him: "That Ulysses don't scare worth a damn!" So that was that, Grant recalled.

My image was fixed. I must bear good or bad news with no sign of fear or excitement.

Someone coughed, and Grant turned around. A thin orderly, covered in mud and missing his forage cap, waited at attention despite the obvious fatigue that creased his young face. "Message from General Sherman," the man said as he saluted.

Grant returned the salute. This is it, he realized. He forced his hand to reach slowly for the crumpled slip of paper, then stopped. "When did you last eat, son?" he asked the courier.

The lad started and blinked in confusion. Generals didn't show concern for a lowly private. Instead, they barked at them, or so his sergeant warned him. He stuttered, "Not since yesterday, Gen'l. That's as best as I can remember. Just a bit of hardtack then. I've been too busy swamping for Gen'l Sherman. Lord, but we near drowned hauling his skiffs over them swamps. You'd think enough water to drown a man would float a boat, but it ain't so, General. I know for a fact it ain't so."

Grant nodded. This soldier could not be much older than Fred, who slept nearby. Dark rings of fatigue beneath the boy's eyes showed plainly even in the gloom. But pride and excitement shone in his eyes as well. "Get this lad a hot meal and a place to sleep," he ordered. He winked at the boy as he took the message. "Good work, soldier. I'll mention your conduct to General Sherman when I see him."

"Won't do no good, General Grant," the lad replied with a streak of independence that marked the men from the West. "Uncle Billy wouldn't know me from the back end of his horse. I ain't of much importance."

Grant placed both hands on the messenger's shoulders. "You're wrong there, Private. You're the most important part of this army. In fact, *you are the army*. Don't ever forget that. Generals like Sherman and me are a dime a dozen, but good fighting men are hard to come by."

The youth straightened his back and his tired face broke into a wide smile. "Yessir, thank you, General. I won't forget what you said." With that he spun on his soggy boots and marched off with an aide.

Rawlins stepped to Grant's side and chuckled. "You sure put the spring back in that boy's step, General." His face turned serious when he looked down at the paper in Grant's hand. What that message contained would make or break his friend.

Rawlins felt sweat run down his shoulder blades, and he shivered in the damp air. He marveled how steadily Grant held the note. Clamped between thumb and forefinger, the exposed scrap of paper would quiver if Grant's hand shook in the slightest. Yet, the hand and the paper were rock steady.

Grant looked around at his staff. "Well, shall we see if Sherman's message puts the spring in our steps, gentlemen?" While the men murmured in reply, Grant opened the dispatch. A staff sergeant passed a lantern to Rawlins, who held it up to illuminate the letter.

Grant read aloud. " 'The squadron is fit and in fighting condition. Although all have received damage from cannon fire, each vessel is seaworthy and capable of performing its duty. Only the *Henry Clay* was sunk. Not a single soul has been lost.' "

A wild cheer broke out from his staff. Carried away by their enthusiasm, junior officers and generals alike rushed forward to pat their general on the back. Grant's skill and luck still held.

Grant turned to his wife, who now held Fred, awakened by the cheers but still half asleep. He smiled widely at her.

Then he turned to his grinning staff and said, "Let us prepare for another run down past Vicksburg with more supplies...."

# FIVE BATTLES

Ulysses Grant sat on a fallen log beside the churned road leading to the sleepy hamlet of Port Gibson. A slight breeze ruffled the map lying across his knees. As was his habit, Grant bent closely over the map like a man with a broken back, keeping his face inches from the printed surface. To one side Rawlins studied another map, this one captured from rebel scouts. His own map in hand, Grant rose from his seat and scuttled across to Rawlins. Remaining bent, he studied Rawlins's map intently for a good two minutes. Without a word he found what he wanted and stumbled back to his seat.

While his junior officer chafed at the bit, Grant reprised the events of the days since Porter's gunboats ran the Vicksburg blockade. The second run with more supplies fared only slightly worse than Porter's miraculous run. The transport, *Tiger,* broke in half and sank after being hit thirty times with solid shot. Half a dozen men were wounded, but otherwise Grant's charmed existence continued. With his army assembled at New Carthage, he prepared to assault the rebel fortifications at Grand Gulf. Capturing

Grand Gulf would gain him a precious toehold on the east bank. Then his luck ran out.

Why did I pick McClernand of all men to take Grand Gulf? Grant wondered for the hundredth time. Because I couldn't spare Sherman or McPherson for the task, he told himself. As much as I wanted to use Cump, I couldn't. I needed him to screen our move down to New Carthage. I planned on sending his 15th Corps back up the Yazoo so Pemberton would think I was going to attack Haines' Bluff. I needed Sherman's threat to keep Pemberton's forces spread out between Haines' Bluff, Grand Gulf, and Jackson, utilizing as few troops as possible at Grand Gulf.

McPherson's 17th Corps was halfway here from Milliken's Bend. They wouldn't reach the embarkation point before the rebels brought their cannon up. That left McClernand's 13th Corps for the job. It didn't hurt any that Lincoln and his crew in the War Department thought McClernand could walk on water, Grant begrudgingly admitted.

But I told McClernand the key was to capture that first bluff. I agreed with Porter that Grand Gulf was too tough a nut to crack, but the first bluff was weakly defended. When I reconnoitered the area from a tug, I could see the enemy fortifying it, but they had not yet moved their cannon into position. A frontal assault under bombardment of Porter's gunboats would carry the bluff. But you have to be quick about it, I told McClernand. The rebels won't wait.

Quick? Ha. I might have saved myself the trouble of advising him. I don't believe McClernand knows what that word means.

The damned fool arrived with his bride! He disobeyed a direct order of mine not even to bring his tent or his horses. Instead, he arrived with his new wife, her servants, and all their combined baggage. He must have thought he was still on his honeymoon.

Then he puttered about, reviewing one of his brigades, scattering his transports up and down the river, and fretting about a thunderstorm. By day's end not a single Union soldier nor one piece of artillery reached the enemy shore.

All surprise was lost. The next day Grant sat aboard a tug and watched Porter's gunboats fighting both the strong currents and the batteries of Grand Gulf, and he knew an assault would fail. The current kept spinning Porter's ironclads around so they could never concentrate their fire, while exposing their thinly armored sterns to the rebel shot.

It was a disaster, Grant thought. But two things saved my bacon. First, Rosecrans had just slugged it out with Braxton Bragg at Stone River. The papers are calling it another Shiloh with heavy casualties on both sides. That takes some of the attention away from my foul-up. Best of all, Stone River and the mischief that Grierson's cavalry raid is causing keeps Bragg from reinforcing Pemberton. Second, a Negro contraband worker in camp showed Grant a way to cross the river between De Shroon's Plantation and Bruinsburg.

Grant traced his finger over the map. The road from Bruinsburg was penciled in. Like the water moccasins his men had battled in the swamps, the road snaked its way over dry land directly to Port Gibson. A narrow gauge railway leading from Port Gibson was the only way the rebels could resupply Grand Gulf. Take Port Gibson, he thought, and the troops in Grand Gulf must evacuate or surrender.

Grant looked up from his map and followed the curve of the road. They had spent all night crossing without being opposed. Now that the army was across, Sherman's role as a diversion was over. Grant would send Sherman word to join him.

He rubbed his hands together and straightened his back. So, here we are, he thought. I've never felt more relieved in my entire life. I've got my feet planted in the same dry land as Vicksburg has, and I've got 35,000 fighting men with me.

His trained ear turned to the sporadic pop and crackle of musket fire up ahead. Since daybreak scattered shots announced contact between Union pickets and enemy scouts. Well, they know we're here, he thought, but they have no idea how many of us there are.

The abrupt sound of volley fire brought Grant to his feet. A second later the dull thump of field howitzers added to the disturbance. The crackle steadily grew in intensity, rolling over the land like a heavy wind. To Grant, it sounded like more than a skirmish.

A moment later he was mounted and riding hard to the sound of the fighting, guiding Kangaroo, his horse, around the wagons and marching men that choked the road. Rawlins and the rest of his staff struggled to keep pace with their leader.

The road ahead divided: the heaviest firing came from the right. Grant guided his horse in that direction and reached the smoke-filled lines. Soldiers in blue, huddled in tight clusters, fired into the heavily wooded hills that overlooked the road and crawled along the gullies and ravines that the rains had carved in the sides of the rising land. Matted canebrakes and snarled brambles further hampered the men's movement by obscuring the carefully placed rebel riflemen without providing solid cover.

Grant dismounted and found Brigadier General A. P. Hovey red-faced and coatless, pacing back and forth along his line, shouting and waving his sword. When Hovey saw Grant, he hurried to his side.

"General," he growled as he saluted, "we've run into a damnable mess here for sure. This land is all broken up and filled with rebels." He thrust his sword into the dirt and paused to wipe his perspiring face on his sleeve. "There's a lot of the devils, too. We're taking a lot of casualties, but they haven't pushed us back. Neither have we been able to dislodge them."

"Have you seen General McClernand?"

Hovey shook his head. "Not all day."

"Whose men are those on your flanks?" Grant asked, forcing his voice to remain level in spite of his rising anger at McClernand's apparently abandoning his men. Now, Grant noted powder burns on the right side of Hovey's cheek. Neither of them flinched as a volley of musket fire raked the trees behind them, showering the two men with leaves, bark, and branches clipped by the bullets.

Hovey turned, ignoring the leaves on his shoulder straps, to look at the broken lines of blue soldiers wreathed in smoke on both sides of his position. "A. J. Smith and Carr's men, I believe, General. The rebs jumped us just as we reached the fork, and the field has been much confused. I think Carr and Smith were behind me on the line of march, and they rushed their men up to cover my flanks."

"Have you any idea who you're facing?" Grant asked. He knew that

Hovey was an attorney from Indiana, short on temper, but a good officer to have in a tight spot. Though capable of improvising when the situation warranted, he sometimes acted without solid intelligence.

Hovey's head bobbed excitedly. "John Bowen. We captured a reb belonging to the Sixth Mississippi. He told us General Bowen rushed here from Grand Gulf with the Sixth, reinforced by a Missouri brigade."

Grant looked about. Through the smoke he could see the broken ground rising to both sides of the divided road. "Well, Bowen picked a fine spot to fight us. He's got our forces split in two at this fork. These hills and ravines are too high to enable us to concentrate a counterattack of useful strength. Bowen's interior lines are shorter than ours, too. We must pass across his front if we wish to flank him, and this ground looks too broken to allow a frontal assault." Grant pointed a gloved hand to the left, where similar smoke and gunfire marked an ongoing battle. "Is that General Osterhaus's regiment along the left fork?"

Hovey waved his own hand in a gesture of futility. "I just don't know, sir."

Grant nodded. He placed his hand on Hovey's shoulder to steady him. "You're doing well here, Hovey. Keep up the pressure on your end."

An appreciative gleam showed in Hovey's eyes. "Thank you, sir. It's not been easy."

Grant gave Hovey's shoulder a firm squeeze before withdrawing his hand to rub his chin. "I suspect Bowen's task here is to pin us down until reinforcements arrive from Vicksburg or Jackson," he thought out loud. "He must have fewer men than we do. Otherwise, he would have attacked us outright down the road where those fields we passed would allow him to deploy his troops. If we keep up the pressure on his center, he must weaken his flanks."

From the sound of the firing, the heaviest fighting continued to be on the right. Unfolding his ever-present map, Grant discovered this place was called Thompson's Hill, after a nearby plantation of the same name. From what he could see, the terrain permitted easier maneuvering near a farmhouse on the left.

Grant carefully refolded his map. Well, that's the way we'll go, he decided. Osterhaus held the key along the left fork in the road. Quickly, he reviewed what he knew of that general officer. Peter J. Osterhaus was a likable fellow, jovial and easygoing, but in battle he could become easily distracted, losing his ability to concentrate. Grant knew that Osterhaus would need someone else's presence to steady him. Waving Rawlins and his staff on, Grant set spurs to Kangaroo, and his horse pranced forward on his hind legs in the characteristic bound that earned him the name. Just after the horse and rider galloped away, an explosive shot tore apart the ground where they had just stood. The last rider in Grant's party slid from his saddle with a bloody hole in the back of his tunic.

Grant located a flustered Osterhaus on the road to the left and settled his staff nearby as he had planned. Osterhaus seemed more composed then, and threw himself into the desperate struggle with renewed determination.

By late afternoon the outcome was still much in doubt. Lines seesawed back and forth across the scorched soil along the road with neither side quitting the field. Wherever the tumbled land afforded cover from the deadly hum of the minié balls or respite from the hand-to-hand fighting, wounded men gathered. Gray and blue uniforms, made similar by the blood of their wearers, filled these scattered sanctuaries to overflowing.

Not an hour passed without couriers arriving from McClernand with requests for reinforcements. Grant refused each demand. Were McClernand to study his front, Grant brooded bitterly, he would realize his position would not allow for more men. There was simply no room for them. They would only stack up on the narrow road, obstructing movement along that lane, and be exposed to fire without the opportunity to add the weight of their numbers to the front line. No, Grant repeatedly informed McClernand, your half of this engagement is not the place to make a move.

Instead, Grant sensed the rebels' line on the left was weakening, so he rushed fresh troops from John Logan's division to support the exhausted men of Osterhaus's regiment. At first nothing happened that would justify Grant's faith in strengthening his left. Then the opportunity he needed presented itself.

A clamor arising from a tangle of brambles caught Grant's attention. The roar appeared to come from the very ground itself. He looked closer and saw movement within a hollow hidden by the underbrush. Directly ahead of him the men of the 49th Indiana boiled out of that ravine in a frantic charge for the shattered farmhouse directly ahead that anchored the enemy's left flank. Roaring at the top of their parched throats, the Indiana men followed Colonel Keigwin as he raced headlong to the house. The few startled defenders quickly fell or raised their rifles butts first in surrender.

Just behind the house, the ground crested at a fence high enough to afford good protection. All day the Sixth Missouri stubbornly anchored this crucial end of their line. Now, Keigwin's rush threatened that flank. Taking that rise would turn the tide, Grant realized.

Grant spotted this opening, and hoped the gallant colonel did as well. Urging his horse forward, Grant waved his hat and shouted. "Take that fence, boys! Keep going! Take that fence!"

The 49th Indiana never heard his words. Racing after their colonel, their dash carried them past the farm and on to the fence, where they tumbled behind the barrier. Breathless and spent, the men peered over the fence. Less than thirty yards away, men of the Sixth Missouri rallied around their waving battle flag, fixed bayonets, and regrouped.

Grant saw the red, white, and blue flag with its distinctive diagonal cross streaming in the wind and the glint of sunlight on the upturned spikes. His heart raced. The rebels were preparing a counterattack on the thin blue line of the 49th. He prodded Kangaroo forward over the fallen cane and trampled brush. A ravine running at right angles to the front line held throngs of blue-coated men foraging among the bodies of the wounded and dead for ammunition. Grant recognized the colors of the 120th Ohio.

The flash of sunlight on silver braided eagles on a pair of shoulder straps caught Grant's attention. He leaned from his saddle to yell down at the officer. "Colonel Spiegel! Advance forward and support the 49th Indiana with all haste!"

Colonel Marcus Spiegel, who was crawling about on his hands and knees looking for a cartridge pouch to reload his pistol, jumped to his feet and spun around, startled at this sudden command. Spiegel had just spied a dead major still clutching a pistol in his nerveless fingers. His mouth dropped open when he saw Grant standing over him. By God, Spiegel, thought, it's General Grant! He's actually here on the front line ... and he knows my name!

"Yessir, at once, sir!" Spiegel stammered. His eyes followed the direction of his commanding general's arm. "Advance and support the 49th Indiana," he repeated in a daze.

"Hurry, now, Colonel," Grant prompted. "We can carry the field this day if you can get your men up there in the next five minutes."

Without another word, Spiegel ordered a charge. Waving his unloaded revolver, he led his men out of their ravine toward the crucial fence.

Rawlins rode forward and seized the reins of his commander's horse just as Grant made to ride forward with the Ohio men.

"Best let those Ohio boys clear out them Johnny Rebs first, General, before you move up," Rawlins cautioned. "You get any closer to them, and they'll be inviting you to share their cornpone."

Grant stood in his saddle to watch. "Do you suppose those Missouri boys have any head knock or white lightning with them?" Grant asked mischievously.

Rawlins frowned. "Another reason I don't want you too close to them," he replied sternly. "Getting shot is bad enough; getting drunk would be just as bad. Stanton and McClernand are waiting for just such an opportunity to have you sacked."

Grant pulled his reins free. "Well," he shouted, "they can't relieve me for failing to make progress, Rawlins. We're across the river and—"

The piercing rebel yell filled the air and cut his words off. Grant winced. Spiegel will be a minute too short, he realized. He won't reach the fence in time to support the 49th.

Racing toward the high fence was a sea of gray, bristling with bayonets, howling and waving battle flags. The charge rolled toward the crouching Indiana soldiers like an enormous wave, threatening to overwhelm the weary men. Grant watched spellbound. Less than ten yards separated them now. In another second it would be over.

Without warning, the men of the 49th loosed a volley directly into the face of the charging Confederate line. Firing as one, their tenuous line erupted in a cloud of dense smoke. The hail of lead raked the attackers with deadly effect.

Stunned, the attackers fell or stumbled over their fallen comrades. The charge staggered, then ground to a halt. Another volley raked the milling survivors. Half the bright flags fell or sagged under the fire. A shocked silence filled the void while Union soldiers hurriedly reloaded.

Then a frightful moan arose from those men still standing and those not yet dead. Companies and squads broke apart and the attack disintegrated as men fled back across the field. A line of crumpled and writhing bodies marked the high water mark of the fateful charge of the Sixth Missouri like flotsam carried forward by the high tide. Yet, this debris was no waterlogged wood, but shattered and shortened lives.

Grant spurred his horse up the hill to the fence. All along the road, Union soldiers were moving forward as the Confederate flank recoiled. In minutes their entire line collapsed in upon itself like the walls of a punctured balloon. Firing became sporadic while Bowen yielded his position and retreated to the safety of Vicksburg.

Reaching the cheering infantry at the fence, Grant shouted out to Keigwin. "Well done, Colonel. Well done."

"Thank you, General Grant." The exhausted officer saluted before slumping down against a bullet-splintered fence post. He turned his head to gaze at the line of bodies piled in front of his command. He could say no more. With a sob he lowered his head into his hands.

Colonel Spiegel ran to Grant's side and saluted. "We got here as fast as we could, General, but we were not needed. There was nothing left for us to do but cheer."

"You might have been sorely needed, Colonel," Grant admitted. "It was a close thing. A very close thing, indeed."

Rawlins rose in his stirrups and stared past Grant down the road leading from Bruinsburg, where the army had crossed that night. "Well, I'll be goddamned," he swore. "It looks like the last of our reinforcements has finally arrived. It's a damned good thing the rebels didn't see what is coming to greet us. They'd think for sure we were down to our last reserves and scraping the bottom of the barrel." He laughed. "It would have strengthened their resolve to fight on instead of quitting the field."

Grant turned to look. He shook his head in amazement and soon joined Rawlins in laughter. Approaching them were two of the most unlikely additions to his army he had ever seen. Trotting toward them were a pair of enormous draft horses with swayed backs, bloated bellies, and muzzles snowy white from age. The worn and cracked saddles and tackle for these animals matched the horses' advanced state of dilapidation. Astride these nags rode Fred, his twelve-year-old son, and Charles Dana, Grant's own especially assigned government spy.

## RAYMOND, MISSISSIPPI. MAY 12, 1863

Eleven days had passed since the battle at Thompson's Hill. During that time events moved at a heady pace for Grant's army. Used to slogging over flooded swamps and dragging supplies and cannon across bayous, the men suddenly found themselves racing along solid roads with little opposition other than the occasional brush with mounted patrols. Pemberton's loss of his cavalry to Bragg now seriously hamstringed any reconnaissance in force he could mount and hampered his ability to hinder the Union advance.

Flying down the roads while filling their pockets and haversacks with fresh peaches, figs, and strawberries whenever they paused, Grant's men scarcely realized the momentous decision their commander had made for them. An army travels on its stomach, Sherman had quoted Napoleon to Grant. Nothing was more sacrosanct to military dogma than a secure supply line. Men could not fight without bullets or food. Napoleon understood that, and so did every field officer in this war, whether they wore blue or butternut.

But the little man with the ever-present cigar realized something far different: an army tied to its supply lines can never maneuver freely. This dilemma faced his army. Relying on Porter's Mississippi River flotilla for food and ammunition would force Grant to attack Vicksburg along that river. Confederate planners expected that and strengthened their fortifications in that area. The vast majority of Vicksburg's heavy guns faced the river, as Farragut, Porter, and Grant so painfully knew.

Attacking from the western side decreed a prolonged, bloody, pointless siege, probably resulting in a stalemate—something that Lincoln and his cabinet would never abide—especially with Lee invading Maryland. The peace movement in the North gained strength with each day the South endured and with each day the newspapers printed the rising toll of Northern dead. To succeed, Grant realized he had to produce rapid results. Besieging Vicksburg's strong side would not do that.

So Grant resolved to attack Vicksburg from the east, where its fortifications were weakest. But how could he do that and still supply his army? Here Napoleon's dictum vexed him. Hooking around from the east would spread his divisions all over the spiderweb of dirt roads east of the fortified city. Too many men would have to be detailed to protect his supply lines as he drove deep into the Mississippi countryside and swung around the Confederate defenses. That was the Gordian knot facing Grant. Unlike Alexander, Grant chose a third option.

He abandoned his supply lines and cut his forces free. From now on they would have to live off the land.

Sitting on a makeshift camp stool outside his pitched tent, Grant pulled the front of his shirt away from his chest and searched for an irritating itch near his collar. *A good thing Julia isn't here,* he thought. *I haven't washed or changed my clothes since we crossed the Mississippi. A small price to pay,* he reasoned. *Things are going well, almost too well—better than I had hoped. My idea to forage for food is working. The countryside has plenty, and my men have become expert at procuring their victuals. Pemberton has not yet united with Joe Johnston, and we've just won another battle today.*

He slipped his hand into his coat pocket and withdrew a ripe peach. Grant bit into the fruit and savored its fresh taste. He chuckled out loud. A present from Fred. His son was proving quite adept at finding the best the country had to offer. The men took to his boyish excitement and shared their spoils with him. The lad ate with them whenever he could, and the men had readily adopted him as their mascot. If anything, he reminded them of home, and that made their task less arduous.

I wonder if the soldiers would be so free with their booty if they knew a portion of it fell into my hands, Grant mused. Probably, he decided. Since the crossing and the fight at Thompson's plantation, Grant had noticed a change in his men. As he rode along the line of march, the soldiers now cheered him. They shared their jokes with him and swapped stories about horses and farming back in the Midwest.

Not like when I first took command, Grant recalled. The 124th Illinois Volunteers, what a pack of rascals they were when I first reviewed them! I never asked for that command. Governor Yates appointed me over my protests that I ought to earn the office before he gave it to me. I even had to borrow money for a uniform to review the regiment; my old army greatcoat was in rags and filthy from working at my father's tannery.

Grant paused in his reflections. He pitched the peach pit into the darkness, listening in satisfaction as the stone hit a tree trunk with a solid thump. Funny how soldiers sense the smallest weakness in their commanding officer, he thought. I was unsure when I received the 124th, and the men spotted it. Men hooted and jeered when I called them to attention. One even shouted out that I was no fit officer.

Maybe they were right. I wasn't then, but I knew how to whip them into shape. I drilled them and marched them day after day until they formed a proper outfit. They looked good then, although the rumors persisted behind my back. They knew about my drinking, my forced resignation before the war, and my queasy stomach.

Things have changed. Now, the soldiers call me a proper fighting general. The boys want me to take on Lee in the East after we take Vicksburg. All in due time. The important thing is that they know now we will take Vicksburg.

Grant stopped to stare beyond the light of his fire. The darkness, the unknown, surrounded him, waiting, watching. He scratched his beard. He knew that anything could happen, and that he would have to adjust his plans to meet those uncertainties. Adaptation was the key to this war. Most of the officers didn't realize how different this war was from all those in the past. But Grant did, and he knew how to use his newfound knowledge to his advantage.

Marshal Kutuzof had laid waste to the lands around Moscow in order to defeat Napoleon's army, but Grant sensed that the Confederate government would never order the people of Mississippi to do such a thing. So his army would be able to supply itself as they advanced.

Grant looked again at the shadows. Nothing to fear out there, he reassured himself. So, why am I feeling that restless urge, that darkness inside me that drives me to drink? He unfastened the top two buttons of his blouse and withdrew a small silver locket on a thin chain from around his neck. Inside the locket resided a strand of his wife's hair. Grant clenched the pendant in his hand.

I wish Julia were here, he thought. Dare I send for her while the army moves ahead at such speed? Every day without her heightens my craving for a drink of whiskey. And once I start, only the devil knows if I can stop. His fingers loosened their urgent grip. No, I must wait. It is too dangerous for her to be here, he decided. Maybe in another day or two.

Two shadows approached his fire. Deftly, Grant replaced the locket inside his shirt and fastened the buttons. As usual, his sentry leaned tiredly on his musket and allowed anyone to pass unchallenged. Charles Dana and Sylvanus Cadwallader strolled casually over to Grant.

"General, may we join you? It is a lovely evening tonight, is it not?" Cadwallader asked, bowing with an exaggerated flourish.

"It is not raining if that is what you mean, Mr. Cadwallader," Grant responded. "And you both are welcome to join me." He pointed with his lit cigar at sawn stumps arranged around the fire for his staff officers. Looking meaningfully at Charles Dana, he said, "I am not preoccupied at this time with any critical dispositions of the army that Secretary Stanton need know about."

Sylvanus Cadwallader guffawed loudly at this remark, while young Dana blushed so deeply that the dim light of the fire revealed his color. You may well flush, Mr. Dana, Grant thought, but that was another reason I ordered the bridges burnt behind us and all lines of communication severed.

So that you could not wire Stanton what I was about. I know he would order me to halt and consolidate my line of resupply. I would lose precious time, which I cannot spare. Pemberton is unsure as to my intentions, and I must take advantage of his uncertainty.

Grant crossed his legs, grasped his knee and leaned back. He puffed furiously on his cigar until a cloud of smoke surrounded his head. By the time I receive any orders to halt from Halleck or Stanton, I will have accomplished what I set out to do. It will be too late then.

Dana made the best of an awkward hand. He withdrew a rumpled paper from his pocket and held it close to the fire to read. "I did receive a message from Secretary Stanton on May fifth, the day we . . . ah, lost further communications. This is the first opportunity I have had to mention it to you, General. Your headquarters has moved so rapidly, I've just now caught up," he lied. He was saving Stanton's note for just the right moment, and this was the time. "May I read it to you?"

Grant waggled his cigar in assent, and Cadwallader moved to the edge of his stump. His reporter's nose for news twitched in anticipation.

Dana read. " 'Grant has full and absolute authority to enforce his own commands, and to remove any person who, by ignorance, inaction, or any cause, interferes with or delays his operations. He has the full confidence of the government, is expected to enforce his authority, and will be firmly and heartily supported; but he will be held responsible for any failure to exert his authority. You may communicate this to him.' " He folded the paper and looked up.

"I hope this means you'll sack that boob McClernand," Cadwallader crowed. "His bumbling cost us Grand Gulf for certain."

Dana concurred. "This communication was in response to the Secretary being informed of General McClernand's delaying at New Carthage until all chances of taking Grand Gulf were lost."

Grant listened impassively. Thank you, Dana, you did me the favor of writing Stanton, he thought. And you'd write the Black Terrier about me, too, if I slipped and fell, wouldn't you? I agree McClernand may be a fool and close to incompetent, but I'll never tell you two. Whatever he is, he is a general officer under my command, and he deserves more than having his name splashed across the newspapers and smeared in the back rooms of Washington. But there was a more important consideration, which he knew had not occurred to the two of them. McClernand's men were used to seeing him, accustomed to him leading them. Even more important, McClernand's men followed him into battle, and they might not risk their lives for someone they didn't know.

They were racing around behind Vicksburg, eating off the land, and trying to stay two steps ahead of Pemberton and Joe Johnston. Grant knew they had to be quick to keep the two Confederate generals from uniting and destroying his forces, and that the Union Army could not afford the slightest delay if it was to succeed.

No, my eager friends, Grant thought, I'll have to make do with General McClernand until I can find a better replacement. I have no one to replace him at this time.

Grant withdrew his cigar and studied the glowing end. "What did you think of today's victory over General Gregg, gentlemen? I think General Logan and General Crocker did rather well."

The other men realized the subject was changed.

Cadwallader shrugged. "What are you calling this battle?" he asked.

"Well, it took place across a place the map calls Fourteen Mile Creek, but the boys of the 20th Ohio and the 23rd Indiana are calling it the Battle of Raymond," Grant answered. "I believe the men who did the fighting ought to name their poison, so Raymond it is."

Dana looked down at his feet. "I missed it altogether."

Grant withdrew his cigar. "So did I, Mr. Dana. I was conferring with General Sherman when news of the victory reached us. Fortunately, General Logan's and General Crocker's boys saw no need for our services."

Cadwallader jumped to his feet. "I was there, General, and it was glorious!" His hands fluttered before his face and wove wild patterns like an ancient Greek storyteller. "At first it was not unlike the fight outside Thompson's plantation. The ground was identical: ravines, brush, and canebrakes. Bullets flew hot and heavy, while charge after charge struggled over contested hollows. Few had time to fix their bayonets, the action was so furious! In the center, the 50th Tennessee stubbornly held on. Their muskets did terrible execution on our cavalry. Then suddenly their whole line broke, and they ran. In a minute it was all over. Happily, I followed our soldiers into Raymond, where they paraded through the streets without a single gray coat to be found."

Grant pursed his lips and flicked an inch of ash from the tip of his cigar. "We captured a few officers of the 50th Tennessee. Colonel T. W. Beaumont's infantry. They told me Gregg ordered a retreat, fearing he'd be cut off from Jackson." He leaned forward, aimed his smoke at the two civilians, while his voice hardened. "I hope you gentlemen realize it doesn't take much to turn a gallant stand into a rout—just a crack in the line, or even the hint of a crack, and the dike gives way. An army is *only* strong when it is unified." He hoped they would take his meaning. He wanted no more plotting in his camp.

An awkward silence followed.

Grant resumed puffing away like a steam engine. "Well," he said at length, "General Gregg is mistaken if he thinks he will find respite in Jackson. He will soon find General Sherman hot on his heels. I have ordered Sherman to advance directly on Jackson and take the town before Gregg can regroup."

"Jackson?" Dana appeared confused. Jackson was even farther east of Vicksburg than Raymond. Why were they attacking Jackson?

"Jackson is the center of all rebel supplies to Vicksburg, and the convergence of four separate railroads. Destroying it will deny Vicksburg any reinforcements whatsoever by rail. Equally important, supplies will also be cut off. No ammunition, no food, no heavy artillery can reach Vicksburg if we destroy their railroad." Grant grinned like a Cheshire cat. "And we won't have to hold the town. Sherman will start tomorrow."

Dana's eyes widened. "But General Grant, you will be further dividing your force! That is against Jomini's *Principles.*"

Grant resumed unfazed. "I have intercepted a dispatch from General Johnston intended for General Pemberton. Johnston is marching toward Jackson to support Gregg. He suggests Pemberton advance eastward to join with them."

Cadwallader sucked in his breath and laced his fingers across his ample belly. They were deep in the heart of the Confederacy, cut off from their supplies and all lines of communication, and about to be caught in the jaws of a vice. What was Grant thinking?

"Will we not be surrounded, then?" Dana said, asking the obvious.

Grant shook his head. "Johnston has only a few thousand men, not more than six thousand, I believe. Jackson has less than ten thousand, even with Gregg's men, and Pemberton has about eighteen thousand. But they are widely separated. I believe General Pemberton feels his main obligation is to defend Vicksburg, and I feel he will act very slowly and cautiously in advancing too far from Vicksburg. So we may be within the jaws of a trap if the Confederates have the sense to spring it, but I firmly believe Pemberton's part of the trap will not close in time."

"Why do you say that?" Cadwallader asked.

Grant smiled. "A hunch, nothing more. But you must remember Pemberton's situation. He is a high-ranking officer in the rebel army, but he is a Northerner, raised in Philadelphia, and a classmate of McClellan. Although his sympathies are with the rebels, many of those of the South still regard him with suspicion. He holds the favor of Jeff Davis, but not many others. His actions are closely watched and often criticized." Grant paused for effect. He tilted his head back and blew a perfect smoke ring over the dying campfire. "Criticism tends to make some generals overly cautious."

Grant guided the end of a smoldering log deeper into the fire with the toe of his boot. *Not all of us crawl into our cages, thank goodness,* he thought. *We all make mistakes, but how we deal with them is another matter.*

Sylvanus Cadwallader coughed politely. He was remembering how Sherman handled journalistic criticism. It was Sherman's actions that led to Cadwallader being attached to this campaign. He had wanted to cover the war with General Lee at first, not this backwater affair along the Mississippi. The battles out East were where the action was. Instead, he was sent to obtain the release of his editor's brother-in-law.

Cadwallader still carried a faded copy of the message Grant had sent to Sherman concerning Warren P. Isham, brother-in-law of Wilbur Storey, editor of the *Chicago Times*. For all the times he had read and reread it, Cadwallader could quote the directive by heart. It stated:

> MAJOR GENERAL W. T. SHERMAN, COMMANDING UNITED
> STATES FORCES, MEMPHIS, TENNESSEE.
> AUGUST 8TH, 1862.
>
> GENERAL: Herewith I send you an article credited to the Memphis correspondent of the *Chicago Times*, which is both false in fact and mischievous in character. You will have the author arrested and sent to the Alton Penitentiary, under proper escort, for confinement until the close of the war, unless sooner discharged by competent authority.
>
> I am very respectfully
> Your Obedient Servant.
> U. S. Grant, Major General

Isham never knew when to use common sense. He delighted in pushing his journalistic rights to the point of treason, and sometimes beyond. In fairness, Grant had warned Isham several times, but this last offense went too far. Isham fabricated a story about a fleet of rebel ironclads at Pensacola, Florida, claiming to have received the information from the "grapevine" telegraph of the Southern Confederacy.

That story, which Isham later admitted was pure cock and bull, exceeded Grant's leniency. Cadwallader admitted to himself that Grant had chosen the right officer to make the arrest. Sherman hated reporters with a passion. Arresting Isham was a labor of love, which Sherman executed with relish.

Sensitive to the papers calling him crazy, Sherman had arrested all the reporters who followed his march out of Memphis. With one sweep, Sherman jailed representatives of the *Chicago Tribune*, the *Cincinnati Gazette*, and New York's *Tribune*, *Herald*, and *World*, not to mention one obnoxious brother-in-law from the *Chicago Times*. It finally took Lincoln to effect their release.

"Well, suppose you are wrong in your assumption?" Dana asked. "Suppose Pemberton does follow Johnston's orders?"

Grant winked. "In that case, I ordered General McPherson to march his troops to Clinton. Tomorrow he will secure the crossroad and the rail line there. Clinton is directly in line between Vicksburg and Jackson. Pemberton cannot link up with anyone without first going through Clinton."

"But that still leaves Joe Johnston," Cadwallader protested.

"Speed, gentlemen," Grant instructed them. "Speed is the essence to our success. Johnston will not reach Jackson for several days. By the fourteenth at the latest, Sherman will have captured the city. If I know Sherman's tendencies to be a merry deconstructionist, as he calls himself, he will have destroyed the rail lines beyond any repair and burned everything at all useful to the South's war efforts."

"Will not Johnston then attack Sherman?" Dana asked.

"No." Grant shook his head. "Faced with Sherman awaiting him in a useless city, Johnston will retreat from Jackson, while still trying to link up with Pemberton. The farther he moves west, the more he will expose his flanks to Sherman and McClernand's forces, while McPherson still keeps him apart from Pemberton."

Grant watched a new light shine in both men's eyes as they bobbed their heads in understanding. Perhaps it is only a reflection of the fire from that newly kindled log, he told himself. Or is it a newfound admiration for me? Dana's dispatches to Stanton must speak highly of me. Why else would Stanton react so warmly? Is my star rising in Washington? Who knows? Well, at least now both men will understand the importance for rapid movement. We must destroy the rebel forces in detail before they have a chance to unite and overwhelm us.

Feeling restless, Grant got to his feet and looked about him. The usual noises of camp greeted his ears, men laughing, tin plates clanking, and the rattle of muskets being stacked. Out in the darkness a mouth organ played a soulful tune, accompanied by an out-of-tune fiddle. Grant could not discern the tune, but the wafting strains made him all the more mournful.

He straightened his coat. "Gentlemen, if you will excuse me, I must make my dispositions for the morning and write my dispatches."

Dana and Cadwallader made to rise until Grant motioned for them to remain seated. Both men watched the general walk in the direction of his tent. Then, inexplicably, he stopped and veered off into the darkness in the direction of a lone source of melancholy music coming from the other side of the camp.

Not long after midnight, Sylvanus Cadwallader awakened with a start. He sat upright on his army cot and struggled to see through the darkness within his tent. Across from him his tentmate, Chief of Artillery, Colonel William Duff, also sat bolt upright. Faintly flickering light from the bivouac showed a figure standing between them.

General Grant looked down at them.

"General," Duff stammered, "may I help you, sir?"

"I believe you have a supply of corn liquor secreted hereabouts?" Grant asked slowly.

"Ah ... why, yes, General," Duff answered uncertainly. "Governor Oglesby did bring a barrel of whiskey with him on his recent visit—a small barrel, which he gave to Mr. Cadwallader and me. He remarked that Sylvanus and I were the only two in camp trustworthy enough to keep it."

The colonel's jest fell on deaf ears. Grant sat heavily on the edge of Duff's cot. His hand slipped beneath his coat, and the dim light flickered on a tin cup.

"May I trouble you for a drink?"

Without speaking, Duff removed a canteen filled with whiskey from beneath his pillow and handed it to Grant. The general filled the cup to the brim and drank it dry. He cleared his throat.

"Would you care to join me?" he asked the astonished men.

Cadwallader declined, but Duff found his own cup and held it as Grant filled it.

Duff raised his drink. "May this campaign of yours, General, have great success and confound the Confederacy no end," he toasted.

Grant said nothing, but emptied his cup just as quickly. At last he spoke. "I am quite worn-out by my duties, gentlemen, utterly exhausted. I have much work left to do tonight, and this stimulant is sorely needed."

He drank another full measure before rising and vanishing into the night as silently as he had come.

Duff and Cadwallader exchanged guilty looks. The reporter suddenly felt ashamed, as if he had participated in a crime of capital importance. Strange, he thought, I should feel elated. I now have my evidence that Grant was drinking, perhaps heavily by the looks of it. His editor at the *Times* would give his eyeteeth for this story, not to mention what he might receive from those papers that were decidedly anti-Grant.

But the veteran reporter could not bring himself to reveal this unprepossessing little man's weakness. A solid truth hit Cadwallader: Regardless of whether Grant was drinking or not, *he was winning victories*. Victories deep within the bowels of the Confederacy. And he was succeeding by using what he was given instead of whining for more of everything like so many of his fellow generals. Grant was succeeding with a rare finesse that Cadwallader could not help but admire. No, the newspaperman resolved, he would not pull him down. Grant's drinking might very well be his undoing, yet he would not cast the first stone.

As if reading his mind, Duff spoke softly. "I believe a discreet silence is called for concerning what took place tonight, don't you, Sylvanus? General Rawlins already suspects me, I'm afraid. Besides, it would do this army great harm to lose General Grant at this juncture."

Cadwallader grunted his agreement. He slipped back beneath his covers still feeling dirty.

## JACKSON, MISSISSIPPI. MAY 14, 1863

Union troops, spattered with mud and streaked with powder and red clay, stamped their feet in the muddy street and slapped their hands against their musket stocks. With a single voice they shouted, "Grant! Grant! Grant!" until the sides of the buildings shuddered to their wild cheers. Their cadence took on the sound of the marching feet of their general's army.

Ulysses S. Grant paused briefly on the steps of the Bowman House in Jackson to raise his floppy hat in recognition. He cast a bemused glance back at his son, Fred, skipping about excitedly in the mud to the wild cheers while Charles Dana clapped his hands in time to the chant. On the landing above stood Sherman and McPherson with their staffs.

Sherman's face glowed a beet red. His fiery complexion matched his hair, which was plastered to his head by rain. Grinning widely, Sherman paced about and slapped his gauntlets against his muddied thigh. Beside him stood James B. McPherson, quiet, resolute, and the opposite of the high-strung Sherman. Both men appeared dirty and tired.

My two fighting generals, Grant thought, always dependable in a battle, always ready to take whatever hill I order them to capture. With them I can take Vicksburg within the month. He climbed the remaining steps and returned their salutes.

Grant turned to look back at the captured city. Panic gripped the residents. Never in their darkest dreams had they expected their city to fall to Federal forces. Throngs of elegantly dressed citizens intermingled with bedraggled slaves, forming a jostling line that streamed past the rows of bluecoats and clogged the road leading east. Every single person, black, white, or soldier, carried whatever their hands could hold. Like the march of army ants, the collection of goods wended its way down the street. I'll wager half of what they carry is stolen, Grant mused. But my men will be blamed for all of it.

Sherman spoke first as he grasped Grant's hand and began pumping it. Crowing in a high-pitched staccato, he addressed his commanding officer. "Welcome to Jackson, Grant, the capitol of Jeff Davis's home state. I've taken extra care to incinerate the necessary properties of their war industries in this seat of sedition."

Releasing Grant's hand, he ticked off what his men were already putting to the torch. "The foundry, warehouses, arsenals, carriage shops, train depots, anything that might prove useful to their forces. We are also wrecking the rail lines. My engineers are burning the wooden cross ties for fuel to warp the iron rails. Ingeniously, they then wrap the red-hot rails around whatever trees or telegraph poles they might find. I've even heard some refer to these twisted rails as 'Sherman bow ties.'" He chuckled at that statement and added. "Sherman's bow ties, yes, I like it. I'm rather proud of that appellation."

Grant looked about at columns of smoke arising from all quarters of the city. To the east an explosion rattled the glass panes in the Bowman House.

"I think that was the arsenal building," Sherman explained blandly. "It was quite full of powder and shot. It was damned thoughtful of the rebels to provide us with the necessities. My men took all we could carry, but there was simply too much. So, I gave orders to torch the rest."

"I believe you have an arsonist's heart, Sherman," Grant commented. "However, as I entered the city, I passed a Catholic church in flames. I do not recall that that denomination has declared for the Confederacy."

Sherman's grin evaporated. He looked down at his mud-caked boots. "Ah, to be sure, that was an unauthorized act, committed, I'm told, by mischievous soldiers. Someone also fired the Confederate Hotel in their exuberance. We are looking for the men responsible for that work. I lay the blame partially on the hotel by reason of their seditious name, but I cannot use that excuse for the church. As you well know, Sam, my dear wife is Catholic, and I respect that institution."

Sherman twitched nervously, his loose-jointed limbs jiggling briefly; Grant could see why his hated reporters might use that mannerism to call Sherman unhinged. "I am relieved to hear that, Cump."

"You know the proprietor of the Confederate Hotel protested to me than he was as good a Unionist as ever drew a breath. But his sign betrayed him. 'United States' was faintly painted out and 'Confederate' painted over it. The cheek of that man!" Sherman's face screwed up in a conspiratorial look. He bent closer to Grant's ear and whispered, "I am informed that some men of Prentiss's division, captured after Shiloh, were brought to this very hotel as prisoners and were denied supper here and insulted by our good Unionist because they could only pay with greenbacks. Word has it that they may have torched the place."

Sherman paused, undecided, then continued his confession. "I might as well tell you the rest for you will hear it too soon from other lips. The cotton factory in town and the penitentiary are ablaze as well. But these acts I believe to be the work of released convicts."

Grant's eyebrows raised. "Are we releasing convicts now?"

"Not at all. Confederate authorities freed the felons, but for what mischief, I cannot fathom. I can only surmise they hoped their action might bedevil us." Sherman looked innocently at Grant. "Their scheme appears to have backfired on them."

"Quite so."

Sherman's enthusiasm rekindled. "I wish you had been there, Sam. It was glorious. In spite of the heavy rains, my men slogged through the roads like seasoned troopers. In some places they waded up to their waists in mud. The artillery had to be dragged forward by hand. The horses could do no useful service. Still, we kept pressing onward. When you last visited me, we were less than two miles from the enemy's entrenchments. Then my boys got the bit in their teeth and I could not hold them back. They forgot the rebels' battery fire, threw off their fatigue, and charged straight into the city."

Grant looked to General McPherson. "Your Wisconsin boys fought as well, I'm told, General."

McPherson smiled modestly. "That they did, sir. We all have much to be proud of today. And I have intercepted important news." He withdrew a leather pouch from his jacket and handed it to Grant.

Grant took the dispatch and turned it over in his hand. A dark stain covered half of the front flap. A pungent smell, all too familiar in war, reached his nose. Fresh blood, Grant realized. Is it from one of their gallant men or one of ours? I wonder what high price was paid for this information? With reverence, he opened the pouch and withdrew the single folded sheet of paper it contained. He read the dispatch several times before looking up.

"Do you believe this document to be authentic?" he questioned McPherson. "You do not think it was produced to mislead us?"

McPherson shook his head. "No, sir. I believe it to be authentic. This dispatch was carried by a young captain whose badges identified him as being on General Johnston's staff." McPherson added solemnly, "He gave his life to protect that message."

Grant nodded. "I see. Well, we must assume it is authentic, then. According to this document, Joe Johnston expects Pemberton to move on our rear and attack us while Johnston swings north of us to join him."

McPherson gestured to a major on his staff, and the officer stepped forward and handed General Grant a map. Grant draped the map over the railing and studied it intently. He paused to light a cigar before tracing his finger over the chart.

"Bolton Station on the Vicksburg and Jackson Railroad is the closest place where Johnston can reach the only passable road. All roads converge on that depot." Grant looked up, but his finger remained fixed on the map. "Evidently, the design of the enemy is to get north of us, cross the Big Black River at Smith's Ferry, and beat us into Vicksburg. We must not allow that to happen."

McPherson and Sherman crowded around the map. "Let me go after Johnston," Sherman pleaded.

"No. Your men have borne the brunt of today's fighting. Finish your work here. I trust to you, Sherman, to do a thorough job here in Jackson. General McPherson, you will turn your forces around and make for Bolton Station in all haste. You must prevent the joining of Johnston with Pemberton."

"Many of my companies are on the road in line of march from Clinton to here," McPherson added.

"Good. Wheel them about in place and march them to Bolton Station. Sherman will follow as soon as he has accomplished his task here. Gentlemen, we will keep the enemy's forces divided and run down Pemberton before he has time to retreat behind his fortifications at Vicksburg. We have drawn him out. Now we have him where we want him. Destroy his forces, and Vicksburg will have no defenders. They must then surrender and—"

A tug on his coattail interrupted the general's orders. He turned to see the disappointed face of his son with his ever-present shadow, Dana the spy, and Sylvanus Cadwallader. Both men appeared flushed and out of breath.

"Papa," Fred sulked as he released his father's jacket.

"Yes, Freddy, what have you been up to?"

Fred looked disgusted. "When we first entered this town, I saw a great Confederate flag flying above the capitol building."

Grant nodded like the doting father he was. "Yes, I saw it, too."

"Well, I meant to have it, and I raced Mr. Cadwallader here up the capitol steps, but a cavalryman beat me. He was already at the top of the steps with the flag draped over his arm."

"It was the only part of him that looked presentable, General," Cadwallader added. "The rest of him was ragged and coated with mud."

"Order him to give it to me," Fred demanded. "I believe I saw it first, and I might have got to it first, too, except I had to wait for my friends to catch up with me."

Grant replied to his son, "Fred, you should never use the good company of your friends for an excuse. You should be happy to have them, regardless of what it might cost you. Friendship is a rare commodity in these times."

Fred sighed and wiped his nose.

"As to the flag, it appears that soldier beat you to it fair and square. You would not ask me to order him to hand over to you something he fought so hard for, would you?"

"No, Papa. You are right. It would be wrong."

Sherman bent down close to Fred. "I am certain there are other battle flags to be found in this city," he said gleefully, "and my men are expert at finding all nature of things."

Fred's eyes sparkled. He looked from Dana to Cadwallader. "Yes! We'll help find them!" he cried, and raced off with the weary spy lagging behind. Cadwallader stayed.

Lieutenant Colonel Wilson, on Grant's staff, stepped forward with a scowling man in civilian dress at his side. Wilson saluted. "Sir. This man is the proprietor of the hotel. He demands payment in advance for tonight's lodgings."

Sherman glowered back at the manager, but the man held his ground. "The great General Joseph Johnston and his staff stayed here last night; and being Southern *gentlemen*, they were courteous enough to pay in advance."

"A good thing, too," Sherman sneered. "You might not have had your bill settled, as they left in a proper hurry."

Grant smiled knowingly. "Colonel Wilson, I imagine we can do as well as General Johnston. Pay the gentleman, if you please, as General Johnston would."

A gleam of understanding showed in Wilson's face. "Yes, sir. How much will our bill be?"

"Sixty dollars."

Wilson whipped out a hundred-dollar Confederate bill and handed it to the man. The innkeeper's jaw dropped and his eyes bulged. "But—But . . . I expected you to pay with greenbacks or U.S. coin!" he stammered. "If I had known you would pay in Confederate money, I would have asked for more."

"Very well," Wilson replied. "We are paying as did those Southern gentlemen you spoke so highly of. Charge what you will, you'll only get rebel currency."

"Well, ninety dollars, then," the man mumbled.

## CHAMPION'S HILL. MAY 16, 1863

The rapping of his adjutant, John Rawlins, on his tent pole brought Grant instantly awake. Fully dressed, he sat upright on his cot, swung his feet onto the ground, and rubbed his eyes. He cocked his head and listened. The heavy rains had ceased. Only the scattered cry of a night warbler and the muffled clink of a too-full coffeepot reached his ears. He heard no firing, so assumed there was no attack. That meant important news, he deduced.

"What time is it, Rawlins?"

"Just past five in the morning, sir." Rawlins turned aside and coughed into his handkerchief. Flecks of blood speckled the cloth that he pressed to his mouth. Turning partly aside so that his commander could not see, he carefully folded the bloodied square and replaced it inside his breast pocket.

Grant pretended not to notice and squinted past his friend at the first rays of dawn leaking between the oak and sweet gum trees. The scent of magnolias and lavender lay heavily in the still air. Poor Rawlins, Grant thought. He thinks I don't know that the consumption is killing him. He ought to be ordered back home to Illinois to rest. But I cannot spare him. I need him here. Besides, he would refuse to go.

Grant rubbed both his hands, palms down, on his knees. "Well, John, what have you got for me?"

"Two men, sir, railroad workers on the Vicksburg and Jackson line. We stopped their engine as it entered our lines. They're waiting outside. I thought you would want to know what they have to say about Pemberton's force."

Grant rubbed the sleep from his left eye, grinding his fist into his socket until he saw flashes of light behind the closed lid. "Do you believe them, John?"

"Yes, sir, I do. They're both old men with no kin in the rebel forces. They appear to believe strongly in the Union and are chagrined by the action of their home state. I suppose that is why they are mere track workers, as the rebel government does not trust them entirely. The engineer and fireman are die-hard secessionists. They would give us nothing other than a string of oaths, consigning our troops to the deepest hells."

Grant scratched his beard. "Show them in, John, and we'll listen to their story."

A bulky sergeant ushered the two informants into the tent. In the gloom, Grant judged both men to be well into their sixties, maybe even seventy. Both had straight white hair, cropped jaggedly about their ears, matching hoary beards and thin, lined faces. Each man cupped a steaming tin of coffee in his gnarled hands. Grant noticed the edge of a tin of beef protruding from the shorter man's pants pocket. Rawlins was getting quite adept at rewarding informers.

The aroma of fresh coffee made Grant's stomach groan, but he ignored it. He addressed the taller man. "Colonel Rawlins informs me that you saw some reb—ah, Confederate forces from your train."

The tall man stared in disbelief at the nondescript man in the rumpled, mud-spattered coat who was the commanding general.

"Tell General Grant what you two saw last night," Rawlins commanded.

"A whole lot of soldiers marching along the Jackson Road as our train passed them," the man replied hesitantly. "Nigh on near the bridge over Baker's Creek, it was there we encountered them."

"And how many soldiers did you see?" Rawlins prompted.

The shorter man stepped forward and addressed Grant. He touched his knuckle to his forehead in a kind of salute. "I was in the Mexican War, General, so I knows something about the military. Served under old General Taylor, I did. Got me a scar on my leg from one of them Mexican lancers."

Grant smiled. "I also served under General Taylor. He was a good teacher and a fine officer."

"That he was. None of that fancy braid nor feathers for him. I see that you took after his method of dress," the short man said, looking Grant up and down slowly. "Well, sir, I counted their guidons as we steamed by. Eighty regimental flags there was, and ten batteries of field artillery."

Twenty-five thousand men, Grant thought. "And they were heading toward Vicksburg?" he asked.

"Hell no, General! They was a-marching east, coming straight for you."

"East? Are you certain?" Grant worked hard to keep his voice level and disinterested.

"No doubt about it. They was marching down the road in the same direction we was traveling on the train. East. They're a-heading straight for you for sure, General."

Grant's face remained calm despite the excitement he felt. "Thank you, men," he said. "The sergeant will see that you get a warm breakfast." With growing excitement he watched the soldier march the two men in the direction of the cook fires.

Rawlins's face glowed. "East, did you hear them? By God, those troops must be Pemberton's. No one else west of us has that many regiments. He must not know Sherman has driven Johnston out of Jackson and we have turned to move against him. He is coming to meet us!"

"Bolton Station," Grant replied. He struck his fist into the palm of his other hand. "That is where Johnston ordered Pemberton to meet him."

Grant lit the lantern on his camp table and hunched over his map. Thinking out loud, he assessed his army's disposition. "We still have the enemy's forces divided. Sherman holds Jackson with his divisions and thus protects our rear. Johnston might outnumber him, yet I feel Cump is up to the task after he has undoubtedly destroyed every bridge and trestle he could lay his hands on. Johnston will not know that Sherman does not represent our full strength. He will be reluctant to attack in force. I think Sherman could spare Blair's division. We will attach it to McClernand's corps."

Rawlins followed Grant's finger to the junction of the rail line from Raymond with the Jackson and Vicksburg line.

Grant continued, "If I were Pemberton, where would I deploy my forces? Yesterday's rains have slowed his march." Grant bent closer to the map until his nose appeared to touch the paper. "Somewhere with good ground. Here!" His finger jabbed the map. "Here is where we will find Pemberton waiting for us. Drawn across the road between Bolton and Edwards Station where Baker's Creek protects the left of his line."

Rawlins focused on the fine printing Grant had penciled across the map. "Champion's Hill," he read. "I recall that place. I rode over it with McPherson. There is a nasty rise that commands the surrounding countryside. Damnable good ground to defend. Let us hope Pemberton does not have the good sense to recognize its value."

Grant straightened. His hand fished about in his pocket for a cigar. Ten thousand of the finest Cuban cigars had arrived by wagon two days after the fall of Fort Donelson. A gift from a grateful Northern businessman, starved for a victory, which I provided, Grant remembered. I gave up my pipe then, and took to smoking these cigars. Sherman thinks these Cubans are too good for me. He says I ought to smoke those wretched cheroots of his.

Grant found his cigar and lighted it from the chimney of the oil lamp. He puffed away thoughtfully. Ten thousand cigars at fifteen or sixteen a day, he calculated. I've barely made a dent in them despite the boxes I've given away to my officers. At this rate my supply will last me for years to come—far longer than this war, I hope.

He turned to Rawlins. "John, Pemberton may be many things, but he is not blind. To expect him to meet us in an open field is more luck than we could expect. He will entrench as much as he can and wait for us to attack him, all the while anticipating Johnston to strike us from behind. With the good ground of Champion's Hill, we shall be engaged in our business today."

By ten that morning Grant had ridden forward to witness his dire prediction come true. Galloping after a rider from McPherson, Grant raced along the road from Bolton Station. Soon he found McPherson astride his horse, arguing with the excitable General Hovey. Before them a line of smoke hung over a hill fronted by a steep-cut bank. Thickly wooded forest and tangled undergrowth choked a ravine leading away from the hill. Clusters of soldiers pressed into whatever hollows the lower ground afforded, rising only to fire at the top of the bank. Standing upright in his stirrups, Grant could see a continuous line of flames spurting from the tree line, marking the enemy's rifle pits.

"Gentlemen, what is your disposition?"

McPherson nudged his horse between Grant and Hovey to enable him to speak first. He saluted. "Blair's and Smith's divisions hold the road from Raymond to Edwards Station, south of here. Smith first encountered the enemy's pickets and drove them back. But he has stopped at the main line. Osterhaus and Carr are pressing slowly forward on the middle road under heavy fire." McPherson pointed to Hovey and then to the steep abutment. "General Hovey's division is here."

"We are under heavy fire, General," Hovey interjected. "I followed your instructions not to engage until we were entirely ready, but my men have been drawn into increasingly spirited action. I have great need of reinforcements."

McPherson sounded exasperated. "I cannot move my men to support General Hovey as long as his baggage train blocks the road," he pleaded to Grant.

Hovey blinked uncertainly. In the commotion he had forgotten that his supply wagons choked the Bolton road behind him. Now he felt foolish.

"Order the roads cleared so that McPherson's corps can move forward," Grant commanded Hovey, and the man passed that order on to his staff. A dark-bearded captain galloped away.

"Who is first in your line of march?" Grant asked McPherson.

"Logan," McPherson answered.

"Good. Good. Logan will give good execution wherever he is needed." Grant pointed to a clearing about four hundred yards north. "Move Logan to that field at right angles to General Hovey's line. They will threaten the enemy's flank there and be in a position to move where they will do the most good."

An exploding shot burst overhead and Grant's horse bolted sideways. An ordinary rider would have fallen, but Grant remained astride. Pressure from his knees redirected the frightened animal. "Have you any idea of the guns on that crest?" he asked.

"The First Indiana Cavalry make out one battery of four guns. Six-pound field pieces, I believe," Hovey shouted.

More missiles crashed overhead. Off to the left a horse shrieked in mortal agony. A steady stream of torn men, bloody and pale, crawled or limped back to the aid stations hastily being organized in a grove of oak trees. By an act of perversity, a round shot struck the turf, sailed high over the lines, and careened off one of the larger trees into a waiting ambulance. The wagon with its team of horses erupted in a cloud of splinters and crimson spray.

The din of battle steadily rose even as the men spoke, and soon they had to shout to be understood. Grant's adjutant, Rawlins, rode up with a dozen staff officers close behind. Rawlins stood in his stirrups to survey the battle. "Champion's Hill," he said sadly, although no one heard his words. Grant was right. Pemberton had picked the best of all possible sites to defend. He would do all in his power to hold this ground, expecting Joseph Johnston to come crashing into the Union rear. There would be much of the heavy toe-to-toe slugging fight today that his commander referred to as "the business." Silently, Rawlins said a prayer for the soon-to-be-lost souls.

Before anyone could utter another word, a roar rose from a thousand throats along the line directly to their front. Rising as a single man, a blue tide erupted from cover and charged headlong up the steep slope. Flashing bayonets followed waving blue regimental colors and the Stars and Stripes. Slipping, sliding, and tripping over roots and crumbling ground, the wave of screaming soldiers clawed toward the rim.

The men reached the crest and dove for cover just as the rebel battery fired. The battle-hardened soldiers could not have timed their dive more closely. An iron sleet of canister and grapeshot scythed through the air inches above their heads. In an instant the men jumped back to their feet and rushed the rifle pits. With a howling fury they fell among the cannon emplacements before the startled artillerists could swab out their smoking cannon.

Grant rose in his stirrups to watch in awe. "Who are those men?" he asked.

"General George McGinnis's 11th Indiana and 29th Wisconsin," Hovey shouted. "McGinnis is a high-strung Irishman, and his blood is up. Carry the hill, my gallant boys!" Hovey shouted. "Carry the hill!"

To the right, the 46th Indiana joined the charge, sweeping forward like a sickle to silence two artillery pieces just within the tree line atop the hill. The 24th Iowa followed on the left to slaughter horses and gunners of a battery of six guns. A hand-to-hand struggle ensued as desperate men battled for possession of the field pieces. In the melee a nine-pounder cascaded down the slope and came to rest on its side with its upright wheel spinning crazily.

"Now they must hold their ground," Hovey cried grimly. "Surely, the rebs will do their damnedest to push them back."

The rebel yell rose from the tree line behind the crest, followed closely by a sheet of flame as the enemy fired in volley. Gray-and-butternut-clad figures emerged from the cloud of their musket fire and charged the fragile Union line. The lines wavered, forced back in places, then stabilized.

A hatless officer, wearing the tattered coat of a general officer with its brass buttons clustered in the characteristic groups of threes, raced toward the watching officers. The left sleeve of the man's coat was torn and bloody, his scarlet sash plastered with mud. An empty scabbard flapped at his side.

"General Hovey!" McGinnis shouted, forgetting to salute. In the smoke and confusion, he completely overlooked Grant. "General Hovey, I must have reinforcements or I cannot hold the crest. We are hotly pressed on all sides. For God's sake release the 16th Ohio to me!"

Hovey blinked rapidly in alarm. The battle, while fierce, was still young. Should he hold his reserves for later? By then McGinnis would certainly lose what precious ground his men had gained. All the while, Hovey imagined the eyes of his commander on his back as if they were hot coals. He must appear cool and decisive like Grant, Hovey reminded himself. Inside he felt far from calm.

Mustering all his self-control, Hovey managed a nonchalant wave. "You may have them, General," he spoke to McGinnis. "Take the 16th and hold your ground."

McGinnis saluted as he dug his knees into his horse's sides and wheeled away. Hovey looked over his shoulder at Grant. To his chagrin, Grant was hunched in his saddle, smoking his cigar. His right leg thrown across his saddle and encircling his saddle horn served to support a large map over which Grant pored. Colonel Rawlins and General McPherson crowded around the map, gesturing and shouting in their commander's ear. Grant merely puffed away and stroked his beard as if he were scanning the morning papers.

Good Lord, Grant is oblivious, Hovey thought. I hope he saw how decisive I was. Hovey's heart sank as he realized his little show for his commander might have been missed.

Hour followed hour as the battle for the center seesawed back and forth. Silent piles of bloody rags dotted the hill, marking the dead. Ever-increasing lines of wounded struggled to the rear. To Hovey, each hour saw his division steadily reduced in men and ammunition. Stubbornly he threw the last of his reserves into the fray.

At noon Hovey's nerves could stand no more. He tore his eyes away from the meat grinder that chewed away at his once-proud division and wheeled his mount around. "General Grant, I must have support," he pleaded. "My reserves are used up, my ammunition is gone, my troops are exhausted."

The cloud of gun smoke that shrouded the trees where Hovey last saw Grant and his staff rolled past, clearing the site. Hovey nearly fell from his saddle at what he saw. Nothing! General Grant and his entire staff had vanished. At this critical juncture, Grant was nowhere to be seen.

Hovey bit his lip. His command was doomed. He turned back and spurred his horse closer to the firing line. He would fall with his men, he resolved. A glorious but futile death would be his reward for following this drunkard. He hoped his wife would receive his embalmed body. He had made those arrangements back at Holly Springs; but here in the heart of the Confederacy, Hovey feared his body would be dumped in a mass grave by the Southern victors. Damn Grant for abandoning us, he swore as he rode forward.

The disheartened General Hovey did not realize that his commander had not abandoned him. Half a mile away, in a newly planted field, Grant reined his bay to a halt near an old well, just behind the rear line. While the splintered and weatherworn walls of the well offered sparse protection, it was the only cover around from the constant fire. As many men as could manage huddled on the ground beside the well and pressed close to its flimsy sides. Musket fire from the tree line patterned the dust like giant raindrops striking the field.

Grant waved to Rawlins. When his adjutant drew near, the general pressed a dispatch into his gloved hand. "Hovey is in jeopardy of being overwhelmed. Take this to Crocker. He is to speed a brigade to Hovey's support. McPherson will also reinforce him with two brigades."

Rawlins's horse shied as a cannonball tore across the field a dozen yards away, bouncing along and casting great patches of turf into the air wherever it touched down. A low moan rose from the two rows of infantry drawn up across the clearing.

"Come back with us, General," Rawlins pleaded. "The fire is too heavy. It is not safe here."

Grant looked around at a hundred expectant faces watching his every move. If I run, so will they, he thought. A general must always lead by example. He waved Rawlins away. "Take my message to Crocker, and send the staff to McPherson. I will join you there shortly."

Protesting, Rawlins rode off, followed by the six other staff officers. Grant dismounted and leaned against his mount while he studied the sheet of fire coming from the wooded belt at the base of the hill. Grant's horse was the only animal in the field.

"Hey, General, can I join your staff?" a voice in the rear line shouted. "I'd be right partial to quit this darned field."

A dozen or more nervous laughs followed. Grant half smiled and shifted what remained of his cigar to the other corner of his mouth.

"Well, then," the frightened voice continued, "could I move a mite to the left, General? Your horse is the only one here, and it's drawing the attention of them Johnnies' sharpshooters."

"Shut up there, you," a color sergeant growled. He leaned forward on the planted staff of his flag like a man facing the wind. "If the general and I can stand here, so can the likes of you."

Grant studied the ash on the end of his cigar. It had grown to over an inch while the tobacco burned down to a mere stub. Watching the flash of rifles and the clouds of smoke surrounding Champion's Hill, Grant now saw his chance. With Pemberton shifting more and more of his men toward the center in an attempt to drive Hovey back, he was weakening his flanks—especially that along the north and west side of the rise. Already, Blair's and Smith's divisions pressed the rebels' right flank, fighting in the forest that anchored that side of their line. The key was the north side of the hill. These men beside him would screen an attack on the rebels' left flank.

He turned to the officer of the men around him. "Colonel, move your men a little by the left flank," he ordered quietly. Grant's low, steady voice electrified the men. Here was a general to lead them who had ice water in his veins, a general who remained cool under fire, one who could stand in an open field alongside them and calmly smoke his cigar while bullets buzzed around his head. Here was a general to lead them to victory, one after the other.

A roar of approval came from the troops. Eagerly, they fell into step, wheeled about, and marched forward. From their new position they could engage the enemy that tormented them where they stood. Now they could return fire on that stand of timber that harbored the rebels and drive them back.

The battle plan formulated in Grant's mind. He would move Logan's fresh troops within the arc of the Jackson to Vicksburg rail line until they commanded the road crossing Baker's Creek. Pemberton's clever use of the creek would now seal his fate. With Logan holding the road, the Confederates' line of retreat would be cut off. Grant slapped his fist into his palm. He would destroy Pemberton's army today, and Vicksburg would fall like a ripe pawpaw.

Behind him the officers shouted, "Fix bayonets! Fix bayonets and forward, double quick!" With a cheer, the two lines moved forward.

Grant watched the lines rolling up to the woods, saw the tongues of flame licking at each other, almost touching, as each line poured volley after volley into the other, and he heard the cries of the fallen. He mounted Kangaroo for a better view. Half an hour passed before scattered bluecoats retreated from the forest back into the field. The line wavered, tried to hold, only to fall back again.

Grant frowned as he saw the Union line crumble under a rush of gray. Men now ran toward him in headlong flight. He set spurs to Kangaroo and galloped to an artillery battery at the far edge of the field.

"Colonel, place your guns in line across that field," Grant ordered as he pointed to the well where he had watched the ill-fated charge. "Load with canister and grapeshot and wait until our boys have passed through your line before firing."

"Canister?" The officer squinted at the cloud with its emerging soldiers. He started to see the gray figures close behind the fleeing men in blue. "Yes, sir! At once, sir!" He saluted and raced away. In minutes the caissons and six-pounders rattled across the field.

Grant watched as his soldiers reached the line of guns. Abruptly, the guns fired, spurting flame at point-blank range into the faces of the pursuing rebels. The report of the massed fire struck his ears a second later. The gray line staggered, stopped, then reversed direction and fled across the clearing. In the blink of a heartbeat, only dead and dying littered the field.

A messenger found Grant. "Message from General Hovey, sir. General Hovey's compliments, and he must have more reinforcements, or he cannot hold."

Grant chomped sourly on his cold cigar. "There are none to spare."

The messenger looked sick. His kepi sported a torn brim, and the gold braid flapped alongside his neck from a single button. His blouse bore patches of powder burn and red clay. "Ah, he must have—" the lad began to repeat, obviously having been urged by Hovey to get more help or else.

Grant held up his hand and the youth fell silent. He's not much older than Freddy, Grant realized. He wondered where in that swirling line of fire and smoke his son was. Silently he hoped Dana had the good sense to stay back of the fighting.

"Please, General, I was told not to come back without help."

Grant sighed and his forehead knitted into deeper wrinkles. He scribbled a message on his field book and tore it off. Pressing it into the lad's hand, he ordered: "Take this to General Logan. He is down that road by the creek. Logan will save your General Hovey."

The boy's face brightened. "Yes, sir, and thank you, sir!" He raced off.

Grant's face clouded. Logan would now shift to his left instead of moving right to block the creek crossing. He would support Hovey, but the trap would go unsprung. Pemberton's army would escape through that opening and live to fight another day.

Unless . . . unless McClernand with the rest of his 13th Corps arrived to hold the Baker's Creek crossing. Where the devil was McClernand? Over two hours ago he reported that he was less than two miles from here, Grant recalled. I keep sending him dispatches to push forward, but he has not arrived on the field. There is only a woods separating us.

Grant rode on, slouched forward in grim determination. His clenched jaw nearly bit his fresh cigar in half. Presently he reached Rawlins, who was waiting with the rest of his staff and General Logan. Charles Dana sat astride his purloined plow horse. Fred Grant was nowhere to be seen.

"Another glorious victory, General." Dana saluted Grant. "We have gained the day."

Logan shook his head, a pained look spreading across his face. He plucked nervously at the buttons on his coat. "No, no, the day is lost. Cannot you hear those cannon over there? They will be down on us right away! In an hour I shall have twenty thousand of the enemy to fight."

"Those are our guns, General Logan," Grant gently corrected his friend. The gallant warrior from Cairo fought with the bravest, undaunted by fear and unencumbered by doubts during the height of battle, but when the engagement was won, nervous exhaustion filled his mind with gloom. Grant long ago recognized this idiosyncrasy and now ignored it.

Rawlins passed his dispatches to Grant and sat astride his mount while Grant read them. "General Hovey has succeeded in driving a wedge between the forces of General Bowen and General Stevenson," he added.

"And what is the latest news of Major General Loring?" Grant asked. "I would expect Pemberton to use him to good advantage against Hovey." Grant searched his memory for his recollections of William Wing Loring, native of North Carolina and a major general in the Confederate Army. Loring's corps had not yet made its presence felt upon the field.

Is he a Stonewall Jackson, who might suddenly appear on my rear to spread panic among my soldiers? No, Grant reasoned. The Loring I recall is well-loved by his troops, but vain and insubordinate. From what I have read in captured Southern newspapers, both Lee and Jackson found him troublesome and difficult to command.

Grant chuckled inwardly. Perhaps that is why he was assigned to the West, to the area of little consequence to the men in Richmond? Banished to the backwater of glory, like me. How wrong they are! When Vicksburg falls, the South will be split in two, and a sally port will open for Federal troops to further cut the South into quarters. Old Winfield Scott saw it, but few else.

Rawlins blurted out his best piece of news. "We captured a Confederate major who called Loring a scared turkey. According to him, Loring has been marching his men back and forth under a flurry of confusing orders from Pemberton. He meant to drive us away from the Baker's Creek crossing and turn our right flank."

Grant's cigar dropped from his mouth at that news.

"But Pemberton countermanded that effort. So, in a huff, Loring has left the field. Word has it that he is retreating south toward Crystal Springs to join with Joe Johnston."

"As I have so often said, gentlemen: Two commanding generals in the field are one too many," Grant quipped. "Let us ride on in hopes we might encounter word of General McClernand. He appears to read from the same manual as General Loring."

The party rode along, directing their animals among the blue and gray piles of dead, clustered along splintered rail fences and scattered along the sunken road. Every declivity and imperfection in the ground appeared a magnet for the killing.

Grant reined in his horse at a clearing where they burst upon a field hospital. Upon every inch of the meadow lay a wounded or dying man. Kangaroo pawed the blood-slicked grass and shivered at the pools of clotted blood where a man had bled to death. Grant's stomach churned. He tried to back his horse from the grisly scene, but his staff pressed too closely to enable a swift detour.

To one side a pile of bloodless limbs, mostly legs with a smattering of arms, rose above the darkened grass, wan and out of place in the forest, like shattered pieces of pale Greek marble. In the open, surgeons with soaked aprons wielded knives and saws on wounded of both sides. Boards, fence posts, and planks served as operating tables. Despite the lack of ether, none of these operated upon had the strength left to scream. Most moaned softly, ground their teeth, or mouthed incoherent words. Blood loss, fatigue, and dehydration left them nearly dead before their next ordeal.

Grant struggled with wave after wave of nausea. His eyes caught the gold looped sleeve of a Confederate colonel to one side. The man sat propped against a stump with his right leg splinted by a cut sapling. A dark-stained tear in his upper pant leg told a grim story.

"General," the man cried after he spotted the shoulder straps on Grant's coat. "If you please, sir, do not let them take my leg off, I beg you!"

Grant stared at the officer. Despite his pale appearance and the clay that clung to his uniform, the man's elegance was notable. His thin face sported a trimmed mustache and goatee, and his uniform was cut to fit and tailored of the finest gray wool.

Beside the wounded officer stood a haggard surgeon, stripped to the waist save for his long johns, wiping his hands on an apron that once was white. His right hand held a curved metal probe, and he saluted Grant while still holding the instrument. "Dr. Kittoe, of the 45th Illinois, sir."

"Oh," the colonel lamented, "I cannot go home to my wife, my beloved Ivalee, on one leg. She loves dancing so."

The weary surgeon grunted. "Well, it is either that or not go home at all."

The Confederate officer swallowed hard.

John Logan slipped from his saddle and removed a small silver flask from his pocket. He looked for an instant at Rawlins as if to say: "I have saved this for just such a purpose, so spare me your sermonizing." Rawlins turned away, saying nothing.

"Here, my good man, take a drink and prepare yourself," Logan said as he offered the flask to the man. "I am sure your wife would prefer most of you to none at all."

Grant battled his stomach while the colonel emptied the flask. The man returned the bottle to Logan and clasped his hand warmly. He sighed deeply and straightened his shoulders. "Yes," he said softly, "I think that now I am in a condition to wear a wooden leg home."

Grant watched the orderlies carry the colonel to one of the makeshift tables made from an old door. Another soldier cast a bucket of river water across the blood-soaked wood before they placed the man upon it. Grant turned away as Dr. Kittoe raised his long knife.

"For God's sake, gentlemen," a voice called out, "is there a Mason among you?"

Rawlins looked down at the speaker. "I am a Mason," he replied.

"I am dying," the man whispered. "As a brother Mason, will you not comfort me in my last hour?"

Rawlins looked at Grant. He was relieved to see his commander nod his assent. Rawlins slid from his horse and knelt by the man. He lifted a corner of the blanket and quickly put it down. A solid shot had nearly cut the man in half. Blood and clay coated the remnants of a butternut uniform. His brother Mason was a Confederate. Rawlins knelt beside the man and stroked his tangled hair.

While they waited, the sound of musket fire faded into scattered crackling from skirmishing, then ceased altogether. The smell of cooking fires spread across the silent hill. Their ears, long accustomed to the cries of battle, tuned out the pleas of the wounded and focused on the crickets and cicadas that ventured forth from their hiding. Dispatch riders came and went with casualty lists.

Grant studied these to keep his mind from the carnage around him. He retired to the edge of the field and tallied the grim findings. At length he rose and walked over to where Logan was sitting on a splintered stump, chewing a plug of tobacco. "I estimate that we had fifteen thousand men absolutely engaged with the enemy today," he said. "I make our losses to be close to twenty-five hundred, with half of those killed, missing, or wounded coming from Hovey's division."

"And the enemy's?" Logan asked.

"I figure seventeen thousand to eighteen thousand engaged, with losses of thirty-six hundred."

Rawlins approached them. "Make that thirty-six hundred and one. My brother Mason has passed away...."

---

BIG BLACK RIVER BRIDGE. MAY 17, 1863

General Osterhaus removed his hat and wiped his face with a square of tablecloth that now served as his handkerchief. His horse stood astride the railroad tracks and struck its hooves nervously against the cross ties. Ahead, the rail line vanished into the night.

Osterhaus cursed to himself. That black smudge to his right must be a forest, but he could hardly see. The general hummed nervously to himself while his division moved up from the road paralleling the train tracks and spread along the left of the forest. He fished inside his coat and withdrew his pocket watch. Opening the gilded cover, he held the face of the watch close to his eye. Four in the morning, he guessed, since he could not discern the hands of his clock.

Osterhaus couldn't believe they were positioning for an attack. They'd just fought a bloody engagement less than twenty miles back, and now they were about to have another go. He could hardly see ten feet ahead, yet they were moving into position. He hoped to God his men could dress their lines in the darkness. He envisioned half of them marching at right angles to the rest.

A voice spoke out of the gloom. "General Carr's division is to your right in those trees, and your left is covered by Smith. Ahead is a plowed field, and the rebel lines are just beyond that clearing. They have thrown up an earthworks of cotton bales and dirt. A bayou protects not only their flanks but the railroad bridge directly ahead. The river is high, and a good foot of water fills the swamp, along with trees fallen by the enemy."

"How the devil do you know that?" Osterhaus snapped. "I can't see my hand before my very face, sir!"

"I rode over there to reconnoiter," the voice answered calmly. A red eye flared suddenly in the dark as the speaker blew on the burning tip of his cigar.

"General Grant!" Osterhaus coughed. "I did not recognize you. You must excuse me, sir. I do not have the vision of a night owl."

Grant ignored the apology. He leaned forward in his saddle and watched the soft dark edges filling the field ahead. "There will be some fog which I think might be to our advantage. You might be wondering why we are pressing Pemberton so closely instead of resting after yesterday's battle."

Osterhaus started to open his mouth, thought better of it, and closed his jaw.

Grant continued. Osterhaus was a good man and an even better fighter when he understood the overall strategy. "I was afraid Pemberton might cross the Big Black River and take the road north to join Johnston. We have them divided, and I'd like to keep them so. Pemberton would do us the most harm by combining with Johnston, but that would abandon Vicksburg. He has shown a great reluctance to do that. I have ordered General Sherman to move west on the upper Jackson road and cross the Big Black at Bridgeport. Hopefully, he can get behind Pemberton."

The fog appeared to lift. Osterhaus now could see the irregular line that marked the enemy's rifle pits. Behind him the sky grew lighter. Dawn would come soon, but the lowering clouds would let little of the sun through.

Clattering down the tracks, an officer on horseback approached the two men. Neither Osterhaus nor Grant recognized the man's face. Thick muttonchops flowed from beneath his forage cap to cover his cheeks as far as his collar. He saluted both men, then withdrew a dispatch from a pouch strapped to his saddle and handed it to Grant. "Message from General Halleck," he said crisply.

From Halleck? How the devil did he find me? Grant wondered. "Have I seen you before, Major?" he asked. The face was unfamiliar.

"No, sir. I'm with General Banks. General Halleck sent his message through General Banks as he was uncertain as to your whereabouts, sir."

Osterhaus had never known any welcome news to come from Never Positive Banks. The fact that Banks had chosen a field grade officer to deliver the message made Osterhaus even more nervous. Grant's response and reaction to this dispatch would be carefully noted and reported back to Banks and Washington.

Grant tore open the envelope and held the paper close to his face. The dispatch bore the date of May 11. Grant surmised that Halleck had sent it to New Orleans, where it was forwarded to General Banks's headquarters. He read slowly, rereading the lines before looking up at Osterhaus. It was as Grant had expected. Halleck was blindly issuing orders that would hamstring him. A good thing I cut off all my lines of communication, he thought. This war cannot be fought from an armchair in Washington. "This dispatch is dated the eleventh of May. General Halleck orders me to return to Grand Gulf and wait there until General Banks can cooperate with us in attacking Port Hudson. Then, we are to return with our combined forces to lay siege to Vicksburg."

"What?" Osterhaus blurted out in disbelief. "This is madness. We are on the verge of taking Vicksburg this very week. If we march down to

Grand Gulf, the rebels will make good use of the respite. Johnston will surely unite with Pemberton, or Richmond will send more reinforcements."

Grant carefully folded the message and slipped it into his coat pocket. He eyed the courier levelly. "This message has come too late. The situation has changed since General Halleck wrote it, and I do not believe he would issue this order if he knew our present position."

The major had been carefully rehearsed. He was to insist the order be carried out, no matter what. He straightened his shoulders while his hands locked on the pommel of his saddle. "General Grant, this is a direct order from General Halleck, your superior. You must obey."

Grant looked at him with a wooden face. Only the deepening of his frown showed his displeasure.

"No doubt General Halleck has a far-reaching plan of which you are not acquainted," the major said, pressing his point. "Your command is only part of his master scheme. To disobey will jeopardize the overall tactic."

What master plan? Grant wondered. Some harebrained scheme, I'll wager, hatched in the back rooms of the War Office with Stanton sniffing about and Lincoln wringing his hands. Why, even the maps they send us are out of date and useless in the field.

Seeing Grant's silence, the major opened his mouth to continue. Suddenly, a wild bellow erupted from the right of the Union line and cut his argument short. Grant turned in the direction of the shout.

Stripped of his blouse, and with his shirtsleeves rolled above his brawny forearms, Brigadier General Michael K. Lawler lifted his 250 pounds onto his saddle and waved his arms wildly. Too large around to buckle the standard sword belt, Lawler wore his scabbard slung over his shoulder, looking like a misplaced musketeer. Clutching his sword and his rosary, he roared again and charged the startled Confederates. A screaming line of blue soldiers followed his galloping horse, yelling and laughing at their coatless leader.

I'll have to thank that crazy Douglas Democrat from Shawneetown, Illinois, Grant thought. His attack has given me the excuse I need. "I must see to the disposition of this battle!" he shouted to the startled major. With that, Grant drove his heels into his horse's flanks. Kangaroo leapt, carrying Grant away toward the action.

We'll show this major how to win battles, Osterhaus decided. He drew his sword and ordered his men forward.

When Grant reached the advancing Union line, the major was nowhere to be seen.

The Confederate line collapsed as men fled back to their only means of retreat, the railroad bridge over the swollen Big Black River. Grant followed his eager troops as they leapt over trenches and clambered across the once dreaded cotton bales and earthworks, hard in pursuit. He reined in Kangaroo when he saw dark smoke rising from the river. Pemberton was burning the bridge.

A rout followed as panicked men dove into the river and tried to swim across. Many drowned as the current swept them under or pinned them beneath snags. Some died as the Union soldiers shot them like fish in a barrel. But most Northerners grounded their muskets and cheered after their fleeing foe.

The loss of the bridge prompted Grant to spread his jubilant army along the east bank in search of means to build new bridges. Abandoned supplies and cannon littered the abandoned breastworks. Couriers arrived with news that Sherman faced the same problem at Bridgeport. A day would be lost constructing means to cross the swirling Big Black. Night fell to the sound of axes felling trees.

Sherman's lanky frame emerged from the evening mists, riding loose-jointed in his saddle so that his body swayed with each cautious step his horse took. Unlike Grant, who rode as if he were fused to his mount, Sherman's awkward riding habits made it appear as if he were constantly in danger of falling off his animal.

Head down as he rode, Sherman appeared to be asleep. On approaching Grant, the animal halted, the rider raised his head, and a weary Sherman peered out from beneath his slouch hat.

"Why, good evening to you, Sam," Sherman said, surprised at seeing his commander at Bridgeport. On second thought, Sherman decided Grant would be found wherever important events were taking place, so it was natural to find him here. "I hear you've had a productive day."

Grant looked up from the log on which he was sitting and nodded.

Sherman dismounted and handed his horse to an orderly. He sought a place on the log and lighted up one of his crooked cigars. Both men smoked in silence for several minutes.

"If we'd got that bridge before the rebels burned it, we'd have captured Pemberton's whole army today," Grant said at last. "But I believe their army is dispirited and ready to surrender."

"I'd be dispirited, too, if I'd lost five battles in so short a time," Sherman answered. "They seem to be surrendering in droves. Blair's men met with an entrenched company of rebs holding the opposite bank when they reached the river. He ordered Captain Ewing with some of his men from the 13th Regulars to strip their artillery horses and swim across under fire. That seemed a bit reckless to me, so I positioned a battery behind that corncrib and lobbed a few shells into the rebel position. No sooner had the first shell struck than a lieutenant and ten men popped out with their rifles held butt upward. You wouldn't see them giving up that easily before."

"I believe so, too, Cump."

Sherman peered at the canvas and rubber pontoon bridge that his engineers were lashing together, even as company after company of soldiers marched across the swaying structure. All along both banks of the river, torches of pine pitch and sweet gum illuminated the dark waters. The burning pitch filled the air with pine scent. The tramp of the crossing soldiers set the pontoon bridge to swaying, casting ever-widening ripples in the water. "By God, this makes a fine war picture," Sherman crowed. "Someday we should get an artist to paint it."

Grant scoffed. "With us standing in one of those heroic poses with hand stuck inside our coats like Napoleon. No, thank you."

"How do you like these newfangled pontoon boats?" Sherman asked.

"They look good. McPherson likes them, too. He has thrown one across where the burned bridge stood. His is not as fine as yours, though. He substituted cotton bales for many of the India-rubber boats. General Ransom prefers cutting down trees for his bridge. Lieutenant Hains of the

Engineer Corps built a raft bridge. All in all, we have three different but equally good bridges to cross the Big Black."

Sherman, ever one to find it hard to keep still, wriggled his boots in a patch of soft clay. "An amusing thing happened as I passed Bolton Station. I saw a small log cabin with a well in the backyard where my soldiers were drawing water. I stopped for a drink and saw a book lying on the ground with several other things the men had scattered about while foraging."

Grant shook his head. Sherman's men surpassed all others in their expertise at helping themselves to whatever they could use. He was glad Sherman used the word "foraging," for he had issued strict orders against looting.

"Well, I retrieved the book, and do you know what I found? It was a volume of the Constitution of the United States, belonging to none other than Jefferson Davis, the president of the Southern Confederation."

"Jefferson Davis?"

"I swear, his name was written on the title page. I asked a Negro standing there if this place belonged to the famous Davis, and he said it did. He also told us that Jeff's brother Joe had a plantation close by."

Sherman paused to gauge Grant's reaction. Grant merely continued smoking his cigar.

Sherman continued unabashed. He knew Grant was listening. "So we paid Joe Davis a visit as well."

"And?"

Sherman cleared his throat and stretched his leg before him. "Well, then we marched on," he said simply.

"And?" Grant knew there was more to this story.

"Unfortunately, several of my staff officers appropriated two of Joe Davis's fine carriage horses. And, I had the men bring along a fine black pony that looked like it might be lonely without the other horses. We named him Jeff Davis after his contributor to the Union cause. I'm making him a gift to you, Sam. You'll like little Jeff, but his ride is a mite stiff. Poor Joe and his niece were most distressed to see his countryside swarming with Federals."

"And?"

"And, then Mr. President Davis's log cabin caught fire and burned to the ground, not unlike the Confederate Hotel in Jackson that I told you about."

"Not more escaped convicts, I hope?"

Sherman pursed his lips and placed his hands together as if praying. He studied his dirty and broken fingernails. If my wife could see me now, what would she think? he mused. He shrugged. "Well, I don't know for certain just who started the fire, Sam, but I am making inquiries."

# VICKSBURG

MAY 22, 1863

Ulysses Grant's heart sank as he stood beside Sherman. Staring down the Graveyard Road, he sensed the attack had stalled. Worse than that, he feared his troops might be routed.

Four hundred yards ahead, the orderly blue lines and flapping banners of Sherman's 15th Corps had simply vanished. Column after column marched forward into a wall of cannon smoke. Then all order evaporated.

Moving steadily up the slope toward the Confederate parapet, the cohesion of the regiments splintered as they threaded along twisting gullies and stumbled into steep-walled ravines. Instead of concentrated lines, the Union's advance dissolved into clusters of tired, desperate men.

Scouting reports warned of broken ground before the enemy's fortifications, but now the true extent of nature's impediment became fearfully clear. The steep bluffs which frustrated the Union's attack on Vicksburg from the river's side and rose three hundred feet above the surrounding bayous and swamps sloped down to solid ground that trailed off toward

Jackson. But, the soft, eroding red clay sliced the ground into sharp ravines and gorges that swallowed whole companies and made it impossible for the horse teams to deploy the artillery.

Added to this, the defenders constructed rifle pits and earthworks to enfilade this approach with deadly fire. Crawling ever upward sapped the advancing men of their strength even as they faced increasing cannon and musket fire.

And this was the second attack to fail. While Grant wore his customary determined look, he ground his teeth as he viewed the bodies of his troops littering the road so appropriately named for the nearby graveyard. Beside him, Sherman chewed his lip as he swiveled his field glasses back and forth along the front.

To make matters worse, a spirited barrage of canister, exploding Hotchkiss shells, and grapeshot slaughtered the struggling infantry. Whoever survived the artillery encountered volley after volley of well-placed musket fire, devastatingly directed in cross fire. The Confederate troops that bolted at the Big Black River bridge mere days before now rallied, fighting with fierce determination and showing no inclination to collapse.

I've seriously underestimated the enemy's will to fight, Grant admitted. Since the Confederate troops were beaten in five successive battles, I felt certain they would break as we attacked. Yesterday, I thought the ground defeated our advance. I believed that if we could cross this broken land in force and come to grips with the enemy, they would surrender. How wrong I was! Both the ground and the enemy forces defeat us. Back behind their well-prepared defenses, Pemberton's army has regained its confidence.

With each exploding Hotchkiss shell that chewed dirty gray holes in the sky and rained flying shards of metal on his hapless troops, the error of his decision grew more evident. In response, his stooped shoulders sagged even more and his characteristic hunched posture deepened. Grant folded into himself in frustration. His right hand reached inside his shirt and grasped the locket with Julia's hair.

Sherman lowered his glasses and turned to his friend. His sharp tongue summarized their failure. "My men are making no progress," he said sadly. "Not a single company has breached the rebel entrenchments. The steep ravines confound them and serve to aid the enemy. Those of my men that claw their way to the tops of the parapets are mowed down by rifle fire. The rest have gone to ground like woodchucks." He hid behind his glasses as he searched in the smoke and fire for the other wing of the attack. No Federal flag flew above any of the rebel lines. He sighed, removed his handkerchief and haphazardly wiped the lenses. "McPherson, I fear, has done no better. His corps has not breached the enemy's breastworks, either."

Grant withdrew his pocket watch and snapped open the cover. "Almost noon," he said.

While Grant pondered his next move, a breathless courier rode beneath them along a ravine parallel to where they waited. His head passed at the level of their horses' hooves. The man reined in his mount, looked about in confusion until he spotted a passable route to the generals. He switched back twenty yards, vanished from sight before reemerging to struggle up a draw to their right.

Grunting from the effort, the rider coaxed his blown horse forward. He saluted and handed a message to Grant. The general noted blood streaming from the flanks of the messenger's horse, and the man's face and forage cap were spattered with blood. The man swayed in his saddle while his animal shivered nervously.

"Another message from McClernand," Grant noted sourly. McClernand's corps constituted the left wing of the assault. As usual, the bridegroom general had besieged Grant for reinforcements and requests for Sherman's and McPherson's corps to divert the enemy from his front. The general chose to ignore everything except his own ideas and continued to act as if the other two corps existed solely to support him.

Grant's frown deepened as he read the note. " 'We are hotly engaged with the enemy. We have part possession of two forts, and the Stars and Stripes are floating over them. A vigorous push ought to be made all along the line,' " he read out loud. Grant reached for Sherman's field glasses and scanned the sector where McClernand's corps operated. Only flashes and smoke met his gaze. "What does he mean?" Grant asked. "I see no evidence of our flag."

He looked again before handing the glasses to Sherman, who looked as well. No evidence of a breakthrough was apparent. Grant crumpled the paper in his hands. "I do not believe a word of it," he snorted.

Sherman protested. "This is an official dispatch. Surely, General Mc-Clernand would not make up such a report. He must have gained a foothold. If I were to renew my attack, McClernand might exploit his advantage."

"And if he has gained nothing, your assault will only lead to useless losses ... and to no avail." Grant contemplated his next move. Decided, he reached for his field book and scribbled a note. "I will instruct McPherson to detach General Quimby's division to support McClernand. Quimby abuts McClernand's right." Grant handed the message to the courier. The man saluted and backed his mount down the slide. In an instant he vanished.

Grant turned his horse and trotted after him. He stopped to call over his shoulder to Sherman, "I'm going to look at this breakthrough myself. I'll ride along the line. If you have not heard from me to the contrary by three o'clock, give it another try."

Grant never reached McClernand's position. A barrage of shells separated him from the rider and diverted him into a deep ravine. Inside the depression, Grant passed wounded and exhausted men lining the sides. Most still clutched their unfired muskets. Those who had the strength left looked up as he rode past. He could still see their faith in him reflected in their upturned faces. Here was their commander riding among the shot and shell to direct them. Most were too spent to cheer.

Grant resolved to stay in the saddle even as puffs of clay and dust rose about the makeshift trench with each shell that exploded overhead. Minié balls whined past while Grant paused to light another cigar before moving on. Carefully, he guided his horse around the outstretched legs of those wounded that filled the bottom of the gully.

His progress stopped as he reached a sharp-angled wall where a griz-

zled sergeant and three men struggled to wheel a six-pound field piece into
position. The jumbled approach made horses useless, forcing the men to
move the gun by hand. Time after time the team manhandled the cannon
to the brim, only to have it roll back. On their last effort they made it. Just
as they got the wheels onto level ground, a shell screeched past and exploded directly overhead. Shrapnel patterned the dirt and flung hunks of
brush and cane into the air. When the smoke cleared, only Grant and the
veteran sergeant remained alive.

"Well, that's the last of the Chicago Mercantile Battery!" the sergeant
cursed. "And I don't know where in the hell Captain White is." In frustration the man slipped back into the ravine and lay pressed against the wall
staring at Grant. "Them's our own damned shells, you know, General," he
muttered in a heavy Irish brogue. "Hotchkiss shells with the wooden bases
fastened to the shell casings with tin strips and bits of wire. Only the cheap
contractors sold us faulty shells, the bastards! They ain't built proper, you
see. Bad fuses and all. The wooden bases blow off before they should." He
glared defiantly at another puff of dirty smoke above his head, refusing to
flinch as more fragments whined past. "Right over us instead of them! The
damned things are killing more of us than Johnny Rebs."

The man eyed the water bottle hanging from Grant's saddle hungrily.
He licked his parched lips. "Say, General, you wouldn't be up to sharing a
drop of your water with a poor fighting man, would you?"

Grant tossed him the canteen. "You've earned it, Sergeant. Take all
you need."

The man drank slowly, closing his eyes as the water ran down the
back of his throat. Satisfied, he handed the bottle back to his commander.
"To think of all the time I cursed the water. When we was up to our waists
in it digging them damned useless canals in the bogs, I never thought I'd be
praying for a drop of the blasted stuff." He coughed, looked warily at
Grant. "Was them canals your idea, General?"

"Yup." Dozens of engineers and staff, even President Lincoln, contributed to Grant's efforts to find a water route past Vicksburg, but Grant
shouldered the blame. "And so was this attack today," he added.

The sergeant nodded thoughtfully. "Don't be taking it too hard, General.

None of us is perfect. Praise be to God, you got us out of the damned swamps and onto solid ground." He picked up a handful of clay and crushed it in his fingers. "A man could grow a potato or two in this dirt if he could straighten out the blasted land," he said matter-of-factly.

"Not like the soil in Illinois," Grant responded. "I raised a fair stand of corn myself near Galena, but the bank panic made my crop worthless."

"I'm no farmer myself." The sergeant grinned for the first time. It was a wry smile, lopsided and revealing a rotten tooth. "And I gather neither are you. Stick to fighting, General," he advised, "you're better at it than farming...."

Grant touched his hat and rode on, leaving the man by his ruined gun. All along the line he saw the same thing. None of the regiments could advance as a unit because of the ravines and tangled cane and matted brush.

Minutes stretched to hours as Grant studied each stronghold that blocked his soldiers. Twice more couriers brought heartening dispatches from General McClernand. The enemy's earthworks were breached, McClernand wrote, and he could press on if only he had more support.

But wherever Grant passed, officers sought him out to complain or ask for guidance. Well into McClernand's sector, Grant realized that McClernand's subordinates lacked clear orders from their general. No one knew if a portion of the rebel fortifications had been carried or not.

An increase in the sound of battle behind him drew Grant's attention. Were the rebels counterattacking? Suddenly, he realized it must be three o'clock. A quick check of his watch confirmed what he feared. Sherman was attacking as ordered.

Grant stared sullenly in that direction. If McClernand's claims were untrue, Sherman's efforts were wasted. He dismounted and climbed to the edge of the ravine for a better look.

"General Grant! General Grant! Thank God, I've found you," a voice shouted.

From down below, stumbling toward him, Grant recognized the figure of Sylvanus Cadwallader. Clay and brambles coated the reporter's clothing and filled his hair, and his face was so smeared with dirt that Grant hardly recognized him.

"Mr. Cadwallader. Have you been with General McClernand? I am trying to locate him. He has reported breaking through the enemy's fortifications."

Cadwallader sank onto his knees. "There is no breakthrough," he said bitterly. "No small measure of victory, except what exists in General Mc-Clernand's head."

Grant climbed down. "What do you mean?" he asked.

Cadwallader stared at the clay on his hands and wiped them on the front of his equally dirty shirt. Three passes showed him the futility of his efforts. He sighed, dropped his hands and looked sadly at Grant. "Nothing of General McClernand's enterprise has succeeded, I'm afraid. I was there. I saw what transpired. Nothing succeeded. Nothing." He winced and ducked his head as a shell burst close overhead. "You know about those infernal Hotchkiss shells?" he asked Grant.

Grant studied the puff of smoke hanging above their refuge. "Yes, ours are defective," he said flatly. "Tell me what you saw."

"I had found shelter behind a rise of ground that prevented the rebel sharpshooters from seeing me. McClernand's advance came within plain view of my place of shelter. As his line moved forward, the Confederate shot and shell so tore it to pieces that in minutes it failed to resemble any line of battle whatsoever. They pressed forward despite the ragged holes in their ranks. Soldiers and officers rushed ahead pell-mell with no attention to alignment.

"Still, they advanced until the cannon could do them no more harm. Mercifully, they were below the guns, whose muzzles could not be depressed sufficiently to bring them to bear on those that were left. Here they met some respite, for the ditch in front of the earthworks also shielded them from musket fire. But as they climbed the glacis, wave after wave of musket fire mowed them down. The struggling blue line grew thinner and thinner. Those that did reach the summit were instantly shot or pulled over the breastworks and taken prisoner."

"And nowhere along the line was a lodgment made? No colors planted on a captured section of the earthworks?" Grant questioned.

Cadwallader looked up. "In one place I saw our flag planted halfway up the embankment. Its color party fell to musket fire almost immediately. There it lay, forlorn and abandoned, until a dreary Confederate soldier ventured out of his trench to retrieve it and carry it back inside as a trophy of war. Those who remain of the gallant charge now take refuge in the ditch and wait for nightfall to crawl away."

Grant ground his cigar into the ground. "Useless, useless," he repeated.

"But there is more," Cadwallader insisted. "Seeing this abject failure, General McClernand persisted. He ordered the troops of General Quimby's division to attack along the same deadly path."

"But I ordered Quimby to support McClernand, not to spearhead his drive."

"A detail lost on McClernand. He seemed obsessed with pressing the attack. I have heard rumors that he personally promised Secretary Stanton, President Lincoln, *and his bride,* that he would capture Vicksburg. Colonel Boomer and Colonel Sandborn of Quimby's division attacked with their brigades under his direct order. They suffered the same fate, and now McClernand blames them for his failure. It is most unfair! Especially as one of McClernand's own colonels refused to make a second assault. He refused to send his men to certain death, he said, and would rather accept the consequences of his refusal."

Grant's face turned hard. Disgust and disappointment filled his features, something Cadwallader had not witnessed before. Between his clenched lips, his cigar had gone out. Using a supreme effort of will, Grant removed his cigar and carefully lighted it again. His fingers neither shook nor showed the slightest hint of the fury that engulfed him. Unseen to the reporter, he snapped the still burning match between his fingers.

"Then this last attack by Sherman and McPherson only increased our casualties without any benefit whatever," he said bitterly.

Cadwallader poured out his woeful story. He would write all this down sometime, he vowed, in reports to his paper and perhaps in a memoir.

But now he felt the need to tell Grant the whole awful truth. Someone needed to expose McClernand's shameful behavior once and for all.

"General, I must tell you of a distressing event that I witnessed. Mc-Clernand ordered Colonel Joseph Mower to advance his brigade. The colonel, on seeing the ground over which he was to move, exclaimed: 'Good God! No man can return from this charge alive!' But his general insisted, so the gallant colonel handed his watch and what money he had in his pocket to a personal friend who remained behind. He requested his friend forward his effects to his wife. Then he drew his sword and marched bravely forward at the head of his men. He fell dead at the first volley the Confederates fired. The whole affair was miserable and inexcusable to a point beyond endurance."

Cadwallader buried his face in his hands. He could say no more. He wept openly as Grant rose and mounted his horse. From his saddle Grant could see his troops pinned down against the slope. Safe from cannon fire, they still suffered from sporadic rifle fire as the rebels thrust their muskets over their trenches and blindly fired down into the ditch. Landing amidst the packed bodies, even the random shot did damage. Here and there the Confederates rolled lighted cannon shells or threw hand grenades into the moat.

Grant studied the sun. It would be a long and terrible wait before darkness gave them cover to creep back to safety. He directed his mount back to his headquarters. Slumping forward in the saddle, his shoulders hunched, he pushed aside his anger as he wrestled with the problem he now faced. He was exposed above the rim of the ravine, and sharpshooters' bullets whirred overhead, but he ignored them. The wind from an exploding shell threatened to dislodge his hat. He pulled the brim tightly down on his head with no more thought for his danger.

Throughout his life Grant hated to backtrack, and even this return path to his staff rankled him. A fierce resolution grew in his breast as he was forced to retrace his route. He had come this far by moving forward. There would be no turning back now. His determination fired his mind, and it worked methodically, formulating a plan. Vicksburg was indeed a tough nut to crack. Frontal assaults would only fail. Still, his troops encircled the city by land. Porter's gunboats and ironclads ruled the river. No food and no reinforcements could reach the city.

He had much to do.

To the east, Johnston and Loring lurked. Johnston now reoccupied Jackson. Grant dismissed any immediate threat to his back. Johnston would find little of use in the capital. Sherman had done his job well. The roads, bridges, rail lines, factories, and warehouses no longer existed. Federal troops held the crossings at the Big Black River and Bridgeport. Any sign of Confederate troops, and Grant's men would burn the pontoon bridges. Any attempt to relieve Vicksburg would take weeks while Johnston rebuilt what the Confederates and the Federals had wrecked.

To be safe, a double line of fortifications must be built, Grant decided, one encircling Vicksburg and another, wider arc built facing east to protect his back from Johnston, or Bragg, or whomever the South might send against him. Hopefully, Rosecrans would keep Braxton Bragg occupied, but Grant knew he could not depend on that. Nothing of use to Vicksburg must be allowed through the double lines.

A double line? Grant found he could chuckle inwardly. What would his old professors at the Point say if they knew he was using a bit of the ancient military history they struggled so hard to cram into his head? In this modern year of 1863, he was besieging Vicksburg exactly like Julius Caesar trapped the Gallic chieftain Vercingetorix at Alesia in 46 B.C.

At the same time, Grant realized his men desperately needed supplies of coffee, bacon, and bread. Since cutting free of his supply lines, his men had lived off the land—and done well at it. But a steady diet of confiscated chicken, turkey, and duck made them crave bacon and even hardtack. He would give orders to construct supply lines to bring those things down from Holly Springs and La Grange and to extend roads to the Yazoo River with its steamboats. With Pemberton shut up, Johnston in Jackson, and the rebels' cavalry transferred to Bragg, cavalry raids were unlikely. Grant still had his cavalry. They would watch Johnston and screen the supply trains.

Vicksburg might be a tough nut, but he would break it if it took a year, he vowed. If he could not crack this nut with a swift, hammerlike blow, he would break it by squeezing it, slowly, steadily, from all sides, until the shell could take no more. Only the deadly, dirty means of a siege could do that.

Grant resolved something else as he rode back: Major General John Alexander McClernand must go.

# CLEANING HOUSE

Grant looked up from his writing desk as the tent flap parted. General Mc-Clernand stood in the entrance, head drawn back and shoulders squared in defiant arrogance. His narrow, deep-set eyes glared down his long, hooked nose at the seated man.

Well, Grant thought. I am in my shirtsleeves and carelessly tied cravat working on plans for the siege, and you are wearing your tailored uniform with its stiff collar and rows of polished brass buttons. You think you are superior to me in every way, don't you? I may not look as fancy as you, McClernand, but I am never inattentive to the business of fighting battles.

Grant's attention returned to his desk. "Come in, General McClernand," he said stiffly. "I will be with you in a minute."

McClernand stepped inside and looked around. He sniffed disdainfully, while his lip curled into a sneer that buried the tip of his nose in the shambles of his dense beard.

Grant placed his pencil down. He jerked his head to Colonel Rawlins, who waited beside the table. Rawlins edged past McClernand and disappeared out the opening. Grant's fingers searched among the papers on his camp desk until they found a single sheet of paper. Grant held it close to the standing man's face. "General McClernand, did you write this order?"

McClernand's face paled. Then, misjudging Grant's anger, he made a grievous mistake, his face recovering its disdainful look. His dark, curly beard wavered across the front of his tunic collar as he wiggled his jaw. "That, sir, is a congratulatory order I issued for the troops under my command. It was addressed solely to my troops and to no others. As such it carries the nature of a private communiqué. I am surprised you have a copy of it."

"Your private communiqué was printed in a newspaper in St. Louis," Grant barked. "The *Missouri Democrat*, to be precise."

McClernand took one step back but stayed his course. "I cannot attest to how the papers came by it, but it was intended for my men alone," he lied. He knew all too well that his wife supplied copies of the letter to every reporter in camp.

"From the copy I saw, you take credit for every victory since the crossing at Bruinsburg. You go so far as to equate yourself to . . . to, what was the phrase? To the 'honored martyrs of Monmouth and Bunker Hill.' Sherman was right when he advised me that this so-called order was addressed to your constituency in Illinois, not to your soldiers."

Grant pressed his attack. "Do you deny that you wrote that you succeeded in making a lodgment in the rebel defenses in Vicksburg but were forced to withdraw because General McPherson and General Sherman failed to fulfill their parts in the overall attack?"

"I did breach the rebel fortifications," McClernand added uncertainly, skirting the question of the other two generals' performance. "My men were the only ones to make a breakthrough. Had I been sufficiently supported—as I begged you so many times during the attack—Vicksburg would have fallen."

Grant rose. "You are a liar. And to impugn the bravery and ability of capable officers like Sherman and McPherson makes your falsehood doubly offensive. Worst of all is the fact that your lies caused me to order another attack that only led to needless bloodshed!" Grant's voice did not rise at all, but his tone hardened to a knifelike edge.

McClernand's face drained of color. "I—I did make a lodgment," he protested. "My men overran their defenses. We raised our colors atop their earthworks!"

"You did not, sir!" Grant's fist struck the desktop, launching the pencil into the air. "I have it on the best authority that your soldiers succeeded only in capturing a small, outlying lunette, and not a single point in the main parapet. As you well know, our engineers reported that the Confederates built many of these V-shaped lunettes across points where they wished to shorten their lines. *They're built outside of the main fortifications!* Those of your men inside that lunette were killed or taken prisoner because it was open to the back, facing the rebel earthworks, and available to the full force of their guns."

"I—I protest your implications, sir!"

"Protest as you like." Grant advanced menacingly on the taller man. "I can only draw one of two conclusions. Either you lied deliberately about your success, or else you are too ignorant to recognize the main fortifications of the enemy."

McClernand's mouth worked furiously, foam speckling the corners of his lips. "May I remind you I have the ear of President Lincoln himself, and Secretary Stanton, not to mention General Halleck," he cautioned Grant. "My influence in Washington far exceeds my rank as Major General."

Grant glowered at him. "You do not have to advise me of the meddling hand of Washington. I have to contend with that all too often. But I may also remind you that Washington favors those who win battles—above all else! Thanks to your poor performance, you have lost what favor you once had."

"Secretary Stanton?" McClernand swallowed hard. Stanton's support advanced with each victorious charge and withdrew with each retreat.

"Your inaction at Grand Gulf cost you his support. Both he and Halleck authorize my removing you from command. Your failure at the battles at Champion's Hill and the Big Black River further strengthened their resolve. And now your disgraceful action against the enemy ramparts—"

"President Lincoln," McClernand bleated. Grant knew that this was a particularly stunning blow. For a politician to abandon someone who could deliver that many votes was nearly inconceivable.

Grant's hand chopped the air inches from the general's immaculate sash. "Lincoln is above all things a shrewd politician. He needs victories to remain in office. Your actions only weaken his position." Grant paused to study the effect of his words. "The President is strangely silent as to your support. I would hazard the opinion that if asked about you this very night he would profess not to know you well."

"But, my men? Surely, they would not follow a new general officer, one unknown and strange to them?"

"That is the saddest loss of all. By callously ordering brigade after brigade to their certain death, you have squandered the affection of your own corps. Like that colonel who refused your order, your men will no longer follow you."

McClernand's shoulders sagged. He grasped the tent pole for support.

Grant continued. "I had hoped to remove you quietly after Vicksburg had fallen by asking you to take a leave of absence. I felt that would be best for the morale of the troops, and it would allow you a graceful exit with your pride and honor intact. But by your deceitful actions and this disgraceful letter, you show that you have no honor to speak of. By submitting your order for publication in the press, you have violated my direct order as well as War Department orders. That alone is grounds for dismissal."

"Dismissal?" McClernand croaked out the words. His fingers rose to his throat to fidget at the polished button fastening his collar.

Grant leaned forward like a bulldog and rested both hands flat on his desk. "General McClernand, you are dismissed from your command. If you, your baggage, and your wife are not gone from this camp by noon tomorrow, I will appoint an escort to hurry you along." From his pocket, Grant withdrew a sealed envelope and handed it to McClernand. "Colonel Rawlins wrote this order at my directive. It relieves you of command of the 13th Corps and authorizes you to proceed to any point in Illinois," he said.

I only wish it were China, Grant thought. The first thing you'll do is run straight to Governor Yates and start trouble for me.

McClernand hung his head. His eyes fixed on his polished boots, and he found it impossible to tear his gaze free from the gleaming leather. They were a gift from his wife—new, above-the-knee boots for him to wear as he entered Vicksburg as its victor. Now he was sacked, disgraced. A dark corner of his mind urged him to fight this dismissal, to go public and speak to the press. But he knew he would lose that battle when the full truth came out. His best chance was to publish an authorized biography that slanted the facts in his favor and muddied the waters of history. It worked for Napoleon, and it would work for him. Adolph Schwarz of the Second Illinois Artillery came immediately to mind as his official biographer. The man wrote well and once served as his chief of staff.

"Who ... who will replace me?"

Grant had not expected McClernand to ask. Begrudgingly, he gave the man credit for more backbone than he realized. "Brigadier General Edward Ord."

"Ord?" McClernand laughed derisively. "The man knows no proper military etiquette. He mopes around the camp in a wretched, old white linen coat and hat, without even a collar to his shirt, and complains about everything under the sun. Why, just yesterday he filled me with lurid tales of his recent bout with bilious diarrhea and showed me how the chiggers had ravaged every inch of his body. The man is no corps commander."

"He has one thing you lack, General McClernand. He has the nose to scare up a battle and the will to fight." Grant decided against reciting Ord's military pedigree. The man had faced Seminoles, Mexicans, Indians in Oregon and Washington Territory, as well as Confederates at Bull Run and Ball's Bluff. However Ord dressed, he fought.

McClernand drew himself up. With a crisp tug he straightened the front of his tunic, aligning the gleaming brass buttons. "Having been appointed to this command by the President, I might challenge your authority to dismiss me, but I forbear to do so at present," he said coldly.

With that, he spun on his heel and left the tent.

# BESIEGED

Night and day, hour upon hour, the air rang with the sound of picks and spades digging away at the red clay surrounding Vicksburg. In the nearby forest, axes added their note as tree after tree fell to supply wooden planking and logs for the Union trenches. Ditching, supporting, and entrenching replaced marching, foraging, and direct assault.

Little coaxing was required to turn infantrymen into would-be engineers. The stench of their still unburied comrades rotting before the Confederate earthworks was all that was needed to convince the foot soldier of the wisdom of this new direction. The occasional doubting Thomas had only to raise his head above the parapet to see his friends sprawled in grotesque forms of death and bloating in the hot sun. Within a second, minié balls whizzed past the reckless viewer. But there was no need to look. The air reeked with the stomach-churning stench of rotting meat.

Wherever the Federals dug, the defenders of Vicksburg posted sharpshooters. Exposing oneself, even for an instant, meant almost certain death. Rarely was the distance more than a few hundred yards, and often as close as a few feet. Where cannons could not be depressed enough to fire on the trench, the rebels devised another use for their artillery shells. Lighting the fuses, they rolled the sputtering shells down the slopes at their besiegers. Then a race with death would galvanize the attackers to cut the fuse before it ignited the shot or to roll it back up toward its owners. Explosions flashed throughout the night as hand grenades exploded along the line.

The Union troops countered with sharpshooters of their own and piled logs on top of their parapets so that men could pass without crawling. Slabs of wood thick enough to stop a rifle bullet roofed especially exposed trenches.

Around the clock the deadly business continued as Grant's men inched closer and closer, zigzagging their lines ever nearer, and creeping forward behind the protection of sap-rollers, bales of cotton, and barrels filled with dirt wired together rolled ahead of the diggers. Men on both sides taunted and joked with their foe as they moved within speaking distance. Hungry Confederates took respite from hurling bombs and threw plugs of tobacco in exchange for hardtack tossed back.

Even the cannonade grew familiar. A rebel eighteen-pounder with a rifled barrel earned the name of "Whistling Dick" because of the eerie, high-pitched shriek it imparted to its spinning cannonballs. For their part, the Federals devised the Coehorn mortar, a short section of a gum tree, strengthened with iron hoops and bored out to fit a six- or twelve-pound shell. These crude mortars proved quick and easy to build and capable of lobbing their shell over the parapet into the rebel trenches.

Everywhere along the tightening noose of trenches, Grant prowled. Inciting, encouraging, and prodding his men, Grant worked equally hard to keep his battle face. For all its deadly work, laying siege held little charm for him. He missed the spontaneity, the uncertainty, and the need for improvisation of a fluid battle. Each day as his forces ground down the trapped Pemberton, the tasks of supplying his own men ground down Grant. The task of writing the endless lists for equipment, rations, munitions, and troop dispositions he bore alone, sharing little of his burden with his small staff of less than a dozen officers.

But from the very beginning, he realized his need for engineering help. Unlike Lee, experienced in the Engineering Corps, Grant's experience in the Mexican War was in artillery. For this reason he issued a call to all graduates of West Point under his command. This morning, one such graduate stood before him.

"Good morning, sir." The chief quartermaster officer saluted.

Grant poured the dregs of his cup of coffee onto the ground and motioned the young officer toward a log that served as a side bench. Behind him, Grant could hear the hacking, consumptive cough of John Rawlins, hovering about inside Grant's tent under the pretense of copying some orders.

Grant turned his attention back to the heavyset officer standing before him. "As you know, this siege requires engineering skills. My command has only four officers of the Engineering Corps. Captain Prime is the chief engineer. He started the overall direction of this siege, but his health has given out, and I have relieved him for medical cause. Captain Comstock is now in charge, but he sorely needs trained assistants."

"But I am a commissary officer," the man protested.

"You are a graduate of the academy, and as such had to study engineering."

The man shifted his bulk on the log. "It embarrasses me to state that engineering was one of my weakest subjects, sir."

Grant smiled sympathetically. "Not one of my best classes, either. Had I known what lay ahead for me I might have applied myself to my engineering lessons with greater diligence."

"My thoughts exactly, General." The man rose slowly to his feet. His face bore the grim acceptance of a convicted man standing before the hangman's scaffold. "Nevertheless, I will not be called a slacker. I will do as you wish, working on the trenches in addition to my regular duties. But truthfully, sir, there is nothing along this line that I would be good for except perhaps to be a sap-roller."

Grant studied the officer. The man was far from tall, and quite heavy. He is a good advertisement for our commissary, Grant thought. No one would accuse him of missing meal call. The general tried to picture the officer pushing wired bales of cotton ahead of him as men dug behind and bullets thudded into the bales. Most of the officer would extend beyond the rolling barricade.

"How much do you weigh, may I ask?"

"Two hundred and twenty pounds, General."

Grant sighed. "I am afraid even our largest sap-roller would not afford you adequate protection from the rebel sharpshooters' rifles. You would only get yourself killed, and I would be short a fine commissary officer. As the men need to eat in order to fight, I could not afford to lose you. Therefore, you are excused from adding your, ah ... limited engineering skills."

"Thank you, sir." The officer saluted and lumbered happily back to his duties.

Rawlins emerged from Grant's tent to watch the retiring officer. "That was very kind of you, General," he said.

Grant lighted a cigar. "Kindness has nothing to do with it. The man would stick out all over his sap-roller. He wouldn't last more than five minutes before he was shot. Then I would be short an inefficient sap-roller as well as my best commissary officer," he said gruffly.

"Nevertheless, it was kind of you," Rawlins replied. "I understand he has a wife and two young children back home." He deposited a sheaf of orders beside Grant and disappeared inside the tent.

Grant eyed the papers as he would a nest of vipers. More papers! Orders, dispositions, correspondence; I'm turning into a damned clerk, he fumed. He rose and stood puffing away furiously while he studied the idyllic setting around his camp. Five miles back from the front lines, little evidence of war met his eye. The hawthorn and crab-apple trees scattered their petals in the light breeze amid flitting birds. Overhead, white clouds dotted the intensely blue sky. Only the constant thunder of the distant artillery duels and the crack of musket fire betrayed the grueling siege that he commanded.

The peaceful surroundings only aggravated Grant's restlessness. He found his hat under the pile of papers and stuffed it on his head. Trailing a cloud of smoke, he stomped off toward the river. Rawlins raised the tent flap, found Grant gone, and hurriedly set off in search of his charge.

Less than a mile from the landing, Rawlins found Grant watching a caravan of over a hundred escaped slaves rolling unevenly into the edge of the camp. Carts, wagons, and carriages of all description jostled and rocked over the raw road cut for the purpose of moving supplies from the Yazoo.

On both sides of the road, soldiers lounged on their rifles and watched the circus.

Men, women, and children of all ages rode or stumbled along the trail. Some were singing, others moaning, but most shuffled along, staring silently at the armed soldiers with wide, frightened eyes. Grant marveled at the variety of dress the contraband wore. Field workers limped along in tattered rags and cobbled scraps of cloth that barely covered their bodies, while escaped house servants arrived in brocade jackets with ruffled collars, silk hose, and silver-buckled shoes.

Fine polished carriages with matching horses shouldered alongside ox carts and hand-pulled vegetable trucks. Furniture, feather beds, ornate cabinets, and finely carved furniture of all kinds filled the wagons. A ragged escapee passed with an oval mirror within a gilded frame strapped to his back. Behind him walked two small boys, each lugging a silver candelabra.

"Do you suppose they stole all this?" Grant asked Rawlins.

"Some did, no doubt. I suspect the surrounding owners abandoned their plantations with its furnishings and slaves when they fled into Vicksburg for protection. These liberated contraband simply took whatever they thought might be useful to trade for food or shelter," the former lawyer replied tactfully. He knew that a few arrived boasting they had forced their masters to part with their riches, but those were the exception. Their scrambling owners had left most to fend for themselves. "You'll notice the lack of foodstuffs and provisions—no pigs, cattle, or ducks. Only a few have a chicken or two. Probably the owners and rebel soldiers took all useful supplies into the city."

Grant stroked his beard. "Every day more and more arrive. They fill the camps and clog the roads. It is a vexing problem. They must be fed and sheltered, but simply to do so without allowing them opportunity to earn their keep continues their status as property and not as liberated persons."

Rawlins shrugged. "Their status is not at all clear. They are not legally freed persons, rather they are abandoned, and yet they have come to us for help. Not a single one of their former owners appears willing to leave Vicksburg to lay claim to them."

Grant considered the issue for a minute before making his decision.

"Rawlins, we will employ them. Treat them as free, entitled to wages for their labor. Issue orders to hire the able-bodied. They can earn their way and relieve the soldiers of camp duties. We can use their help in digging our fortifications, building revetments, and hauling provisions. The women can sew, and cook, and do laundry. Make certain they receive a decent wage for their efforts. Since our friend the chief commissary officer has been spared as a sap-roller, he can handle their employment."

"Shall we pay them in Confederate script?" Rawlins asked mischievously. "We have plenty at hand, and it would place no strain on our paymaster."

"No. Greenbacks or U.S. coin," Grant cautioned. "I am sure Father Abraham would want no less and will sanction the added expense."

A guard party marched along the outside of the river of contraband with a recently captured prisoner. The man looked tired and ill fed. The sole of one boot flopped loosely from broken stitching, and his knees protruded from torn trousers. The sergeant in charge approached the officers and grounded his musket smartly. Grant recognized the collar insignia of the Eighth Missouri, attached to Sherman's 15th Corps. Raised from a border state, these men fought courageously, often against their own neighbors and friends.

"What have you here, Sergeant?" Grant asked.

"A Johnny we caught making out of Vicksburg with a message for Old Joe Johnston," the soldier proclaimed proudly. Opening his cartridge box, he removed a letter and handed it to Grant. "He never made it past our rear lines."

The captured man spit on the ground, disrespectfully close to the officers' boots. "Shoot, if'n they'd give me a decent horse, you Yanks'd never caught me in a month of Sundays." He glared defiantly at Grant. "Yer boys had to shoot my animal out from under me as it is."

"You're lucky we didn't shoot you, reb," the sergeant growled.

"Well then, Yank, you done us both a favor. We was going to eat that old bag of bones tomorrow, anyhow. He probably appreciated dying a hero rather than a ration."

Grant opened the letter and read its contents. He handed it to Rawlins. "More of the same. Johnston has crossed the Big Black to support a breakout by Pemberton. Joe has no expectations of holding Vicksburg or attempting to liberate it. He urges Pemberton to leave at once."

"I certainly hope Pemberton tries that," Rawlins said as he rubbed his hands together.

"Pemberton won't," the rebel interjected. "Most of our men would rather die inside yer trap than skedaddle. We'd never be able to face our neighbors and kinfolk if we run away and left them to you."

Grant reached inside his coat pocket and withdrew a bundle of cigars. He handed one to the sergeant and each member of his detail. As an afterthought he gave one to the prisoner. Rawlins supplied the matches, and within minutes all present were puffing away like old acquaintances.

"Say, what are they feeding you boys?" Rawlins asked in a conversational tone. Rumors from the escaped contraband told of dire shortages of food.

"Well, it ain't no secret," the man sighed as he exhaled his smoke. "We're on half rations. Mostly we got a quarter pound of bacon, half pound of beef, and a measure of cornmeal. Sometimes we git some peas and rice, sometimes not. Sometimes molasses or sugar for our chicory."

"Half rations?" Rawlins replied, trying not to show too much interest.

The prisoner nodded. "I prefer to eat all my rations at once and skip the next day. At least that way I git one good meal out of the bargain. Besides, the way your artillery is pounding away at us, I could git myself blowed up before the next meal call. I'd surely hate to die with un-et food in my haversack."

"A wise decision," Grant agreed.

Warmed by these friendly officers, the captured soldier grew loquacious. "We're better off than the civilians, I have to admit. We're soldiers, so we're used to living in holes and missing our feed. Most of them are starving. I ain't seen a mule nor a horse belonging to the townfolk in some time. They all been et. General Pemberton has detailed guards to keep watch on the army's storehouses. The womenfolk are mixing field peas and tree buds with their cornmeal to stretch it out a bit. Folks are eating rats when they can catch them."

"He had another note on him, General," the sergeant said. "I thought it was a joke or something at first, but this reb says it's serious." He retrieved another crumpled scrap.

"A fellow in my company gave that to me. He said in case I got caught to give it to one of you Yanks."

Rawlins unrolled the paper and studied the scratchy handwriting before reading aloud. " 'We are pretty hungry and dreadful dry. Old Pemberton has taken all our whiskey for the hospitals and our Southern Confederacy is so small just now we are not in the manufacturing business. Give our compliments to Gen. Grant and say to him that grub would be acceptable, but we will feel under particular obligations if he will send us a few bottles of good whiskey.' "

Grant smiled, but Rawlins clenched his jaw. Every mention of liquor in Grant's presence set the adjutant's teeth on edge. He knew Grant was chafing at the bit with this siege.

The Confederate expanded on the note. "By and large what whiskey any of us had, well, that's gone by the way, even in the hospital. One of your shells blew the corner off the hospital and with it all the alcohol and drugs. Blew off one of the surgeon's legs in the bargain. I guess now that doc will know how many of my friends feel minus one of their pins."

"That was never our intention, to shell the hospital," Grant said. "My artillery officers have orders not to fire on that building, but shells often go astray."

"Mistakes is made—on all sides, General."

"Are you still getting beef as your meat?" Rawlins asked.

"Not no more. Major Gillespie, he's in charge of feeding us, issued an order three days ago that the meat ration would be half pound of mule. The boys don't much enjoy it. Not horse, neither. Only the fellows of that Louisiana brigade takes to it. They like small deer and rats, too. 'Course, most of them is French."

The prisoner stopped and looked back in the direction of Vicksburg. The rolling thunder of the constant barrage from the land and the river grew louder. He looked down at his worn shoes. "I ain't too sorry to be caught," he admitted. "Most of us is living just like the rats themselves, in hollowed-out caves. I was a farmer before all this started. The sun started my day and the sun ended it. I don't much cotton to living underground and not seeing the sun." He looked earnestly at Grant. "General, what's going to happen to me now?"

"You'll be held until you're exchanged or paroled. First, you will receive a decent meal. My men don't eat rat."

The man saluted Grant. "I am much obliged. If you turn me loose, I think I'll just go back to my little farm. It ain't much, just a few acres of bottomland where Bayou Pierre touches Keller's Creek below Pine Bluff, but it's all I got to feed me and my family. I'd be mighty late for planting as it is."

Grant studied the man. He appeared worn-out. "That might be best," he said.

The prisoner nodded. "I reckon I seen my share of glory, and it ain't worth much," he said slowly.

Rawlins waited while the detail led their captive away, then he and Grant began to walk as well. "Pemberton is desperately short of percussion caps along with rations," the adjutant said. "The boys found hollowed-out logs filled with caps that rebs across the river tried to float over to Vicksburg. We also intercepted six men attempting to cross the swamps with a supply of caps. Each man carried ten-thousand percussion caps."

"Percussion caps?" Grant echoed.

Rawlins nodded. "Would you believe a boy of ten was acting as their guide? The lad had the cheek to say he didn't think we'd hurt him, as he was so little. Well, the men gave him a good strapping."

Grant stopped their stroll and watched as a dozen somber, black-coated men carrying Bibles in their hands crossed the road with little interest in the sea of contrabands they parted.

"The Sanitary and Christian Commission," Rawlins said, answering Grant's unspoken question. "Since the roads are open, visitors of all nature arrive on the hour. The commission has brought food, blankets, and medical supplies. Believe it or not, we also have a singing concert scheduled tonight—the famous Lombard Brothers, Frank and Julius, from Chicago. I have arranged for front row seats for you, General." Rawlins hoped the show might distract Grant for the moment and provide him with some diversion.

Grant scratched his beard. "Not for me, thank you. I'm sure the men will enjoy the singing, but I have no ear for music." He patted the crestfallen Rawlins's arm. "I only know two tunes, Rawlins. One is Yankee Doodle and the other isn't."

Grant turned and walked back briskly to his headquarters. He found Kangaroo saddled and tied to a nearby tree. Grant swung into the saddle. "Stay here, Rawlins, in case Sherman sends me further news of Johnston. His cavalry is scouting along the Big Black in search of Johnston. I am off to McPherson's sector."

"Do you expect an attack there?" Rawlins asked anxiously.

"No. I want to look at the mine General Ransom is digging near the Jackson Road. If we can explode it and advance into the breach, we can beat Johnston to the punch. I worry most about what that man might do. He is the most able commander in this theater and ought never to be underestimated."

Grant cantered off, happy to be moving even if only for a few miles. Along the road, men stood or waved as he passed. To these he nodded curtly, all business. Grant did not realize it, but the image his men held of him was just that: Grant, the no-nonsense businessman of war; Grant, the hammer, without frills without flourish, "Unconditional Surrender" Grant, who got the job done.

"Why, General Grant!" Brigadier General Thomas E.G. Ransom appeared at the tunnel entrance and blinked at the bright sunlight. "Welcome to Mine Ransom, General. This is, indeed, an unexpected surprise." He straightened his back, brushed dirt from his shirt, and pulled his braces up while he searched about for his tunic. Powdered red clay lined Ransom's youthful face. His dark eyes stared out from the clay mask, and powdery dust coated his bushy muttonchops, making him appear older than he was. Unable to find his coat, Ransom judged it improper to salute in his state of undress, so he extended his hand.

Grant shook hands. Despite his youth, Ransom's straight nose, broad forehead, and clenched lips revealed his fierce drive and determination. He was one of Grant's best officers, always ready to undertake an expedition or face a new challenge.

Grant looked up at the imposing fort. Every attempt to take it had failed. Cannons from here, along with "Whistling Dick," had so battered the *Cincinnati* as it passed downriver that the gunboat sank.

Ransom read Grant's mind. "Fort Hill. The boys have dubbed it 'Fort Hell.' She's a sharp thorn in our side. Did you know Colonel Andrew Jackson, Jr. of the First Tennessee Artillery commands its guns? With Andy Jackson's kin in charge, it is no wonder Fort Hill is such a tough nut to crack."

Grant stroked his beard. "Yes, I've heard that." Secretly, he hoped the colonel would be away at the appointed time. Blowing up a descendant of the seventh President of the United States bothered him.

"What progress have you made, Thomas?" Grant asked as he crawled into the narrow trench.

Less than twenty feet in front stood the enemy's parapet, looming over the trench like a brooding giant. Only the piled logs and timbers erected about the rim of their excavation hid them from view and shielded the miners from sniper fire. A sputtering grenade rolled down the steep glacis, bounced over the wooden roof, and landed close to Grant's feet. A Union sharpshooter who had been watching the officers nonchalantly reached down, picked up the smoking bomb, and hurled it back over the Confederate walls. A muffled explosion followed shortly after.

"Most excellent progress, sir." Ransom beamed. "We have undermined their fortification and the mine is charged."

Grant peered into the dark hole, only to see pairs of eyes blinking back at him. "Can you give me the specifics?" he asked.

"Major Hickenlooper would be most happy to explain in detail."

Ransom moved aside to allow another head to emerge into the light. Hickenlooper grinned, showing even white teeth in his blackened face. No general of Grant's rank had ever visited their work, let alone expressed an interest in the details of digging a mine. They simply ordered one and forgot about the backbreaking effort mining required.

Hickenlooper, who believed mines to be an important facet of any siege, often felt ignored and snubbed. For Grant to ask was a dream come true. Before he was halfway out of the tunnel, he began his lecture.

"Well, General, we've been working in one-hour shifts. Two men picking up front, two men shoveling the loose clay into grain sacks, and two men handing back the earth-filled sacks. The heat tires a man, so after an hour he must be relieved. We started this drift some ways back so that it is quite deep where it lies underneath their fortifications. The drift is usually three and one-half feet high and two and one-half feet wide. The main galley is forty-five feet long, with secondary galleries branching off at forty-five-degree angles. Ever so often I probe the ground ahead and under us with this." A dirty hand held out a long iron rod. "I use this rod to look for countermines. If they dig a tunnel under us, we'd have to abandon this mine."

"Any evidence of that?" Grant asked.

"Oh, they're digging all right, looking for us. They know we're tunneling. They can hear us, just as we hear them, but so far they haven't found us. It was my idea to start this drift a ways back so that it's much deeper under their barricade than they suspect. The rebs are above us, and they don't know it. They think they are below us." He handed the rod back. "They fired off a countermine this morning. It missed us, but I'm ashamed to admit it frightened my boys away for several hours. But it's only a matter of time, General."

"McPherson tells me the charges have been laid."

"Yes, sir," Ransom answered. "Explosives laid and fuses cut. Twenty-two hundred pounds of powder supplied by the navy, eight hundred pounds in the main gallery and seven hundred in each of the two lateral tunnels. We had to dodge the rebs' cannon as we brought the powder up. Twenty-five pounds at a time. We'd time the interval between shells and make a dash with the powder. I'm proud to say I didn't lose a single man or a bag of powder. The explosives are all in place. She's ready to go."

Hickenlooper nodded excitedly. "I've personally laid the fuses in double strands to cover the possible contingency of one failing to burn at the proper speed. All it needs now is your say-so, General." The major hoped Grant sensed his urgency. That last attempt by the enemy came very close. Their next try might prove right on the money. Hickenlooper hated to think of all his work going for naught.

"Good. You will explode the mine at three o'clock today. I will order a heavy artillery barrage to accompany the explosion. General Logan will move his troops into position to take advantage of the breach. I talked to him on my way here. He has ten men picked from the pioneer corps ready to go forward first to clear any obstacles. The 31st and 45th Illinois and the 23rd Indiana will charge after them into the breach."

"Wonderful!" Ransom rubbed his hands together in expectation. "It should be quite a show."

An hour and a half before the appointed time, Grant and his staff, shadowed by their faithful reporters, rode to a ridge where they could watch. General McPherson sat his mount alongside Grant. General Logan, whose Indiana and Illinois regiments waited to attack, stood beside them with his field glasses pressed to his eyes.

Grant chewed his cigar and waited. He refused to look at his timepiece. It seemed to him unnecessary, as the men around him fidgeted with their pocket watches at five-minute intervals. Finally, he judged the hour close, as every one of his staff stopped talking and turned their eyes toward the cone-shaped rise in the land called Fort Hill.

"Three o'clock." McPherson snapped his watch face closed and turned to say more.

He stopped short as the ground beneath their feet jolted like an earthquake. His horse reared and crashed into Kangaroo. Grant controlled his mount easily, but several of his staff struggled to stay in their saddles as their frightened horses bucked and kicked wildly.

An eerie silence followed, filling the air for half a second. Then a muffled roar rose from the ground itself, followed by a deep crash that struck the men with sudden force. Grant stared at the fort.

The hill grew, bulging toward the sky. Vast sections of dirt broke loose from the smooth contour and flew into the air in all directions. A crimson tongue of flame shot upward from the broken center like a massive flare and then quickly vanished. The masses of flying dirt shattered into smaller and smaller pieces until only a cloud of dust and dirt billowed over the hill.

The cloud of soil settled, to be followed by sudden flashes as bag after bag of powder exploded. Plumes of smoke spiraled from deep rents in the ground. Then the hill collapsed on itself, sinking lower beneath the horizon, until a wide crater replaced the fort.

Grant's eye followed the thick cloud. It appeared to be dropping dark objects of various shapes. He looked closely. Planks, cannon, canvas from shelters, and bodies of men rained in all directions. He bent his head down as dirt and splinters showered him.

Twenty yards ahead a tattered Negro slave fell to earth at the feet of an astonished staff lieutenant. The soldier rushed to the man's side. He shouted back to General Logan, "My God, General, the man is still alive!"

"Bring him here," Logan commanded.

Two soldiers half dragged the trembling slave. They held him by his shoulders as the lieutenant checked for wounds. The man shivered, blinked his eyes, and struggled to comprehend what had happened. A moment before, as a slave to a citizen of Mississippi, he had been digging in the countermine. Now he was contraband, captured Confederate goods, in care of the Federal Army.

"Are you hurt?" Logan asked.

The man shook his head.

"How high did you go up?" Logan questioned.

The man swallowed hard. "I don't know, massa," he answered, "but I think about three miles."

Logan laughed. "Take him to my quarters. I will employ his services, for he is remarkably fortunate today."

A loud roar, coming this time from men's throats, called their attention back to the crater. The men of the Indiana and Illinois regiments rushed into the gap. Their blue battle flags advanced into the crater and climbed the mountain of dirt thrown up by the mine. Behind that waited the hurriedly assembled line of rebel soldiers.

A volley of musket fire met the attackers. The flags wavered and dipped under the hail of bullets, then with a cheer that reached back to where Grant waited, the sea of blue charged over the ridge.

McPherson stood in his stirrups and waved his hat. "Go at them, boys! Go at them!" he yelled.

His men appeared to hear, for they continued their headlong rush. Without warning the ground ahead of them erupted in smoke and flame. Canister and grapeshot cut great holes in the blue line. The charge wavered, came to a halt in the face of this intense cannonade. Then the line fell back into the crater to escape the shells.

General Logan stared through his glasses. "My God, the rebels have constructed a second line of breastworks behind their fort!" he cried. "They have concentrated their cannon there."

"They must have suspected we would explode our mine, and prepared a fallback position in case their countermining failed to stop us," McPherson noted grimly. "If our boys cannot take that second line, they will be caught in the crater like fish in a barrel."

Grant leaned forward in his saddle. Already, a counterattack of gray boiled over the rim, only to be met by men wearing blue. The figures grappled and fell in deadly hand-to-hand fighting. Grant watched as a rebel colonel sprang onto the rim, shouting and waving his sword. A dozen Union rifles fired at once, hurling the officer backward in a cloud of blood and tattered cloth.

Secondary flashes and puffs of dirty smoke sprang up along the rim and inside the bowl as both sides resorted to hurling hand grenades. Larger concussions reached their ears as Confederates rolled lighted shells over the rim. Desperate Union soldiers carried these back to the rim under heavy rifle fire. Some succeeded. Others vanished as the shell exploded.

As the battle inside the crater chewed up unit after unit, fresh companies poured into the caldron. Wounded and exhausted, those who survived dragged their weary bodies back to safety, still holding their broken and fouled muskets. Hour after hour passed. The fury of the battle sucked more men into the pit.

Grant winced as the smoke cleared enough to disclose the once proud blue battle flags. Fluttering on the fractured parapet of the fort, little remained of the colors but tattered bits of smoking blue cloth. Grape and shot had reduced them to unrecognizable scraps.

General Logan watched ten men drag an enormous cypress log a good fifteen inches in diameter up to the crater from the Union trenches. Bullets kicked up dust and dirt around the men as they rolled the log over the rim. Inside the bowl, the soldiers struggled in the crumbling earth to push the timber up the other side. As one soldier after another fell, a new man took his place. Chinks cut from the undersurface notched the entire length of the log. Placed lengthwise along the lip of the pit, it would provide cover for riflemen. Just as the soldiers got their makeshift barricade into position, a cannonball hit the log squarely, hurling it back into the crater and decapitating the men behind it.

General Logan tore his glasses from his tear-filled eyes. He turned away, unable to watch anymore. "My God! They are killing my bravest men in that hole!" he wept.

McPherson shook his head. "It is all for naught. We have destroyed only a portion of the fort. The rebels have simply moved their line back beyond where our mine exploded and constructed a second breastworks. Their cannon fire not only confronts us at point-blank range, but the rest of their works may very well enfilade our line." He paused to watch a handful of his men pushing a howitzer into the crater. As they struggled to drag the gun up the other side, the wheels mired down in the pulverized dirt and sank up to their hubs. A fusillade of rifle fire raked the artillerymen, leaving their bodies strewn about the useless cannon. "We have not even planted a battery on that cursed rim," he said in disgust.

Grant sensed danger in their failure. He withdrew his dispatch books and wrote hurriedly. He handed his orders to an orderly. "Take these to General Ord and to General Steele."

"General Steele, sir?" the courier looked confused.

"Yes, he is currently commanding that portion of 15th Corps entrenched along the north of the cemetery road while General Sherman is maneuvering along the Big Black River."

"Yessir." The orderly touched his cap and galloped off.

Grant saw the puzzled look of his generals and explained. "Our failure to break the enemy's line with our mine has weakened this section, General McPherson. The enemy may concentrate on this weakness and force a breakout to reach Johnston. I don't want that to happen, so I have ordered Steele and Ord to intensify their attacks on the breastworks facing them, to take the pressure off of this area."

Grant waited until he saw recognition in their faces before he turned his horse back toward his headquarters. He rode along, avoiding the stares of his men. More of them would die or be maimed because of today's failure. They peered at him silently from the caves and holes in the ground they had dug for protection from the Confederate shelling. Not a single tent flapped within range of the enemy guns. Thousands of burrows honeycombed the front instead. His army had vanished underground like moles.

# A SERIOUS TOOT

Two weeks after the fiasco of the exploding mine, a small steamboat thrashed around the river's bend, reduced speed, and altered course to intercept the *Diligence*. A handful of Union soldiers wearing the long curved sabers and gold flashing of cavalry lounged along the foredeck. As the two vessels approached within shouting distance, General Grant appeared at the port rail and hailed the other steamer.

"Ahoy, *Diligence*," he shouted, slurring his words. "Is Captain McDougall in command?" Grant swayed and hung on to the railing as the wash from both vessels rocked his ship.

Captain Harry McDougall, formerly of Louisville, Kentucky, appeared at the pilothouse. He hurried down to the main deck when he saw who hailed him. With a smart salute, he greeted his department commander.

"Yes, sir, General Grant. I am here," McDougall called back with his megaphone. Since his boat was traveling downriver toward Vicksburg, he expected Grant to ask him to carry a message back to the Union lines. "What are your orders, sir?"

Grant wobbled slightly, but this time there was no wake. "Captain McDougall, I wish to come on board with Captain Osband and my cavalry escort."

"Sir? Are you turning back?"

"No." Grant shook his head. His hat, usually firmly placed on his head, flew off and landed on the deck. Grant stooped to retrieve it. He appeared above the railing a moment later with his slouch hat firmly back in place. "You will turn about and head back upstream. I wish to go *upstream* on your vessel."

A voice behind McDougall complained. "We have just been upriver to Satartia and are heading downriver."

McDougall turned to face Sylvanus Cadwallader. "That may well be so, Mr. Cadwallader. You and I have just been to Satartia, but General Grant has not. He is my commander, and I must follow his orders. If he desires to go upstream, we will go back upriver. The *Diligence* will take on the general and his escort and turn around. You may disembark if you wish."

Grant staggered, again, and clutched the rail with both hands.

"By God, is he drunk?" Cadwallader whispered. He looked closely at the figure on the other ship. Nothing in Grant's dress appeared unusual. His private's coat with its shoulder straps sewn on looked as rumpled and soiled as ever. The carelessly knotted tie, stained shirt, and mud-spattered boots he wore constituted his routine attire. Only his speech and loose-jointed movement caught Cadwallader's attention. For all his disregard for dress, Grant's movements and speech were always clipped, sparse, and to the point. Even the night Grant had filched those cups of whiskey in their tent, he remained in rigid control. Cadwallader had never seen Grant like this before.

"Drunk or sober," the nervous captain said, "we will obey his orders."

The ships' crew tossed lines and grappled their vessels together while the pilots kept the paddle wheels turning sufficiently to keep their ships in midstream. Grant staggered on board and pushed past Cadwallader. He disappeared down the steps into the bar room. As the *Diligence* was a commercial steamboat just recently appropriated by the army, her saloon still contained a well-stocked bar.

Cadwallader watched as the cavalry escort transferred their horses and the two ships parted company. With foreboding, he headed in the direction of the saloon. Pausing outside the etched-glass windows of the doors, he watched Grant down three full glasses of whiskey. Standing in the corner of the room, the reporter saw Lieutenant Towner, whom he recognized from Chicago.

Cadwallader entered and slipped past Grant, who leaned heavily on the bar contemplating his tumbler, his back turned to the saloon. While the general muttered incoherently, the journalist scurried to Towner's corner.

"Towner, you must get the general to stop his drinking," Cadwallader urged. "He is intoxicated beyond ability to carry out his duties!"

The officer swallowed nervously while he cast anxious glances at his general's back.

Cadwallader stepped in front of the lieutenant, blocking his view of Grant. "He can hardly stand, let alone speak. If unfriendly eyes see him like this, he will be ruined. Can you imagine what friends of General McClernand might do with this information? Grant will be removed, and the siege of Vicksburg will fall apart."

Lieutenant Towner blinked at Cadwallader in terror. "What can I do, Mr. Cadwallader? I am only a junior officer acting as aide-de-camp."

"You must stop him!"

Towner shook his head. "If I interfere, the general might resent it. When he becomes sober, he will remember what I did. Then what would become of me? He would surely punish me."

The door opened and Captain McDougall entered. He approached Grant cautiously, hoping for further orders; but upon seeing his commander's condition, he retreated to the far corner of the room to join Cadwallader and the cowering Towner.

"In Heaven's name, Captain," Cadwallader pleaded. "Do something to stop General Grant's drinking. Surely, you command this vessel and have some say."

McDougall watched the general dispose of two more glasses of whiskey. He turned back to Cadwallader and shrugged grimly. "This ship is under the command of the Department of the Tennessee. General Grant is commander of that department. Therefore, he has the full power to do what he pleases with this boat and whatever it contains. I cannot order him to stop."

Cadwallader shook his fist in McDougall's face. "You will close this bar at once," the reporter ordered, "or I will see to it that you are clapped in irons the very moment I return to headquarters! Your inaction is shameful and disgraceful."

McDougall scoffed. "Who would you report me to? Grant outranks everyone."

"Colonel Rawlins!" Cadwallader hissed. "You must be aware of how vindictive Rawlins acts to anyone indulging the general's weakness. The last man who Colonel Rawlins caught offering the general a drink was strung up by his thumbs."

The captain blanched. "Yes, yes, I heard of that." He glanced back and forth from Towner to Cadwallader. The snarl on the reporter's lips demonstrated his resolve. McDougall could picture himself in irons. He sighed deeply. "All right. But what can we do?"

Cadwallader had already thought of that. Grant by now was stupefied, mumbling incoherently and draped over the bar for support. "I will help the general to his room. After we leave, lock this room. You do have the key, don't you?"

McDougall searched inside his pocket and withdrew a large key ring heavy with brass keys. "Yes. Here it is."

"Good. Lock the bar room as soon as we leave. And for God's sakes, man, lose the key until the general is off the vessel!"

Cadwallader moved to Grant's side and slipped his arm around the general's waist. The reporter judged the little man to weigh less than half what he himself did. He easily lifted him off the bar and turned him in the direction of the exit. Grant looked up, bleary-eyed, as Cadwallader half carried him out the door of the saloon and aft to his cabin. Grant said nothing during his removal. Once inside the cabin, the newspaperman placed Grant on his bunk and locked the door. With his back to Grant, Cadwallader slipped the key into his waistcoat.

To his dismay, the small table beside the bunk held five bottles of whiskey. Cadwallader opened the one small window and pitched a bottle through the opening and over the railing. The bottle hit the water with a splash. A cry arose from the cavalrymen on deck at this waste. Ignoring them, Cadwallader quickly threw the remaining bottles over the side.

Grant awoke with a start. "What the devil are you doing?" he demanded. "That's good whiskey you're tossing."

"You have had enough, General. This is for your own good."

"What the hell do you know about that? What do you know about a siege, or an army corps, or even a company for that matter?" Grant swore. He sat upright, propped on his elbows and glared at Cadwallader. "I didn't give you permission to be in here. Get out of my room!"

"No. I will not. I am staying until you recover some of your sense. Someone must watch you, General."

"Then let me out. Unlock that door. I need a drink!"

"The door is locked," Cadwallader said with a note of finality. "The key is missing."

"Damned lot of nonsense with keys on this boat. I heard what you whispered to McDougall about hiding his keys. Unlock this door and get out, now!" Grant swung his feet onto the deck with a heavy thump. He braced his arms on the cot.

Cadwallader moved to the louvered door, folded his arms over his ample girth and stood with his back pressed against it. His bulk blocked the entrance like a cork tightly wedged into a bottle. "General Grant," he began, "it is no secret that I work for a paper that many would call a copperhead rag. My editor would delight in printing a story of you in your present condition. He and many others would be happy to see you relieved of command for being drunk."

Grant swayed on the edge of his bunk. "What do they know about running an army ... the heavy responsibility ... all those men killed by my mistakes.... It's too heavy ... too much for any man...." His voice trailed off as he stared at his muddied boots.

Cadwallader looked down at the little man. Save for the gold stars on his shoulder straps, he might be a bum on Chicago's Skid Row. But here was no wino, but a general of rare talents who understood the changing nature of this terrible conflict.

No matter that the differences between North and South were so vast—the Union must be preserved; and Cadwallader sensed only Grant could win the war for the North. No one else but this drunken little man held the key to victory.

Cadwallader realized he must protect Grant. It was a concept he had been backing into since he first met the little general and found him unlike any of the malicious stories circulating about him.

"General Grant," he said, "you may not believe it—" Cadwallader wiped the perspiration from his forehead with his pawlike hand. "And I am surprised myself when I realize it—but I am the best friend you have in the Army of the Tennessee." He straightened his shoulders and pulled down on his vest, feeling embarrassed by these events. "I have no ax to grind, no promotion to desire, nothing to gain from helping you, other than to see you successfully conclude the siege of Vicksburg. If you don't, so many lives and so much effort will have been for nothing."

Grant wiped his beard and studied this impediment to his finding another drink.

"You have drunk more than is prudent today," the reporter continued, pacing now about the small cabin. "God knows you are entitled to do so, yet you are no ordinary man. You command a great army, and that army needs your guiding hand. So, say what you like, I will not let you out of this room until you are sober." With that the reporter backed against the cabin door again and set his feet in a wide stance.

Grant studied Cadwallader. "I suppose you are too big for me to wrastle," he said resignedly. "It is so hot in this cabin. Cannot I go on deck for some fresh air?"

Cadwallader shook his head. "No, General, but I can improve your situation." He removed Grant's coat, vest, and boots, and picked up Grant's dispatch book from the bed. As he fanned the general, Grant sank back onto the cot and fell asleep.

Only an hour or two passed before a knock on the cabin door awakened Grant. "General," a voice called out, "we have reached Satartia."

Grant sat upright, wiped his hand across his mouth, and rocked into a sitting position. He looked about for his boots and coat and began to dress himself. His right boot fell from his grasp onto the floor.

Cadwallader rose from the chair he had propped against the door. Obviously, Grant was still quite drunk. "General, where are you going?" he asked.

Grant squinted up at his guardian. "Tell Captain Osband to disembark my horse and my escort. I plan on riding back to my headquarters outside Vicksburg."

Cadwallader started. "General! Vicksburg is miles away and this land is still hostile country. Who knows what rebel troops or their sympathizers are about? Riding in the dark with so small an escort is dangerous."

Grant looked about tiredly. "I can't find my other boot," he said.

"Best get some more rest while the *Diligence* ties up until the moon has risen. Then she can steam downriver, perhaps to Haines' Bluff, if you'd like."

Grant wobbled his head in agreement. "Haines' Bluff, make for Haines' Bluff," he directed with a wave of his hand before he flopped back into his bunk with his left boot still on.

The moon came and went as the steamer churned the dark waters on its way downstream again. By early morning the landing at Haines' Bluff appeared as the ship rounded the bend. Within twenty minutes the vessel touched the dock and made fast. Cadwallader, Captain McDougall, Osband, and Lieutenant Towner lined the foredeck by the gangplank, waiting expectantly. To their amazement and relief, Grant emerged from his now unlocked cabin, fresh and alert and wearing a clean white shirt.

Grant lighted a cigar with steady hands and greeted them crisply. "Good morning, gentlemen, we are at Haynes Landing, are we not? Good. General Kimball's camp is close by. Osband, I want you to take six men and ride to Kimball's headquarters. Return with whatever news you can obtain. We will await your return before sailing down to Chickasaw Bayou."

Osband saluted and hurried off. Grant walked down the gangplank to the collection of shacks and sheds lining the water. Cadwallader watched him strolling among the buildings with his hat on the back of his head, his hands in his pockets, and puffing a trail of smoke. Relieved, the reporter returned to his own stateroom to wash his face.

An hour later the reporter lounged on the port railing sipping steaming coffee from a tin cup. A great heron stalking among the reeds at the river's edge caught his attention. Cadwallader watched as the bird slowly lowered its head until its long beak nearly touched the water. With a lightning thrust it impaled a small silvery fish. The drama ended, the reporter straightened and shifted his footing to look back at the landing. He choked on his coffee at what he saw.

Grant had returned from his stroll, obviously as drunk as the previous night. Wobbling up the plank with two large bottles of the home-brewed sour mash that the soldiers called "rifle head knock," he stopped in front of Cadwallader and the astonished McDougall. "Cast off as soon as Osband returns. Make for Chickasaw Landing."

"Yes, sir." McDougall saluted Grant's back. He waited until the general felt his way toward his cabin before staring at Cadwallader with wide eyes. "Mr. Cadwallader, Chickasaw Bayou is no more than five hours from here. We shall arrive at noon. At that time the landing will be filled with transport trains, officers of every rank, and companies of men. Everyone will see the general's condition. Nothing you or I do then can keep his binge a secret. We are lost, and so is he!"

Cadwallader seized the officer's arm. "Get hold of yourself, Captain! We must think of ways to delay our arrival until after dark."

"But how?"

Cadwallader scratched his head. A smile slowly spread across his face. "Green wood," he said.

"Green wood? Of course! We could let the boiler fires die out and say we got a load of green wood. It will take several hours to load dry wood from the landing and to relight the boilers." McDougall's burst of enthusiasm faded. He wrung his hands together in despair. "Even so, I fear even that subterfuge will not delay us sufficiently until nightfall."

The reporter clapped his own hands on the guardrail. For all his education, the captain showed little imagination. Cadwallader realized he must do all the scheming himself. "Find a sandbar to ground your vessel upon. It happens all the time, so General Grant will not suspect anything unusual."

"Am I to wreck my vessel, Mr. Cadwallader? I will surely lose my command if I sink the *Diligence*. I would do that if needed, but it will mean the end of my career."

"Nothing that drastic is needed, Captain," his coconspirator reassured him with a pat on the shoulder. "Find a good, safe sandbar, one with no rocks or deadheads to endanger your ship. A nice clean sandbar with a gradual slope will do nicely. Have your pilot and linesman keep a sharp lookout for one far enough from here and the bayou to be safely out of the way. Then reduce speed and gently nudge her onto the bar. We can play at how difficult it is to free the boat until dusk."

Their plan worked perfectly. Another day vanished before the *Diligence* drew alongside the landing at Chickasaw Bayou. The vessel slipped beside a larger, three-decked steamboat tied to the landing.

Cadwallader's heart stopped when he saw the ship. It was the headquarters steamer of "Wash" Graham, the chief sutler for Grant's army. To foster goodwill among those officers who ordered his supplies, Graham always kept an open bar, well stocked with cigars and liquor. No officer was ever charged for whatever he drank or smoked.

Before the general appeared, Cadwallader pushed his way past the milling guards, leapt to the dock, and boarded Graham's boat. He found the sutler directing the unloading of a pile of canvas tents.

Graham turned to greet the reporter. Graham's narrow face and sharp pointed nose and furtive eyes gave many the impression of a rodent endlessly searching for a piece of cheese. His habit of wiping his hands together added to that image. "Good evening, Sylvanus, would you care to purchase a thousand good canvas tents? I'll give you a good price. Just my luck that Grant's army surrounding Vicksburg prefers to live in holes in the ground rather than use my tents."

Cadwallader studied the sutler's beady eyes. "You would burrow underground, too, Wash, if you faced the hellish cannonade his men experience daily from John Pemberton's twenty-pound Parrotts and Whitworths."

Graham shrugged. "That may well be, but I am a businessman, and I need to move these tents. Another month in this damned heat and humidity and the canvas will rot."

"I am sorry to hear that, but I have a more pressing problem. I need your help."

"Yes?" Graham folded his inventory book and glanced suspiciously at the reporter. Cadwallader had never asked for his help before. If he gave it, the man would be obligated to him. That might lead to a profit. "What can I do to help you?" He smiled.

Cadwallader paused to consider what he was doing. Could Graham be trusted? What other choice did he have? Sylvanus asked himself. None. He pressed onward. The general would appear at any moment. "General Grant drank heavily last night—it was a rare celebration of a breach in the Vicksburg fortifications," Cadwallader lied. "But he has not yet recovered from the effects of that party." A party of one, the reporter thought.

"I see."

Cadwallader continued. "Under no circumstances must you give him anything to drink. We have a long ride ahead of us back to headquarters."

"I understand completely. I will see to it that the general gets only cider or lemonade. You have my word of honor on that, Sylvanus."

"Thank you, Wash." Cadwallader pumped the sutler's hand. "I must hurry back to pack my satchel and help unload the horses." He spun on his heel and headed back to the *Diligence*.

An hour later all the animals were ashore and saddled, and the cavalry escort mounted and ready. Grant was nowhere to be found.

"Where the devil has he gone to?" Cadwallader asked Captain Osband.

"I have not seen the general since we docked," the escort commander replied. "He is not in his room, nor anywhere aboard ship. I sent my first sergeant to search the vessel, and he found no trace of him."

A burst of raucous laughter escaped from what was once the ladies' cabin on board Graham's steamer. The noise escaped along with a shaft of yellow light when the door to the saloon opened. As the door closed, the light and sound vanished.

Cadwallader looked at Osband. "You don't suppose ...?"

Not waiting for the obvious answer, the newspaperman stormed off. Corks popped just as Cadwallader opened the door to the saloon. He found the room thick with smoke and packed with laughing officers. Seated at a table loaded with bottles of rye and baskets of champagne, Wash Graham poured a dollop of whiskey into a cut-glass tumbler held by the missing General Grant. Grant swallowed the contents as soon as he saw Cadwallader enter.

The reporter pushed his way to the table and glowered at Graham. The sutler grinned back lopsidedly. Grant's face grew stormy. His brows knitted deeper while he struggled to focus on his self-appointed guardian.

"General," Cadwallader snapped, "your escort is ready. *Your men* are waiting. Kangaroo is saddled. You must leave at once."

"Humph," Grant grumbled. He pushed himself to his feet, using both hands on the crowded table, and walked out the door.

Only Cadwallader noted the overly careful steps and unnaturally stiff way Grant carried himself. He's drunk again, Cadwallader moaned inwardly as he followed Grant outside. God in heaven, will he never stop? How can I shield him if he persists in this reckless behavior? He must be found out if this continues. Is that what he wants? Does he wish to be ruined?

Grant sprang into his saddle. Kangaroo reared back and jumped forward. Grant jabbed his spurs into the horse, and the two of them raced away into the dusk.

Cadwallader jumped onto his horse and yelled back at the cavalry escort milling around the dock. "There goes General Grant! Follow him!"

Galloping along the narrow road snaking from the landing, Grant urged his horse onward. A series of bridges crossed the winding bayou, with sentries and tents pitched at each checkpoint. Astonished guards sprang to the ready and leveled their bayonets as this lone rider thundered down upon them. The dangerous rebel cavalry leader Nathan Bedford Forrest continued his lightning raids along the Union supply lines, striking out of the blue, so these men stood ready to fire.

"Don't shoot!" Cadwallader screamed as he clutched his saddle horn and galloped after Grant. "It is General Grant! Don't shoot!"

The general hugged his horse's neck as the animal hurdled the dumbfounded sentries. Men leapt into the water cursing and shouting, tents crashed down, and sparks scattered from campfires as Grant bounded over the barricades and raced past.

Outpost after outpost suffered the same treatment as Grant considered them part of his private steeplechase. Any nearby corral only added to the obstacles without forcing Grant to slow his breakneck speed. The speedy Kangaroo pulled farther ahead of Cadwallader and his animal, but the reporter followed the cries and curses. He was too far behind for his frantic warnings to be heard by the guards ahead, so he could only pray that Grant was not shot from his saddle or bayoneted by one of his own soldiers.

Cadwallader knew of the South's Stonewall Jackson being shot in the dark by his own men just weeks ago. Was this to happen to his general? What irony that would be. As he galloped after, he waited for those telltale shots. But none came.

The night grew darker and the moon showed no signs of showing its face for hours to come. In the darkness, Cadwallader despaired at finding Grant, but he galloped on. Sweat covered him while his horse lathered until white foam coated its shoulders and made its neck slick. On rounding a bend, he was astonished to see the general directly ahead, riding along at an easy walk. Cadwallader spurred his blown horse alongside and snatched the reins from Grant's hands. A tussle followed but the reporter held firm to the lines and finally looped them around his saddle horn.

"General, you cannot race about on these roads in the dark. You are lucky you were not shot by the sentries or fell from your horse and broke your neck."

Grant sagged in the saddle. "Shot?" he mumbled. "Why not? What makes me so different from anyone else? Thousands of men have been killed and no end is in sight. Hundreds die each day, many by my orders. Ought I not pay the same dues I demand of others?"

"General, you must not talk like this. The army needs you," Cadwallader pleaded as he directed their horses off the road and into a thicket of willows skirting the foot of a steep bluff. There at least, he judged, they would be safe from the accidental encounter he feared.

Grant continued his rambling. "Winfield Scott foresaw this mad killing, and no one believed him. Sherman, too, and everyone called him crazy..." His words trailed off as he slipped from his saddle and tumbled to the damp earth.

Cadwallader secured the horses to a half-rotted stump and removed their saddles. One he placed beneath Grant's head. The general snored away loudly. Then the reporter sat down to ponder his next move. He had little time to think.

"Halloo, anyone there?" a voice off to the right called.

Was this a bummer, those uniformed criminals of both armies, or a search party? Cadwallader sprang to his feet and peered into the darkness. He held his penknife in his hand, ready to cut the shoulder straps from Grant's coat so that he might go unrecognized in his drunken stupor. He decided he would claim his friend was named Smith if discovered.

The shadow of the horseman closed on their hiding place. "Halloo!" he called again.

"Walters? John Walters? Is that you, Sergeant Walters?" Cadwallader recognized the voice. It was one of the cavalry escort.

"Mr. Cadwallader? Where are you? Have you seen General Grant?"

Cadwallader moved in front of the snoring Grant. He stood there until Sergeant Walters reached his side. He could smell the man's sweat and the lather of his wheezing horse long before he could see him. The trooper stared down at the body of his general.

"Is he dead, sir?" Walters asked with trepidation.

"No, sound asleep." Cadwallader tried hard to keep the mixture of relief and disgust from his voice.

"He's damned lucky he didn't break his fool neck, galloping off like he did." Walters sighed in obvious relief. "He gave the boys and me a start, he did. We're spread all over the place searching for him. I never saw him do that before, but he got on one serious toot."

Cadwallader grasped the cavalryman's boot. "Listen, Sergeant. Ride directly to headquarters and find Colonel Rawlins."

"Rawlins," the man repeated.

"Yes, Rawlins, and no one else. Say nothing to anyone who might inquire about General Grant, other than Rawlins. No one else must know about this. Do you understand that?" Cadwallader gave the boot a firm squeeze to emphasize his point.

Walters nodded sagely. "Yes, sir, I do." He leaned from his saddle to gaze at Grant. The general lay snoring with open mouth. His left arm lay at his side, flattening the crown of his hat into the moss. "Not a word. We don't need to be fueling them rumors about our general, do we?" he added craftily. "We need him, drunk or sober, to take Vicksburg, and that's the plain truth."

"Exactly. Tell Rawlins the general is not hurt, but I need an ambulance with a safe—and discreet—driver to bring the general to camp. The colonel will understand. Then you must guide that driver to this spot. Come alone with the driver, just the two of you."

The sergeant touched his cap. "I'll gather up the escort and keep them safely out of sight. There's still a passel of bushwhackers hereabouts." He wheeled his horse and rode off. While this reporter held no rank, his orders would help Grant, and that agreed with Walters. The sergeant wanted Grant to stay in command. For all his shortcomings, he felt Grant did all he could to keep his losses down.

Grant awoke as the ambulance rattled to a stop on the road. He got to his feet, searched about in the darkness until his hand contacted his hat, and pulled it firmly on. "I will ride back to camp on my horse," he asserted firmly. "I will not ride in an ambulance like an invalid."

Cadwallader shook his head. "Your condition is too obvious, General. You must ride in the ambulance. If it will help, I shall sit inside with you. We can saddle the horses and tie them to the back of the wagon. I have some papers and a map in my pocket, which I will take out. That way it will look as if you are using the ambulance for transportation while you are planning your next move."

Grant squinted at the reporter and said thickly, "That is clever, Mr. Cadwallader. Perhaps I should watch you more closely. You may be too clever."

Cadwallader followed Grant to the ambulance and settled opposite him on a crude bench. The general managed a tense smile. "Please, don't tell General Sherman of your assessment," Cadwallader begged. "He will clap me in irons for spite."

The ride along the road in the jostling ambulance wagon gave both men pause to think of how much the wounded who rode inside must suffer. While the iron leaf springs of the ambulance were far superior to the carts and supply wagons used by the Confederates, every rut and rock in the trail translated into a stiff jolt. The two men's silence only made the jolting ride more painful.

At last Grant sighed deeply, raised his head, and removed his battered hat. He peered at the darker shadow inside the unlighted wagon that was his companion. The general pulled a handkerchief from his pocket and wiped the damp headband inside his hat, then his face and hands on the large square of blue gingham.

He cleared his throat. "Mr. Cadwallader," Grant began, "for the last two days, you have gone far out of your way to protect my reputation—much further than I have any right to expect. I am deeply indebted to you for that." He paused to shift uneasily on the wooden plank. "My actions during this time have been irresponsible, my conduct totally unbecoming a general officer, *or any officer, for that matter.*"

Cadwallader tried to soften the recrimination. "General, you have been under enormous strain, directing the crossing, the siege, the—"

"There is no excuse," Grant interrupted. He folded the handkerchief into a neat square and returned it to his coat pocket. His fingers touched a bundle of his cigars, but he decided against lighting one. He would speak his mind first. "*There can be no excuse.* My burden, however great, is my duty, and I must bear it just as the infantryman must follow the order to charge even though he harbors great misgivings about that order. With my high rank go equally high responsibilities."

He looked earnestly at the shadow, and the strain of his shame made his voice low and hoarse. "It is no secret that drinking was the reason for my resignation from the army in 'fifty-six. I was found unfit to carry out my duties and was given the honorable choice of resigning my commission." He winced in the darkness, thankful that Cadwallader could not see him. "When I am away from my family—my wife, Julia, especially—for long times, I fall to temptation. One drink leads to another so that I cannot stop. Colonel Rawlins understands this and has struggled to keep me sober despite all my actions to the contrary. He is a rare friend to put up with me."

Grant paused to exhale heavily. He rubbed his hands together, feeling their roughness return as his body overcame the alcohol in his system. "I suppose I have a weakness to drink, an addiction. I tell you this as an explanation of my disgraceful actions. But it is no excuse."

"I understand, General."

"You have every right, Mr. Cadwallader, to expose what I have done. It would make headlines, no doubt, and confirm what so many hope to hear. However, I don't think you will. You wouldn't have gone to such pains to shield me from exposure as you did. I can only surmise that you are a true friend like John Rawlins."

Now, Cadwallader felt awkward. "I hope to be considered your good friend," he said softly. "You are a great general, sir. Great generals, however, have few close friends."

Grant reached across the darkness and grasped the reporter's hand. "Consider yourself my close friend. Even better, consider yourself an officer on my staff. You may give any orders that you feel are necessary in my name, and I will back them up. I will tell Rawlins to issue that directive. I will also see that all assistance is afforded you in posting your dispatches to your newspaper. It is the least I can do to repay your kindness."

"Thank you, General." Cadwallader said no more. He struggled with his emotions. He had compromised his profession as a journalist, and in doing so gained a friend. To his amazement, he felt good about it. At the same time he felt a deep sadness for this rumpled man who sat across from him in the gloom. For all the power he wielded, for all the thousands of soldiers under his command, he had less than a handful of friends.

Not another word passed between the two after that. Grant sat with his elbows propped on his knees, staring at his boots, and Cadwallader leaned against the canvas side of the ambulance as the wagon continued to test the limits of its leaf springs over the primitive trail.

Close to midnight the ambulance jerked to a stop at Grant's headquarters. The camp waited quietly—almost expectantly, to Cadwallader's mind. The campfires had burned down to tired red eyes of glowing coals, tent flaps were closed and laced, and only the singular clank of a tin pan broke the stillness. In the distance the unceasing rumble of the cannon spoiled the warm spring night. Colonel Rawlins waited outside his tent with Colonel John Riggin at his side. As soon as they saw the ambulance, their conversation ceased.

Cadwallader disembarked and walked to the waiting officers. He opened his mouth to speak. He was about to explain Grant's sorry state when the general appeared on the tailgate of the ambulance. Surely, Grant's condition would speak for itself, the reporter thought. No need to pour salt in the open wound. Rawlins could see for himself.

Grant hopped lightly out of the back of the wagon, shook his shoulders as if working out the stiffness from his ride, and pulled his vest down. He adjusted his hat and brushed the nettles from his coat.

"Good evening, Rawlins," he said. He nodded also to the other man. "Riggin. I am off to bed. Wake me at five o'clock." With that Grant squared his shoulders and marched straight to his tent without looking back. Not the smallest sign of instability affected his gait.

Cadwallader blinked in astonishment at this transformation. Grant seemed sober as a church deacon! Rawlins only scowled as his eyes followed Grant until he disappeared behind the canvas tent flap. Riggin, none the wiser, saluted the general before he walked to his own tent.

Cadwallader waited until Riggin left before facing Rawlins. The menacing look in the colonel's eyes sent a shiver down the reporter's spine.

Rawlins's gaze warned that he would tear Cadwallader into a thousand pieces if he were to blame.

Cadwallader shook his head and defended himself. "Colonel Rawlins, you must think that I was the one intoxicated, not the general, but I assure you the message I sent you was true!"

Rawlins moved close and sniffed Cadwallader's breath. His teeth clenched so tightly that the newspaperman heard the grinding in the dark. "No! No, you are not to blame. I know him. I know him. All too well. He has played this game before. I want you to tell me the exact facts—and all of them—without any concealment. I have a right to know them, and I will know them."

Cadwallader related the last two nights' events with apprehension. Rawlins listened without interruption. The reporter finished his report and wiped his brow. Despite the cool evening air, he was sweating. "Now, I fear the general will send me out of the department," he lamented. "While I may have acted offhandedly to him and not in keeping with his rank, what I did I did in his best interests."

Rawlins grunted. "Did he thank you?"

"Yes, most profusely. He said I was a true friend, like yourself."

"Then you are safe. Grant is a man of his word, whatever else his failings. Even in his drunken state he had the good sense to recognize you protected him and meant him well. Besides, I am indebted to you as well for your care of him. No one will send you out of this department while I remain in it. The general has too few friends and far more enemies. I must keep his allies close at hand."

Glad that this sorry encounter was over, Cadwallader thanked Rawlins and made for the tent where the other correspondents slept. He would get little rest that night. How Grant treated him in the morning would tell whether or not he had any future as a military correspondent.

Rawlins watched the reporter leave, then he walked to Grant's tent and rattled the tent fly to announce his presence.

"Come in, Rawlins. I've been expecting you," Grant answered.

Rawlins untied the flaps and entered the blackened tent.

"Sit down, John."

"No, sir. I will stand."

"As you wish," Grant sighed. Here comes my Sunday-go-to-meeting sermon, he thought. John Rawlins's forceful oratory could breathe fire into a cause, bring men to tears, and drive women to the vapors. His stirring speech on the Union had so affected Grant that he asked Rawlins on the spot to be his adjutant general. Now, like an errant boy, Grant hunched his shoulders as he sat on the edge of his cot and hunkered down for his well-deserved tongue-lashing.

But no words poured from his faithful friend from Galena, Illinois. Speechless, Rawlins stood in the dark and openly wept. His shoulders shook as the tears poured from him, uninterrupted except for a single racking cough from his consumption-wrecked lungs.

The effect was far more devastating than words. Grant swallowed the lump in his throat. "John," he said softly, "you have every reason to be disappointed with me. I have no excuse."

Rawlins wiped his eyes on his sleeve. "You, this army, this campaign, and maybe our great cause of Union for which so many thousands have laid down their lives or lost their limbs are ... finished if you continue your drinking. Providence has shown fit to place you in this position—at this crucial time in our history—to vanquish our foe. Providence shields you from harm when men all around you are killed."

"John—"

"Yet, you will destroy yourself. You will do to yourself what no rebel bullet has done, and I cannot stand to see that happen. I wish to be relieved of my duties. I will issue my own orders conveying me to General Rosecrans's command. It will be my last duty for you."

Grant drew in his breath. He rose from his bunk and stepped forward to grasp Rawlins's hand. "My friend," he sighed, "what would I do without you?"

Rawlins only hung his head in reply.

Grant stared up at his friend. "John, I drink to forget those fields of white crosses we leave whenever we move on, all those piles of legs and arms stacked beside the surgeon's tent, and all those lifeless, twisted bodies lying in the field." His grip tightened on Rawlins's hand until the man felt his bones might break.

Grant searched for understanding in his friend's eyes, but in the darkness he saw only sorrow and disillusion. "At times I feel all those I ordered to their deaths are waiting in the shadows for me—waiting for me to explain why my poor orders got them killed or maimed. Then I wonder what I could have done better." Grant shook his head and dropped his gaze. "The thought is so crushing that I can hardly stand it. That is why I take a drink. I know I have a weakness for liquor. Once I take one drink I cannot stop. But it is the only relief I have when Julia is not with me." He released his grasp and sank back onto his cot.

Now it was Rawlins's turn to speak. "For God's sake, man, no general in this war can win a battle without losses. The men know that. They accept that, too. They march into battle knowing it might be their last day on earth. But they take that risk because they know their cause is right, and they are prepared to die for it! And because they trust you! You, Sam, *their* general. They know that you will not throw their lives away without just cause, like so many of our other generals. They understand that."

"The papers call me Grant the Butcher."

"And they would call you Grant the Coward if you stayed in camp and never fought a single battle," Rawlins snapped. "Even then, you could not help but lose men. As many die from typhus, dysentery, and pneumonia as fall from bullets. Can't you see, Sam? Your drinking will leave Lincoln with no other choice but to dismiss you, and that will only cause more men to die—without advancing our army. You produce victories. You win battles, and strategic ones at that. In the East our boys fight and die and then retreat back across the Rappahannock. All their sacrifice is for nothing. Lee and his generals thwart all Lincoln's efforts to take Richmond."

Rawlins paused while a spasm of coughing shook his frame. He swallowed back the blood and continued. "Only here in the West is progress made, and you are the reason for that success. With you gone, this department will become just like the East."

Grant buried his face in his hands. "It is too heavy a responsibility to bear. Perhaps Sherman—"

"It is too heavy a responsibility *not* to bear," Rawlins protested. "Have you thought of that? Without you, Joe Johnston will break the siege, and Pemberton and all his men will escape our trap. All our labors will be for naught. How much heavier will your burden for your losses be if you throw away victory at the eleventh hour? All the soldiers who died will rise from their graves and point an accusing finger at you because you had forsaken them." Rawlins jabbed his own finger at his friend.

"Sherman cannot survive without you. Good as he is, Sherman needs your presence to give him confidence. Do you not notice how he grows in assurance under your command? With you gone, he will sink back into mediocrity and—"

Rawlins's impassioned oratory dissolved in a fit of coughing. He reached for his handkerchief and held it tightly to his lips. The salty taste of blood filled his mouth. It mattered little to him. He had said all he meant to say.

Grant stared at the canvas wall. A barely perceptible glow lit that side, making the canvas lighten from black to a soft gray. The night was finished. In an hour dawn would come, a new day with all its tasks, all its trials, and all its opportunities.

He rubbed his hand back and forth over his mouth. His fingers reeked of stale whiskey, and the odor turned his stomach. His hand dropped to his knee and he rubbed it against the coarse weave of his woolen trousers to scour it clean of any memory of the last day's spree.

Rawlins's sermon had done its job. His dismissal would not bring his dead soldiers back to life, nor would it erase those lives from his conscience. Even if he were a broken, disgraced drunkard hiding on his ruined farm in Galena, Grant knew those painful memories would still haunt him. He could never escape from himself. His best course was to win victory for those he had ordered to their deaths. Nothing less would do.

The words his men sang while they marched filled his mind. *He has loosed the fateful lightning of his terrible swift sword . . .*

Was he that terrible, swift sword, as Rawlins prophesied? Was he alone the savior of the Union? He doubted that. He was only one man among thousands. Any day a bullet might strike him from the saddle. Then his burden would be lifted and he would join his fallen men. Until that day came, though, he would not be free.

One thing he was sure of: *He had been struck by that same fateful lightning, and his life would never, ever, be the same.*

"Thank you, John, for speaking to me as you have," he said when he had recovered his voice. "And thank you for striving to keep me sober. I know it has been a long and frustrating task—one, up to this time, without thanks. You should go to your tent and try to catch at least a few hours sleep. We have a busy day ahead of us."

Rawlins backed to the entrance. He stopped when his head brushed the tent flap. "And what of your weakness? Will you continue this race along the road to self-destruction?"

Grant smiled wanly. "From this day forth," he said, "your job will be lightened. I will drink no more."

# WHITE FLAGS

Four weeks had passed and Grant remained true to his word. Not a drop of liquor touched his lips as he tightened the noose around Vicksburg. But while he kept his word, rumors of his constantly being drunk flourished like the summer's weeds. There seemed no end to the attacks, published and private, directed to Lincoln and members of his cabinet. Copperhead publishers singled out Grant with relish.

Now, as he stood alongside General McPherson, Grant read another poisoned letter Sylvanus Cadwallader had slipped into his pocket just minutes before. The reporter refused to say how he had gotten hold of personal correspondence from Murat Halstead, editor of the Cincinnati *Commercial*, to Salmon P. Chase, Lincoln's Secretary of the Treasury. Instead, the reporter winked and laid his finger alongside his nose while he walked away.

Grant knew Halstead to be one of his enemies. For all his power and wealth, Murat Halstead affected neutrality in his public dealings with Grant, yet labored in private to drive a knife into Grant's back whenever the opportunity presented itself. The letter suggested that Cadwallader had contacts in high places with rapid means of transporting news, which he would use to help Grant. Halstead wrote:

> You do once in a while don't you, say a word to the President, or Stanton or Halleck, about the conduct of the War?
>
> Well, now, for God's sake say that General Grant, entrusted with our greatest army, is a jackass in the original package. He is a poor drunken imbecile. He is a poor stick sober, and he is most of the time more than half drunk, and much of the time idiotically drunk.
>
> About two weeks ago, he was so miserably drunk for twenty-four hours, that his staff kept him shut up in a stateroom on the steamer where he makes his headquarters . . .

Wind whipped the paper closed. Without emotion Grant unfolded the letter and read on. His eye traveled to the bottom of the page.

> Grant will fail miserably, hopelessly, eternally . . .

The general folded the letter and returned it to his coat pocket. Word travels fast, he admitted, especially damning ones. But this time Murat Halstead was wrong. Vicksburg would fall tomorrow on the Fourth of July, and nothing the editor from Cincinnati could say or do would change that. At this moment he and McPherson stood formulating the last details of their proposed attack for the next day. Neither man held any doubts that a general advance against the entire Confederate line would now succeed. The enemy was starving.

Suddenly, white flags sprang into the air. Fluttering opposite General McPherson's sector, they caught Grant's attention instantly. A small party of Confederate officers, carrying the flags, rose from their fortifications as all firing stopped. Grant ceased talking to McPherson and leaned against a stunted and twisted oak tree to watch as the party approached. No cheering followed the assembly, but along that section grinning Union soldiers poked their heads from their rabbit warrens and watched in anticipation.

Grant recognized Major General John Bowen, once his neighbor in Missouri, leading the party. The once dapper Bowen looked haggard and worn, his face sallow and drawn with great, dark circles beneath his eyes. Bowen drew himself up to his full height before Grant and saluted.

"Sir, may I present Colonel Montgomery, General Pemberton's aide-de-camp. General Pemberton has ordered me to present his letter to you." Bowen withdrew a letter from his gauntlet and handed it to Grant.

Grant read the letter. He looked up. "As I wrote yesterday, I have no conditions beyond the unconditional surrender of the city and the garrison."

Bowen winced. "Quite so. The general will meet with you at a place of your choosing at exactly three o'clock."

Grant ran his hand along the rough bark of the misshapen tree. How it had survived the weeks of bombardment or the axes of his men who scavenged every scrap of wood for their foxholes was beyond his comprehension. "I will be waiting at this tree," he said. "Three o'clock."

Three o'clock came and went without sign of Pemberton. Grant's face grew stormy with each passing minute. Thirty minutes late, John Pemberton finally rode out of his fortifications. A deep scowl dragged down the corners of his mouth. His whole attitude spoke of annoyance, as if he were being put upon to attend a meeting with subordinates. He reined in his horse a good thirty yards from where Grant waited, dismounted, and walked forward two paces. There he stopped and waited with arms folded across his chest.

Neither man spoke. Pemberton waited, his face a dark and blank mask, pretending not to recognize his old classmate. He appeared intent on acting as if he were the winner and forcing Grant to cross over to him and speak first. Grant in response raised his granite facade and leaned nonchalantly against the gnarled tree. As triumphant party, he felt no compulsion to open the conversation.

Minutes of awkward silence followed. Union soldiers surrounding the area grinned and winked at each other. Their tough Old Uncle Sam was staring down this Confederate dandy, beating him at his own game just as he had whipped him in battle. Finally, Colonel Montgomery stepped up and introduced the two generals.

Pemberton spoke, his voice thick with insolence. "What terms of capitulation *do you propose to grant me?*" he sniffed haughtily.

"Those terms stated in my letter this morning," Grant answered bluntly.

Pemberton's face flushed. His eyes blinked furiously. "If that is all you have to offer, the conference may as well terminate."

Grant's frown deepened until it looked as though his right eyebrow was trying to climb over his left one. Conference, he thought to himself, what conference? This is a meeting of surrender. But he looked directly at Pemberton and shrugged. "Very well, I am quite content to have it so," he said. He spun on his heel and pointed toward Cincinnati. His orderly hurried forward with the animal. Today, instead of Kangaroo, Grant rode Cincinnati, whose easy gait favored the rider's injured leg.

"Sir!" General Bowen showed his alarm. "Might not General McPherson and General Smith retire a ways with Colonel Montgomery and me to ... ah, informally talk over the matter? Hopefully, we could suggest such terms as might be proper?" Bowen emphasized the word "proper" and kept his voice level, but alarm clearly showed on his face. Despite Pemberton's disdain, Bowen and the rest of Vicksburg's generals knew they could not repulse another assault. Each commander knew his starved men had not the energy to effect a breakout. They could march or they could fight, but not both.

"Very well," Pemberton asserted. He walked over and sat down on an ammunition crate.

Grant sat down on the ground and leaned his back against the tree. He lighted a cigar and proceeded to pull tufts of grass from the ground around him. He watched the officers withdraw and begin their discussion. "It's been some time since we served together in the Mexican War," Grant said to his old classmate. "We've both gotten grayer since we were in our old division."

The Confederate general's face softened and he nodded. "A long and unhappy time. My family has expressed fears that I shall be singled out for special punishment since I am a Pennsylvanian, a Northern man, who chose to fight for the Southern Confederation."

Grant paused in his act of weeding. "No, John, I have no special instructions to that effect. You will be treated as any other captured officer until you are paroled."

Pemberton stared straight ahead. He had expected to be shot by a firing squad. "May I have your word that the rights and property of the citizens of Vicksburg will be respected? I have heard terrible things about General Sherman's activities."

Grant chuckled inwardly. Sherman was proving as effective a bogeyman as a field commander. "I do not propose to cause any undue annoyance or loss to the civilians. General Sherman and his corps are not scheduled to enter the city." Grant stopped there. Informing Pemberton that Sherman's forces were arrayed along the fords of the Big Black River to hold back Joe Johnston was dangerous and unnecessary. No use fanning any sparks of hope that might flame into more resistance, Grant reasoned.

A sudden thought struck Grant. His terms of unconditional surrender might prove difficult to implement. Under the current rules of prisoner exchange, his prisoners—all thirty thousand of them—would have to be shipped by rail to Washington and Baltimore. Then river steamers would move them to Aiken's Landing on the James River, where they would be exchanged for captured Union soldiers. The cost and logistics would be a nightmare.

If he modified his conditions to allow the captured men to be paroled, they could march away as soon as the papers were signed. He would not have to feed or clothe them. Grant pondered the idea. Theoretically, those paroled men gave their word not to raise arms again against the United States. Some broke that promise, he realized.

However, most of these men lived near Vicksburg or within the state of Mississippi. Most of that territory now lay within Union lines. From talks with captured soldiers, he learned that these men were tired of fighting. Drained, hungry, and diseased, they looked upon the defense of Vicks-

burg as their duty to their state. To that end they fought courageously, but
that defense was finished. With the fall of Vicksburg, most felt their obligation ended. Now they simply wanted to go home.

Grant hoped they would melt away to their farms and homes, never
to fight again. If his hunch was right, he could accomplish the same purpose
with no cost.

The returning men broke Grant's train of thought. He rose to
meet them.

"Would you modify your terms to permit our troops to march out
with the honors of war, carrying our battle flags, small arms, and field artillery?" Bowen asked.

"No." I don't want to face their muskets and cannon a second time,
Grant thought.

Bowen's face dropped, and Pemberton sprang to his feet and walked
about in agitated, jerky short steps. A. J. Smith, one of Grant's own generals who had supported the proposal, studied the tops of his boots in
embarrassment.

Grant considered for a moment. "I will modify my terms," he added.
"I will allow the men to be paroled. Then, you will be permitted to march
out of our lines. The officers may take their side arms and clothing, and the
rank and file will be allowed all their clothing, but no other property. Field,
staff, and cavalry officers may take one horse apiece."

Bowen cast a glance at his superior. Pemberton ceased his stomping.

Grant continued. "I will put those terms in writing and place them in
your hands by ten o'clock this evening."

Pemberton nodded gravely. A sigh of relief leaked from Bowen. The
men saluted Grant, mounted their horses, and rode slowly back to tell their
men. The Union lines watched in silence. Not a single cheer rose from the
hundreds of holes.

Soldiers hurried to the twisted tree and tore it down. Branch after
branch, roots and bark disappeared into men's pockets as souvenirs. In minutes nothing remained but a hole in the yellow clay.

General McPherson pointed to the empty hole. "The men will have their remembrance of the tree where Pemberton surrendered to Grant," he remarked.

"Yes," Grant snorted, "and I have no doubts that more pieces of that poor tree will be produced and circulated among the soldiers than fragments of the True Cross."

Ten o'clock the next day, Porter's gunboats and ironclads appeared on the river with pennants and signal flags strung from bow to stern. Firing their unshotted cannon in continuous salute, the boats converged on the remnants of the Vicksburg landing near the center of town like shining water beetles on a carcass. Outfitted in their best dress whites, the sailors and officers lined the deck and cheered as they docked.

On land, the defenders marched out of their fortifications with their own colors held high and their own bands playing. On an open hill they stacked their arms and returned to camp to await their parole. Grant's army marched up the road where so many had died, into the center of town, and down the north end of Cherry Street.

Haggard citizens of the town lined the street, but no one jeered or fired upon the men in blue. Most of the onlookers watched in mute wonder, dazed and befuddled by the sudden silence. Cannon fire and exploding shot had been so much a part of their lives for so long that most simply stood in shock. Not a single building remained without missing shingles, gaping holes in masonry walls, or scorched streaks rising from shattered windows.

Grant rode along, obscured by the flags and banners carried by his troops. At the head of the column, the men of the Eighth Wisconsin marched with their mascot, a bald eagle named Old Abe, flapping from his cross perch. During the heaviest fighting, Old Abe flew above the Wisconsin, screaming and diving through the hail of bullets. Despite numerous attempts by rebel sharpshooters, not a bullet touched the eagle's feathers.

Grant watched as men in blue opened their haversacks and shared their bread with their hungry prisoners. Shy smiles and thoughtful looks passed from man to man, but not a single word of animosity. In the long siege, both sides had exacted a deadly toll on the other, and in doing so had earned the grudging respect of their foe. Now both armies acted relieved they were alive and mollified that their worthy foe also lived. He overheard one private say as he pressed a piece of hardtack into the hand of a Louisiana man, "We were holding you prisoner all these weeks, Johnny, and making you feed yourself, but I guess now we've got to feed you ourselves."

The Confederate soldier replied, "When one of you Yanks yelled across at me that he was planning to eat his dinner in Vicksburg, I yelled back that he'd better catch his rabbit first." The man fingered the hardtack like it was a lump of gold. He smiled wryly. "Well, I guess I been catched."

Grant rode silently on to the courthouse in the center of town. On the top flight his junior officers sang "The Star Spangled Banner" off-key and waved their flag and a captured Confederate signal flag. As Grant mounted the stairs with Logan, Rawlins, and McPherson at his side, a colonel of artillery, obviously drunk with something besides his enthusiasm, lurched from the railing and clutched Grant's sleeve.

"General Grant," he slurred, "have you observed the ironwork of the staircase upon which we stand?"

"Hold your tongue. You are drunk, sir!" Colonel Rawlins fumed as he glared at the officer, but Grant held Rawlins back. He recognized the man as one of the officers who had struggled to drag a field piece into the pit created by the first mine exploded under Fort Hill.

"Let him speak," Grant ordered. "He has paid a heavy price to stand on these steps." Grant gave Rawlins a knowing look. "He didn't offer me a drink, John," he said. "Even if he should, I will refuse. You have my word, I have given up drinking."

The colonel of artillery drew himself up and smiled. "Have you noticed the maker of this iron stairway, sir?" he asked.

Grant shook his head. "No, I have not."

"General, it was manufactured in Cincinnati."

"Cincinnati?" Rawlins repeated.

"Yes, Cincinnati, up north," the man grunted. "It was not built here in the South at all. Damn the impertinence of these people, these people of the Southern Confederacy, who think they can whip the United States. Damn them if they think they can whip us when they can't even build their own staircase."

# LINCOLN

Grant opened his eyes. A pencil, worn to a stub, hovered as a blurry image just beyond his open fingers. His face rested on pages of foolscap, covered with writing. He raised his head, ignoring the ache in his jaw, and blinked until his eyes focused.

A shimmering glow through the lace curtains of his bedroom window announced the birth of another day even though dark rain clouds still lingered sullenly in the sky. The half-open window admitted the clean, sharp smell of air scrubbed clean by the rain.

Grant rubbed his beard, avoiding the lump in his neck, and looked about. It was an hour before sunrise, he judged. His right hand was asleep where his head had rested on it, so he massaged it until the leaden numbness gave way to tingling.

He was still alive. He had not choked to death in the dark as he so greatly feared. He must have moved from his bed to his writing table during the night. He remembered being unable to sleep, the memories of

Vicksburg flooding his mind, but he could not recall leaving his bed to write them down.

A pang of anxiety hit him. What had he written? Was it gibberish or the work of a drugged mind? He found his spectacles and held them up while he studied page after page. Precise sentences greeted him on every sheet. He sighed in relief. The work was coherent and well-written. The Vicksburg campaign jumped from the pages.

His heart slowed. While his pain grew in intensity with each day, taking medicine for it only fogged his mind, and he knew he was running out of time. He made a mental note to refuse the laudanum supplied by Dr. Shrady. The opiates confused him. He was reliving the War Between the States as he feverishly worked on his memoirs to the point that at times he lost track of the present. Grant realized he could not afford to lose his focus, so the painkillers would have to go. He steeled himself for the constant, penetrating pain.

Pushing himself out of his chair, he walked to the window, moving softly. Any undue noise would bring Julia and Fred running to his aid. A fitful breeze battled against the oppressive heat. The rains had done little to temper the sweltering night. He dressed quietly and returned to his desk.

The cancer is sapping my strength, he thought, just as I encircled Vicksburg, like an anaconda tightening its coils as its victim wears itself out in fruitless struggling. I suppose my end will come with exhaustion, just as Vicksburg fell on a whisper or a sigh instead of a shout or a bang. I was surprised then, and I suppose I will be surprised when my end comes. One never expects death.

He picked up his pencil. Vicksburg, he thought, that was the end of the Confederate hopes, although few realized it at the time. One thing it did for me. It won me the unwavering trust of Abraham Lincoln.

Grant adjusted his spectacles as he shuffled the papers stacked in neat piles on his desk. He found what he was looking for and held it up to the growing light from the window. It was a letter, worn and frayed at the edges, yellowed with age, but still unstained, with the writing clear as that day he had received it. He read it to himself, as he had a hundred times before. Even now the words warmed his heart, yet filled him with remorse for the great man.

JULY 13, 1863

MY DEAR GENERAL

I do not remember that you and I ever met personally. I write this now as a grateful acknowledgement for the almost inestimable service you have done the country. I wish to say a word further. When you first reached the vicinity of Vicksburg, I thought you should do what you finally did—march the troops across the neck, run the batteries with the transports, and thus go below; and I never had any faith, except a general hope that you knew better than I, that the Yazoo Pass expedition, and the like, could succeed. When you got below, and took Port Gibson, Grand Gulf, and vicinity, I thought you should go down the river and join Gen. Banks; and when you turned Northward, East of the Big Black, I feared it was a mistake. I now wish to make the personal acknowledgement that you were right, and I was wrong.

Yours very truly,<br>Abraham Lincoln

The words dissolved as tears flooded Grant's eyes. He bowed his head and wept as he had that day he sat in the corner of the East Room of the White House with a black crepe band encircling his left arm and watched the long lines of mourners file past Lincoln's casket.

Robert Todd Lincoln stood at the foot of the coffin, pale and somber. Grant sat at the other end. Unable to look upon the murdered President, he stared at a cross of lilies resting against the catafalque. While Lincoln's oldest son played the man, Lincoln's general, the conqueror of the South, broke down and wept like a child. It was the saddest day of his life.

Had it been twenty years since Lincoln fell?

The door opened hesitantly. Fred stood in the opening carrying a tray with a dark amber bottle, a glass of water, and a small glass syringe. His face registered alarm when he saw his father weeping. Grant hardly ever cried.

"Father, what is it? Are you in pain?" Fred blurted out. He stood frozen with the tray clutched in his hands. "I have your medicine here. Let me give it to you," he pleaded.

Grant waved him off with his hand. Spasms locked his throat, precipitated by his tears. He struggled for his breath as well as his words until the spasm passed. "No more laudanum," he gasped. "It confuses my mind."

Fred set the tray on the hall table and returned to hover by his father. More anxious minutes passed before Grant's breathing slowed to normal. With supreme effort Grant cleared his throat. A congealed clot of blood dislodged with his coughing filled his mouth, and he spit it into his handkerchief, taking care to conceal it from his son. At last Grant winked at his son and managed a weak smile.

"My tears were for President Lincoln, Fred," Grant said at last, "not for myself. I was reading a letter he sent me after the surrender of Vicksburg. And I was recalling when we first met. When he summoned me to Washington." He decided not to mention Lincoln's funeral. Fred appeared too distressed as it was.

Fred nodded. His body relaxed and he managed a smile. The younger Grant moved to the window and opened it wider to admit what fitful breeze there was. "I remember that, too. We stayed at Willard's Hotel in Washington. It was the first time I had ever been in so grand a place."

"Yes, your mother thought I ought to take you along. She feared your education in the battlefield needed tempering with exposure to the capital. I believe she was correct in that regard. You felt at the time the whole war was being waged solely for your benefit."

Fred flushed with embarrassment. "You certainly gave that hotel clerk a start, registering as 'U. S. Grant and son, Galena, Illinois.' I believe he took you for a captain or even a major. That must have been why he gave us that tiny room on the fifth floor. He never dreamed you were a general on your way to meet with President Lincoln."

Grant refolded his letter from Lincoln with infinite care and slipped it into a side drawer. "It was a good room. You must admit the view from that fifth floor was worth the climb. It almost reminded me of the stairs of that house we rented in Galena."

"Yes, but when officers from the War Department came looking for the newly appointed Lieutenant General Grant, the only general to hold that exalted title since Winfield Scott, the shaken clerk could not find us in any of the grand staterooms. Only after he checked the register did he realize where he had placed us—in the fifth floor walk-up. The poor man nearly died."

"Sherman was more upset than anyone when he found out where I was. I remember he cabled me: 'For God's sake and your country's sake, come out of Washington.'" Grant paused to look out the window. "He was right. I should have heeded his advice, especially after the war."

Fred placed his hand lightly on his father's shoulder. "You were a good President, Father. The people loved you. They voted you in for a second term, and they would vote for you again, I'm sure," he said warmly.

Grant looked reproachfully at his son. "I was anything but a good President, Fred. I know that all too well. I suppose I failed to realize that politicians couldn't be commanded like soldiers. They never say what they mean or come at you directly like a fighting man, instead they smile and scrape and trick you. Washington is the only place on this earth that I know where you advance by backing up. It was the worst place for me. As you know, I'm superstitious about retracing my steps. But bad President or not, I was a good general. I'll admit that to you and your mother—in private—but not to anyone else."

Fred smiled. "Do you want to dictate to me this morning?" he asked. "I don't have to go into town until this afternoon, and I can cancel that if you want."

Grant waved his hand. "No. Thank you, Fred, but I think I'll reread what I wrote last night before I come down for breakfast. Tell your mother I'll only take tea and some mush this morning." He knew he could hardly swallow even that soft cereal. No sense wasting food on me that I cannot eat and that my family can, he reasoned.

As a diversion, he patted his waistcoat, feeling his ribs through the layers of worn material. His jacket, vest, shirt, and undershirt made him appear heavier than he was. He kept himself dressed in front of Julia, his family, and friends to conceal how thin he had grown. "I'm watching my weight," he joked.

Fred smiled dutifully and went out to find his mother. Grant knew she would be downstairs in the pantry or the kitchen, fretting over how to stretch their meager supplies. She would rank up there with the best commissary officers. Even when we were poor as church mice, he thought, she kept us fed.

Grant ran his pencil through an awkward line and reworked it until it satisfied him. His memoirs were like a battle, he had come to realize, attention to detail being so very important. He knew his constant editing set Mark Twain's teeth on edge, but he wanted to get it right. Hardly a day passed without a letter or telegram from Twain begging for the manuscript. At their last meeting the humorist clearly appeared shaken by the change in him.

He fears I'm going to die before I complete my task, Grant thought. I could see it in his face, in his eyes, although he did his best to try to hide it. He needed propping up like a faltering battle line. I hope I relieved his anxiety when I looked him directly in the eye and said: "I mean to complete my memoirs."

Grant paused to reflect. "Meaning" is one thing and "doing" another. Lee meant to defeat me, yet he failed. But I must finish my book. If God will only grant me the strength to finish it. *Man proposes and God disposes,* he thought. I like that phrase. I might use it in the opening. Quickly he wrote it down. Man proposed and God disposed. Lincoln proposed to bring the South back into the Union with all the care offered the prodigal son. But . . .

He opened the side drawer and withdrew Lincoln's letter. He opened it and stared at the writing. The even script drew his thoughts back to that period in time, back to his first encounter with the President from Illinois.

Grant entered through the side door. He paused and stared as the attendant held the door open for him. Somewhere out of sight a band played a tune Grant did not recognize. It certainly was not "Yankee Doodle." The music underscored the buzz of guarded conversation. People dressed in their finery filled the entire hall. Ladies floated about in flowing gowns with flowered corsages and tightly ringed hair, blushing and whispering behind fluttering lace fans. Men in uniform and evening dress stood about in tight clusters. The gold braid, epaulets, scarlet sashes, and razor-creased trousers of the officers made his rumpled uniform look out of place.

It was the best he had. Julia herself had mended a tear, brushed the jacket, and tried to press creases into the worn woolen pants, but the trouser legs stubbornly remained baggy and shapeless. Freddy even polished the brass buttons, with limited success. Most were tarnished and dented beyond repair. His uniform was no match for even the lowest lieutenant in the room. He felt very out of place.

At least I own my uniform this time, he reminded himself, not like when I first took command of the 24th Illinois Volunteers. Then, I had to borrow money to buy my uniform, and the one I bought was shabby at that. None of the men thought me grand enough to be their colonel. Well, I showed them that I was their commanding officer. Regardless of how I dressed.

He looked at his hands, glowing strangely at his side in white gloves like something not a part of him. He felt thankful now that Julia had insisted he pack a pair of white gloves. You must wear them when you meet the President, she counseled. It is the proper fashion in Washington, and I have heard white gloves are even worn in the field by all the generals in the Eastern Theater.

Grant stepped inside. He hunched over and tucked his bearded chin into his collar to make himself less conspicuous while his gloved hands balled defensively into fists at his side. A black servant paused momentarily before him with a silver tray loaded with crystal punch glasses. Grant reached for one, decided against it, and withdrew his hand. The servant frowned disdainfully down at Grant before he whisked the tray away to more deserving men.

Several men glanced at him with indifference before turning back to their conversation, and two women studied him briefly over the tops of their fans. Without the gold trappings to announce his rank, few noticed the faded stars on his shoulder straps. From his attire, they judged him to be a misdirected footman. His unsmiling face held little attraction for the ladies, so they resumed their conversation behind their fans.

Grant could not help noticing the spotless and shining patent leather shoes the men wore. Not a single spot soiled their boots, not at all like the mud-covered attire of his fighting men. His soldiers around Vicksburg wore its yellow clay like a second skin. Those men had fought and died for these dandies, he thought bitterly. I wonder if they appreciate it.

Suddenly, Grant wished he were back in his headquarters tent on the Yazoo. The heavy French perfume filling the room made his head spin and he longed for the clean scent of the pines and magnolia trees. Most of all he wished Julia were here.

"Why, here is General Grant himself," a voice called out over the undercurrent of conversation. The voice was high-pitched, almost nasal, carrying the iron-edged twang of Kentucky and southern Illinois.

Grant stiffened. The room grew still, and like Moses parting the waters, the crowd separated. All eyes turned to watch him. Grant found himself standing alone, staring down the empty expanse of the ballroom at a mismatched couple.

At the far end stood a tall, thin man whose pipe-stem trousers and black frock coat made his legs and angular arms appear twice their normal length. Looking like a scarecrow marionette cut loose from its strings, he stood with his loose-jointed limbs dangling inside his suit. The man's tie had tilted wearily to one side like a sinking ship and abandoned all pretense of encircling his loose collar in any orderly fashion.

At the man's side stood a short, plump woman wearing a plum-colored dress thickly strewn with satin flowers. A similar bouquet wreathed her black hair and decorated her lace-gloved wrist as a corsage. Despite her smile, the woman eyed Grant with dark misgivings, like a farmer appraising a gathering thundercloud. Fiercely protective of her husband, she viewed each new hero as a potential threat to Lincoln—and not without cause. McClellan openly spoke of opposing her husband in the next election.

With grave reluctance Grant marched forward stoop-shouldered, and bowed to his commander-in-chief. While Mary Todd Lincoln kept her distrustful look, there was no coldness in Lincoln's smile as he grasped Grant's hand and shook it warmly. The President's firm handshake carried with it the memory of a working man. Their clasp communicated a thousand unsaid words of the hard work that had callused their skin, Lincoln from splitting rails and Grant from hauling green hides. Moreover, the President's lined and rawboned face instantly put Grant at ease. His gray eyes carried within them the image of the prairie with its lonely rolling hills and biting winter winds. Here was a man Grant could talk to, and, he realized, one who would listen.

Lincoln kept hold of Grant's hand as he spoke to the assembly. "I am certain that everyone here will wish to congratulate you, General, on your splendid victory. When they are finished, would you be so kind as to join me in my office. We have much to discuss."

"I would be happy to meet with you right now, Mr. President," Grant added hopefully.

Lincoln's eyes twinkled. "No, General, enjoy your moment in the sun. With the clouds of war hanging about our heads, the sun shines so infrequently it must never be ignored—as you well appreciate," he added knowingly.

"Oh, Father, must you work again tonight," Mary complained. "It is such a lovely ball."

Lincoln released Grant's hand and took his wife's. Grant noticed how her soft, pudgy hand almost vanished within his bony fingers. But the hand that might easily crush hers held it with loving care.

"My dear, I'm afraid I must, but you stay and enjoy the evening. All the young blades are dying to dance with you, and I promise not to be too jealous." He smiled at her, ignoring her pout, before walking away.

Grant found himself facing the icy glare of the President's wife.

"I suppose you harbor aspirations of replacing my husband," she said sharply. "All his generals do. But they come and go. You will see it takes more than one victory to ensure success, General Grant. Many before you have made that mistake."

"Madam," Grant replied, "my sole concern is the defeat of the South. Nothing more."

Mary's eyes narrowed. "My family supports the South. Did you know that? My mother, my brother, my half brothers are all against the President. In every corner of this city there are whispers against me because of them. But those slanderers are wrong. I am loyal beyond question. I wish all my brothers were killed or wounded."

Her statement shocked Grant. His frown deepened. "How so, madam? They are your own family." To him his family was more precious than life.

Mary's face grew cold and dark. "Because, sir, they would kill my own husband if given the chance," she hissed vehemently. Then her face lightened. She looked around at the curious faces of the guests standing at a respectful distance. "I don't suppose you dance, General Grant?" she asked.

"Not well, madam."

"Good." Mary spun around in a great swish of satin and crinoline and disappeared into the crowd.

Grant watched her vanish into her sea of sycophants. He was glad now that Julia had not come. He was certain his wife and Mrs. Lincoln would not get along. Strange, he thought, in so many ways they are so alike. Both are southern born, both come from well-to-do families, and both are fiercely loyal to their husbands. But there the resemblance ceased. Mary Todd Lincoln showed signs of instability, unlike his Julia, who was a rock of certainty. No, he corrected himself, he was mistaken; they are not that alike at all. They would not be friends. In fact he saw good reason for them to be enemies.

Grant finally extracted himself from his well-wishers and made his way to the President's room. He knocked on the oak door, opened it, and stepped into the office. Papers and maps were strewn about the floor, covering the desk and every available chair. To his surprise, he saw a child's set of wooden soldiers arranged on the carpet.

"Come in, General Grant," Lincoln called from behind his desk. His long legs stretched out from under the desk like creepers. A pair of wire-rimmed spectacles perched on his nose, and a pencil rested behind his enormous ear. He looked to Grant more like an overwhelmed bookkeeper than the President of the United States. Lincoln saw Grant staring at the toys and remarked: "The army may be mine, but that company of infantry belongs to my son, Tad."

"A well-ordered company, Mr. President," Grant remarked.

"Not at all like mine," Lincoln replied as he looked over his glasses at his general. "Or my desk for that matter. I trust it does not resemble yours?" he added perceptively.

"No. My desk, while smaller, is better organized. But you must know that from Mr. Dana's correspondence."

"Ah, yes." Lincoln smiled slyly. "Mr. Charles Dana, Stanton's spy. Yes, he has written in detail about you, and Stanton dutifully passes on his correspondence to me. Now, Dana has become your avid supporter; he does nothing but sing your praises."

Grant stared at his gloved hands. "I hope Mr. Dana's enthusiasm for me does not exceed my abilities. I find it is easier to surprise my critics than to satisfy the overly generous expectations of my supporters."

"Well said, General. Now you have a feel of my own situation. But you need not trouble yourself about Charles Dana. Stanton is quite pleased with his reports. He plans on appointing him to the post of Assistant Secretary of War." Lincoln looked about his cluttered office. He swung one leg over to push a stack of books off the chair to his right. The books crashed to the floor. Grant noted one was Jomini's *Life of Napoleon*, translated by Halleck. "Sit down, General. It will be easier on both our necks. I am unaccustomed to looking *up* at people." He winked at Grant. "Besides, we need to look after each other's necks, for I believe they are both in the same noose."

"I agree."

"Good. As to the arrangement of my office, in politics it is best to conceal what is important to you. What appears disordered to you confounds my detractors, but is orderly to me. It is my best protection against ... ah, shall we say well-intentioned tampering."

"I'm not sure I understand," Grant said as he settled into the recently cleared chair.

"Well, General, you are blessed with the trust and directness of a soldier." Lincoln added prophetically, "But in politics that can be fatal."

Grant stared at the lined face. Lincoln was not as he first appeared. Beneath his facade of backwoods bonhomie, Grant detected a shrewd and calculating mind, one capable of making hard decisions. Such minds could be dangerous if left unchecked, and the powers Lincoln had usurped gave him control far beyond that intended by the Founding Fathers.

Lincoln correctly perceived Grant's assessment. "You realize I am not as simple as the papers make out," he said. "I am not the baboon the cartoonists portray."

"Yes."

"And you are asking yourself: 'Am I serving a dictator? How far will this man go to preserve the Union? Am I fighting one threat to my country while supporting another one?' Well, I will answer your question with a question. How far will you go, General, to defeat the South?"

"I will use whatever means at my disposal."

Lincoln leaned back in his chair, drew up his right knee and locked both hands about it. "A good answer. And I will do the same to preserve our rightful government—*whatever means at my disposal.* To answer your other question: once this dreadful war is won, I will revert back to the role of a normal President because my conscience will not permit me to do otherwise. Not to do so would destroy the thing I am fighting so hard to preserve."

Grant smiled.

"Good. I hoped my response would agree with you, and I see you can smile as well. When I first caught sight of you entering the ballroom tonight you looked as cheerful as a man attending his own wake."

Grant scratched his beard. He craved a cigar, but he knew the President did not smoke. Instead, he crossed his legs and leaned forward in his chair. "Mr. President, I am a plain man. I am out of place at a soiree. What I do best is fight battles."

Lincoln slapped his knee. "Exactly. You not only fight battles, you keep on fighting them. And you win. You win." Lincoln paused as he picked at his bootlace. "I'm reminded of a story about a great war between the animals. Well, one side had the devil of a time finding a commander with enough confidence to lead the other animals. But finally Jocko the monkey came forward and said he would feel comfortable being the leader if only his tail were longer. So the other animals chipped in and spliced more tail onto Jocko. It looked good to him, but he thought a little more would be even better. Well, sir, he kept on asking, and the other animals kept on splicing until the tail grew so long it filled the room and coiled around Jocko's shoulders and neck until it strangled the foolish monkey."

"Like McClellan."

Lincoln's smile folded his face into bottomless creases. "Grant, you are the first real general I have had in three years of fighting. Can you believe it? Of all those men to choose from, and you are the first. Never once during the whole Vicksburg campaign did you ever ask for reinforcements. You went ahead with what you had and got the job done. Not another of all my other generals has done that. They keep asking for longer tails."

Lincoln withdrew a paper from the clutter and handed it to Grant. "Your patron saint from Illinois, Congressman Elihu Washburne, had his hand in this. He felt a general who could fight without needing a longer tail at least ought to have another star on his shoulders. So I'm promoting you to the rank of Lieutenant General. Only you and Winfield Scott hold that rank, and I'm appointing you Commander-in-Chief of all the Federal forces. Your victory at Vicksburg and Meade's at Gettysburg have saved my political neck."

"Thank you, Mr. President. I am honored. I never expected this."

Lincoln opened a side cabinet and withdrew two carafes, one holding water and the other brandy, and two glasses. He placed these on his desk close to Grant. "Perhaps you would like to celebrate your promotion, General? I'm a teetotaler myself, but I have no objections if you'd like something stronger than water for your toast."

Grant looked at the brandy without visible emotion. The tormented face of John Rawlins rose in the back of his mind. "Water will be fine, Mr. President," he said. "I am on the wagon."

"Water it is. For us both." Lincoln smiled. Grant's drinking problem was no secret to him. But Grant had passed Lincoln's little test. He studied Grant over the rim of his glass as both men toasted the promotion. The general obviously needed a new uniform. "Is there anything else I can do for you, General? Now is the time to ask. I am feeling uncharacteristically generous tonight."

"My chief of staff, Colonel John Rawlins, deserves much of my credit. Could he be promoted?"

Lincoln masked his surprise. He had expected Grant to ask for a raise. "John Rawlins? Of Galena, Illinois?"

"Yes, that is the same Colonel John Rawlins."

Lincoln could not resist pulling Grant's leg. "Oh, well, he is not one of my supporters. I believe him to be a Douglas Democrat. I'm afraid that would not do."

Grant's face dropped. "Oh—"

Lincoln waved his hand as he chuckled. "I was merely teasing, General. It is a weakness of mine that my Mary says is unbecoming a President, but it helps to ease my burden. Of course the good Colonel Rawlins may receive his promotion. I will issue orders to elevate him to the rank of Brigadier General at once."

"Thank you, Mr. President. I will draw up plans immediately to coordinate my forces in the West with the Army of the Potomac—"

Lincoln shook his head and his glasses slipped from his nose. He caught them before they fell to the carpet. "I've given you the molasses, General, that's your promotion. But there's sulfur to be swallowed along with the molasses. Now, the sulfur is you can't stay out West. You will have to command the campaign against Virginia. The legislators are tired of Lee and his army dancing circles about our boys. Those same lawmakers are scared to go to bed for fear Lee will capture Washington while they sleep. And, to tell you plainly, I'm fed up with it myself. You can control the Western Theater, but you must do it from the soil of Virginia. I want Richmond captured and General Lee's army destroyed. I hope you have some ideas to effect that goal."

As he customarily did when concentrating, Grant leaned farther forward. This was the question he prayed Lincoln would ask. During the trip to Washington, he had formulated his plans. Now he could present them to the President. He folded his hands together and locked his fingers tightly.

"Mr. President, our armies in the West and in the East are never coordinated. When one is attacking, the other is sitting in camp or waiting behind fortifications. We outnumber the South, but this piecemeal approach allows the enemy to transfer their soldiers back and forth to reinforce the active regions. By doing so they effectively negate our superiority of numbers. One week Longstreet's Third Corps is helping Lee. The next week he is in Tennessee supporting Bragg."

Lincoln contained his growing excitement. "And what do you propose?"

"Attack the Confederacy on all fronts so that he must fight where he stands and cannot move to support another department. General Meade and the Army of the Potomac should cross the Rapidan and go after Lee's army. With luck he will get Lee to stand and fight until his army is effectively destroyed. General Butler with his Army of the James should advance on the rail lines that supply Richmond from the South. Richmond will be cut off, so that if Lee retreats to that city he will be without supplies. Place General Sherman in charge of the West. He can drive across Georgia and capture Atlanta. General Banks should move up from Louisiana, attack Mobile, and link up with Sherman."

Lincoln could hardly believe his ears. He gobbled up each sentence like a starving man consumes each new dish presented to him. When Grant finished, the President clapped both hands together with joy. "Just what I have been urging on my generals for the last two years!" he exclaimed. "But they gave me nothing but excuses as to why exactly what you propose cannot be done. Logistics, supply problems, lack of communications, the list was longer than my arm and grew longer each time I renewed my request. Now, I admit to being ignorant to military science, but nothing I have read precludes attacking on all fronts."

"It can be done, Mr. President."

"General, you have no idea how your plan warms my heart. I can see an end to this terrible conflict at last. It may be a ways off, but I can see the end shimmering on the horizon like a new day. But where do you fit in? Remember, your place must be here in the East."

"I will make my headquarters with the Army of the Potomac." Grant swallowed hard. That would take some delicate steps, he judged. Despite his sudden promotion to Commander-in-Chief, General George Meade was senior to him on the army lists. How Meade would take to him as his superior remained to be seen. Could he be ordered or did he need coaxing? Then there was Meade's well-known temper. His biting nature made his own men call him "a goggle-eyed snapping turtle." The crusty, cautious, and cantankerous Meade would strain his patience, but Grant saw no other option.

"Yes, I can see it taking place." Lincoln rose from his chair and walked about excitedly. He repeatedly clasped his hands together as he paced, like a man receiving wonderful news. In his movements he passed close to Tad's wooden soldiers and knocked one over. He appeared not to notice. "General, you have lifted a heavy burden from my shoulders. I feel I can place the disposition of the army squarely in your hands, and you will not disappoint me. We will go after the enemy on all fronts, and skin 'em whenever we can. And those generals not skinning can hold a leg."

# ONE LAST CIGAR

Alden Goldsmith leaned against the rail fence and beamed with pride as his friend, Ulysses Grant, admired his horses. Beside the former President stood C. B. Meade, Goldsmith's neighbor and a nephew of General George Meade. The three men stood outside the barn and watched as grooms led one horse after another past them.

"I am so pleased you could come, Mr. President," Goldsmith said. "I knew you would appreciate my trotters. This year they are in fine form. In fact, I've never had as good a stable to enter before. I have high hopes of winning the Hambletonian at the Good Time Track."

Grant reached out his hand and patted the sleek coat of the horse in front of him. Since childhood he loved horses more than any other animal, and with each year his love of horses still continued to grow.

Grant ran his hand along the muscular flanks. "You know, Alden, this animal reminds me of a pacer I once owned when I was in Washington. She was a beauty. I'd take her out and hitch her to a one-horse shay and away

we'd go. We'd fly like the wind down the streets if I'd let her have her head."
He stopped to look sheepishly at Goldsmith. "I confess I encouraged her.
Once, a policeman stopped me as I was flying past and said I was speeding."

C. B. Meade's face brightened. "But you were serving as the President
then. Did the policeman not recognize you?"

"Not at first. I was alone in the carriage. He threatened to issue me a
ticket for reckless speeding before he realized who I was."

"Surely not!" Goldsmith protested.

"Yes. The poor man's face blanched and he hemmed and hawed after
he made me out. But, you see, he had already committed himself. He had
his ticket book out and was starting to write. He was caught between doing
his duty and fearing I might have him fired."

"So he decided not to," Meade responded.

Grant shook his head. "No. I told him to do his duty and no harm
would come to him. He had found me breaking the law, and he should act
accordingly. So he gave me a ticket for speeding. I had to go to court and
pay the fine."

"That is unbelievable. The President of the United States and hero of
the War Between the States issued a speeding ticket by a policeman."
Goldsmith shook his head in disbelief.

Grant looked at him evenly. Goldsmith was born to money and often
expressed his belief in special privilege for the upper class. "No, Alden, you
shouldn't be surprised. I broke the law. No man is above the law," Grant
said simply. "That is what makes our country so great."

"What did Mrs. Grant say when she found out?" Meade asked.

Grant smiled. "Julia accused me of not acting my age. She said I
ought to act more dignified."

The groom paraded the last trotter past. A handsome bay, the animal pranced about nervously, tossing its head, until Grant's gentle hand
calmed him. The horse swung its head and watched Grant with its liquid
brown eyes.

"A good breadth on this one's chest, Alden. He reminds me of
Cincinnati."

"Ah, yes, the famous Cincinnati, almost as famous as his illustrious rider. He ranks up there with Lee's Traveler in notoriety."

"Cincinnati had more spirit than Traveler, even on his off days," Grant stated flatly. He disliked the comparison that inevitably arose between him and Robert E. Lee. Now their horses were being rated. Since Lee's death fifteen years ago, forces at work in the South sought to canonize their former commander, often at the expense of Grant and his Northern generals. For all his ability, Grant thought, Lee made mistakes just as I did. He was not perfect.

Lee was the last of the cavaliers, Grant reasoned. His cause was one of the worst ever for which men fought, but he commanded well and nobly. Nevertheless, he failed to recognize the changing face of the war. Sherman and I only realized the difference when it was forced upon us—after Shiloh. We realized that winning the war had become a matter of attrition, that no single victory in one battle or another would spell ultimate success. Had we been successful in the early part, like Lee, we might never have noted that change.

Lee misunderstood the war until it was too late. He believed he would be victorious by winning battles and capturing towns. In the past that was all it took. And it almost worked. The Peace party came so close to upsetting Lincoln. But Lincoln held Washington's feet to the fire that blazed so brightly in every hamlet and backwoods town in the North: The idea that men gave their lives for—freedom and equal justice for everyone, regardless of their social status.

The country was changing as well from one of wealthy landowners whose power lay in their inherited place in society to one where a man's future blossomed from the quickness of his mind and the cleverness of his hands.

*The noble Lee was content to suffer the meager rations of his men and sleep alongside them on the ground. I preferred to see that my men were well-fed and slept in tents whenever possible. That was one crucial difference.*

*The railroad, telegraph wire, and the supply trains did more to win than brilliant tactics. If Lee and his generals realized that men on either side would not give up the fight until they were too weak to strike a blow or no longer had the means to load their muskets, they would never have started the conflict in the first place. The South never had a chance against the industrial might of the North, especially not after Sherman and I waged total war upon them.*

Meade noticed the darkening of Grant's face and mistook it for displeasure over his remark about Traveler, so he tried to correct his faux pas. "Ah, yes, I think your horse is a much finer animal than any I have seen. Do you still have Cincinnati, sir?"

Grant gave a minuscule shake of his head; any more would have brought a surge of lancinating pain on top of the boring ache he had come to live with. His eyes glowed as he recalled his favorite horse. Not as showy as Lee's Traveler, Cincinnati worked harder and complained less than any animal he had ridden. "No, I presented him to the veterans of the Grand Army when they were raising auction funds for those crippled in the war. They auctioned him off. Old Cincinnati went for ten thousand dollars, I'm proud to say. I don't recall another animal going for that high a price. Even after the war he continued to do his part."

"A noble deed worthy of a noble steed." Meade reached into his pocket and produced a handful of roasted chestnuts. He had picked them from the trees nearby that morning. The trotter eyed the nuts and swung his head over to be fed. Meade handed one to the horse before the groom returned the mount to its stable.

The three men wandered past the fence and climbed the rolling hills. The sun broke through the soft white clouds to cast warming rays over the fields. Grant paused to study the lay of the land. Below him, the winding waters of the Wallkill River meandered through the hills. The sunlight glinted off rocks and ripples in the river, and they shone like silver fish scales. Groves of trees stood guard along the stream's flanks. A light breeze, warmed by the sun, turned their leaves at random, exposing their pale undersides.

Grant pressed on until he reached the crest of the ridge, then stopped. Too many years of waging war led him to automatically seek the high ground. Meade sauntered along, playing with a handful of his roasted chestnuts.

"Those chestnuts remind me of those I used to roast in my room at West Point," Grant remarked. "I'd wait until after midnight so that the provost would not catch me after lights-out. I had to be careful. Unlike General Lee, I had more than my share of demerits," he joked.

"I collected these this morning. They are quite fresh," Meade responded. "My uncle George told me his men roasted them during the Battle of the Wilderness."

"Yes," Grant replied. "I remember that all too well. Most of the chestnuts came already roasted by the fearsome fires that raged throughout the battle. The men had only to scoop up the hot nuts from the burning ground." Grant sighed sadly. He remembered the endless burning brush and the cries of the wounded who could not crawl to safety. Many a good man on both sides roasted alongside the chestnuts in that conflict; many who might have been saved by the surgeon found themselves encircled by fire and burned to death where they lay.

Again Meade misinterpreted the former President's reaction. "Would you care for one, sir?" Meade offered. "They are quite delicious."

Grant looked longingly at them. He could not recall the last time he had eaten a chestnut; but his mind remembered the taste, and his mouth watered. "I would love one, but I'm afraid I could not swallow even the smallest piece because of my throat."

Goldsmith stepped forward. "I can boil some for you, Mr. President, until they are soft as velvet. Then you can eat them like mashed potatoes."

Grant considered the offer. "I have not had boiled chestnuts."

"My old nurse used to prepare them for me, and I can vouch that they are delicious as well as soft."

Grant nodded. "All right, Goldsmith, I'll let you be the doctor."

The dying hero sat on a log while the other two scurried around like boys on a camping trip. Branches were laid and set afire while Goldsmith returned from his house with water, a spoon, and a battered tin pot he had borrowed from the stable hands. In minutes the water boiled and the nuts were placed into the pot to cook. While Grant watched with a bemused look on his face, Alden Goldsmith mashed the nuts into a white pudding. When he was satisfied with his work, he presented the pot to Grant.

"My apologies for the mean nature of the dishes, Mr. President. I'm sure this is nothing like the fine china you used in the White House and have in your home."

Grant took the pot in both hands as if it were a rare gift. Since Christmas he had subsisted on tasteless cold soups and milk. Hot or solid foods threw his throat into spasms so painful that he would be forced to leave the table and walk the halls until the fire in his throat subsided. He did this so that Julia and his family would not see the tears in his eyes. Still, he insisted on joining the family for dinner. In the best and worst of times, his love for his family never wavered, and what little time he had left he wished to spend with them. Meals gave him that opportunity. He still led his family in grace and presided at the head of the table. But weakened as he was, he allowed Fred to carve the meat that he could no longer swallow.

Water burned his throat above all else. On bad days he might go all day without drinking to avoid the pain.

"This looks equally grand, Alden. Better than anything I used during my campaigns. Besides, the White House china always made me nervous. I constantly worried about breaking my place setting."

"How so, Mr. President?"

"Well, Alden, it was quite expensive and did not belong to me."

Goldsmith smiled at his friend's utter lack of pretense. Young Meade looked away in embarrassment. How could this man to whom the nation owed so much fret about breaking a dish? Surely he had the right to trash the entire White House if he wanted to.

Grant continued. "As to the dishes at Mount MacGregor, we have only plain crockery. Julia insisted on adding her fine china and silverware to the settlement of my debts."

"I am so sorry to hear that, Mr. President," Meade blurted.

"Oh, don't be," Grant added with a smile. "It is quite serviceable and rather sturdy. I need not fear breaking it."

Carefully, Grant raised the spoon to his lips and tasted the mush. His face brightened. It tasted better than he had remembered. While his companions watched, he spooned tiny portions into his mouth until the pot was empty. He set it down on the grass and turned his gaze back to the restful river. His right hand searched inside his jacket and withdrew a single cigar. Grant held it, turning it over in his fingers, while he studied the rolled tube of tobacco. This one would be special.

Meade saw Grant contemplating the cigar and remarked, "You are famous for your cigars, Mr. President. Everyone associated you with a cigar in your hand," Meade blundered on, unaware that he had touched on a sensitive subject.

"Yes, but I smoked a pipe at one time. I could not afford cigars. One can always find something to smoke in a pipe, as I recall, even when you have no money to buy tobacco. Corn silk will do in a pinch. After the fall of Fort Donelson, a grateful merchant sent me an entire wagonload of cigars. I believe I estimated there were more than ten thousand—all of the finest Cuban tobacco. I gave box after box away to my staff, my visitors, to whomever I could. But I hardly put a dent in the pile. So I took to smoking them myself. *Harper's Magazine* published a drawing of me with one of those gift cigars, and then there was no end to it. More gift cigars kept coming, faster than I could give them away or smoke them up. Perhaps I have smoked too many," he added gravely.

He recalled asking Shrady if his smoking had caused his throat cancer. The surgeon replied the malignancy was due to the nervous tension placed upon Grant by his taxing role as commander of the Federal forces and as President, and Grant had no reason to doubt his answer. However, Shrady warned that his continued smoking was irritating the lesions in his throat and might lead to fatal bleeding. His beloved cigars might just be the straw that broke the camel's back, the doctor suggested. It would be best to stop.

Every day now was borrowed, Grant knew, and there was still so much left undone. His manuscript was far from finished. There was no question of choice. For himself, death meant a blessed release from his constant torment, but he knew he must press on. Completing his memoirs was his last and only chance to save Julia.

Grant looked wistfully at his cigar. He held it up to them in a curious salute. "Gentleman, this is the last cigar I will ever smoke. The doctors tell me I will never finish my work if I do not stop."

While Goldsmith and Meade watched in silence, Grant took a match from his vest and lighted his cigar. He turned away from them to watch the river while he smoked. Behind Grant, Goldsmith bowed his head and pressed his hand to his eyes in a fruitless attempt to hold back his tears. With no further interruptions, Grant puffed slowly on his last cigar until nothing remained but ash.

# OUT ON A LIMB

Mark Twain bounded up the stairs to the library two steps at a time. Tucked safely inside the breast pocket of his white vest he carried a letter that added fuel to his irrepressible zeal. The note from his partner, Charles L. Webster read: "There's big money for both of us in that book and in the terms indicated in my note to the General we can make it pay *big*." With his new book, *The Adventures of Huckleberry Finn,* selling out on its first printing, Twain had every reason to burst with enthusiasm. Grant's memoirs would be the biggest thing to hit the readers that he could remember. He could hardly wait to tell the general.

The faces of those waiting for him on the upper landing stopped him cold. Their somber expressions quenched his glee.

"What is it?" Twain gasped as he struggled to catch his breath. His breathing reminded him that a fifty-year-old ought not to be galloping up steps like a child. "Is it the general? Has he taken a turn for the worse?"

Fred Grant stepped forward and grasped Twain's hand. His handshake stopped the author's forward progress, and turned him away from the door to the library. "Have you not been keeping current of my father's progress?" Fred whispered.

Twain looked from one face to the other. Three doctors barring his way could not mean good news. "Only what I've read in the papers. They say the general is progressing well with high hopes of recovering," he blurted in bewilderment. A moment ago his heart soared with excitement; now it sank. "Is that not correct, Fred?"

"Those reports are untrue."

Dr. Shrady, standing behind Julia, nodded solemnly, confirming Fred's pronouncement. To his left, Dr. Douglas dropped his head in agreement. Shrady lowered his voice, casting anxious glances at Mrs. Grant as he spoke. While Twain was not a member of Grant's immediate family, both Julia and Fred urged the doctor to be frank with the writer. "The disease has progressed rapidly since you last spoke with the general," Shrady said. "He is much weakened and in considerable pain. His sleep is fitful and so disturbed that he is on the brink of collapse. And—" He stopped, overcome with emotion for this patient he had come to love and admire.

Dr. Barker spoke bluntly. "We fear the general will not live beyond three weeks."

Julia buried her face in her son's shoulder and stifled a soft sob. Fred released his grip on Twain and patted his mother's head in comfort. The physicians shuffled their feet uncomfortably.

"Good God," Twain gasped. "I had no idea." His heart sank even deeper. His last correspondence from Grant stated that the general had finished a rough draft on Vicksburg. That might do for the first volume, but what of the second volume? He needed the Wilderness campaign and Appomattox for that. "What of the book?" he blurted out.

"We are of a divided opinion about that," Douglas answered. "Fred, Dr. Shrady, and I think his writing is keeping him alive."

"I do not agree," Julia countered. "I think his commitment to finishing it creates great anxiety for him, and that saps his remaining energy. Dr. Barker agrees with me."

"And the general?" Twain asked.

Julia smiled ruefully. "Nothing any of us say has the slightest influence over my husband. He is determined to continue writing."

The humorist looked from face to face. Outside these walls his company's agents were selling subscriptions to this work at a feverish pace. He himself exhorted them to keep attacking, to keep pouring the hot shot on, as he put it, until everyone imaginable had signed up.

Thank God for Grant's stubbornness, Twain reasoned. But three weeks! The book would not be finished. He could find no humor in that prospect, not even dark humor.

"May I see the general?" Twain asked softly. Suddenly the business end seemed trivial. He wanted desperately to see the great man at least one more time.

Shrady looked at Julia. She nodded. "If your visit is too tiring," he said, "I shall ask you to leave."

"I understand."

Walking on tiptoe, the writer followed Fred and Julia into the study. Grant's ever-present shadow, Harrison straightened from adjusting the blanket covering Grant's crossed legs and backed into the far corner. Silently, he returned to his wicker chair, although his eyes never left the general. Neat stacks of notes covered the top of the writing desk in front of the seated Grant, and an unfolded military map marked with bold crayon lines draped across a folding table behind him. Grant sat sideways in a wicker chair, with his legs crossed and a writing pad on his lap. His right hand held a worn pencil. At the sound of their footsteps on the creaking wooden floor, he turned slightly to greet them.

Not even Mark Twain's darkest expectations prepared him for what he saw. The writer's solid, unpresuming hero had withered away into a shadow. His body, despite all attempts to hide it with vest and jackets, appeared shrunken in size to a miniature version of the man. Most distressing of all was the gray color that suffused both skin and beard. Grant seemed to be fading away. Even the air in the shut-up room smelled of death and decay. Twain held his breath as he approached for fear his words might shatter the image before him and reduce his idol to a pile of dust.

"Ah, Twain." Grant smiled. "It is good to see you again. How have you been? Well, I hope?"

A lump formed in Twain's throat. How typical of the man, dying as he was, to ask after his own well-being. The author swallowed. "I am well, General." He stopped short of asking after Grant's health. The man's appearance spoke all too eloquently of his illness.

"I am just sorting my notes about the Wilderness. Tomorrow I hope to begin writing about that dreadful place. If I could only get a good night's sleep, I could write faster." He forced a smile. "Julia, do you remember that I told you how easily I slept during that battle? I knew we would prevail even though my officers had grave doubts. I could sleep untroubled then. Now I can barely close my eyes, yet I have no enemy on my flanks." He stopped to correct himself. "That is not entirely correct. I fear I face the most terrible of adversaries, one who has never been defeated. He will win the war, but all I need is to win one last battle and I shall be content. One last battle is all ..."

"General ..." Twain found himself at a loss for words. "How is your writing coming?" he asked, instantly hating himself for asking.

Grant peered at him over the thick rubber rims of his eyeglasses. He scratched his beard with clawlike fingers, and his shoulders moved beneath the embroidered shawl like bones threatening to protrude through some exotic hide. "I figure my writing to three hundred words a page," he calculated. "On good days I manage ten thousand words."

"Ten thousand! Great Jehoshaphat!" Twain exclaimed to the startled looks of the family and physicians. "Ten thousand words in one day, why it would kill me to write even half that!"

Grant studied his friend earnestly. Without pretension he answered. "But my writing is not as good as yours. Elizabeth has been reading portions of *Huckleberry Finn* to me. Your words make the Mississippi spring to life."

Twain could not find words to reply. He simply stood and ran his hands through his unruly hair.

Grant motioned to Harrison to draw up another chair and changed the subject. "Please sit down. You might give me an uncensored report of the bill to place me on the retired list as a Lieutenant General. Fred and Julia refuse to provide me with the details."

Mark Twain slumped into the chair and his face grew hard. "You heard it failed to pass the House."

"Yes. I had hoped it might pass. It would give Julia my pension of five-thousand dollars upon my death." He smiled at his wife.

"A damned shame, General," Twain interjected. "I read an editorial in the *New York Times* that said 'Thus, four Confederate brigadiers, eleven colonels, one major, five captains, two lieutenants, and twelve enlisted men did to Grant in Congress what they couldn't do in the field.' I believe no truer words were ever spoken. I know they spoke for me, and I was once a Confederate myself."

"I'm sorry their animosity against me runs so deeply. The war has been over for twenty years, and our country must put those hatreds behind us. As I said in my inaugural speech: Let us have peace."

"Well, you knew William Rosecrans joined the Confederates in voting against the bill?"

"Rosecrans? No. He was a classmate of mine at the Point."

"Yes, the jackass! Not only did he speak against your bill, he had the audacity to say your abilities as a general officer were highly overrated."

Fred winced at Twain's bluntness. He and his mother had worked hard to keep that piece of news from his father.

Grant's eyes twinkled over his glasses. "Well, well. I'm afraid Rosecrans has never forgiven me for pulling his bacon out of the fire at Chattanooga. He let Bragg pin him up in the town, and his army almost starved to death. They were eating their starved mules and picking seed corn up from the wagon ruts when I broke through with a relief column."

Grant motioned to Harrison, and the man sprang forward and handed him a polished wooden box. Mark Twain wondered how the servant could read Grant's mind, but said nothing. Grant ran his fingers over the satin surface, turning it over and over to view all sides as if it were a rare gem before passing it to Twain.

"This is one of my most prized possessions, a briarwood cigar box that was carved by one of Rosecrans's trapped soldiers. He gave it to me when we marched into town. He jumped up and grasped the stirrup of my horse. I believe it was Jeff Davis I was riding at the time. He cried, 'Hurrah, General, God bless you and General Thomas. This is for you, General. I carved it out of a single piece of briar to keep me from chewing on so fine a piece of wood. I was so hungry I'd have done it if I hadn't used it to whittle on instead. I'd be mighty pleased if you'd accept this as a token of my thanks. You opened the Cracker Line and saved me and my buddies so we can git this war finished.'" Grant looked knowingly at his doctors. "Of course, I no longer have it filled with cigars. I keep my pencils in it instead." He opened the box to reveal a dozen stubby pencils, each carefully whittled to a sharp point.

Dr. Shrady nodded approvingly.

Grant waited until Twain passed back the box. "Well," Grant continued, "I took General Rosecrans to task for getting himself into such a situation. There was no excuse for it. Somehow, the fact that I had him standing tall before me got into the papers. There was quite a row. Several editorials called for his resignation. It could have been my old friend Sylvanus Cadwallader who leaked it. He knew General Rosecrans would never miss an opportunity to give his side to the press—a side that always favored him at the expense of other officers. And, I suppose, Cadwallader wanted the truth told and beat Rosecrans to the punch. Whoever published the story, it was unflattering to General Rosecrans, but accurate."

Twain nodded. "It is still disgraceful. The man is trading on your success, victory that you provided, General. Without your leadership he would not have the glory that got him elected from California." The writer paused to reflect. "Of course, that state favors the extreme. It may be the heat. When I was there it caused men to do some strange things, things lacking in common sense. Not so bad as Nevada, mind you. That place has the lock on blistering lands. You know, Nevada only has one tree that I can recall, and that one is so blasted by lightning as to be unrecognizable." Twain paused for effect. A thin smile on Grant's haggard face encouraged him. The natural raconteur could not contain himself. His well of humor spilled over, and he pressed on. "And I've heard tell that men sent down to Purgatory from Nevada find the change refreshing."

He was gratified to see Grant chuckling. With the general's laughter, the room lightened. Twain thought back to the first time they met and how his speech brought tears to the general's eyes. Silently, the writer thanked his gift. He loved his friend better than a brother and would do anything he could for him. If he could not restore Grant's health, at least he could lighten his burden with laughter.

Laughing proved too much for Grant, however. He broke into a fit of coughing that wracked his body. Fighting for air, he gripped the arms of his chair, his chest bent forward, and he struggled against the spasms that blocked his throat. Julia and his doctors rushed to his side, but he waved them off. They stood helplessly around him while he coughed and wheezed. Mark Twain watched, looking anguished.

After several minutes, the attack ceased. Grant wiped the sweat from his brow and settled back into his chair. Harrison rushed forward to replace the fallen lap robe.

In despair, Fred turned to their visitor. Now was the time to enlist the writer's help. "Mr. Twain, you see how weak Father is. Yet, he insists on testifying in the upcoming trial over that scoundrel Ward. Can you not convince him otherwise?"

Twain frowned. What madness was this? With his physicians saying he had less than three weeks to live, the general wanted to give his deposition? "Surely you are not strong enough, Mr. President?"

Grant shook his head. "I want to prove that I knew nothing of Ward's schemes. This chance may be my last chance. The court has consented to take my testimony in the library."

Fred stamped his foot in disgust. He turned to Twain and waved his hands in frustration. "He does not believe that his testimony will only result in ridicule."

"Ridicule or not, I want the truth on record. We were taken in by Ward—all of us."

Fred sighed. "Father is only letting you see that the Grant family is a pack of fools."

Grant reached out to pat his son's arm. He knew Fred's concern was for his reputation and not for his own. "Ward swindled the president of the

Erie Railroad out of $800,000 and falsely sold part of Senator Chaffee's sil-
ver mines to a banker for $300,000 without a deed or a single letter of au-
thorization. No one ever called these men fools, yet they were taken in just
as we were. I do not think the fact we trusted a man and believed his word
will reflect too badly on us."

Twain raised his eyebrows. Naiveté had its limits, bordering on fool-
ishness, as Fred predicted. No wonder this man was shorn by the politicians
during his presidency.

Dr. Shrady interceded. His perceptive ear noted the weakness in Grant's
voice and the effort this discussion required. "There has been enough excitement for today. My patient should rest now," he stated firmly.

The party filed out the door, leaving Harrison to his watch. Grant
reached out to grasp Twain's sleeve and hold him back. He waited until Julia, the last to leave, stepped outside. She turned back, but he waved her on.

"Mr. President?"

"I would be a fool, though, if I did not believe you might have con-
cerns about my finishing the manuscript, Twain," Grant rasped over another spell of coughing. "Do you have much riding on my work?"

"Do not give it a second thought, Mr. President. My concern is for
your health. If writing the book is harmful to you, you ought to stop. I will
not be injured financially," Twain lied. He presented his best poker face and
hoped Grant believed him. Without thinking, his fingers touched the letter
from his partner inside his pocket. Pay big, Webster had crowed. Now it
might not pay at all.

I'm really out on a limb here, Twain thought, a shaky limb that might
break at any minute. All my royalties from *Huckleberry Finn*, over $55,000,
are tied up to publish Grant's work—and $200,000 I borrowed. If the mem-
oirs are not completed, I'll be ruined. Still, I can't tell Grant that. I can't
cause a dying man to drive himself into an earlier grave to fill my purse.
His friendship means more to me than my fortune.

The dark side of the writer's personality flickered into his thoughts. All
my debts are tied to subscriptions and sales contracts for the book, he calculated. I could cancel them now and cut my losses. A prudent businessman

would do just that. But then sales of Grant's book—if it does get finished—will dwindle to nothing. Subscriptions amount to the bulk of the orders.

Grant read his publisher's mind. Without his memoirs there was no hope for Julia. His fingers gripped the writer's arm. He fixed Twain with a look of iron determination. "Disregard what the doctors say. All my life I have been underestimated. Many voices predicted what I could not do, and I fooled them all."

The grip tightened. *"I mean you shall have the book!"*

Outside the library, Twain looked back at the dying general. Julia had returned to Grant's side. Here was a love that transcended wars, bad times, and politics, the author noted. So much between them went unspoken, but their feeling was nearly palpable. Someday he might write about them if only he could find the right words to do them justice. For all his skill, he doubted he could.

Mark Twain quietly closed the oak door to the library. Prudent businessman be damned! He had the general's word. Tomorrow he would issue press releases to all the papers. He was going farther out on the limb.

# THE PENSION

The pounding on the front door threatened to knock the heavy wood from its thick hinges. Behind the door, Tyrell Harrison adjusted his starched collar and squared his shoulders for another battle. Over a hundred attempts by reporters to see his master this day brought his patience to an end. How could he be expected to care for the general and fend off the hoard of newspapermen who incessantly attacked the house?

No end was in sight. Reporters bribed the deliverymen, hid inside their wagons, climbed through unlocked windows, and even sneaked through the laundry chute. All in an attempt to see his dying friend and master. But none reached the general. Harrison saw to that. More vigilant than the finest army picket, he beat them all back. The house was not the only site of attack. Writers, posing as patients, bombarded Dr. Shrady and Dr. Douglas to the point that the doctors wore various disguises to check on their patient.

Since word broke that Grant lay on his deathbed, the newspapers drove themselves into a frenzy to reach the dying man. The nation that still loved him wanted to know every detail, and the papers saw great profits if only they could supply the facts.

But this late in the day was too much, Harrison decided. He would teach this one a special lesson. Carefully, he selected a stout walking stick from the umbrella stand, testing it against his hand with a solid whack. He raised the stick, selected his best scowl, moved to block the entrance, and swung open the door.

"Jesus, Harrison, it's me!" William Tecumseh Sherman cried as he dodged the blow. "Don't fire! I am friendly."

Harrison blanched. He stammered and quickly hid his club behind his back. But he still kept it ready. Behind Sherman a dozen carriages lined the street and clumps of reporters circled the streetlamp. As they rushed forward, Harrison pulled Sherman inside and slammed the door. Muffled voices outside screamed in protest.

Sherman shook the rain off his cloak. "Outflanked them, did we, Harrison? The sons of bitches!" He glared at the door. "By God, I hate them worse than body lice. Lice at least never called me crazy. If I could, I'd roll a cannon out your door and give them all a taste of grapeshot. Either that or sic Custer's Sixth Michigan on them. Now that was a cavalry unit that would scatter those parasites." He threw off his cape and tossed it on a chair, where it dripped water onto the rug.

Harrison collected the dripping coat and hung it inside the closet. Turning his back to Sherman, he sponged up the puddles of water with a towel he kept in the closet for that purpose. While frequent visitors like Mark Twain shook off their wet coats outside, Harrison knew Sherman never did, preferring to charge inside and do his dripping in the foyer. "The general will be mighty glad to see you, General Sherman."

Sherman's face dropped. "How is he, Harrison?" he asked earnestly.

Harrison lowered his eyes to the floor. Tears blurred his vision, but he kept his voice steady. "Not well, sir. Not well at all. Every day when those reporters ask me, I say, 'He's much better today, thank you. I think he's growing better every day.' But he's not."

"Well, I've got some news that ought to cheer him up. May I see him?"

"He's upstairs in his bedroom, General Sherman. Go on up." Harrison pointed to the staircase. "I'll be up presently. First, I better double check that all the windows and doors are locked tight. I don't want a reporter slipping past me."

Sherman caught sight of himself in the hall mirror as he turned. He blinked. An old man stared back at him. So many gray hairs, he reflected. *There was a time when my beard and my hair were fiery red. We were young and immortal then. My face was always seamed, but my hair was red. Now, I've grown old and gray, and my friend is dying. I can't imagine him not being here. I never expected that of him. He seemed indestructible to me.*

Outside the bedroom, Sherman drew himself up to his full height. He opened the door cautiously. Grant was slumped in his wicker chair, bundled like a mummy. Julia sat beside him, looking even paler than her husband. Grant appeared thinner than their last meeting. *How much more can the man take?* Sherman wondered. *He never was robust to begin with. From the looks of him, he must be nothing but skin and bone by now.*

Sherman noticed a white-suited man sitting on Grant's other side. Mark Twain rose to greet this new arrival, but Sherman rushed forward and announced his news directly to his old commander.

"Sam, I've got great news. The bill to reinstate you passed! You are returned to your former rank of Lieutenant General, retired."

Julia jumped to her feet. She kissed Grant on his forehead. "Hurrah! Our old commander is back!" she cried.

Twain slapped his knee and rushed forward to pump Sherman's hand. Even the poker-faced Harrison broke into a wide grin. But Grant showed little emotion.

"I am gratified the thing has passed," he said. He was thinking of the small pension Julia would receive now. It would help, but it would not clear his debts. *Nothing really had changed. Everything hinged on the book.* "You are wholly responsible, Cump. I cannot thank you enough."

Sherman flushed self-consciously. He hoped Grant had not heard about him exhorting his friends to cut their way back into Congress to press the reconsideration of Grant's pension. He would not tell Grant that news of his dying had shamed many of the representatives into changing their vote. "I can't take all the credit. You had help from the most unexpected quarters. Even from the Honorable Representative from Kentucky, James Speed."

Twain's eyes twinkled. "Speed? A reconstructed Confederate like me, I hope?"

"Yes, it was the former Attorney General who carried the Confederate veterans to your side. Those who voted against you at first changed their vote after he published his letter."

"What letter?" Twain asked.

Sherman explained, all the while keeping his eyes on his friend. Unfortunately, his wonderful news only appeared to drain Grant even more. "Speed wrote in his letter what you told President Johnson after General Bradley Johnson was arrested as he returned home to Baltimore."

"General Bradley Johnson?" Julia looked puzzled. She turned to Twain, but he only shrugged and arched his thick eyebrows.

Grant spoke. "Bradley Johnson was a native of Baltimore who fought for the South. He surrendered, and I released him on parole like all the rest. When he returned home, the civil authorities arrested him for bearing arms against his state and charged him with treason." The explanation exhausted Grant, and he slumped back in his chair.

Sherman continued, "Speed said you went to President Johnson and argued that the man was released on military parole and could not be arrested by civilians."

"So?" Now Twain appeared confused. He could not see how this action would sway Grant's former enemies into changing their vote.

"Well, President Johnson had his eyes set on bigger fish. He asked Grant how he could arrest Robert E. Lee as a traitor if he could not hold General Johnson on the same charges. He was planning to jail Old Marse Robert. Sam here told him that he couldn't, not unless Lee violated the terms of his parole. And . . ." Sherman paused for effect.

"And?" Twain took the bait. He rose from his chair as if he were planning to drag the words out of Sherman.

"And Sam told President Johnson that if Lee were arrested, he would resign as Commander-in-Chief of the Army!"

Twain's face lighted. He turned toward Grant, who averted his eyes and studied the worn tops of his slippers to avoid the man's admiring gaze. "So you kept Robert E. Lee out of jail, did you? How come no one ever heard of this before, General? It would make you an instant hero of the South."

Grant shrugged. "It was a private matter."

"Well, now it isn't," Sherman crowed. "Every veteran of the Southern Confederation knows the good turn you did their beloved General Lee. They all feel indebted to you."

"My my," the writer chuckled. "I can see how that would work, but did it convert the prodigal son, Rosecrans?"

Sherman grinned maliciously. "I petitioned the son of a bitch myself. Just between us, I may have blackmailed him. I threatened to dredge a little knowledge I had on him." He stopped to stroke his close-cropped beard. "Something about a comely Southern maid in Chattanooga."

Mark Twain guffawed loudly. This intrigue was better than a dime novel. Julia appeared shocked. "Why, General Sherman—"

Sherman slapped both hands over his heart and rolled his eyes toward the ceiling in a mocking look of repentance. "Begging your pardon, Julia. I wasn't about to let that pompous demagogue block our efforts. If Rosecrans had been any sort of a general, I might have given a second thought to extorting him. Anyway, you knew I was nasty the day we first met, and my wife confirmed it to you."

Julia frowned. "Still ..."

Sherman removed one hand to tap the side of his nose with a finger. "I am allowed to do the unorthodox when it is required, Julia. It is one of the few benefits of being labeled insane."

Grant wished to change the subject. "How did this pass?" he asked Sherman. "George Childs telegraphed me on March third that Congress was set to adjourn, and he saw little hope of the bill being reintroduced."

Sherman could not resist the chance to place another dig at his hated newspapermen. "Well, that only shows that men like your editor friend of the Philadelphia *Public Ledger* are usually wrong. Still, it was a close thing, Sam, a damned close thing. It truly did not happen until the eleventh hour. Childs was correct about one thing: it did not make it on the third, the last day of Congress."

"But how, then?"

"The House forgot an important appropriations bill in their haste to adjourn, funding for the Brooklyn Navy Yard, I believe. So the Speaker reconvened the House the next day, the fourth, and ordered them to backdate what passed to the previous day."

Grant looked puzzled. "But Cleveland's inauguration was the fourth. As I recall, the Constitution prohibits the old House from meeting past noon on that day, requiring it to give way to the newly elected House."

"True, true. As I said, it passed on the eleventh hour to a resounding chorus of ayes. The bill was rushed to Cleveland to sign. It was his second official act as the new President. Robert Todd Lincoln"—the outgoing Secretary of War—"presented the papers himself."

Julia placed her hand on her husband's shoulder. "His father signed your first appointment as Brigadier General." Her eyes grew misty. She looked at Twain and said, "Did I ever tell you of my conversation with the late President, just before the surrender at Appomattox?"

"No, I do not believe so, Mrs. Grant."

"Julia," Grant chided his wife gently, "I do not think Sherman cares to hear of that. He must have important things to attend to."

"No," Sherman protested. "I would like to hear this. Lincoln was the only politician I ever liked." He corrected himself. "I never considered you a politician, Sam."

Julia folded her hands in her lap and began rocking in her chair as if telling a story to little boys. "I was staying with the children in one of those little log cabins the general built at City Point. My, there were a slew of them, over forty as I recall. Mr. Lincoln was staying on the *River Queen* in the harbor, and Ulys was using the grand Appomattox Manor on the hill as his headquarters. Well, one day there was a knock on the door, and Mr. Lincoln stooped his head to step inside. He was looking for Ulys."

"If we only knew then that Lincoln had only three more weeks to live," Grant added. "He spent two of those last three weeks living on that gloomy steamer."

"Yes." Julia smiled sweetly, pleased her story stirred her husband's interest. His desire to finish his writing drove him to exclude all else these days. "Well, I asked the President if he had made any peace arrangements with the Confederate peace commissioners. I guess my question took him aback. He probably thought I should mind my own business, but he was polite. He frowned and said: 'Well, no.'

" 'No?' I said. 'Why, Mr. President, aren't you going to make peace with them? They are our own people, you know.' He looked very tired and sad. 'Yes,' he said, 'I do not forget that.' Then he took a large, folded piece of paper from his coat pocket, unfolded it, and read the terms to me. I thought they were most generous. 'Did they not accept those?' I said. 'No,' he said sadly. 'Shame on them,' I replied. 'Those terms are most liberal.' Lincoln shook his head wearily and smiled. 'I thought when you understood the matter, you would agree with us,' he said.

"While the President waited for you, Ulys, I gave him a cup of tea. He looked so worn-out my heart ached for him. I'd watched what the war did to you, how you lost weight and how lined your face became, but it was ten times worse with Lincoln. To cheer him up I told him I had had my own discussions with the Confederate commissioners."

"You did?" Grant appeared surprised. This was the first time Julia had mentioned this part of her conversation with the late President. He leaned forward.

"I told Mr. Lincoln that my own brother was a prisoner in the South and that I related that fact to the commissioners. His incarceration was ironic for he was an unrepentant secessionist. The commissioners asked why my brother was not exchanged, and I replied because he was a civilian, not a soldier, arrested while he was visiting in Louisiana. Lincoln smiled and asked if I had spoken to you about seeing to his release."

Grant frowned at this.

Julia ignored his look. " 'Yes, I have, Mr. President,' I told Lincoln, 'but my husband refused to intervene, saying that he could not ask for that while so many brave Union soldiers who had fought for their country were imprisoned.' Then, Lincoln said that his wife had lost much of her family fighting for the South, and he prayed the war would end soon."

"Well said, Julia," Sherman grunted. "With the Southerners in Congress embracing Sam, that breach is healed except for one last devil—me. I fear the South shall never welcome me back into their fold." He shrugged. "But I don't lose any sleep over it."

Mark Twain rose to his feet and cast a meaningful look at Sherman. Already Grant showed signs of fatigue. "Best we take our leave on this high note, General. We don't want to overstay our welcome." He walked to the door, making sure that the exuberant Sherman moved ahead of him.

But Sherman got in the last word. He balked at the doorway and waved to his friend. "March thirty-first, Sam. Expect your first paycheck on that date!"

"March thirty-first," Grant echoed hollowly as they closed the door.

In the hallway a pale Fred Grant encountered them. "Did I hear you say March thirty-first?" he asked.

"Why, yes," Twain replied. "That is the date of your father's first pension. It should not be cause for alarm."

Fred shook his head. "March thirty-first is the day an astrologer predicted my father would die."

# LIES, DAMNABLE LIES

The weather that March was the worst people had seen in thirty years. The skies themselves seemed to be grieving for the dying Grant. Day after day passed without the sun ever showing its face. Instead, rain pelted the streets and the silent throngs that held their deathwatch outside the general's home while cold winds added to their misery.

Each day, Shrady trudged to the house and found his patient closer to the grave. Weakness kept Grant from moving from his bedroom, and pain kept him from eating. He slept little and then only fitfully, preferring to doze in his chair, where breathing came more easily for him. Whenever the general lay down, the swelling in his throat threatened to close his wind-pipe, slowly choking him. Fits of coughing racked his body and further sapped his remaining strength.

Grant's ordeal bound the nation in a mood of sympathy not seen be-fore. Unlike Lincoln's death, which came suddenly and grieved the North, Grant's protracted illness weighed heavily on both North and South. Robert E. Lee's son sent his best wishes, as did Congressman Rosecrans, who now tried to make up for his shameful behavior with kind words. Even Jefferson Davis prayed for comfort for Grant's body and peace for his mind.

Only P.G.T. Beauregard remained unrepentant. Even after all these years, his bloody encounter with Grant at Shiloh still weighed heavily on him. "May God have mercy on his soul," he snapped when asked for a statement.

Sherman snarled as well at his hated reporters, but for a different reason. He was losing his father figure, the rock that had enabled him to endure the confusion of the world. He hid his sorrow behind bluster. "When General Grant dies, President Cleveland will have something to say," Sherman seethed. "After that the rest will have our say. Until that time comes, I will have nothing to say."

Madmen and charlatans added their voices. One prayed fervently for Grant to renounce coffee before a policeman removed him. Quacks pestered Shrady and Douglas with new, miracle cures by the hundreds. Policemen stationed themselves along the street to keep the curious and the mourners at a respectful distance from the Grants' front door. Each paper strung a direct telegraph wire from a house across the street to their offices.

Old military friends made their pilgrimages to their leader. Ely Parker, Grant's assistant adjutant general at Appomattox and a general in his own right now, visited Grant along with Horace Porter and General John Logan.

Mark Twain came daily. He would sit in the library with head bowed or visit the general while his thick brows drooped in sorrow. Asked if he prayed for his friend's deliverance, Twain replied that he wished he could, but he did not believe in God. Never once did he mention to Julia or Fred his impending financial ruin if the general's book was not finished.

Five days before the dreaded thirty-first, a convulsive spasm of coughing hit General Grant. Wave after wave of choking and coughing followed. Injections of morphine and cocaine did little good. Everyone feared the spells would precipitate bleeding which the man's constricted throat could not handle.

On March 31, the day prophesied by the astrologer as Grant's last,

Shrady injected a strong dose of morphine to quiet the general's restlessness. Silently, he watched Grant sink into a deepening stupor. Packing his medical bag, the doctor left the house never expecting to see his patient again alive. The dreaded day had arrived.

Five hours later Tyrell Harrison knocked on the doctor's door and summoned him back to the Grant house. Stepping from his cab, Shrady collided with Dr. Douglas. Outside the front door, a reporter from the *Times* snagged Shrady's arm and refused to let go.

"Doctor," the man called as he braked Shrady's run, "is it true that you have decided against excising the tumor from General Grant's tongue to help his breathing? Is it true such operations carry a one in four mortality rate?"

Shrady stopped, sending the man sprawling on the mist-slicked paving stones. He looked down, regarding the man with a curious mix of contempt and compassion. These were the same men who had hounded him after he performed the autopsy on President Garfield. Their sensationalizing his findings tainted him and scandalized his profession for years to come. He wished they would leave him and the Grants in peace. But he knew that would never happen.

Still, if he said nothing, the man might print something outrageous. Even now, reports appeared in print of Grant's miraculous recovery alongside papers purporting his illness to be a hoax designed to get his pension. Whatever the case, Shrady hoped to block a media frenzy similar to what had followed the assassination of Garfield. He marshaled his reserves, ordered his voice to be steady, and replied, "It is doubtful that the general's heart would stand another choking attack. But we have decided he could not survive a tracheotomy for very long."

For all his reserve, Shrady found he could hardly speak. He regarded Grant as too close a friend. The lone light in the upstairs bedroom drew his attention, beckoning to him with a faltering urgency.

While the reporter hastily scribbled down his words, Douglas and Shrady bolted through the front entrance. Harrison threw his weight against the door and slammed it shut. Inside they found Mrs. Grant on the upper landing in tears, with her head pressed against her son's chest. Fred tried hard to maintain his composure.

"I have had Reverend John Newman baptize my husband," Julia wept. "I ... I never knew if he had been baptized before, and I thought it wise to ..." Her voice died away.

Shrady climbed the stairs two steps at a time and made his way to the bedroom door. Steeling himself, he opened the door. Douglas hobbled behind.

A single electric lamp glowed dimly by the general's bedside. Harrison moved to his chair just outside the cone of light, prepared to spring to his master's need. Shrady paused inside and listened. Only the creaking of the wood floor beneath his feet reached his ears. The strident, labored breathing of his patient could not be heard.

Shrady stepped to the bedside and slipped his fingers around Grant's wrist. He expected to find the hand cold and without a pulse.

The pulse was faltering but still present.

Grant opened his eyes at Shrady's touch. His brow, smoothed in sleep, resumed its characteristic corrugated look of determination. He smiled weakly. He motioned for Shrady to bend closer.

"If you doctors know how long a man can live underwater, you can judge how long it will take me to choke when the time comes," Grant whispered. That effort triggered another spell of gasping and choking.

Shrady turned to his colleague. Douglas produced a syringe from his bag and filled it with brandy. Both men hoped the brandy would break the choking spell. At worst, the injection might help the general to slide into oblivion.

Unexpectedly, injecting the entire syringe into a vein in Grant's right arm produced no result. Shrady could scarcely feel a pulse at all. In desperation, Douglas filled another syringe and emptied it into the general's arm.

The pulse quickened. Grant, strangling on his back, forced himself onto his elbow in search of air. Gagging, he rolled to one side and retched. A chunk of rotted tissue plugging the back of his throat broke loose and shot from his mouth onto the bed. A flood of hemorrhage followed for end-less seconds. Miraculously, the bleeding stopped.

Grant forced himself into a sitting position and inhaled the first clean, unobstructed breath he had in weeks. His chest rose and fell easily as he savored the fresh air. Shrady grasped his patient's wrist.

The pulse beat strongly and evenly.

Douglas and Shrady crowded around the bed while Harrison prayed silently from his chair in the corner. Grant drew in a deep breath and blinked up at his astonished physicians. He shifted his right hand to pat Shrady's arm.

"I am much better," he said simply, although his voice was reduced to a hoarse whisper. "Tomorrow, I hope to resume my writing."

The next day he did just that.

And each day afterward. While Reverend Newman claimed it was his prayers, and Douglas and Shrady the brandy, Grant left them to argue as he renewed his attack on his memoirs, dictating hours at a time until he regained the strength to write. Like all of his campaigns, his mind held each individual move as well as the overall plan, whether it was army troops or book chapters. Day after day Grant's writing produced enough work to fill twenty-five printed pages.

To Twain's dismay few of the chapters arrived in sequence. Little did the author realize that Grant often wrote his field commands out of order during the war only to shuffle them into proper arrangement at the end. Grant considered his memoirs his final battle and attacked it with old and proven methods.

To Mark Twain's delight, however, the general was now well into the second volume.

By April's end Grant raced along, leapfrogging over obstacles in a fashion reminiscent of his swinging around Cold Harbor to capture Petersburg. On one bright clear spring morning on the last of the month Grant looked up from his work as Mark Twain burst into the library with Fred hot on his heels.

Grant recrossed his legs, adjusted his writing pad on his lap, and laid down his pencil. He removed his glasses and studied the red-faced humorist. Twain appeared about to suffer a seizure. His face glowed beet red from his collar line to the roots of his unbridled hair, and red veins suffused the whites of his eyes.

"Twain?" Grant greeted his favorite intruder.

"Those goddamned sons of bitches!" Twain swore as he struck a folded paper against his opened palm like a man testing a cudgel. "Goddamn them straight to hell!"

"What is the problem?" Grant asked, looking from the writer to his son and back again.

Twain waved the paper about. "The *World*, that's what! That daily issue of unmedicated closet paper has printed the most scurrilous lie since the serpent whispered into the ear of Eve! I shall sue them for libel! I have already retained Clarence Seward to that end. Apologies will not do, nor will retractions. We will press for punitive damages. Damages that will cripple—yes, disable—that paper financially!"

Grant ordered the pile of papers on his lap. "What did they write that is so destructive?" he asked.

Twain thrust the newspaper at Fred. "Read it, Fred. I cannot. I am so distraught."

Fred unrolled the clinched paper and read from its torn page. " 'The work upon his new book about which so much has been said is the work of General Adam Badeau. General Grant has furnished all of the material and all of the ideas in the memoirs, but Badeau has done the work of composition. The most the general has done upon the book has been to prepare the rough notes and memoranda for its various chapters.' " Fred lowered the paper to glance at the stack of handwritten pages stacked around his father.

"Lies, damnable lies!" Twain shouted as he stomped around the room. "I'll have their livers, I'll—"

Grant held up his hand to silence the seething writer. His eyes twinkled. "Oh, I thought it was something serious. Adam Badeau, although my friend and a novelist in his own right, is not writing my book. I am."

"It is serious," Twain insisted. "If everyone believes your memoirs are not your own work, they will not buy your book."

Grant replaced his glasses and searched for a clean sheet of paper.

He found one. "Well, the best approach then is a frontal assault." His pencil raced across the page, but he spoke as he wrote. "This letter will be sent to the Charles Webster Publishing Company for you to print in the newspapers."

My attention has been called to a paragraph in the *World* newspaper of this city of Wednesday, April 29th of which the following is a part.

"The work upon his new book about which so much has been said is the work of General Adam Badeau. General Grant, I have no doubt, has furnished all of the material and all of the ideas in the memoirs as far as they are prepared; but Badeau has done the work of composition. The most that General Grant has done upon this book has been to prepare the rough notes and memoranda for its various chapters."

I will divide this into four parts and answer each of them.

First—"The work upon his new book about which so much has been said is the work of General Adam Badeau."

This is false. Composition is entirely my own.

Second—"General Grant, I have no doubt, has furnished all of the material and all of the ideas in the memoirs as far as they are prepared."

This is true.

Third—"but Badeau has done the work of composition."

The composition is entirely my own.

Fourth—"The most that General Grant has done upon this book has been to prepare the rough notes and memoranda for its various chapters."

Whatever rough notes were made were prepared by myself and for my exclusive use.

You may take such measures as you see fit to correct this report which places me in the attitude of claiming authorship of a book which I did not write and is also injurious to you who are publishing and advertising such a book as my work.

Grant lowered his pencil and looked up to see Twain grinning widely.

"A damned fine attack, General," the mustached author crowed. "It puts me in mind of a piece an old riverboat captain used to say whenever he saw one of his competitor's steamboats run aground: 'Well, if that don't get their attention at least it'll sink 'em.' I think your letter will definitely sink them."

But the next day, Adam Badeau marched into Grant's study and slapped a sealed envelope onto the desk in front of the hunched-over writer. Before Grant could open the package, his friend spun on his heel, marched back out, and slammed the study door so hard it jarred the pictures on the wall. Badeau's action left little doubt that his visit was not friendly. Fred Grant stared after him. His hands balled into fists while his mind wondered where he could find a horsewhip.

His father hefted the thick envelope in his hand as he stared at the closed door. "Badeau has always been a quarrelsome and arrogant man," he reminded his son. He looked at the letter. "Do you suppose, Fred, that this is another attack on my flank? By one whom I thought was my friend?"

"By Heaven, if it is ... I'll—I'll cane that pompous jackass myself!" Fred stammered.

Grant looked over the rims of his glasses at his son. "Fred, where did you learn such speech? You must be associating too much with Mr. Twain, or is it the influence of Sherman?" Although he chided his son, Fred's loyalty caused his breast to swell. "You know I never put much stock in swearing. I felt it never did much good other than to inflame a situation." As if his own example was not sufficient, Grant added. "Lincoln never swore, you know."

Grant tore open the envelope and studied the five pages of ultimatum.

"What does it say, Father?"

Grant shook his head. Adam Badeau had been his friend since the Civil War. Despite his quick temper and overbearing nature, Badeau had risen to the rank of Brigadier General on Grant's staff and been wounded in the service. A writer in his own right, he had offered suggestions while Grant was writing his pieces for the *Century Magazine*. Fearful that he might die before he added his scattered notes into his memoirs, Grant had asked Badeau if he might assemble the chapters if the worst came to pass.

Grant frowned. That was my mistake, he thought. Even though Badeau declined, saying he was working on a novel about Cuba, now he thinks we have a commitment. He read on carefully, rereading passages several times. At length he looked up at his son.

" 'Yours is not and will not be the work of a literary man, but the simple story of a great general,' he writes."

"Goddamn him!" Fred spit. Instantly, he held up his hand. "Sorry, Father, but Mark Twain would have said far worse."

Grant continued, "He says, 'I am willing to agree to complete the work from your dictation in the first person ... to claim, of course, no credit whatever for its composition but to declare as I have always done that you wrote it absolutely.' "

"Badeau should have no difficulty saying that for it is the truth. You wrote every line yourself."

Grant carefully folded the paper. "In exchange he wants ten percent of the book profits and a retainer of a thousand dollars a month until the work is done."

Fred's face turned purple. "A thousand dollars a month!"

Grant's eyes twinkled. "He has grossly overestimated our poor finances, to be sure. When was the last time we saw that amount of money?"

"What will you do?"

Grant searched for another clean sheet of paper. His face resumed its serious mask. "Time for another direct attack." He wrote:

> My name goes with the book, and I want it my work in the fullest sense. I do not want a book bearing my name to go before the world, which I did not write. I have to say that for the last twenty-four years I have been very much employed in writing. As a soldier, I wrote my own orders, plans of battle, instructions and reports. As President, I wrote every official document, I believe, usual for Presidents to write, bearing my name.

Now came the hardest part, yet Grant knew it was necessary. There must be no confusion after he was gone. Julia's future depended upon it. "You and I must give up all association so far as the preparation of any literary work goes which bears my signature," he scrawled.

He looked up sadly. Fred stood waiting, so he handed his letter to Fred and turned back to his writing. Over twenty years of friendship gone with the stroke of a pen. It was just as swift and cruel and final as a well-placed bullet.

A single well-aimed minié ball was all it took. Staring at the blank page, he could recall the wrinkled and whiskered face of Major General John Sedgwick squinting beneath the downturned brim of his weathered slouch hat, its tarnished gold bullion cord and frayed acorn ends serving as the only indication he was a general. A hat not unlike my own, Grant mused.

Old Uncle John, loved by his men, was standing in his stirrups when a Confederate sharpshooter saw his gold-braided slouch hat and killed him with a single bullet that struck Sedgwick beneath his left eye. A moment before, the general had ridden forward and joked to his men, who lay cowering behind tree stumps, that those same sharpshooters could not hit an elephant from there.

I retired to my tent and cried when I heard of Uncle John's death, Grant recalled. That was at Spotsylvania Courthouse just after the Battle of the Wilderness. The Wilderness—where I first faced Robert E. Lee.

# THE WILDERNESS

As dawn broke across the roads converging on the shallow crossings of the Rapidan River, the sunlight peeled back the shadows on a striking scene. Clouds of ocher dust boiled along the length of the roads, half obscuring the dark blue uniforms that choked the line of march. Thousands of bayonets glinted and shimmered in the rising heat so that the columns of soldiers looked like a gigantic centipede wriggling along, bristling with steely spines. Scattered along this writhing path, battle flags and regimental colors rose above the dust, fluttering like blue-, yellow-, and red-striped wings.

The Army of the Potomac was marching south. Hours before, cavalry brigades splashed across the river at Germanna Ford and Ely's Ford, east of Lee's fortifications upriver at Mine Run. Driving away the few Confederate pickets, the horsemen fanned out to guard the crossing. Behind them, Federal engineers dove into the waters and strung lines across the swirling current. India rubber and canvas-covered pontoon boats followed as men sweated to push them from their wagons into the river. Within minutes pontoon bridges spanned the crossings and men marched across.

As the sun rose the day grew warm. The dust rose higher in the sky and drifted aimlessly on the light wind. The columns of marching soldiers continued unbroken, but soon discarded blankets, knapsacks, and great-coats speckled the sides of the roads. Rumbling across a separate bridge, the supply wagons, each bearing the emblem of their respective corps stitched on their canvas covers, jostled up the far bank and into the gloom of the dense wilderness ahead. Dried apples, potatoes, pork, and molasses rolled along with black powder, cartridges, and bandages.

Twisted clumps of stunted trees, scrub, and thorn brush from a deci-mated forest swallowed up the columns on the far side. The vegetation cut off the sunlight without moderating the heat. Only patches of daylight shone across the scattered openings. Most large trees in the region had been burned for fuel for the tin and iron mines in the region, and their re-placement with tangled brush was Nature's retaliation for the damage done her. Movement outside the dark, narrow paths met constant resistance from the brush. As the men and wagons vanished into the forest, the clink and rattle of tin cups and wagon chains grew muffled and still. The Wilder-ness appeared to be devouring the unending line of soldiers.

Sitting astride Cincinnati to watch the army pass below, Grant de-cided that the Wilderness was an accurate name for the place. For hours, from the front steps of a broken-down farmhouse on the bluff, he had watched the forest swallow up his forces, and it left him uneasy, so he mounted his horse and rode along the hills.

By noon his heart rose as he spotted the swallow-tailed flag of a corps headquarters flutter past. A white St. Andrew's cross emblazoned the center of the dark blue forked flag. Grant took a deep breath. John Sedgwick's Sixth Corps was crossing. Warren's men were across. With any luck, Gen-eral Warren's Fifth Corps flag with its Maltese cross would be planted be-side the Wilderness Tavern by now.

Grant closed his eyes against the glare from the Rapidan. He could picture Hancock leading his Second Corps with their three-leafed-clover banner across Ely's Ford and down the five miles to Chancellorsville. Hav-ing Hancock's corps in support of their rear made good sense even though it divided his army. Second Corps was the most seasoned of the Army of the Potomac, and Hancock was now fit and able for the first time since his wound at Gettysburg. After a bent nail was pulled from his groin wound, the festering ceased, the wound healed, and Hancock now commanded his corps from his horse instead of an ambulance wagon. Hancock carried the nail as a lucky piece.

Grant turned his horse and headed down the Germanna Plank Road, deeper into the forest. So far we have been lucky, he realized. He half expected Lee to attack while they forded the river, or cross the Rapidan himself and strike north at Washington. Just in case, Grant had left Burnside's Ninth Corps across the river if Lee should head north.

General Humphrey, Meade's chief of staff, had insisted that the advance troops bivouac near Wilderness Tavern, inside the forest. He claimed the artillery and supply trains could not keep up with such a rapid march.

A rider galloped up to Colonel Horace Porter, Grant's newly appointed aide-de-camp and a full-blooded Indian. The rider saluted and thrust a dispatch into the colonel's gloved hand. Porter tore open the message.

"Enemy moving in strength toward New Verdiersville!" Porter shouted. "Lee is coming out! General Meade passes along a signal he intercepted from General Ewell. It says: 'We are moving. Had I not better move D. and D. toward New Verdiersville?' "

Grant flicked his cigar eagerly. Lee was coming out from behind his fortifications at Mine Run like a lion stalking his prey. "That gives just the information I wanted. It shows that Lee is drawing out from his position and is pushing across to meet us."

Grant looked at the dust-covered rider. His horse was panting and covered with sweat. "Son, can you take a message to General Burnside?"

"Yes, sir!" The boy saluted smartly. "I know right where his headquarters are." The red patch of cloth in the shape of an escutcheon sewn on the top of his forage cap denoted he was from Burnside's own Ninth Corps.

"Good. Tell him to come quickly." Grant spoke to the boy as he scratched out his dispatch. "Lee is not attempting to cross the Rapidan. He is coming out of his fortifications and making for us."

Grant watched the youthful rider wheel his mount and gallop down the road. It would take the rider a good two hours to reach Burnside. Time was essential.

The general looked down at the line of black telegraph wire strung on trees and cross sticks that snaked back along the twisting woods. The line ended in a wagon drawn off the road. A set of flags with red, white, and black squares in their centers leaned against the wheels. The men were heating a pot of coffee on a small fire.

Within the flat morass of the Wilderness, Grant realized those telegraph wires would be essential. No one could see signal flags in this place, and there were no hills to signal from. Yet, constant contact with his commanders was vital.

Grant withdrew his watch from his vest and snapped open the cover. It was one-fifteen P.M. He replaced the watch, extracted a cigar from the opposite vest pocket, and lighted it. He puffed for a minute before studying the ivory-colored thread gloves he wore. He thought they looked foolish, but Julia had told him it was the fashion for officers in the Army of the Potomac. She had sewn the circle of gold braid on his hat and made him promise to wear the gloves.

He withdrew his cigar and pointed it at the wagon. Instantly, the Signal Corps officers jumped to their feet, clustered around their batteries and telegraph key and exchanged eager glances. This might be their first chance to send messages from the front line. No other general had asked them to string wire as the army marched.

"Porter, send a telegraph to General Burnside. Say: 'Forced marches until you reach this place. Start your troops now in the rear, the moment they can be got off, and require them to make a night march.' "

Grant turned to the other riders in his party. A man dressed entirely in black with a stovepipe hat was talking earnestly with Sylvanus Cadwallader. "Gentlemen, if you will ride ahead with Colonel Parker, he will take you to General Meade's headquarters. I hope he can provide you with some lunch. Colonel Porter and I will join you later."

Cadwallader leaned forward in his saddle. The thought of food raised his spirits, and he quipped, "General Grant, about how long will it take you to get to Richmond?"

Grant smiled. "I will agree to be there in about four days—that is, if General Lee becomes a party to the agreement. But if he objects, the trip will undoubtedly be prolonged."

The dark-suited figure barked a deep throaty laugh and kneed his mount to follow the reporter. Cadwallader, finally aboard a passable horse, trotted after the staff.

Colonel Parker leaned close to his new commander and asked, "Who is that man with the reporter? He presents an ominous figure, all dressed in black. I overheard some of the men speculating that you had brought along your own private undertaker."

Grant's eyes twinkled. "I heard the boys say he is a parson brought especially to read the last rites to the Army of the Southern Confederacy. I prefer that rumor. Actually, he is neither. That man is Congressman Elihu Washburne of Illinois. I owe my third star to his efforts." Grant watched the receding figure. "I suppose he has come along to see how well I handle my new rank," he remarked dryly. Grant drew one last puff from the minuscule stub of his cigar before tossing it away. "Well, let us ride over to Sheridan and see how he is doing. He also has a new and expanded command," Grant said as he turned his horse down a narrow trail that led from the Germanna Plank Road east past a series of abandoned iron mines toward the Ely's Ford Road and Chancellorsville.

Three hours later a dust-covered Phil Sheridan looked up from a map to see a small party of equally grimy riders approaching from the north. Instantly, he recognized the lead rider and his horse. Cincinnati, Sheridan grunted to himself, a fine bit of horseflesh, but not so fine as my warhorse, Rienzi. He saluted as Grant reined in Cincinnati and dismounted. Sheridan's sharp eye noted that Grant still limped.

Grant returned the salute, immediately sat down on an empty cracker box, and motioned Sheridan to do the same. Grant lighted a cigar before speaking. "I see you've got Gregg's troopers strung along the road from Ely's Ford to here. We passed through their pickets."

Sheridan slapped the map with his hand. "Meade has been issuing or-

ders to my cavalry corps without consulting me!" he fumed. "He still believes the Cavalry Corps should support his forces like the supply service.
He has divided my command for all sorts of purposes other than con-
fronting the enemy."

Grant studied his fiery little commander. When he had requested
Sheridan be promoted and placed in charge of cavalry in the East, everyone but Lincoln questioned the wisdom of his request. Worn down to
barely a hundred pounds from fighting in Tennessee, Sheridan's five-foot-
six frame looked frail. But Grant knew his new cavalry leader was a terrier
who would harry the enemy at every turn. Best of all, if anyone could, he
was the man to neutralize J.E.B. Stuart's horsemen.

Sheridan removed the flat-topped porkpie hat he always wore at a
jaunty angle and wiped the grime from his face with his sleeve. His close-
cropped, jet-black hair glistened with sweat, but the dust on his mustache
made it appear a dull red. "I told Meade my brigades would no longer be
dispersed among the various infantry divisions to be used for patrol and
picket duty. The horses were worn to a frazzle by that, and the men's fighting edge dulled. I'll command my cavalry as a single fighting unit, to reconnoiter, raid, and destroy the enemy's mounted troops. The South is smart
enough to use their cavalry that way, and we should, too."

"And General Meade's reaction to your proposal?"

"He was dumbstruck!" Sheridan stared glumly at his thigh-high boots.
"Absolutely staggered by that suggestion. 'Who will protect my supply
trains, my rear, my artillery trains?' he moaned. I replied he would not have
to worry after I destroyed the Confederate cavalry that was responsible for
his fears. But he was unconvinced."

Sheridan's spirit remained depressed. Even now his First Division—
one-third of his command—under Brigadier General Torbert with Custer
and Devin, remained across the Rapidan, guarding the supply trains from
the menace of Stuart's cavalry—a menace that was nowhere near to them.
To take a mobile force like this and tie it down was pure madness.

For the first time Grant looked around and grew aware of his surroundings. Sheridan's cavalrymen bivouacked along the outskirts of Chancellorsville, with Hancock's Second Corps sprawled beside the road. An

eerie stillness permeated the air. Whether by accident or by design, the soldiers now camped along the site of last year's fierce fighting.

Grant marveled at the irony. For all the vast stretches of land, the exigencies of terrain funneled armies repeatedly to the same place, over and over again. A year to this very day the bloody Battle of Chancellorsville had ended. It was here that Lee and Stonewall Jackson bloodied Hooker's army.

The hastily buried dead from that battle now rose from the ground to greet them.

Bleached arm and leg bones jutted from shallow graves, while the wind waved their tattered scraps of uniform, and polished skulls leered at them from every hollow. Clusters of bright flowers and thick green grass sprang from patches of ground made fertile from soldiers' blood.

With gallows humor, soldiers pitched their tents amidst clusters of shallow graves and sat atop mounds while they boiled their coffee. Some scavenged among the skeletons for signs of identity. Shreds of blue cloth seemed to far outnumber butternut and gray.

Suddenly, Grant realized the veterans of Hancock's Second Corps had been here before, had fought on this very ground. From the way the old soldiers pointed to clusters of graves and clumps of shattered trees and whispered, the general knew they were reliving the battle. He rose slowly and strolled along the road, with Sheridan and Porter following. Stopping in the shadow of a gum tree, he paused to listen to the soldiers.

A grizzled sergeant pointed to the dense brush and shuddered. "Boys, I hope we get through this chaparral without a fight. This is an awful place to fight in."

"How so, Zeke?" a fresh-faced private asked.

"You can't see more than a hundred yards. Chances are you'll be shot at close range. And the wounded that can't move are certain to be burned alive."

"Burned to death?" the private gasped.

Zeke nodded gravely. He pointed to a blackened skull near his foot. "In the battle for Chancellorsville that's just what happened. The dry brush caught fire. Many of the wounded burned to a cinder before we could get to them. Both sides, the fire chose no sides. You could hear their screaming all night long as the fires raged. Men in my squad were shooting those poor wounded they could see burning but couldn't get to."

Beside him a sardonic corporal with a still-red scar across his nose skewered a half-exposed skull within its shallow grave and pried it into the air with his bayonet. He brandished the leering object like a Shakespearean actor performing *Hamlet*. But his soliloquy was far less erudite. "Bobby Lee will find us tomorrow, boys," he predicted, "make no mistake about that. And he'll fight us in this damned thicket like he did before. And ... this place will burn like it did before." He turned the skull over on his bayonet to inspect the face. This was one of the lucky ones, he judged. A bullet hole cracked the center of the forehead. "This is what we are all coming to," he said softly. "Some of you will start toward it tomorrow...."

Porter's and Sheridan's eyes met at that comment, locked in understanding, then looked toward their commander. Grant moved away, returning to where Cincinnati was munching contentedly on the fresh grass. He mounted and rode back toward the Germanna Plank Road. As he passed line after line of dusty blue soldiers, Grant reviewed what he knew of his generals. He would come to know them better by tomorrow, he judged. In the pit of his stomach, Grant felt the same way as the sergeant. Tomorrow they would see fighting.

Hancock and his battle-seasoned Second Corps gave him no cause for concern. Nor did Sheridan. Both men had shown the flexibility and aggressiveness he wanted in his commanders. Whenever the opportunity presented, Grant knew those men would fight.

John Sedgwick and his Sixth Corps would do their part as well. Unmarried and scruffy, Sedgwick's unkempt beard and unruly hair masked a methodical and precise soldier who considered the army his home and his soldiers his sons. "Uncle John," his men called him, and they would charge into hell itself if he asked them to. While he played solitaire in his tent at night, Sedgwick spent his days welding his divisions into a cohesive fighting unit.

Grant worried about Burnside. By all accounts, his Ninth Corps should be crossing the river by now. Still, for all the pretense of his turned-down hat and flashy muttonchop sideburns, General Burnside had a history of dragging his feet. *I may need him to come running if things turn sour,* Grant thought. *I hope he will.*

Another wrinkle forced Grant to deal with Burnside and his Ninth Corps as a separate entity instead of adding it to the Army of the Potomac: Burnside's commission predated Meade's. Burnside was Meade's senior and refused to place himself under Meade. Grant shook his head. A general's pride and personal feelings should never stand in the way of sound military judgment, but it happened—much too often. He could not understand that.

Grant realized he knew little about Major General Gouverneur K. Warren, the newly appointed commander of the Fifth Corps. A scholarly, abrasive man, Warren lacked tact and projected a weak image, which was only made worse by the thick mustache overriding his recessive chin. With his dark hair slicked across his high forehead and curled behind his ears in a stylish pageboy, he often rode about with his too-short pant legs hitched above the tops of his riding boots, and buttoned his tunic askew like a child.

Grant paused in his reflections to consider his own dress. He chuckled to himself. His coat was not buttoned at all.

*Looks can be deceiving,* he granted. Warren taught mathematics and graduated second in his class from the academy. Best of all, Warren could gauge the value of ground. His recognition of the strategic value of Little Round Top had saved the Federals at Gettysburg.

Then there was Meade.

The cold-blooded Stanton had urged Grant to replace Meade. After all, Meade's commission preceded Grant's, the man was years his senior, and a sophisticated Easterner. *How would Meade take orders from this hayseed from the West who had been promoted over him?* Grant had wondered.

But Meade surprised him. During their first meeting, Meade displayed a graciousness that charmed and impressed Grant. Meade volunteered to step aside if Grant felt another could better lead the Army of the Potomac. Winning this war was paramount, Meade went on, taking precedence over personalities and all else. Too much had been sacrificed already. He would serve in whatever capacity Grant ordered—without bitterness or recrimination.

Thankfully, Sherman commanded in the West. He knew what to do: head straight for Atlanta, cutting the South in half and laying waste to anything that supported the enemy's will to fight. What did Sherman say? "I can make this march, and I can make Georgia howl."

Grant swayed as Cincinnati stumbled over an exposed tree root, but both horse and rider regained their balance. Grant released his reins while his right hand sliced the air in the characteristic chop he used when he wished to make a point.

Colonel Porter saw the movement and believed his commander was relaying orders which he had not heard. Porter spurred his mount forward and cocked his ear. But Grant's cigar remained clamped between his teeth and no sound issued from his lips. Hastily, Porter dropped back to let his superior continue his planning undisturbed.

Handling Meade might prove ticklish, Grant realized. Lincoln had related to him how Meade's lengthy delay after Gettysburg drove him to despair.

By five that evening Grant and Porter had reached their camp. A tired rider recognized Grant and handed him a dispatch. Grant nodded and passed it to Porter. Union engineers had completed their third pontoon bridge that day. This one spanned 160 feet of the Rapidan at Culpeper Mine Ford, located halfway between Germanna Ford and Ely's Ford. The packed supply wagons of General Rufus Ingalls would roll across all night, protected by Torbert's cavalry. The three days of food each man carried in his haversack could now be replenished.

Grant dismounted and landed on his sore leg. He grunted in pain as the bruised nerves protested. He forced his mind elsewhere. Automatically his eye studied the terrain.

Meade's staff had pitched his large Sibley tent on a rise beside the Orange Courthouse Turnpike just west of its junction with the Germanna

Plank Road. This modest elevation permitted the best view of this critical crossroads, yet it was little more than five hundred yards from the dense scrub pine and stunted oak. At their backs, the dilapidated roof of the abandoned Wilderness Tavern sagged. Weed, thistles, and brambles covered the clearing while forbidding trees ringed the site.

A bold purple flag emblazoned with a silver eagle fluttered near Meade's tent. Colonel Ely Parker and General Rawlins stepped from that tent to greet their commander.

Grant gestured to the flag. "What is imperial Caesar about?" he joked.

Parker smiled darkly. He had had a run-in with Meade's staff over where to place Grant's less imposing wall tent. "No Caesar, sir, that is General Meade's *personal* flag," he replied. Secretly, Parker hoped Grant might say something about Meade's camp overshadowing that of his superior officer, but Grant merely limped to his tent, removed his coat and tossed it across the tripod supporting a tin washbasin. Other than a canvas cot, two folding chairs, and a camp trunk, the basin was all that occupied the tent.

As darkness fell, Grant finished his cold supper and limped to a camp stool beside a roaring fire of fence rails appropriated from nearby. From Meade's tent came the clink of silverware and china as the general and his staff dined on champagne and cooked meats.

Grant lighted another cigar and leaned back in his chair. Behind him his fiercely loyal staff glared at Meade's party. Not inviting Grant to dine with Meade they judged a terrible breach of etiquette. None of them understood why Grant seemed unperturbed by this, but his mind was sifting the next day's options.

Lee had Dick Ewell and A. P. Hill to throw against him. But Longstreet might be Lee's ace in the hole, Grant realized. Old Pete's corps was down near Gordonsville, at the railhead where the Virginia Central Railroad could transport his troops south to the defense of Richmond, or the Orange and Alexandria rail lines could bring him north to the aid of the Mine Run defenses. Lee might direct Longstreet's First Corps against his left flank, adding its weight to Hill's forces.

Grant's eyes narrowed as he pictured his old friend, James Longstreet, tall, solid with his black beard cascading over the front of his uniform. Grant sighed. They went back a long ways, back to West Point. His friend and best man when he married Julia. Pete runs deep and quiet like the streams of his native South Carolina, he thought. Neither one of us says much.

But Longstreet favors the defense. He's got a theory about assaulting a position which I think is right. Three-to-one superiority is needed to capture a heavily defended position, if I recall. That makes him reluctant to attack if he's unsure about the odds. In this tangle of brush, the strength of my line will be hard to gauge. That will cause Pete to be cautious, and that will give me time to support my left flank with Hancock's men. Hancock will be quick. I think if Lee plans on using Longstreet to turn my left flank, that attack will fail.

A shadow fell across Grant and he looked up. George Meade stood just inside the ring of light with a worried look on his face.

"General Grant, I was not told you had arrived back in camp," Meade confessed. "I would have waited supper for you."

Parker cast a disgusted look at Porter and Rawlins. He had informed a major on Meade's staff as soon as he saw Grant and Porter approaching the camp. But General Rawlins thanked his lucky stars. From the clink of the glasses, he knew alcohol flowed freely inside Meade's mess. Grant had not taken a sip of liquor, to Rawlins's knowledge, since that impassioned speech outside Vicksburg.

Grant merely shrugged. "I only required a light meal." He withdrew another cigar and offered it to Meade. "A cigar, General? They are of the finest Cuban tobacco." Several dozen boxes still remained from the Fort Donelson gift.

Meade accepted the cigar and settled into the other folding chair. Striking match after match, he struggled to light his cigar. But the evening wind blew strongly through the camp, whistling through the treetops like the moans of departed souls, and extinguished each Lucifer match.

Grant removed a small silver tinderbox from his pocket, a gift from Julia, and handed it to Meade. Inside were a flint and steel and a flammable coil of fuse that resisted the wind. Meade struck the flint, ignited the wick, and lighted his cigar.

As Meade handed the box back to Grant, he failed to see the satisfied looks on the faces of Grant's staff. This incident involving the lighting of the cigar in the wind drove home to them the vast difference between their general and General Meade. By himself Meade might try and fail. But they knew Grant would get the job done.

# BUSHWHACKING ON A GRAND SCALE

Since early morning Grant found himself in a new and uncomfortable position, one that gave him greater insight into Lincoln's frustrating situation. Elevated to General-in-Chief of the armies further removed him from direct command and made him more dependent upon his generals.

In the West, Sherman and McPherson acted like an extension of his will, understanding his orders and acting quickly and decisively to effect them. Here in Virginia, both Meade and Burnside acted like a mix between a balking mule and a reticent suitor. To Grant, minutes counted, where to those generals, hours mattered, even days at times. Now the difference became apparent.

Grant's greatest wish was to maneuver Lee out of his barricades at Mine Run and into open ground where the might of Federal forces could be brought to bear. Only half his wish was granted. The gray fox had plans of his own.

The first signs of trouble were the ringing of axes westward down the Orange Turnpike. Grant turned in the direction of the chopping and listened. A heavy silence followed. He rose from his stump and listened again. Nothing.

Like a coiled spring, Grant returned to his seat and resumed whittling away on a stick. Turning the stick over in his hands, he sharpened both ends, shaved off the bark, cut the stick in two and tossed it away. Then he started on another branch, repeating the procedure. Soon, a small pile of sharpened sticks littered the ground at his feet. His thread gloves, now stained and showing signs of wear, remained in place, as he had promised Julia. Only the staccato puffing on his cigar revealed Grant's unease.

I had hoped to be well out of this tangle by now, he fumed. But Burnside is still not entirely across the Rapidan and Meade moves forward at a snail's pace. How far should I go in pressing Burnside and Meade? I can't assume their command. My orders are clear: Move with all possible speed. Yet, this army pokes ahead while Burnside drags behind.

Grant winced again as the chopping resumed. He puffed furiously. An army on the move doesn't chop down that many trees, which means only one thing—the men are building barricades. Without looking, he could picture the frenzied piling of logs into palisades, sharpening the branches to form palings, and heaping dirt into earthworks. Shovels, spades, and hatchets wielded by anxious men.

Grant rose slowly to his feet as a squad of men rushed past. He recognized their badges, 83rd Pennsylvania from Bartlett's Third Brigade of Griffin's division. Griffin was anchoring the end of Warren's line of march! Is the enemy just down the Orange Turnpike? he wondered. He hadn't expected them so soon.

The sharp rattle of musket fire rolling through the dark trees answered his question. More fire, strung out this time, followed. The heavy thud of cannon joined the noise.

General Warren galloped up. His dappled gray mount whinnied and tossed his head in excitement. Warren wore the yellow sash of a major general, and today his pants met the tops of his boots. His widened eyes revealed his alarm. He saluted and pointed toward the sound of battle.

"General, I have just received word from Griffin that the rebels are concentrating on the far edge of a clearing called Sanders' Field. The turn-pike passes directly through that field."

More gunfire caused Warren's horse to shy, and the animal pranced and spun so that Warren lost sight of his commander. He jerked the reins to control the horse. "I have ordered my columns to halt, but my division is strung out along the road to Parker's Store. The ravines and marshes of the Wilderness Run have broken my brigades into pieces," he shouted into the air.

Instantly Grant leapt into his worn saddle. "Let us take a closer look, General Warren," he suggested. Not waiting for an answer, Grant galloped toward the sound of the fighting.

A short ride brought them to the impromptu bulwarks. Powder smoke hung in the air and snaked among the chipped pine trunks. Splinters of wood filled the air, and the sky buzzed and snapped with the passage of minié balls. Everywhere along the line soldiers fired, reloaded, and fired their muskets with battle-honed skill.

The angry hum of grapeshot rattled the trees overhead. A cloud of branches, pinecones, and tree limbs rained down upon the scouting party. Warren straightened his sash, brushed the leaves from his hat, and looked to his chief.

Grant stood in his stirrups to study the clearing. The Union position covered a low rise that overlooked the sunken turnpike. Then the ground rose gradually onto a neglected cornfield. A tree line marked the far end of the field. Puffs of smoke and tongues of flame spurted from the distant trees, and the red and blue colors of the Confederate battle flags waved defiantly amidst the smoke. Across the open field, a ragged line of gray figures bending forward against the iron wind advanced toward the Union line.

The next volley of fire from the Union breastworks saw the attackers stumble, then move slowly back to their own abatis. Grant noted a sol-dier perched in a pine tree to his left watching him. Resting across a limb lay the man's rifle. The slender brass telescope fitted along the heavy barrel identified the weapon as a .45 caliber James target rifle. The man was a sharpshooter.

Pleased that he had caught Grant's eye, the man grinned and touched the tattered peak of his forage cap in an indifferent salute. He pointed to General Warren. "Begging the general's pardon, but that gold sash makes a mighty tempting target. You might as well paint a bull's-eye on your chest."

"This signifies my rank. I wear it with pride," Warren bristled.

The man shrugged and spat a sluice of tobacco between the pine needles. "Makes me no never mind, but I'd ask you to move a mite to your right, General. There's a Johnny over there with one of these rifles he stole from us, and he's a-looking that yellow sash over in his glass right now. He must have been a squirrel hunter in better days for he's a damned fine shot."

"Why should I move?" Warren snapped. "I am no coward. I will not hide."

"I never thought you were, General, but that reb might spot me whilst he's studying you. This here is about the only tree suitable for a man of my profession."

No sooner had the man spoken than a bullet smacked the trunk close to Warren's left shoulder strap. The man's grin widened. Warren held his ground defiantly.

"How far to the enemy lines?" Grant asked.

The man uncoiled the string from a brass stadia sight and held the metal plate the length of the string from his right eye. His other hand adjusted the sliding piece until the man he was measuring filled the aperture, then he read the distance on the graduated scale.

"Three hundred and seventy-five yards, give or take a few feet," he said with authority. He tested the crosswind whistling through the pines with a wetted finger. His fingers fiddled with the knob at the base of his rifle scope. "Needs a mite more windage," he said to himself.

"What else can you see?" Grant called up.

"Shovels and axes a-flashing in the air, General. They're working like beavers to build their own fortifications, just like us. Funny thing, General, when they just sprung out of the air, I figured they'd hit us like always, a-hooting and a-shooting as they charged across this field. But they didn't.

They spread out to the left and right and went to digging. I never saw them do that before."

Grant digested that information. Why didn't they attack? Somehow the rebels had slipped past Wilson's cavalry pickets and had the advantage of surprise. Striking at the gap between the tail end of Warren's departing Fifth Corps and the late arriving head of Sedgwick's column, the Confederates had stumbled onto the chink in Meade's army. A concerted drive would split the line of march at its weakest point.

The enemy is too weak at this time to attack in strength, Grant realized. He is digging in to secure his own position.

Grant looked around. Lee's greatest ally was this wilderness. With the exception of Sanders' Field, the ground surrounding the Union trenches and bordering the cornfield defied description. Dense brush, thickets, and fallen trees prevented any hope of an organized line of attack. Broken ground, rotted stumps, and clumps of scrub pine hid men from their officers, and water-filled pits and swampy ground blocked all effort to roll heavy artillery into place. Concentrating a force to attack would be hard.

Grant recognized General Charles Griffin riding along his line. A hard case, as Meade described him, Griffin's training at West Point and his experience fighting Indians in Oregon made him gruff and outspoken but competent. His thin, youthful appearance and exuberant handlebar mustache reminded Grant of another such officer—George Armstrong Custer, commanding the Michigan cavalry under Sheridan—only Griffin's mustache was dark brown, while Custer's was blond.

General Griffin spotted his superiors and guided his horse along his line to their side. He neglected to salute, which touched another nerve in the jumpy Warren; instead he gestured at the field with an extended brass telescope. The man in the tree shook his head. Now he had three generals and a handful of their staff clustered beneath his tree.

"That's Dick Ewell's Second Corps out there," Griffin exclaimed. He stabbed at the tree line with his telescope, using it like an abbreviated lance. "I spotted a blue flag with the seal of Virginia. It's the Second Virginia of the old Stonewall Brigade for sure." Griffin swiped at his mustache as he paused to reflect. "Good thing Jackson's in his grave and not in charge. He'd have overrun us for sure."

"What is your disposition, Griffin?" Warren huffed. He did not appreciate Griffin's blunt honesty. Pointing out his exposed rear to Grant, whether it was the truth or not, was the last thing Warren wanted. The ambitious New Yorker had worked hard to impress his new commander. Rumor had it that his efforts had paid off and that Grant had mentioned him as a possible successor to Meade. The dashing Hancock loomed as his only rival for command of the Army of the Potomac. If he played his cards right and Meade and Hancock stumbled, he might have another star on his shoulder before long.

Griffin was prepared for Warren's question. Rapidly, he ticked off his reply. "I've placed the 140th and the 146th New York north of here and the First Michigan to the south. The Michigan boys spotted the enemy first. But for them, we might have missed the enemy's advance guard entirely. That would have been a damned pretty mess, me marching my men off down the road to Parker's Store only to have the rebs fall on my rear."

Warren's face flushed. "Where the hell Wilson and his cavalry are is beside me!" he snapped. "His troopers are supposed to be screening this road and the march down to Parker's Store, but I have had no contact with them since last night. I would not have been surprised had he done his job properly." Warren bit his tongue. He remembered suddenly that Brigadier General James Wilson owed his new command of the Third Cavalry Division to none other than Ulysses S. Grant.

But Grant already wondered if appointing Wilson to command cavalry had been a mistake. Despite his brilliant showing during the siege of Vicksburg and again at Chattanooga, Wilson commanded infantry at those battles, not mounted horsemen. Grant realized the absence of reassuring dispatches from Wilson forced Warren's line of march to creep along behind the slow screen of pickets, feeling their way like blind men.

Griffin continued relating his disposition. "I've ordered General Bartlett to push out on the turnpike and probe the enemy's strength. He sent Colonel Hayes out with the 83rd Pennsylvania and the 18th Massachusetts along the turnpike, and ordered the 20th Maine to dig in." He pointed back to a flurry of swinging axes wielded by men stripped of their blouses. "Those Maine boys know how to swing an ax."

The sharp crack of a rifle close by drew the officers' attention. The sharpshooter in the tree continued to look through his telescopic sight while smoke wafted from his rifle's muzzle. "Well, that's one less Johnny Reb who'll wave that blue flag," he muttered grimly. "Beats me how they find men stupid enough to hold them flags, anyway." Hugging the trunk, the man carefully reloaded his target rifle.

Griffin peered through his glass. He focused on the spot where he last saw the flag of the Second Virginia. The banner sagged sharply to the left then vanished behind the barricade. "By God, man," Griffin exclaimed, "that's fine shooting."

"Not bad, with this wind," the soldier called down with a tired modesty. He aimed his rifle again and pressed his eye to his sight. The blue flag reappeared in his field of vision. "Whoa, they just got another fool to wave their flag," he said.

Warren glared up at the man. "Carrying the colors is an honor!" he shouted. "Many a brave man begs to serve on the color guard."

"No disrespect, General, but waving that flag is just begging to be shot—if not by me, then by chance when your soldiers loose a volley. I know infantry aim at anything that stands out in the field, and a flag is almost as tempting a target as a man on a fine horse wearing a gold sash. Being brave don't necessarily equate with being smart."

Griffin laughed out loud, and even Grant turned away to hide his smile.

Warren fumed. "You are nothing more than a—a bushwhacker!"

Rather than take offense, the rifleman nodded gravely. "Yessir. That's all I am, plain as day, a bushwhacker. Of course, we prefer to be called sharpshooters. Some of us have fancy green uniforms like Colonel Berdan's sharpshooters. The First New York Battalion of Sharpshooters didn't hand out anything fancy, except this James rifle. It's not half the rifle the

Whitworths are. Them English guns that the rebs use can do real execution up to fifteen hundred yards."

"A bushwhacker," Warren repeated, unconvinced.

The man in the tree settled his rifle into a notch and pointed to the forest. "Look about you, General. This awful place won't let you fight on your feet. There's no place to line up, except that field out there, and that's going to be a grand killing ground, mark my word. Your soldiers will have to crawl over stumps and dig through bushes as they fight. Both sides will be stumbling into each other before they know it. This battle is going to be bushwhacking on a grand scale."

B y late afternoon the sharpshooter's prediction proved murderously accurate. Hour after hour saw the struggle for control of the dusty turnpike suck both sides further into conflict. Fruitless charges across the open ground of Sanders' Field yielded dreadful results for both blue and gray. Bodies littered the corn stubble. Fanning out on both sides of the Orange Turnpike, clusters of men crept forward and emptied their muskets into brambles and thickets that hid their opponents. Hand-to-hand fighting followed desperate, stumbling, ill-coordinated rushes.

Over all this, the sun beat down like a bronze hammer, adding to the thirst and suffering of the combatants. As the veteran of Hancock's Second Corps forecast, fires broke out everywhere

Grant returned to the knoll by the Wilderness Tavern and waited. Adding to his frustration, he found he could not move freely from that spot without losing contact with his widely spaced command. Despite his urging, his commanders moved slowly, held back by their fear of Lee and the difficulties of the terrain.

Dispatch after dispatch brought nothing but bad news.

Burnside loped along down the plank road as if on a summer's stroll. Warren found his hands full as the tail of his column battled at Sanders' Field while the head of his line of march reached the junction with the Orange Plank Road. Disaster almost followed when eager Union soldiers attacked Confederates they found there. Pushing them back, they suddenly found themselves outnumbered as they ran headlong into the advance units of an entire corps. A. P. Hill's Third Corps had arrived.

Hancock's corps, too far south at Todd's Tavern, now needed to march back up the Brock Road to support the increasingly beleaguered infantry at the crossing.

The wise Sedgwick did what he could by rushing Brigadier General Getty's Second Division down the cluttered road to reinforce the men facing Hill's troops on the Orange Plank Road. He shunted the rest of his command off the Germanna Plank Road to support Warren's right flank. Forced to march down the narrow, twisting Culpeper Mine Road, he found the route little more than an abandoned wagon track branching west to link the Germanna road with the Orange Turnpike. Progress ground to a halt when he encountered rebel pickets and dismounted troopers of the First North Carolina Cavalry holding the road just north of the contested Sanders' Field. By the time Sedgwick cleared the road, the sun was setting and Ewell's entire corps was firmly dug in. All hope of mounting a swift attack before Ewell could strengthen his position vanished.

Throughout the day, Grant smoked one cigar after another, lighting a fresh one from the crumbling ash of the previous. Wood shavings piled about his boots as he whittled every stick in sight. From where he sat, clouds of dense smoke billowed from burning forest, accompanied by the crackle of small-arms fire. While bewildered officers rushed around the camp, Grant worked hard to appear unflappable.

Inside, however, he seethed.

Grant closed his eyes and concentrated. Without resorting to a map, he pictured the entire battle in his head. Lee had thrown Ewell and Hill against the Union line in a two-pronged attack, striking from the Orange Plank Road and the Orange Turnpike into the drawn-out columns. It helped to have local knowledge of those routes, Grant admitted, something the Union lacked.

Colonel Porter approached. Grant looked up. A hundred yards behind Porter, Meade stomped around his purple flag, flinging orders at his staff and snapping at anyone unfortunate enough to come within range. Meade is frustrated and overwhelmed, Grant judged. Should I take over? No, he reasoned. Things are not that bad ... yet.

Porter removed his hat and swallowed hard. Rivulets of sweat streaked the dust coating his face. Tears filled his eyes.

"Sir, I have the misfortune to report that Brigadier General Alexander Hays has been killed."

Grant paused in his whittling. For long minutes he stared at the partially sharpened stick. At last a long sigh escaped from his lips. "Hays and I were cadets together for three years. We served for a time in the same regiment in the Mexican War. He was a noble man and a gallant officer."

"He was killed leading his brigade against the rebels on the Orange Plank Road. His line broke under an attack, and General Hays rushed forward to encourage his troops, and he was instantly killed."

"I am not surprised that he met his death at the head of his troops. It was just like him. He was a man who would never follow, but would always lead in battle." Grant looked up at his aide. "I hope all effort is being taken to see that his body is returned to his family."

"Yes, sir."

"Good." Grant looked bleakly at the falling darkness. The fires continued, adding their smoke to the dusk while casting flickering light through the trees. The cries of wounded men came from every quarter of the knoll. Scattered shrieks rose from where the fires burned fiercest as wounded men, too weak to flee, burned to death. Grant felt as though he were surrounded by screams.

How many men on both sides will vanish in this wilderness? Grant wondered. Sending Hays's body home offers little consolation, but it is something.

Mercifully, the onset of night brought an end to the wholesale butchery. Even the most aggressive fighters balked at shooting in the dark.

Grant ate little for supper. Instead he sat and surveyed the scene, kept company by Porter and the ever-faithful John Rawlins. Grant reviewed the reports of the day's fighting, but the arrival of casualties distracted him sorely.

A constant string of wounded trudged by on their way to the aid stations encircling the ruined tavern. He would watch those who could walk hobble by, turning his head away whenever a horribly injured soldier passed. Lights burned inside the building as surgeons worked on the urgent cases. Each lantern glow marked the return of a stretcher party that had braved enemy fire to drag a helpless man from the flames or roll a man into a bloodied sheet to carry him back.

The carnage appeared to have little effect at Meade's mess tent. Glasses clinked as usual, and laughter followed. Meade eventually emerged, entered his headquarters tent, and finally walked over to where Grant sat.

Before he could sit down, Grant rose and pointed in the direction of Germanna Ford. "General Meade, we must make all preparations to care for our wounded," he said. "I urge you to instruct your commanders to pass those that can be moved back to the rear. General Ingalls has seen to it that we have adequate ambulances for that purpose. Using the supply route over Culpeper Mine Crossing would seem the quickest and safest route."

Meade nodded. "I have issued those instructions."

Grant turned his eyes toward the fiery trees. A cluster of scrub pine burst into flames as their dry needles and pitch ignited. Muffled screams accompanied the sudden blaze. Out in the darkness a wagon loaded with powder exploded into an orange ball.

"Good. No man ought to be left to burn when wounded in the service of his country." Grant tossed another cigar stub into the cook fire. Yesterday his staff had heaped fence rails onto the fire to produce a cheering effect. Tonight the smoldering coals mocked the conflagration that surrounded and threatened them.

Elihu Washburne stepped into the circle of light from Grant's campfire. All his love for his fellow countryman had not prevented him from joining Meade's table. Grant's Spartan meals left much to be desired.

"Does your pronouncement apply to rebel wounded as well, General?" he asked.

"Yes. To all brave men."

"What is your assessment of today's battle?" Meade asked. His own performance left much to be desired, he knew. Somehow, this wilderness with its dark and closing shadows drained him of confidence. He half expected Lee to charge out of every shadow. In fact Lee almost had. Wistfully, Meade longed for the rolling hills and open wheat fields of Pennsylvania. He had done much better at Gettysburg.

Grant recognized his general's uncertainty. The laughter from Meade's mess tent had sounded too forced, too strained. He spoke to reassure Meade. "As Burnside's corps on our side and Longstreet's on the other side have not been engaged, and the troops of both sides have been occupied principally in struggling through thickets and fighting for position, today's work has not been much of a test of strength."

Meade squeezed his eyes shut, feeling the gritty smoke grate beneath his lids, and swallowed.

"Still," Grant continued, "I feel pretty well satisfied with the results of the engagement."

"How so?" Washburne asked.

"Well, it is evident that Lee attempted by a bold movement to strike this army in flank before it could be put into lines of battle and be prepared to fight to advantage; but in this he failed."

Meade exhaled softly.

"Tomorrow will make the difference," Grant said as he thought about his old friend Longstreet. Where will Lee insert him? he wondered. If my guess is correct, it will be along our left flank, between Richmond and us. "I suggest Hancock, with help from Wadsworth's Fourth Division, attack Hill at first light, say four-thirty."

Meade objected. "Half past four is impossible. Six at the best."

Grant shook his head. "We will be attacked first if we wait until six. Five at the latest." He turned to cut off further debate. "We shall have a busy day tomorrow. I think we had better get all the sleep we can tonight."

Washburne rose to his feet and stretched. "It is said that Napoleon often indulged in only four hours' sleep, yet still preserved all the vigor of his mental faculties."

Grant tossed his half-finished cigar into the dying campfire. "I never believed those stories," he replied. He walked over to his tent, closed the flap, and dropped onto his cot. His fingers reached inside his shirt and grasped the tiny silver locket that held a lock of Julia's hair.

Within minutes he was fast asleep.

# WILDERNESS: THE SECOND DAY

The heavy tramp of marching feet jostled Grant from a sound sleep. His dream about wrestling with Freddy while Julia laughed at their antics vanished in an instant, and he found himself sitting upright on his cot staring at the smudged canvas wall. Precious little of the evening cool still remained, and the smell of smoke and gunpowder hung heavy in the still air. Grant pulled on his boots, wincing as his injured leg protested, buttoned his vest, and limped outside.

To his relief, the marching soldiers wore blue.

Grant strained to see the insignia on their caps, but it was too dark. Marching along to one side, a color guard carried a white rectangular flag with a dark shield sewn on its center. The Third Division of the Ninth Corps, Grant realized. Burnside had arrived.

The general opened the cover of his watch and held the face close to see the hands. Four in the morning. They must have marched all night, he decided. A good thing, too, we need to get the jump on the enemy.

Colonel Porter and General Rawlins converged on their commander. Rawlins handed Grant a steaming cup of black coffee. Brewed all night, the coffee had the consistency of molasses. Grant took the cup and sipped the bitter drink. While his eyes followed the marching soldiers, he limped over to a makeshift table consisting of a purloined door thrown across two ammunition crates. Tins of biscuits, smoking slices of ham, and yellow piles of scrambled eggs covered the table.

"We have the makings of a hearty breakfast," Porter commented. He waited for Grant and Rawlins to sit before dropping into the closest folding chair. Although formality was loosely observed at Grant's table, with messengers and staff officers eating on the run, the colonel still waited on his superiors.

Rawlins grunted in agreement as he forked a slab of ham onto his pile of eggs. "A busy day today requires a proper breakfast," he quipped. Holding his tin cup in a salute, he toasted, "Here's hoping we're so busy pressing the rebels that we have little time for lunch."

"Hear! Hear!" Porter added. He looked over to see his general-in-chief studiously cutting a small cucumber into thin slices. Grant poured vinegar over the slices and sat back to eat his meal. He drained another cup of coffee before lighting a cigar and rising to his feet.

"Would you like something more, General Grant?" Porter asked. An impromptu breakfast of a sliced pickle was no meal, to his thinking.

Grant patted his pockets. "More cigars," he answered.

A colored servant hurried to Grant's tent and returned with two boxes. Grant stuffed handfuls of the cigars into both pockets until no more could fit. Turning, he crossed over to the highest point of the camp and paced back and forth while he puffed away like a steam engine. He checked his watch and cocked his ear to the left in the direction of Hancock's position. Quarter to five, he noted.

An unexpected burst of gunfire erupted not from the left but from the right. The fire increased. A rolling rebel yell cut through the sounds of rifle fire before the thump of artillery drowned the cry.

Grant thrust his hand deep into his pocket to keep it from chopping through the air in disgust. Lee's forces had got the jump on them, again. Ewell's men were attacking Warren and Sedgwick before they could launch their own attack. Meade's half hour had cost them the advantage.

Did Lee's attack on his right wing mean Longstreet had arrived and now threatened them along the Orange Turnpike? Grant listened carefully. No, the fighting does not sound like that, he assured himself. I believe Lee still intends to strike us hard on the left. He would have by now if Longstreet were in position. So, Pete must not be ready. Well, we won't wait for Lee. Hancock will attack Hill's position before Longstreet arrives. Any minute now.

A grim humor struck him. Longstreet must be dragging his feet just like Burnside. Unlike Lee, however, my slow Burnside has finally arrived. I've got his Ninth Corps midway between both roads where they can move to support whichever one needs help. My center is weak, he admitted, but the wilderness works as a deterrent. If I can't advance my troops through this jumble of brush, neither can the enemy.

Precisely at five o'clock Hancock's push began. Cannon, rifle, bugles, and battle cries sounded on the left. To Grant's satisfaction, none of the cries were the rebel yell.

"Colonel Porter, ride to Hancock and evaluate the situation. Then bring me back your report." Grant removed his slouch hat and ran his hand through his hair as he watched his aide gallop away. He looked over at Meade's tent, where the general was pacing about and snapping with renewed ferocity. Meade's worried staff cast frequent glances over at Grant. With great restraint Grant found a stump and sat down. Donning his thread gloves as he had promised Julia, Grant commenced whittling again.

After what seemed like two lifetimes, Porter returned, covered with dust and scorched by gunpowder. He dismounted and saluted. A small mountain of wood shavings covered Grant's boots by now.

"General Hancock's attack drove the enemy back on the plank road almost to Parker's Farm," Porter reported in short gasps of breath. "His attack obviously caught Hill by surprise. The Orange Plank Road was strewn with enemy dead and wounded and many battle flags were captured. In fact, our advance progressed so rapidly that Hancock halted his men's rush to restore contact with his rear guard. Word also came of infantry advancing up the Brock Road on Hancock's left. Then, south on the Brock Road, a great fight was heard, and that also prompted Hancock to check his advance."

"Was it Longstreet?" Grant asked.

Porter shook his head. "No. The infantry were recovering wounded returned to duty by the surgeons. They had marched from Chancellorsville and the rear by way of a footpath leading into Brock Road. But the sounds at Todd's Tavern were indeed from a spirited fight. It was J.E.B. Stuart's cavalry seeking to fall upon Hancock's left flank. But Sheridan met him with his own horsemen and defeated the enemy completely."

"Good." Grant smiled. His little Sheridan, the man no one thought was up to the job, was proving his detractors wrong. "Sheridan will press Stuart until he has destroyed him."

Porter's head dropped. "Unfortunately, General Meade believed Sheridan had been defeated. He issued direct orders for the cavalry to withdraw to the east to protect the supply wagons."

"Confound Meade and his blasted supply wagons," Grant muttered. "How can he expect to win this war if he constantly looks over his shoulder?" He caught this uncharacteristic lapse. Withdrawing his field order book from his inside pocket, he scratched an order. "Find General Burnside. Impress upon him the urgency of linking up with Hancock's right and pressing the attack."

Again Porter rode off, this time on a fresh mount. Grant returned to his whittling. Waiting for an order to be obeyed was always the worst part, he remembered. Life was simpler when he could act on his own.

While he waited, a desperate attack by the Confederate forces drove the left wing of Warren's line back. The fighting grew closer to the rise where Grant waited. At first a few shells screamed overhead to explode in the brush behind. The wind blowing from the west drove the clouds of war into the faces of the Union soldiers. Smoke and powder billowed back from the beleaguered line, engulfing Grant at times. As the wind swirled, he would emerge, puffing away while his carving wore holes in his gloves. Lines of wounded straggled back to collapse to the ground around Grant.

Then the shot fell closer, the cries louder and more desperate. Canister and grapeshot scythed limbs from the trees surrounding the camp, filling the air with a constant shower of pine needles and branches. Minié balls hummed overhead. A Shenkl shell flew past with its characteristic high-pitched whine to strike a supply wagon behind the camp. Powder and percussion caps exploded and a black smudged ball of orange flame engulfed the wagon.

A solid shot bounced down the dusty road, scattering a line of men like tenpins. Arms, legs, and parts of bodies flew into the air or slammed against trees, and the sky exploded into a crimson mist. When the air cleared, bloody cloth draped from close-cut bushes. Piles of red-stained blue clothing and mangled parts were all that remained of the company.

Grant turned his head away while his stomach churned. He dug his penknife sharply into the stick he carved, tried to control his nausea.

A major ran to his side and pointed to where an orderly held Cincinnati at the junction of the far side of the camp and the clearing behind the Germanna Plank Road crossing. "General, wouldn't it be prudent to move headquarters to the other side of the Germanna Road at least until the result of this present attack is known?" he asked. Another round of shot crashed into a clump of pine, splintering the trunks into toothpicks. The officer ducked.

Grant followed the path of the last cannonball before turning back to the officer. He blew several puffs from his cigar as if considering the man's suggestion. His eyes settled on the red stripe on the man's trousers, identifying him as an artillerist. With an even voice Grant replied, "It strikes me it would be better to order up some artillery and defend this present place."

"Yes, sir! At once, General!" the flabbergasted man stammered. "Artillery ... yes!" He rushed off and returned in five minutes with gun crews and a battery of twelve-pounders.

Grant resumed his woodworking while the gunners poured point-blank fire into the advancing rebels. The rain of steel stopped the charge and blew the enemy back. A lusty cheer went up from the artillerymen. Their action had saved headquarters.

Several more hours passed before Porter returned. He dismounted in a state of agitation and hurried over to Grant.

"Did you press Burnside to attack?" Grant asked.

"Yes, sir, but I fear his attack may be delayed for another hour—at least."

"What? Why?"

Porter sighed. "His men are still struggling through the swamps and the heavy undergrowth and—"

"What else?"

"Well, when I found General Burnside, he and his staff were picnicking by the roadside."

"Picnicking?"

Porter nodded. "They had a basket opened and were eating and drinking champagne. He refused to hear me out unless I joined him, saying a wise soldier always eats whenever the opportunity presents itself as any future meal is uncertain."

Grant exercised all his self-control to focus on his penknife. He closed the blade slowly and studied the bone handle. Longstreet would not delay forever. If Burnside did not take the offensive, the opportunity would slip through their fingers, and they would be on the defensive once more. When he could speak, he looked levelly at Porter. "The only time I ever feel impatient," he said slowly, "is when I give an order for an *important* movement of troops in the presence of the enemy and am waiting for them to reach their destination. Then the minutes seem like hours."

Grant stood up and walked over to the edge of the rise. Inexplicably, in the face of all the smoke and fighting, a small herd of beef cattle intended for the quartermaster stumbled into camp. Oblivious to shot and shell, the shortsighted civilians driving the animals from the Germanna River Ford had stumbled into the thick of fighting. Intent only on being paid, they had delivered their animals into the center of the hornet's nest. Now they realized their predicament. While the cattlemen glanced about nervously as fires raged and shells exploded, one of the animals broke from the ranks and headed for a small stream below the knoll, directly toward Grant.

One drover shouted over to the general, "I say, stranger, head off that beef-critter for me, will you?"

Porter opened his mouth to protest this man's insolence. How dare this contract worker ask Grant, the commander of the entire Union forces, to herd a cow!

But the farmer in Grant took hold. He spread his arms above his head and bellowed at the cow. The animal stopped, then trotted back to the herd.

I wish I could turn the Confederates that easily, Grant thought.

Burnside might have wished the same. His attack lacking coordination, his men vanished into the brush, losing contact with their officers and diminishing the cohesion of their drive. More men bled and died in desperate hand-to-hand fighting over smoldering stumps and in smoke-filled swamps. In the end nothing was gained and much was lost—hundreds of lives.

As the day waned, both sides advanced, broke, ran, re-formed, and charged again over the same strip of useless land. Both Sedgwick and Hancock found their flanks rolled back by desperate charges, and both generals barely escaped with their lives as butternut-clad infantry, shooting and shouting, swarmed around them.

General Meade shuffled over from his side of the camp. He stared down at Grant's hands. Little remained of the thread gloves but scraps of lace held together by strips of thread. Grant's frustrated whittling had worn them to pieces. His fingertips and nails and most of his hands poked through the material in every possible place.

Meade removed his hat and mopped his brim. Nothing seemed to be working for him today. More than one unit had broken and run, disgracing him and his army. Even Uncle John Sedgwick's plea not to disgrace him had gone unheeded. Perhaps Grant's magic could not work in the East like it had in the Western Theater, Meade wondered. Perhaps Robert E. Lee's magic was stronger.

"I could use one of your cigars, General Grant," Meade asked humbly. For all the confusion over the last two days, Grant had not spoken a harsh word to him, and Meade deeply appreciated it. Everyone else had.

His commander's best chance was when General Griffin tongue-lashed him in the presence of Grant, but Grant turned away as if he were intruding on a personal argument. Meade was grateful for that.

Grant dipped into his coat pocket. All he found was a single remaining cigar. He offered it to Meade. "My last cigar," he said in amazement. "I have more in my chest, but guess I've smoked all that I stuffed into both pockets this morning."

Meade lighted his cigar from a burning branch. "And your gloves, General. You have worn them out."

"I expect I've done enough whittling to last me for the rest of this war." Grant pulled off the ruined gloves and stuffed them into his empty pocket. He had kept his promise to Julia. He had worn her gloves on his first engagement with Robert E. Lee. He would save his last pair of gloves to wear when he accepted Lee's surrender.

Meade surveyed his superior through a cloud of tobacco smoke. "You had quite a few cigars. You smoked them all?"

Grant made a mental calculation. "Twenty cigars. Yours is the last."

The two men stood and smoked while their eyes and ears probed the sounds of battle. Like the day itself, the fighting seemed to be wearing itself out. Both on the left and the right the crash of musket fire slowed and finally settled into the sporadic rattle that marks a stalemate. Both sides wormed deeper into their defenses. Soon, only scattered shots disturbed the roaring fires.

With the relief of the enemy's pressure, more officers drifted into camp for instructions. A haggard courier on foot presented Meade with a message written on the bloodstained wrapper of a cartridge box. Meade read it and reported to Grant.

"General Getty sends word that Longstreet attacked the extreme left of our line earlier today."

Longstreet! Grant thought. Our left flank—between us and Richmond—just as I suspected.

"In the attack, General Longstreet was shot by mistake by rebel soldiers while directing his men. Longstreet was seriously wounded and carried from the field. His condition is unknown. Brigadier General Micah Jenkins riding beside him at the head of his South Carolina Brigade was shot and killed."

Grant closed his eyes. He could see Longstreet's face as clearly as the day of his wedding. Pete spoke little, never more than a few clipped phrases unless pressed to expand. Silently, Grant prayed for his old friend's recovery.

I respect Longstreet and all the rest fighting for their cause, Grant admitted to himself, but their cause must be the poorest that ever surfaced on the face of this earth. He added another prayer that this suffering might soon end. A part of his prayer echoed back at him: The faster I beat Lee and the others, the quicker this war will conclude.

Brigadier General Truman Seymour, commanding the Second Brigade of Ricketts's Third Division stumbled up to Grant. All day long Seymour had appeared befuddled. His brigade's rout led to the collapse of the right wing of Sedgwick's line and almost proved disastrous. Hoping to salvage his reputation, Seymour wrung his hands and blurted unwanted advice to Grant.

"General Grant, this is a crisis that cannot be looked upon too seriously," Seymour exclaimed in short breaths. "I know Lee's methods well by past experience. He will throw his whole army between us and the Rapidan and will cut us off completely from our communications."

Grant sprang to his feet. He snatched the cold stub of his last cigar from his mouth and faced Seymour with a withering glare. "I am heartily tired of hearing about what Lee is going to do!" he snapped. "Some of you always seem to think he is suddenly going to turn a double somersault and land in our rear and on both of our flanks at the same time!"

A murmur of laughter encircled the officers, but Grant's stern look silenced that. He pointed his cigar at Seymour. *"Go back to your command and try to think what we are going to do ourselves, instead of what Lee is going to do!"*

Hastily, Seymour backed into the darkness and disappeared.

# AIN'T I GLAD . . .

The soldiers walking their guard post by the headquarters tents blinked in astonishment as their general-in-chief threw back his tent flap and stepped into the predawn darkness. The men exchanged questioning looks. Grant was the first officer up.

Pouring himself a cup of coffee, Grant replenished his empty pockets with cigars, and paused to light one before settling cross-legged by the campfire. He withdrew his order book and began to write.

A good night's sleep found him rested, alert, and firmly decided upon one crucial point: From now on he would tightly grasp the reins of this army. Issuing general directives to Meade and expecting him to firm up the specifics had not worked. The last two days had proved that. Meade was incapable of acting swiftly, decisively, and aggressively on a moment's notice. Failure to concentrate their troops against the enemy's weakness had squandered both lives and success.

Grant's orders would be specific. Meade would only have to pass them along or implement them. Who, what, where, and when would be spelled out in detail. There would be no room for misinterpretation.

Another realization hovered in Grant's head. He had underestimated Lee's aggressiveness. He would not make that mistake a second time. And Grant now realized he could not defeat Lee in this broken land. The Wilderness was too powerful an ally.

If he gauged the mettle of his adversary correctly, Lee would not be content just to sit behind his fortifications and batter back any further Union assault on his position. He would use his local knowledge to spring surprise attacks where the Federals least expected it.

Grant's pencil flew across the paper. Pages torn from the dispatch book piled up at his feet. Under cover of darkness he would disengage the enemy. Sedgwick's corps would quietly back away, turn east toward Chancellorsville, then swing south toward Spotsylvania Courthouse. Burnside would follow. Warren would march his men past Hancock's line, using them as a screen, and press south on the Brock Road toward the same destination. Then, Hancock's Second Corps would follow. In the night, the two blue snakes would slither south.

In the morning Lee would find himself facing abandoned trenches. The Union Army would be straddling the crossroads at Spotsylvania—on open ground between Lee and Richmond.

As the sun crested the smoking hills, Grant finished his orders and shuffled them into a neat stack. The sky turned a bright red as the sunlight mingled with the dense clouds of smoke. The scattered picket fire and occasional cannon shot confirmed what Grant had estimated. The enemy would use this day to rest if it could.

Sleepy staff officers poured out of their tents as soon as word passed that the general was up. Breakfast was served and eaten hastily and then the aides hurried off, for each officer found a stack of orders beside his plate.

Congressman Washburne wandered around the camp, uncertain if his protégé was a success or a failure, so he asked Grant to assess the last two days.

Grant drew his hand across his beard. "Well, it is in one sense a drawn battle, as neither side has gained or lost ground substantially since the fighting began. Yet, we remain in possession of the field, and the forces op-posed to us have withdrawn to a distance from our front and taken up a de-fensive position."

"A victory, then?" Washburne asked hopefully. He wanted something positive to tell the widows of his constituency.

Grant shook his head. "We cannot call the engagement a positive vic-tory, but the enemy have only twice actually reached our lines in their many attacks and have not gained a single advantage. This will enable me to carry out my intention of moving to the left and compelling the enemy to fight in a more open country and outside of their breastworks."

Washburne turned away, further confused.

The party broke up on that equivocal note, and the officers went about their business. Stealthily, preparations were made. Sedgwick executed his maneuver with finesse, and for once Burnside followed suit. Campfires were piled high as night fell, to lure the enemy pickets into thinking the army had turned in.

Then the time came for Hancock's line to move out. Canteens, sabers, and anything that might clank were wrapped in cloth. Companies stood to as sergeants and captains rushed about whispering orders they nor-mally bellowed. Weary soldiers stumbled onto the Brock Road and dressed their ranks.

An air of gloom hung over the men, adding a darkness to the night that even the burning campfires could not lighten. They had been here be-fore, had done this before. They had fought hard, bled, and died in this hor-rible place. Their friends and comrades lay shattered and dead along the splintered fence posts of the turnpike and the plank road, and whole com-panies were strewn across the trampled corn husks of Sanders' Field. They had given their all. And for what?

The next move was all too depressingly familiar. McClellan, Burn-side, and Hooker had led them into this wilderness to fight, to die, and then to straggle back across the Rapidan like licked dogs. The men hung their heads in shame.

Along the road a party of riders appeared at the head of the cross-ing. The foot soldiers raised their heads. It was General Grant. There could be no mistaking his hunched shoulders and ever-present cigar. He stopped beside the division officers. The men watched Grant raise his arm and point.

He pointed south!

An excited murmur ran through the ranks as orders were issued to about face. They were not retreating, not slinking back, not heading for the Rapidan crossing. They were marching south toward Richmond!

Men leapt to their feet and threw their caps into the air. Shouts, hurrahs, and cheers burst from their throats as they cried out Grant's name. Tears of joy filled the soldiers' eyes. Their sacrifice had not been in vain. The fight went on.

Grant waved his hand to quiet the men, but it did no good. The shouting increased until the whole army cheered. Some men broke into songs. Wheeling proudly, the men shouldered arms and marched south.

Grant rode along slowly. Against a splintered pine tree he saw a wounded soldier waving happily with his right arm. The man's left leg had been blown off below the knee, and a dirty, blood-soaked tourniquet covered the stump. His left arm hung useless within a bullet-riddled coat sleeve. Grant paused to stare.

Tears of joy streaked down the man's grimy cheeks, and he grinned broadly in spite of his obvious pain. "Hurrah for General Grant!" the wounded man shouted. "Hurrah! God bless the Union, and God bless General Grant!"

Grant turned to Porter. "This is most unfortunate," he said with evident embarrassment. "The sound will reach the enemy, and I fear it may reveal our movement."

Porter grinned happily. "It cannot be stopped, General."

Just then a drum corps spotted Grant and struck up a lively tune as they marched past. Colonel Porter and the others burst into laughter at the tune.

General Rawlins, laughing as well, rose in his stirrups and saluted the drummers. "Good for the drummers," he cried.

Grant looked puzzled. "What's the fun?" he asked.

Porter caught his breath. "It is a musical joke, General. Do you not know the tune?"

Grant shook his head. "Well, with me a musical joke always requires an explanation."

Porter smiled. "General, the drummers are playing a popular Negro camp meeting air in your honor. They are playing: 'Ain't I glad to get outta de wilderness. . . .' "

# THE LAST VISITOR

Ulysses Simpson Grant closed his eyes and laid down his pencil. He was finished. All he could write, he had written. His memoirs were completed. He had won his last battle.

His eyes reopened as if under a heavy weight and studied the last few lines he had scrawled. His bold hand had given way to feeble scratches as he struggled to the end.

His skeletal fingers searched among the papers on the velvet-covered writing desk until he found what he was looking for. He slid the two pages out from the pile. He adjusted his glasses and reread what he had written. The first was his dedication, penned on May 23.

*These volumes are dedicated to the American soldier and sailor,* it said. He nodded slightly to himself. A good dedication, he thought, one that honors all those brave men. The *American* soldier and sailor, that means just what it says, North and South alike ... together. I hope this dedication will help to heal the breach that terrible war caused. I feel the common soldiers would have embraced and come together long ago if left to their own devices. Most have, I'm sure. Only Beauregard and Jeff Davis still carry a grudge.

He read the first line of the second paper, his preface, written on July 1. *Man proposes and God disposes . . .* He liked that as well. Where the phrase came to him, he could not recall, but it stayed in his mind.

A choking spell tore him away from his thoughts. He clutched both sides of the table and battled through the episode until it passed. His fit so alarmed Julia that she reached across to clutch his hand, as if her holding him tightly could protect him and stave off the inevitable.

Grant reached across and placed his other hand on top of hers. She smiled bravely. My little soldier, he thought. We have been through so much together. He gently extracted his right hand and scribbled a note to her.

*I'm all right,* it said.

Julia read his note, smiled, and returned her hands to her lap, where she clutched them together tightly as she pretended to read her Bible. Since she had found her husband's note to Fred concerning his funeral, Julia had not left his side while he was awake. She no longer left the house for walks, for visits to friends, or even to visit her grandchildren. If he dozed on the porch, she held his hand. At night she stayed at his bedside, smoothing his beard and hair, now turned white, while he slept fitfully.

For weeks now the stranglehold on his throat had reduced his voice to a harsh whisper that few could understand. So, he scribbled hasty notes to substitute for his lost speech. Many of those about him held his notes as heartrending mementos of their encounter with a great and good man who faced his losing battle with dignity.

Dr. Shrady treasured a note Grant had given him about an encounter he had shortly after the war.

Walking to a reception in his honor one rainy night, a stranger going to the reception had shared his umbrella and his opinions with Grant. "I have never seen Grant," the man confided. "I am going merely to satisfy my personal curiosity. Between us, I have always thought Grant was a highly overrated man." Grant replied that that was his view as well.

Nothing so amused him, Grant told Shrady, than the startled look on the man's face when Grant shook his hand in the reception line.

On another occasion he wrote a note to Shrady after reading about his demise in the papers. "The *World* has been killing me off for a year and a half. If it does not change, it will get it right in time."

Dr. Douglas also carried a poignant note in his breast pocket that read: "The fact is I think I am a verb instead of a personal pronoun. A verb is anything that signifies to be, to do, or to suffer. I signify all three."

It was Douglas who engineered the move from New York City to Mount MacGregor to escape the oppressive heat of the summer. It was the dour but kindly Douglas who snapped up the offer of A. J. Drexel, the financier, for the Grants to use his two-story Queen Anne–style cottage at Mount MacGregor. The cool, clear air near Saratoga Springs would be perfect for his patient, Douglas thought.

Douglas and Shrady moved along to keep an eye on their patient, and for a while the change in climate helped. The swelling in Grant's throat subsided, and he was able to swallow his mainstay of tea, milk, and beef broth with less pain. But soon the general's attrition resumed its mathematical progression. Only his will to complete his book kept him alive now. Douglas feared the worst when it was finished.

Grant leaned back and adjusted the napkin covering the right side of his face. He was done. Twain would be happy, Grant thought. Now the humorist could have the manuscript he so dearly wanted. Grant closed his eyes and pictured the writer's last visit. Clapping his hands together, Twain crowed that he had estimated the first edition ought to weigh close to 330 tons, far more than the forty-five tons of the first run of Thomas Macaulay's monumental *History of England*.

Grant carefully replaced the two pages. He lifted the final page of his work and studied it for the last time. A phrase caught his eye:

> I feel that we are on the eve of a new era, when there is to
> be great harmony between the Federal and the Confederate.
> I cannot stay to be a living witness to the correctness of this
> prophecy; but I feel within me that it is to be so ...

He ordered his writing into a single pile and placed his pencil on top just as Harrison arrived with Fred and Dr. Douglas. The physician bowed to Julia before examining his patient. Grant watched him impassively. Their eyes locked in a moment of understanding. Douglas stared glumly at the finished work and turned briefly away to swallow the lump rising in his throat.

Grant raised his head to scan the horizon, far beyond the borders of the porch railing. Catching Fred's attention, Grant pointed to the promontory called the Eastern Lookout, which offered a panoramic view of the White and Green mountains of the neighboring states of Vermont and New Hampshire. From there, Grant loved to gaze down on the valley where patriots of the Revolutionary War defeated the British Army under General John Burgoyne just over a hundred years before.

On a haze-free day Grant could see Mount Washington, but not today. A feeling deep inside the general warned him that he had no time left to wait for a better day.

He wanted one last look.

Helping Grant into the wheeled Bath chair, the party set out. Harrison, Fred, and Douglas took turns pushing and pulling the general in his chair to the outlook. The route crossed a path strewn with boulders and filled with ruts. Several times progress ground to a halt until Grant struggled from the chair and walked a few yards with the help of his cane.

By the time they reached the outlook, Grant was sweating and breathing heavily. Harrison and Douglas bordered on the brink of exhaustion.

Grant loosened the scarf at his neck and studied the hazy vista with fading eyes. Serenity settled over him, as if the peace of the landscape before him were rising from the valley to cover his body. All the ranting and praying for his soul by Reverend Newman, Julia's pastor, had not done half this much to settle Grant's spirit as this last look.

Far below, the summer breeze gradually transformed the leaves into waving battle flags. Brigade after brigade rose from the shimmering tree line until the rolling hills were covered with ghostly soldiers, both blue and gray.

Why is there no cannon fire? Grant wondered. Why is there no rolling crackle of musket fire, no distant thump of artillery, no cries nor cheers? Surely, I ought to hear the guns from here, he thought.

Slowly, he realized the armies were marching together, not engaged in battle. Banners and blue and yellow regimental colors of both sides fluttered as the lost battalions wheeled onto the field. The Stars and Stripes and the Stars and Bars marched together. The echelon rolled to the edge of the plain and stopped. Then all the flags dipped in salute.

They are marching together at last, Grant thought. He raised his right hand and touched the side of his stocking cap as he returned the salute.

Douglas started as he watched the color fade from Grant's face until the general became deathly pale. Hurriedly, the physician signaled to the others to return his patient to the house. Sensing the urgency, Harrison and Fred doubled their efforts on the struggle back.

Back at the porch, Grant pushed himself out of the wheelchair and struggled toward the steps. Halfway up, he swayed and his cane slipped from his hand and fell clattering down the stairs. Fred rushed to his side, but his father caught himself and finished the last few steps. Reaching the wicker chair where he had done his writing, Grant collapsed.

Eight hours passed. Grant's temperature rose, and his pulse shot to 120, fading to a weakened beat that Douglas could scarcely feel. At times the general awakened and tried to take water, but this only precipitated hiccups that left him gasping for air.

Dr. Shrady slipped into the bedroom and conferred with Douglas. The elder physician shook his head sadly.

Buck, his second son, arrived and joined his mother, his brothers Fred and Jesse, and his sister. Grant opened his eyes and smiled at his son. Buck leaned close and spoke to his father. "Father, General Sherman has left St. Louis by train. He will be arriving soon."

Grant closed his eyes in recognition. "Water," he whispered. Fred dabbed a wet towel to his cracked lips. "I would like to lie in bed," Grant rasped.

Fred and Douglas exchanged fearful glances. Not since coming to Mount MacGregor had Grant lain in bed. Doing so severely restricted his breathing. Sitting upright in his easy chairs was the only way Grant could breathe for long. Both men knew that Grant was asking them to help him go. With sinking hearts they helped the general into his bed.

Shortly after midnight on the twenty-second, Dr. Douglas pried Julia's hand loose from her husband's. She caressed his damp brow one last time before reluctantly leaving the room, not taking her eyes from his face until the door was closed.

As the first rays of sunlight heralded the new day, Grant's breathing faded into a shallow whistle. Douglas ordered Harrison to gather the family. Julia resumed her vigil by the bedside with her husband's hand in hers. Fred, Buck, and Jesse, with their wives, stood close behind her. Fred rested his hand on his mother's shoulder. The ever-faithful Tyrell Harrison hung his head and dabbed at his eyes with his handkerchief.

Ever so quietly the whistling sound slowed. Then, even more gently, without a sigh, without a gasp, it stopped.

Fred moved to the pendulum clock in the corner and stopped the movement of its hands forever. It was 8:08.

Even with his eyelids closed, Grant sensed the light coming from the window. Or was it the far side of the room? It was hard to know which, it was so bright. The light grew in intensity until it flooded the chamber and washed out all but the faintest outlines of the bedroom. With the light came a feeling of peace far stronger than what he had experienced at the Eastern Outlook, and Grant felt his body's release.

A figure appeared within the center of the glow, and Grant strained to identify this last visitor. The beams seemed to bend around the individual as he stepped forward. With the light hurting his eyes, Grant recognized the erect posture, the snowy hair and beard. It could only be Lee. The other general beckoned him.

Grant rose from his bed and followed Lee into the light. His fighting was done.

# A FINAL FAREWELL

In the pocket of his father's dressing gown, Fred Grant found four things, including a woven lock of Julia's hair that Grant carried through all his battles; his wedding ring, which had become too big for his thin fingers; and a final note from Grant to his wife. The general had left one last dispatch for his beloved companion.

> Look after our dear children and direct them in the paths of rectitude. It would distress me far more to hear that one of them could depart from an honorable, upright, and virtuous life than it would to know that they were prostrated on a bed of sickness from which they were never to rise alive. They have never given us any cause for alarm on this account, and I trust they never will. With these few injunctions and the knowledge I have of your love and affection and the dutiful affection of all our children, I bid you a final farewell, until we meet in another and, I trust, better world. You will find this on my person after my demise.

The fourth item was the worn stub of the pencil with which Grant had fought so valiantly to the end.

# EPILOGUE

## JULIA GRANT

Mark Twain published 624,000 copies of Ulysses S. Grant's *Personal Memoirs*. Two subsequent editions were published in 1892 and 1894. The first royalty check to Julia Grant amounted to $200,000. In all, Grant's *Memoirs* earned his wife close to half a million dollars, removing the specter of debt and poverty. True to her husband's wishes, she paid off every penny of the general's obligations. As a wealthy widow, she remained the steady matriarch of her family, traveled throughout Europe, supported women's suffrage, and became close friends with Varina Davis, the wife of Jefferson Davis. She died at the age of seventy-four.

## FRED GRANT

Grant had no cause to worry about his children. Fred served as ambassador to the House of Hapsburg, police commissioner for the City of New York, and colonel of the New York 14th Infantry during the Spanish-American War. He remained in the army and retired with the rank of Major General.

## MARK TWAIN

The mercurial author rose to the pinnacle of success with the release of the *Personal Memoirs*, only to see his publishing company bankrupt by 1894 due to a series of poor choices for subsequent publications and bad financial decisions. Twain, ever the gambler, went bankrupt himself before the age of sixty. Perhaps prompted by the example of his friend Grant, Twain worked diligently to pull himself out of his financial hole by writing and lecturing. Unlike Grant, the effort left him bitter to the end. He died in 1910 with the next arrival of Halley's Comet, as he had predicted he would.

## WILLIAM TECUMSEH SHERMAN

Sherman's wife, Ellen, died shortly after the general moved from St. Louis to New York, leaving him a merry widower who loved the theater. His third and only surviving son, Tom, became a Jesuit priest, much to the anguish and dismay of his non-Catholic father. All his life Sherman had resisted conversion by his devout wife. When his wife once protested, "You knew I was Catholic when you married me," Sherman replied, "Yes, but I did not know you would get worse with each year!" He died in 1891, following a stroke. During his funeral his old adversary, Confederate General Joseph Johnston, acting as one of the pallbearers, stood bareheaded in the freezing rain. When urged by one of his former officers to put his hat on to avoid catching cold, Johnston refused and replied, "If General Sherman were here in my place, he would do the same for me." Within a week Johnston died of pneumonia complicating the cold he caught.

## HORACE PORTER

Thirty-nine years after the Battle of Chickamauga, Porter received the Medal of Honor for his help in stopping the Confederate attack and avoiding a Union rout. Successful in business, he wrote *Campaigning with Grant* in 1897. As Ambassador to France, Porter used his own funds to find the grave of John Paul Jones in Paris and arranged for the body to be moved to its present tomb at the Naval Academy at Annapolis.

## SYLVANUS CADWALLADER

The newspaperman became head of the Washington bureau of the *New York Herald* after the war. For a time he lived with Grant's dying chief of staff, General Rawlins, until the general succumbed to his tuberculosis in

1866. Cadwallader named his son Rawlins after his friend. Living in California, he finished writing his manuscript, *Three Years with Grant*, in 1896, when he was seventy years old. The detailed work was never published and languished as the property of the Illinois Historical Society. Eventually, the bushel was lifted from this candle into Grant's personal and military life and Cadwallader's work was published in 1955.

### GENERAL JOHN RAWLINS

The devoted Rawlins lived long enough to see his deepest wishes come true: to see Ulysses Grant defeat the Southern Confederacy and preserve the Union. Spent by his efforts, the gallant Rawlins died of tuberculosis in 1866.

### DR. JOHN HANCOCK DOUGLAS

Dr. Douglas's fortunes and his own health declined following the death of his most illustrious patient. Penniless, he died in a charity hospital.

### DR. GEORGE FREDERICK SHRADY

Dr. Shrady crusaded for the licensing of physicians by examination through his journal, the *Medical Record*. His efforts resulted in standardized examinations being required to license physicians in New York State. Finishing a series of articles on Grant for the *Century Magazine*, he died in 1908.

### WILLIAM HENRY VANDERBILT

Vanderbilt donated the entire collection of memorabilia that Grant had given him as collateral to the Smithsonian Institute. Within a year of Grant's passing, he also died.

RICHARD PARRY is a retired surgeon who lives in Sun City, Arizona. He is the author of three acclaimed novels on Wyatt Earp.